The Other Side of the River

The Other Side Of The River

Jessica Blair

PIATKUS

Acknowledgements

My sincere and grateful thanks go to Mr Hal Redvers-Jones of the Victorian Jet Works, Whitby, who so willingly gave of his time to talk to me about the jet industry and to show me the remarkably well-preserved Victorian jet workshop.

I am indebted to my wife and family for being my severest critics, and as always to my editor, Lynn Curtis, never failing in her advice.

Copyright © 1997 by W.D. Spence

First published in Great Britain in 1997 by
Judy Piatkus (Publishers) Ltd of
5 Windmill Street, London W1

**The moral right of the author
has been asserted**

*A catalogue record for this book is available
from the British Library*

ISBN 0-7499-0377-5

Set in 11/12pt Times by
Action Typesetting, Northgate Street, Gloucester
Printed and bound in Great Britain by
Bookcraft (Bath) Ltd.

For Joan
whose unfailing magic always lights up the years

Chapter One

Gennetta Turner paused at the gate of number seven New Buildings which occupied a prominent position on Whitby's West Cliff. She looked across the River Esk and the red-tiled roofs of the old town to the ruined Norman abbey high on the East Cliff. It was a view which never failed to thrill her, and the bustle on the quays of this thriving Yorkshire port was always exhilarating. She blew Reuben Briggs a kiss. He responded, and though the length of a well-kept garden lay between them they could sense the warmth in one another's smiles as they waved goodbye.

She hurried down the hill to Bagdale with its row of elegant houses, the homes of merchants, ship owners and captains. This August day in 1845 was hot with not a cloud to bring some temporary relief from the sun. Only a gentle sea breeze tempered the heat. She liked this weather, preferring to enjoy it without hurrying, but hurry she must. Up to two minutes late for afternoon tea with her father on Wednesday, Saturday and Sunday raised a scowl of disapproval; more than that brought a sharp word of rebuke.

Family tea on those days was a ritual, had been ever since Gennetta could remember. It had puzzled her why it should be so until she had learned, eleven years ago when she was seven, that it was really a memorial to her mother, Eliza, who had died when she was born. Prior to that Eliza and her husband Jeremiah had always taken tea together on those days. The others she had entertained wives of the well-to-do whose riches had been garnered from the trade of a port which sent ships to all parts of the known world. Jeremiah had encouraged her socialising, seeing it as instrumental in promoting his own thriving jet business. Now his beloved helpmate was lost to him in death but he kept the memory of her alive with this custom of taking tea with Gennetta and her brother Jack, who was two years older than herself.

1

Gennetta was panting hard when she opened the front door of the house in Bagdale and glanced at the clock in the hall. The burden of anxiety was lifted when she saw that she still had five minutes in hand. She felt some relief from the heat in the coolness of the marble floor. Her father, wanting to impress visitors, had had it designed especially. Roundels and squares in black and dark green patterned a white background. Cleaned and swept every morning by two maids, the floor shone like a new pin. But Gennetta found the whole effect cold and impersonal, and the dark patterned wallpaper and heavy iron balustrade on the stairs did nothing to alleviate the impression. It was the same throughout. There was nothing homely here. It was just a house, a place to find the essentials of living and no more. As she grew older Gennetta grasped what was missing: the loving touches of a wife who would make it into a home for her family.

Gennetta had long since realised that her father did not notice, or was not concerned about, what was lacking. That knowledge came when one day she overheard a conversation between Mrs Bates, the housekeeper, and Mrs Peters, the cook.

She got on well with both of them and liked to spend time chatting downstairs. This particular day the kitchen door was ajar and she stopped outside when she caught them in the middle of an exchange of opinions.

'Oh, aye, I'll grant thee t'master's fair with us, gives us no trouble.' Mrs Bates's agreement was swiftly laced with criticism. 'But he has no warmth or kindness to him. He's as cold as a codling.'

'That's just it,' Mrs Peters solemnly endorsed. 'It's Gen I'm sorry for, poor little mite. She's never known a mother's love.'

'It's all right for Master Jack. He's very much like his father and the apple of his eye.'

'Aye, and t'master can blame him for nowt. It's cruel of him though, to put her mother's death at Gen's door. Natural at the time, I suppose, but to keep it up all these years is beyond comprehension ...'

Gennetta had turned away unseen from that conversation with thoughts which disturbed her until she realised she now had an explanation for much that had previously troubled her.

This put a new interpretation of her father's habitual stern remoteness which, because she had grown up with it, she had accepted as normal. At times she had wondered why he did not take the same interest in her as some of her schoolfriends' parents did in their children. Why he so often brushed aside her enthusiasms and excitements with a non-committal grunt or even a sharp word of rebuke at being disturbed. From that overheard conversation she now had the explanation, and it was only her precious friendship with Reuben Briggs

2

that kept her from being permanently damaged by the knowledge that Jeremiah blamed her for her mother's death.

It explained his stern, sometimes downright tyrannical, ways towards her. Though Jeremiah kept a firm hand on both his children, Jack was never the victim of his harsh and unloving attitude, something which created jealousy in Gennetta and did nothing to promote a cordial, close relationship between brother and sister.

She could fault her father in no other way. He was a good provider. She had a sound roof over her head; she was well-fed, well-clothed, and he had given her a good education at a local dame school, with additional specialist tutors in music and literature and particularly drawing, which she loved. But he showed no special interest in her accomplishments, did not enthuse when she did well or when her teachers and tutors waxed lyrical with delight at her ability. He remained a cold, aloof figure who seemed to think more of his work than he did of his daughter. She felt that, quite apart from his blaming her for her mother's death, his business swallowed up any last interest he might have had in her. He gave the impression that it was his duty to provide for her, since she was his daughter, but beyond that he acknowledged no other obligation. In return he expected obedience in anything he ordered, because he knew best.

Gennetta complied because there was nothing else to do; she was otherwise comfortable, and able to follow her own interests so long as they were within the realms of decorum. But still she longed for the love of a mother, finding a faint echo of it in her relationships with the housekeeper and the cook. Though she was on good terms with them, and they had a great deal of quiet sympathy for her, there was always one final barrier between them: she was their employer's daughter and they his employees.

Gennetta found solace in the friendships she made at school and especially with Reuben Briggs whom she met when she went for special tuition in drawing from Mr Archibald Cooper who lived in a small grey stone house at the north end of Skinner Street. He agreed to teach Gennetta provided she attended at the same time as Reuben, whose great-aunt, recognising his talent and wishing him to develop it further, had arranged for tuition beyond his school work.

So from the age of twelve they had come to know each other, discovering many shared likes and dislikes. In Reuben, Gennetta found everything lacking in her father and brother. He was warm, friendly, always ready with a smile which spoke of his pleasure in her company.

Reuben, for his part, enjoyed the company of someone of his own age for most of his time was spent with his Great-aunt Edith. Edith

3

Briggs presented a formidable figure: tall, with a long face and cheeks which seemed to sag level with her jaw-line. But what she lacked in looks she made up for in good nature, though on first meeting this was not apparent. Her eyes, beneath eyebrows arched exceptionally high, gave the initial impression that she was highly suspicious of the person introduced to her, but on closer examination an observer could detect a twinkle of amusement in those large dark eyes, as if she was relishing the impression she made. Her clothes added to the air of severity for, though they were of the best quality, they were plain, devoid of frills and flounces, and of sombre colours. The only adornment she allowed was an exquisite jet brooch at her throat, carved in the shape of a whale, and a curling lizard, set with marcasites, pinned below her left shoulder.

When Reuben's mother and father had died in an epidemic when he was seven, Edith, as his only relation, had taken him in. Her offer to do so was tinged with a little reluctance for she knew that a young boy would intrude on her reclusive way of life. She cultivated few friendships and even her nephew and his wife had never been close. Reuben knew of her, had met her very occasionally, and viewed her as a formidable personage from whom it was safest to keep his distance.

But given a home by her he had determined to make the best of it, to keep to himself as much as possible and have only the minimum of contact with her. Edith's stiffness swiftly melted when she and Reuben were drawn into proximity. She had to admit that little boys held a special charm, especially when they respected their elders without losing that endearing hint of mischief which lurked beneath the surface.

She realised the pleasure she could gain from watching him grow up and by encouraging him to make the most of his talents, and derived much satisfaction from using for this purpose the wealth she had inherited from her father, made in the boom years of Whitby's whaling trade.

One of Reuben's talents was with a pencil and paper, and accordingly she arranged special lessons in drawing for him. His particular forte was depicting the ships and boats around Whitby's busy harbour. Edith realised that the boy had a special love of the sea and ships, something he must have inherited from a long line of Briggses, and that one day she might lose him to a sailor's life.

She approved his friendship with the girl who shared his drawing lessons and encouraged him to bring her to tea whenever possible. Edith liked Gennetta, a pretty child with silky fair hair which tumbled to her shoulders like a cascading waterfall, indicating care and regular brushing. She had been immediately taken by the child's pale blue eyes which sparkled so prettily. But she saw behind them a guarded sadness. It could be banished in jokes and laughter shared with Reuben but return just as easily. Then a serious expression would cloud her round childish face. It was at those times that Edith's heart went out to the girl for she knew how much someone of Gennetta's age needed a mother's love and resolved to try to impart some of that love without intruding or being obvious about it.

Gennetta appreciated her kindness and repaid her with a special regard.

Edith found great joy in watching the two youngsters grow up: Reuben into a fine, handsome, broad-shouldered young man whose hair seemed to darken as he grew older until it matched the raven depth of her own, a Briggs family trait; Gennetta with a figure which, when it lost its adolescent plumpness, boasted a slim waist which anyone would envy. The rounded cheeks had fined down a little but retained their pink-tinged prettiness.

Edith saw the friendship between them developing into love, though neither of them recognised it until Reuben's sixteenth birthday.

The three of them were having tea together. Mirth filled the cosy dining room with its glazed doors open to a walled garden. There was a small lawn outside and winding paths among rose trees full of blossom which scented the air with an intoxicating fragrance. The table was laden with scones and home-made strawberry jam, Reuben's favourite, red jellies, sponge cakes filled with jam and cream and, in the place of honour in the centre of the table, the birthday cake which had had Cook's special treatment to keep it moist and was delicately iced with the words 'Happy Birthday' in pink on the smooth white icing.

Gennetta had never felt happier. She had bought Reuben a ship in a bottle with money saved from the allowance her father had started to give her. The work of a sailor whose sailing days were over, it was very delicate and lovingly crafted. When she arrived at the house Reuben came hurrying to meet her and in those moments alone she was able to give him her present. His dark eyes lit up at the sight of the ship and when they looked up at Gennetta they held something special. He kissed her on the cheek and her heart fluttered at the touch of his lips. She knew there was a deeper feeling than affection between them now. The childhood days of platonic friendship were over. This feeling was different. There was an empathy between them which made them truly happy only in each other's company.

Gennetta was light-headed. She had never experienced anything like this before. It must be love, she decided, and if it was then long may it go on.

Edith too recognised the change in the young pair she loved so much. She saw that Reuben's excitement over his present went much deeper, stemming at least as much from the pleasure of having Gennetta to share this special occasion. And in Gennetta Edith saw the first love of a young girl for a boy. She made no observation but offered a silent prayer that both would always be as happy as they were at this moment.

She saw that newfound happiness tested only a short while later. The candles on the birthday cake had been blown out amidst excited chatter and laughter. The cake had been cut and passed around. Edith and Gennetta immediately gave their best wishes to Reuben. He thanked them. Then they saw his face cloud over. His serious expression as he glanced from one to the other made them both wonder what was coming.

He took a deep breath and declared: 'Great-aunt, I would like your permission to go to sea.'

In spite of the warm, balmy day, the words brought a chill to the room.

For a moment no one spoke. Gennetta felt her heart thud and a numbness grip her. She wanted to scream, 'Reuben, no! Not now, just when our lives are linked together in love!' She glanced through misty eyes at Miss Briggs and read dismay on her long face.

Though it was something Edith had expected one day, Reuben's announcement had still come as a shock. Edith shot a glance at Gennetta. The girl was hurting terribly. Why had he chosen now to make his request? Why on this happy occasion? Why when they had just discovered their love for each other?

She broke the tense silence with a little cough as if it were necessary to clear her throat for what she was about to say. She took a grip on herself. She did not want to lose Reuben who had become so much a part of her life. He would leave a void she knew she could never fill. But she wanted to be fair, wanted to do what was best for him. He needed her now more than ever. She must be wise for them both – no, for the three of them.

'You've thought about it carefully?' Her voice was soft, neither approving nor condemning. All the while her eyes were focused sharply on him, reading every nuance of his expression, wanting to miss nothing, testing the depth of his sincerity and commitment. At the same time she was fully aware of Gennetta's reaction. She saw a mixture of surprise, horror and disappointment as only a girl in love could unconsciously express them.

6

'Yes, I have.'

'It will mean a rough life. There is no easy way to senior positions at sea. You will have to start at the bottom.'

'I don't mind that. It's what I would expect.' His voice was firm.

'There are dangers, too. Have you considered those? Storms, shipwrecks ... We can none of us see what lies ahead.'

'Yes. They hold no fear for me.' He seemed shocked that his aunt might think him faint-hearted.

She gave a small wry smile. 'Bless you, child, that's the boy in you speaking, but the man in you tells you that there are circumstances in which you would be afraid, and if you were not you would not be a worthy sailor. Fear makes you cautious, which is as it should be. For that caution could one day save your life and those of others.'

Reuben nodded, blushing a little. 'I've thought about life at sea very carefully.'

'You'd be leaving comfort behind. This house, good food, a soft bed.'

'I know.'

'You'd be leaving me and Gennetta.'

'That is the one thing I'll regret.' He glanced from one to the other and his heart ached, for he knew he was causing them pain. He had not wanted to be the cause of those tears trickling down Gennetta's cheeks.

'I have few close friends but those I have are influential, men of position,' his aunt went on. 'It would be easy to place you somewhere on land with prospects – with one of the merchants or shipbuilders ...'

'Great-aunt,' he interrupted gently, 'I would rather you used your influence with a shipowner and a good captain.' His voice warmed with enthusiasm. 'I've always dreamed of going to sea. If you let me go, I know I will do well. You'll be proud of me. You both will.' He glanced at Gennetta, eyes pleading with her to understand.

Edith knew that what he said was true. He would do well in anything he tackled but he would do better in something on which he had set his heart and to which he could direct all his talent and determination to prove himself. Apart from that he would be in a trade in which he would be happy, and his happiness was paramount to her.

'Very well, Reuben. You have my approval. I will see what I can do to get you a position on a good ship.'

In the grip of excitement, he sprang from his chair and ran to her, flinging his arms round her neck and hugging her tightly. 'Oh, thank you, thank you.'

'There, there, now. No fuss,' she returned, embarrassed at the display of affection, though in her heart of hearts she liked it. She

7

patted him on the shoulder and gave him a reassuring smile as he stepped away.

Gennetta was numbed by Miss Briggs's approval. Reuben would no longer be here for her. There would be a large void in her life which would be filled only when he was between voyages. The tears flowed a little faster.

Reuben saw them and came to her. 'Please don't cry, Gen,' he said softly. 'Be happy for me.'

She gulped, nodded and sniffed back her tears. She found her handkerchief and dabbed her eyes.

'Gennetta,' Edith spoke gently, 'we'll both miss Reuben very much but you must continue to come here. Happen we'll be company for each other. Promise me you will?' Apart from the comfort she would find in Gennetta's visits, she knew it was important for her to continue to provide the love and support which the girl so sorely missed at home.

Gennetta nodded. 'Oh, I will come.'

Edith smiled. 'Now I'm going to take a short rest. You two go into the garden. It's such a nice day.'

Out of sight of the house they sat on a seat beneath a willow tree, its weeping branches, lush with leaves, providing a cool canopy from the heat of the sun.

Reuben took Gennetta's hand and with that touch they both knew that they had left their childhood behind. 'Gen, I'm sorry, but please try and understand.'

'I do, really I do. It was just such a shock when you made your request, I was bewildered.' She looked deep into his eyes. 'I don't want you to go, I want you here. But I do realise how you feel.'

He smiled. 'That makes me feel better, for I never wanted to hurt you.' He paused then added seriously, 'Today I realised you meant more to me than a friend. I love you, Gen.'

'Oh, Reuben, I love you too.'

He leaned forward and kissed her lightly.

'You'll think of me?'

'Always.'

'Never forget me?'

'Never.'

They sealed these promises with another kiss lingering a little longer this time.

So it was that Edith Briggs gained a position for her great-nephew as cabin boy on the *Diana*, captained by an old friend, Silas Barrick.

8

Reuben took to the life immediately, showing both keenness and ability. His nimble brain was ever ready to learn and he was considered to be destined for quick promotion.

Gennetta's visits to Miss Briggs continued regularly and they both found solace and enjoyment in each other's company, while always looking forward to Reuben's next leave.

This time, late in his eighteenth year, Reuben had brought the news between voyages that Captain Barrick had promoted him to Able Seaman, and that if he worked well there was no reason why he should not advance quickly to Second Mate.

It was in this knowledge, with the future looking bright for them both, that Gennetta had left him, swearing his love for her, and hurried home to have tea with her father and brother.

There were five minutes to spare. Time for her to wash her face and hands and compose herself to face the ritual. She stepped quickly across the hall towards the staircase. An uneasy feeling touched her, and her steps faltered. Something was different. The door to the drawing room, where her father always took tea, was open. This was unusual. Her father was a stickler for keeping doors closed. She pursed her lips, gave a little shrug of her shoulders and went on, heels clicking on the marble floor.

'Is that you, Gennetta?' Her father's voice held a thick Yorkshire accent, something he had never tried to moderate even though success had brought him a wider social circle.

Its sharp, cold tone brought her to a stop. 'Yes, Father,' she replied, keeping her voice level. Inwardly she felt a little apprehensive. This was not the usual teatime greeting. Normally, once she had entered the room, there was a polite passing of pleasantries, though there was no depth to them. Why was she being summoned this way? Why the open door? Had her father been listening for her return?

'Come here immediately.' The order contained the tone of parental authority that demanded instant obedience.

Puzzled, Gennetta entered the room. Filled with oak furniture, with thick curtains draped at the windows, it had always had a sombre atmosphere which was hardly lightened by the patterned wallpaper. Her questioning glance took in the scene. Her father stood with his back to the fireplace in its heavy oak surround, though on this warm day no fire burned in the grate. He was holding himself stiffly erect, hands clasped behind his back, under his grey thigh-length lounge jacket with black satin lapels. At his throat was tied a muslin stock against the high stiff collar of his shirt. A pale yellow waistcoat, topping dark grey trousers, was his only concession to brightness. His black shoes shone mirror-bright as they always did.

Jeremiah was a fine figure with an air of authority. It was something which had not come to him naturally but which he had cultivated from his early days in the family jet business. Realising that one day, as the only son, he would take over the firm he'd wanted the employees to know who was in charge and must be obeyed instantly. He was their employer and they should know their place. Now his firm jaw was set grimly and his small waxed moustache seemed to bristle as he eyed Gennetta.

'Close the door,' he ordered. 'I've delayed tea until I ring for it.'

She was even more mystified. Their cherished routine was going to be broken. Her father must have something serious to say. She glanced at her brother Jack who lounged in a large leather-cushioned chair, but if he knew the reason for this break from custom he gave nothing away.

His father tolerated Jack's colourful taste in clothes – red jacket, pale blue waistcoat and yellow-checked trousers – for he knew that behind the outward foppery was a young man just as steely as he was. He had seen to that, moulding his son to his own image so that the firm of Turner, Jet Makers, would be in safe hands in the future. He was confident it would continue to thrive and expand on the popularity of the material, mined along the Yorkshire coast and inland on the moorland hills, which could be carved and etched into highly polished pieces currently fashionable with ladies as items of jewellery, brooches, necklaces and adornments to their dress.

Jeremiah eyed his daughter. 'Sit down,' he ordered, indicating a high-backed chair upholstered in a depressing dark red plush.

Gennetta did as she was told, straightened her dress and placed her hands one on top of the other on her lap. She looked up at her father who towered over her.

'It's come to my notice that thy friendship with Reuben Briggs has become much more.'

The words astounded her. How did he know? Her mind reeled but she focused on what he was going on to say.

'I allowed thee to take drawing lessons with him, and thee has become a very competent artist. I thought it helped thy talent so I allowed the association to continue. But I was blind to what the consequences might be as thee grew older, and for that I blame myself. Since he went to sea you've been seeing him whenever he was in port. It must stop forthwith!'

Gennetta sought for words. As honest as she was, her first instinct was to deny the inference. 'Reuben and I are friends ...'

10

Her father bristled. He scowled at her. 'Don't lie to me, girl. Jack saw thee walking hand in hand on the cliffs, saw thee kissing.' A note of disgust had come into his voice. 'Don't tell me that was just friendship?'

Gennetta shot an angry glance at her sneak of a brother and saw the self-satisfied smirk on his face. She could tell he was enjoying watching her being reprimanded by their father. It only heightened the defiance which was rising in her. There was no point in denying her father's accusation now. 'All right,' she replied with a snap in her voice, 'it's not. We love each other.'

'Love?' her father sneered. 'However thee describe it, it will stop. My daughter is worthy of someone better than a common sailor.'

'Reuben has great prospects, Captain Barrick has said so. He'll become a captain himself one day.'

'Thee'll forget him' rapped her father. 'I'll have you marry Cyrus Sleightholme!'

'What?' Gennetta sprang to her feet. 'That fop! Never!' Her eyes blazed in defiance.

'Thee will, for the sake of the firm.'

Gennetta tossed her head and snorted in disgust. 'I see it all. You want me to marry Cyrus so that you can unite the two biggest jet firms in Whitby. All you're thinking about is your own welfare.'

'If Cyrus had had a sister there would have been no need for this, Jack would have married her. Instead he married Grace and she's turned out useless. She'll never give me the grandson I want.'

'Not my fault she can't conceive,' protested Jack from the depths of his chair.

Father and daughter ignored him.

'So you want me to marry Cyrus to get you a grandson with a hand in both businesses?' Her eyes narrowed rebelliously. 'Well, you'll get your grandson but he'll be a Briggs!'

Jeremiah's face flamed with anger. 'Thee'll not defy me! Thee will marry Cyrus. I've already spoken to his father and he approves. It will be good for both firms.'

'I'll not agree,' Gennetta declared. 'You can just untell him!'

'Thee'll do as thee's told,' Jeremiah boomed. 'I've given thee everything thee's had, clothing, food, an education ...'

'Yes, you have, and I'm grateful,' she broke in. 'Everything but the one thing I wanted most of all – love. You've always blamed me for Mother's death and it's turned your heart to ice so far as I'm concerned. I found the love I craved with Reuben and Miss Briggs, and I'll not lose it now. I'll not sacrifice my happiness for the sake of your ambitions. I'd rather leave.' Her chin jutted determinedly.

11

The colour drained from Jeremiah's face. 'Leave and I'm finished with thee. There'll be nowt for thee, not one penny. Think on that.'

'I have no need to. My mind is made up. Keep your money. I'll marry Reuben Briggs and be happy.' She swung round and started for the door.

'Don't come running to me when things go wrong!' her father flung at her as she crossed the room, her back ramrod straight, bristling with anger and defiance.

She took no notice but slammed the door, her final answer.

Chapter Two

Gennetta quickly packed a bag with a few clothes. She would return for the rest when she knew her father and brother would be at the workshop.

Her feet barely touched the steps as she came down the stairs, determined to be away from the house and her father as swiftly as possible. The door to the drawing room was still closed but as she crossed the hall she could hear the clink of teacups. The ritual must go on in spite of the upheaval. Maybe her father had expected her to return repentant, or maybe he didn't care that she was leaving.

Her heart was beating fast at the enormity of the step she had taken. She was gambling that Reuben would marry her. He had professed his love but had never once mentioned marriage. She supposed that he had not done so because he wanted to be in a better position to support her and that this would come with time and promotion. But what would his attitude be now? And would Miss Briggs be sympathetic towards her? Would she understand Gennetta's reasons for leaving home? She was throwing herself on their good nature, after all.

Aprehension started to gnaw at her as she hurried down Bagdale and started the climb to New Buildings, but she thrust the doubt from her mind as she opened the gate to number seven. She paused momentarily, looking at the house. It seemed friendly, always had, and Gennetta drew strength and hope from that fact as she walked up the path.

The sound of the bell echoed in the depths of the house and was soon answered by a maid, neat in her black skirt, white blouse and small mob-cap.

'Is Miss Briggs still at home, Rose?' queried Gennetta.

At twenty Rose was fresh-faced with sparkling brown eyes and a pleasant, ever-willing demeanour. She had been in Miss Briggs's service since she was fifteen. Devoted to her employer, and meticulously trained by her, she quickly brought under control her surprise at seeing Gennetta again so soon. 'Yes, Miss Gennetta.' She stepped aside to let her enter the house. 'Miss Briggs and Mr Reuben are in the drawing room.'

'Thank you.' She dropped her bag and started towards the door but Rose slipped quickly round her. Things had to be done properly.

She knocked on the door, opened it and announced, 'Miss Gennetta, ma'am.'

Gennetta hurried past her into the room. Miss Briggs and Reuben rose from their chairs in surprise.

Concerned at her worried expression, Reuben anxiously searched her face for an explanation as he asked, 'What's wrong, Gen?'

She looked from him to Miss Briggs, seeking understanding and support.

'I've left home,' she blurted out.

'Good grief, child!' Miss Briggs's eyebrows shot up even higher at this blunt statement.

Gennetta's glance was fixed on Reuben now. 'Father said I wasn't to see you again and that I was to marry Cyrus Sleightholme.' The words caught in her throat.

'What?' gasped Reuben. 'You can't.'

'I'm not!' There was defiance in Gennetta's voice in spite of the tears which had begun to run down her cheeks. 'But what am I to do?' She looked pleadingly at him.

He put his arm around her and led her to the sofa. 'We'll work something out,' he said comfortingly as they sat down. 'Won't we, Aunt?' They both looked up, hoping her reply would be favourable.

Miss Briggs, who had watched them shrewdly, answered with a question: 'You expect to stay here, I take it?'

Worry creased Gennetta's face for she thought she detected disapproval. 'Oh, please, may I?'

Edith pursed her lips thoughtfully, leaving the young people in breathless suspense. Her mind made up, she said gently, 'You are placing me in the awkward position of apparently condoning your action – but what would Reuben think of me if I refused?' She smiled when she saw relief replace concern, then sat down in her chair opposite them.

Gennetta and Reuben looked at each other joyfully. He squeezed her hand. Gennetta wiped tears from her eyes as she expressed her thanks profusely.

Edith raised her hand to halt them. 'I've known for some time how much you love each other, and I'm not prepared to see that love destroyed by your father's insistence on a match which, I suspect, has been arranged only to further the interests of two businesses.'

'You are a shrewd judge, Miss Briggs,' observed Gennetta.

Edith gave a wry smile. 'Aye, I may appear to lead a secluded life but I have friends and can draw my own conclusions from what I hear. Now we must think ahead – but first we'll take some tea. Ring the bell, Reuben.'

He went to the long pull beside the fireplace and tugged it twice. A few moments later Rose appeared carrying a tray set with tea things which she placed on a small table in front of Miss Briggs.

Edith poured the tea and sat back in her chair. 'We must treat this matter with care. Both your father and Mr Sleightholme are ambitious men and each would like to take over the other's firm. They feel they could achieve this through your marriage to Cyrus and will stop at nothing to achieve it.'

'But if I'm here they can't reach me,' Gennetta pointed out.

'Nor can you make yourself a recluse.'

'You think they might try to abduct Gen when she goes out?' cried Reuben.

'They wouldn't dare.' She was nevertheless alarmed by a possibility she had not considered.

'Determined men might do anything.'

'Even if they did, I would never marry Cyrus!'

'You'll marry me,' put in Reuben, 'then they can't do anything about it.' His gaze met hers as she turned towards him. 'You will, won't you?'

The smile of joy which wreathed her face gave him his answer but he was still thrilled when she whispered, 'Oh, Reuben, yes.'

He gripped her hand even more tightly as he turned to his great-aunt. 'I hope you approve?'

She smiled and nodded. 'Of course. Ever since your sixteenth birthday, when I saw the special feeling between you both, I've hoped that one day it would come to this.'

'Then it's all settled,' said Reuben briskly. 'Your father can do nothing.'

'Don't be so sure,' Edith warned. 'Gennetta will only be safe after you're married.'

'Then we'll marry as soon as possible.'

'There isn't time before you sail in four days,' Edith pointed out.

'Then I won't sail.'

'And jeopardise your career?' She scowled.

'You mustn't,' put in Gennetta quickly. 'Your prospects are good. You mustn't throw them away after what Miss Briggs has done for you. You mustn't miss your chance because of me.'

15

'But I would do anything for you! You mean more to me than my life.'

'You're happy at sea. It's what you've always wanted to do. How do you think I would feel if I ruined it for you? No, Reuben,' she went on to halt his protestations, 'say no more. My mind is made up. We'll marry next time you are in Whitby.'

What Edith saw and heard enhanced her opinion of Gennetta and she admired the girl's determination to see things the right way.

'That will be in six weeks.' He turned to his great-aunt. 'Keep her safe for me?'

Edith nodded. 'I will, Reuben, I will. You are both very precious to me.' Her eyes were damp and she paused momentarily. 'Now, let's get down to practicalities,' she said briskly. 'You'll need to get some things from home, Gennetta.'

'I've brought a few clothes. The bag's in the hall.'

Miss Briggs cast her a knowing look. 'So you expected me to be sympathetic?'

Gennetta blushed but said nothing.

'Well, as this is to be your home, let me show you your room.'

Her back straight, hands clasped together in front of her, Miss Briggs led the way up the stairs, followed by Gennetta and Reuben who had picked up the bag in the hall.

When Gennetta entered the bedroom she gasped with delight. 'This is for me?'

Miss Briggs smiled benevolently. 'Yours for as long as you like, my dear.'

'Like it, Gen?' asked Reuben anxiously.

'It's lovely.'

'Modelled on my room as I remember it as a child,' explained Miss Briggs.

Gennetta's eyes ranged around the room. The narrow oak-framed bed spread with a multicoloured patchwork quilt looked inviting. Brightly coloured chintz curtains on the casement window matched the flounce around the small dressing table on which stood an oak swivel-mirror and jet trinket tray. The sparkling brass handles enhanced the plain beauty of the oak chest of drawers. On one side of the bed stood a small table, on the other a chair. The walls were papered with a small pink rose motif and hung with two engravings titled 'Northern Whale Fishery' and 'Whalers Entering Whitby', reminders of Miss Briggs's connection with the industry which had once been so important to the port.

'Oh, Miss Briggs, thank you so much.' Gennetta's eyes brimmed with tears of joy and relief. In her elation propriety was forgotten. She flung her arms around the old lady and hugged her.

'Oh, my! Bless me.' Miss Briggs, taken aback by the exuberant display, spluttered and stiffened. To escape she added quickly, 'Now let's show you the rest of the house.'

As they moved from room to room Gennetta revelled in the cosy atmosphere. She sensed a welcome and knew she would be happy here.

In the kitchen Miss Briggs announced to her staff, 'Miss Turner will be staying with us for some time.' She turned to Gennetta. 'You already know Rose, Barbara and Helen, but you won't have met Mrs Shaw or May, the kitchen maid. They are both new, only been with me a month. Mrs Shaw is my cook and supervises the staff.'

'Pleased to know you, miss,' said Mrs Shaw with a smile. Gennetta judged her to be in her late forties, with a well-made figure that carried its weight well. Her round open face and rosy cheeks exuded the friendliness of one who yet knew her place. She carried an air of authority and would rule her kitchen and staff firmly but fairly. Her eyes were those of an understanding woman, one who would be a staunch ally once you had her trust.

'Mrs Shaw doesn't live in but is here most of the day, returning each evening to her own home and husband,' Miss Briggs explained on their way back to the drawing room. 'Well, my child, I hope you will be happy with us,' she added as they sat down.

'I'm sure I shall be more than happy and it will be wonderful to have you for company while Reuben is away,' said Gennetta warmly.

The following day Reuben accompanied her to the house in Bagdale. With her future assured, she had no regrets regarding the step she had taken but felt a touch of nostalgia. After all, this had been her home all her life and now she was leaving it for good.

She packed her belongings quickly and said farewell to Mrs Bates and Mrs Peters, who had sensed something amiss when her bed was not slept in. They wished her well with tears in their eyes when she gave them a final hug. They knew the house would be a sadder place without her.

Gennetta did not look back as they hurried along Bagdale. The past was the past; the future lay with the man beside her.

'We sail on the evening tide, my love, but I must report aboard by noon.' There was a note of regret in Reuben's voice as he took Gennetta's hands in his. Their seat beneath the willow tree in a secluded corner of the garden shielded them from onlookers. 'I'll miss you.'

'And I'll miss you.' There was sadness in the blue eyes which met his loving gaze. 'Take care and come back safe for me.'

'I will, and then you'll become Mrs Briggs.' He smiled reassuringly at her.

'And out of everyone's reach,' she said softly.

A serious expression crossed his face. 'Until then take care, my love. Don't let anyone persuade you against marrying me.'

'You think Father will try?' Alarm clouded her face.

'He might, one way or another. And there are the Sleightholmes also.'

'They can try all they like but I'll not listen to them,' said Gennetta determinedly. 'I'm yours and yours alone. I love you so.'

'And I love you too, and will do forever.' He leaned towards her and their lips met in a kiss which sealed their love.

Reuben's words and kiss were foremost in Gennetta's mind as she and Miss Briggs watched the *Diana* sail on the evening tide.

The lowering sun painted the red roofs of Whitby with a warm glow which was reflected in the waters of the harbour and river. Two ships moved towards the sea, their topsails catching the breeze. Sailors were getting into position, ready to take advantage of the wind once they were clear of the river.

Gennetta's eyes were only for the second ship, the one with *Diana* painted on her bows in black edged with gold. From their position on the west pier, Gennetta felt she could reach out and touch her. Men swung on to the bulwark, gripped the rigging and swarmed upwards to unfasten the main topsail.

Gennetta eagerly scanned the ship. 'There he is!' she cried excitedly, and pointed to where two men stood coiling the ropes which had been hauled on board when they had cast off.

Reuben straightened and, catching sight of them, waved. Gennetta hugged that last moment of contact to her. It was something she would hold in her memory until he returned. She waved vigorously in return while Edith too acknowledged him. Reuben raised both his arms and then stooped to continue coiling the ropes.

The *Diana* slid between the two piers and met the sea, her bow curling back the water to send it hissing and foaming along her side. Orders were obeyed instantly. Sails were unfurled to catch the wind, and as they billowed men scrambled back to deck. The ship dipped into the sea, adjusting to its demands as a course was set which would carry her away from the vicious Yorkshire cliffs before heading south for the Channel.

Stricken by Reuben's departure, Gennetta watched until the *Diana* was a mere speck. Edith waited patiently, not wanting to intrude on these last precious moments.

18

Eventually Gennetta sighed and wiped a tear from her eye. Six weeks! It seemed an interminable period. She had faced such partings before, but then her life had been more settled, she had been caught up in a familiar daily routine. Now, with her life altered by leaving home, the future was unknowable.

As they turned to walk from the pier, Edith linked arms with Gennetta and patted her hand comfortingly. 'We must look forward to his return and prepare for your wedding.'

Gennetta detected a forced brightness in her voice. She shot Edith a glance and saw her swallow hard. Edith too missed Reuben terribly. It must have been hard for her every time he sailed, though she had hidden her sadness from prying eyes. She was not going to let herself be seen as a sentimental old spinster.

They strolled back along the quay beside the river. Weatherbeaten sailors exchanged banter as they prepared to sail to the fishing grounds; seagulls floating on the air currents screeched lazily; bare-foot urchins dodged and chased through the people who milled about the quay; artisans freed from work turned into an inn or hurried home lest they receive a scolding for being late. Whitby buzzed with activity which would only quieten down after nightfall.

Crowds flowed in both directions along Baxtergate. Shopkeepers called their wares, hoping for more custom before they closed. Edith and Gennetta paused to buy some fruit and look at the jet on display. They passed the Angel Inn, a coaching inn where local society met at both public and private functions. They passed the Chapel of St Ninian and the lanes leading to timber yards, hearing the last blows of the hammers in the block and mast-making yard and seeing the workmen leaving the sail manufactory. Everywhere there was bustle and clamour, and it was a relief to reach the quieter area of New Buildings.

The maids soon had a refreshing cup of tea ready and once they had settled in the drawing room, Edith looked seriously at Gennetta.

'I don't want to worry you, my dear, but I think we were followed from the pier.'

'What?' Alarm rang in Gennetta's voice.

'It may mean nothing, I may be wrong, but I think it might be wisest if you did not go out alone.'

'You don't think Father would ...'

'There's no telling what he might do. He may only wish to know what you are doing, where you are. But I do think we had better exercise caution.'

'I'm so sorry to have brought this upon you.' A troubled frown creased Gennetta's forehead.

19

'Think nothing of it. Nobody is going to intimidate Edith Briggs!'

'What's going on, Jeremiah?' snapped Robert Sleightholme as he bustled into Jeremiah's study.

He was sitting behind the large oak desk where he dealt with most of the paperwork concerning his jet business. The room was sombre with its dark oak panelling and three walls lined with bookcases.

Jeremiah frowned at this sudden intrusion by a man with whom he was only reluctantly friendly. The owners of the two foremost jet manufactories in Whitby had always kept a cautious eye on one another and, while outwardly relishing the idea of amalgamation, each schemed to achieve absolue control. Both saw a marriage between Gennetta and Cyrus as a means to overall power for himself.

Jeremiah was sure Jack could outsmart Cyrus, while Robert thought there was nothing more certain than that his son would eventually hold the reins once he had Gennetta's share of the business. But he was perturbed by the rumours he had heard.

Now he towered over Jeremiah, who had remained seated. Robert was a tall man, heavy-jowled, big and round, a protruding stomach showing that he liked good food and plenty of it. His ruddy complexion betrayed his liking for the best wine and he was not averse to taking spirits as well.

Robert leaned forward, his broad hands with their chubby fingers splayed on the desk, and glared at Jeremiah from brown eyes shot with annoyance.

'Well?' he snapped.

Jeremiah leaned sideways to see the door being closed by the maid who had attempted to announce Robert, only to be pushed aside as he burst past her. The door clicked shut and Jeremiah straightened in his chair and looked hard at his visitor.

'Sit down, Robert, and calm thissen. Thee'll have a heart attack, the state thee's in.' He made his meaning clear by glancing at the large stomach and gestured to the bright red face. He knew Robert did not like anyone drawing attention to these aspects of his appearance and derived some pleasure from the way his friend and rival spluttered his annoyance and sat down. 'Now, what's worrying thee?'

'Gennetta – I hear she's left home?' rapped Robert, statement and question following hard on one another. 'Gone to that horse-faced Edith Briggs, apparently. Sweet on that sailor great-nephew of hers. Where does this leave Cyrus? Art thou doing anything about it?'

'Of course I'm doing something about it!'

'Thee'd better. Rumours are she'll marry Briggs – will have to if thee believe everything that's being bandied about.'

'Tittle-tattle by idle busybodies.' Jeremiah dismissed Robert's veiled accusation but it left a nagging doubt in his own mind.

'There's no smoke without fire,' Robert blustered. 'Let's see thee stop this nonsense once and for all. Jack told Cyrus why she walked out, said she intends to marry this damned sailor.'

'She can't do that until he returns from sea. And by that time she'll have seen sense.'

'I hope so. See thee bring her to heel.'

'And thee tell Cyrus to do something about it, if he loves her.'

'Love?' Robert gave a snort of derision. 'Think I loved Maud when I married her? More like saw the chance of getting my hands on her father's firm if I married his eldest daughter, him having no sons. Now here's a chance for our two firms to amalgamate. We'll become equal partners. Build it up to be passed on to Cyrus's children ... and Jack's,' he added hastily, and gave another half laugh. 'Love? Cyrus'll do as he's told. See thy lass does the same.'

Jeremiah nodded. 'She will.' There was a note of determination in his voice. He wanted the amalgamation as much as Robert – more in fact. Equal partners? Maybe for a short while but then ... There would be a test of wills. Robert's could be formidable but he lacked the necessary ruthlessness to ride roughshod over friends and partners. And Jeremiah knew that that was where he could win. But first it needed Gennetta's marriage to Cyrus.

Jeremiah waited two weeks before making a move. Through Jack he learned of the scandal which was beginning to surround his daughter. She was being talked about at social gatherings in the Assembly Room of the Angel Inn, the hub of Whitby society. A dinner never passed without some guest referring to the latest rumour about Gennetta Turner. Her name was whispered wherever gentlemen met to conduct business as they speculated about the outcome for the Turners and Sleightholmes, it being common knowledge that Jeremiah and Robert saw the marriage of their children as advantageous to both firms. Jack brought word from Grace that, at the tea parties she attended, the ladies were shocked that someone like Gennetta should run off with a sailor. That was the way they saw her actions and they had no time for Edith Briggs who appeared to be condoning such scandalous behaviour.

Jeremiah let the gossip rage, knowing full well that housekeepers, cooks and maids relished such talk, adding to it as it was passed along. He knew employers caught the drift of the salacious chatter and that Edith Briggs and Gennetta would not be immune to the scandal being sown around Whitby.

21

So he felt sure of victory as he walked up the garden path to the front door of number seven New Buildings.

The day was bright but still sharp after the morning mist had cleared. It was a day that imparted a feeling of well-being and there was a confident strut to Jeremiah's step. His black frock-coat and black-striped trousers were neatly brushed above highly polished black boots. A black bow-tie was fastened at his stiff winged collar. His top hat was worn at a jaunty angle, and his malacca walking cane with its silver knob tapped regularly on the path.

The ring of the doorbell brought Rose to see who was calling.

'Mr Jeremiah Turner calling to see his daughter.'

Her eyes widened with surprise but she maintained her composure as she had been taught. 'Yes, sir. Please step inside. I'll see if she is receiving visitors.'

For a moment Jeremiah bristled at this reception but he restrained his annoyance, knowing that this was the customary reply when someone unexpected came calling.

Rose closed the door behind him and scurried away towards a room on the right.

Jeremiah glanced round the hall. It was imposing with a curving staircase running to the right. Halfway up it passed a long Venetian window which flooded the hall with light. The walls were covered by a flower-patterned wallpaper in pastel shades adding to a feeling of spaciousness. There was little furniture, only a small table and chair at the foot of the stairs and another small table between two doors to the right. All the pieces were crafted delicately in rosewood. Quite a contrast to the sombre atmosphere of his own hall, he realised.

Rose reappeared. 'This way, sir.' She stood to one side of the open door.

He laid his hat and walking stick on the nearest table and gave her a nod of thanks as he passed into the room.

Edith, her long face serious, occupied the chair to the right of the unlit fire. Gennetta was sitting opposite on the sofa, an open book lying beside her. Her face betrayed no emotion at the sight of her father.

'Miss Briggs.' Jeremiah gave Edith a slight bow which she acknowledged with a tiny nod. He looked at his daughter. 'Gennetta.'

'Father.' Her voice was a monotone, revealing nothing.

He turned to Edith, noticing the jet bangle she wore on her right wrist. 'Miss Briggs, I'm sorry to disturb thy morning but I would be grateful if I could have a word with my daughter alone.' Jeremiah thought it best to come straight to the reason for his visit.

'What you have to say to me can be said in front of Miss Briggs,'

22

put in Gennetta icily. She guessed the reason for her father's visit – to persuade her to return home – but was determined to have none of it.

Edith held up her hand to prevent Jeremiah from saying anything more. She looked understandingly at Gennetta but said, 'My dear, your father has a right to speak to you alone and I think you ought to hear what he has to say without my presence.' She rose from her chair, halting any objections Gennetta might have made. 'I will only be in the next room.'

Jeremiah waited until the door had closed then sat down on the sofa beside Gennetta.

'Thee looks well, and pretty in that dress.' He admired the motif of blue flowers which swirled across the dress with its long sleeves tight to the wrists. A belt of matching material encompassed the tiny waist and a white lace collar adorned the neck.

She was surprised at his observation. It was rare for her father to make any comment on her appearance. Was he going to try persuasion? She knew he could be effective for she had seen him when he had entertained friends or business guests. She must spike any such ruse.

'Father, if you've come here to try to persuade me to return home, you're wasting your time. I'm not coming. And I'll certainly not marry Cyrus. I'm marrying the man I love and that is Reuben.' Her voice was sharp and Jeremiah recognised the task he faced.

'Gennetta, have thee ever considered the consequences of thy action? Dost know what people are saying?'

'Things have reached us,' she replied.

'The scandal!' He rolled his eyes heavenwards. 'Thee running away to marry a sailor must mean only one thing. There's talk everywhere.'

'Then let people talk if it satisfies their evil minds. There's no truth in what they say. You shouldn't listen to their prattle.'

'I never believed that aspect,' he hastened to reassure her. 'But talk goes on and it affects not only thee. It rubs off on thy family, thy friends, and on Miss Briggs. People say she has only taken thee in because thee's a good catch for her great-nephew.'

'That's not true!' snapped Gennetta. 'Miss Briggs is a kindly person. When I first came here she took thought for you even though she knew you showed little affection for me. She made me consider seriously the action I was taking and pointed out all its consequences. But she saw how in love Reuben and I were. Still, she only agreed to allow me to stay here until he returns to port, then we must marry.'

'But ...'

23

'No buts, Father,' she broke in. 'My mind is made up and I'll not change it.'

'I've had Robert Sleightholme to see me.'

'And that's why you're here, at his instigation?' A note of contempt had come into her voice. She was annoyed that her father had not come of his own accord.

'No, no, not that,' he replied, reading her meaning. 'He was concerned about Cyrus.'

'And his precious firm. Just as you are about yours. You both want to use us to further your own ends.' She looked away in disgust.

'No, Cyrus has a great affection for thee and both families expected thee and he would ...'

'Marry?' Gennetta finished for him. 'Well, they'll be disappointed.'

'But with Cyrus, thee'll want for nothing.'

'You mean, I will with Reuben? Well, you're wrong. He has great prospects ...'

'Those will only come about in time, and that can pass slowly for a sailor. Until then you'll have a hard life.'

'I'll endure that for the man I love, as he will for me.'

'Love can be sorely tested when there is no money.' A sudden look of comprehension crossed his face. 'Unless Miss Briggs has hidden wealth?'

'I know nothing of that,' snapped Gennetta indignantly. 'If you think for one moment that Reuben and I are scheming to obtain an old lady's money ...' Contempt sharpened her blue eyes. 'I think you had better leave. The answer is no.' She rose from the sofa, stiff with anger. He hesitated. 'Please go!'

He stood up and looked hard at his daughter. For one moment his heart missed a beat. It was almost as if he was facing his beloved Eliza.

'Gen ...' He reached out.

'Just go.'

He saw it was no use pursuing the matter now, sighed and walked towards the door.

She watched him go with mixed emotions. The door closed behind him and she sank back on to the sofa.

Edith heard the door close and came into the hall to see Jeremiah heading for the front door.

'Mr Turner ...' He stopped and turned back. 'I hope that your talk was satisfactory?'

He stared for a moment at the elderly lady who stood so erect, hands held together in front of her, looking at him with her mournful dark eyes. Into his mind came Robert's description of 'horse-faced' and he wanted to laugh, but her dignity prevented him. 'It wasn't,' he replied testily. 'I do not approve of the encouragement thee's given my daughter. Her rightful place is with me.' After a slight pause he added forcibly: 'But I'll not give up.' Then turned on his heel and left the house.

Chapter Three

Edith Briggs was thoughtful as she returned to the drawing room. She had no doubt that Jeremiah Turner would put up a fight and decided it would take all of Gennetta's resolve for her to stand firm. The girl would be sorely tested but Edith had faith in her and the love she expressed for Reuben. She must be strong for Gennetta, able to give her all the support she needed. She had promised Reuben she would look after his love. 'Keep her safe,' he had begged, and she was determined to do just that.

Edith assumed a confident air as she went into the room. Gennetta, sitting on the sofa, looked sombre and lost in thought.

She did not move as Edith crossed the room, rang the bell and then sat down in her chair.

A few moments later Rose came in.

'Hot chocolate, please, Rose.'

'Yes, ma'am.'

'Well, my dear, from your father's demeanour as he left, I take it you rebuffed him?'

'Yes.'

'And what worries you?'

'He confirmed there is scandal, but I fear it is worse than we have heard.'

Edith gave a little smile. 'People love gossip and like to enlarge on what they hear so that they appear to be in the know. We must take no notice.'

'But it affects a lot of people.'

'Maybe, but time will cure that.'

'I'm not bothered about my father, nor Jack and Grace, nor the Sleightholmes. But I am bothered about you and what people are saying.'

'Ah, so he tried to get at you through me? No doubt he'll try again.

But don't let it worry you. I'm thick-skinned. I have few friends, as you know. I don't think they will view me any differently because of this, and if any of them do then they are not worthy of the name.'

'But if I went home the rumours would stop and you wouldn't be tainted by them.'

Edith straightened in her chair, looking fiercely at Gennetta. 'You'll do no such thing! That's exactly what your father's trying to make you do. Give way, take that one step, and you'll be caught like a fly in a spider's web. There will be no escape.'

She was left to ponder those words as Rose arrived with the hot chocolate. By the time the maid had left the room Gennetta had chastised herself for allowing her resolve to weaken for one moment. She stiffened her back, tensed her shoulders, and, the mask of despondency banished, looked much more in control of the situation as she said, 'I love Reuben too much to let that love be destroyed.'

Edith gave a sigh of relief. For a few moments she had wondered if Gennetta's love was as strong as she had believed. Now, she had no qualms.

'Then stay here and forget what people say.'

Gennetta jumped from the sofa and gave her a hug. 'Thank you for your wisdom and advice.'

The barrier had been lifted and the bond of affection between them strengthened.

Edith patted her shoulder reassuringly and said, 'Now let's have our chocolate.'

As he walked home Jeremiah's thoughts turned to his daughter and her defiance. Maybe he could have shown her more affection over the years, but the loss of his wife in childbirth still pained him after all these years. He had provided for Gennetta, expected her obedience, but had reaped only opposition.

He thought of her in Edith Briggs's house, in that comfortably furnished room, its light chintz curtains framing large windows, allowing light to enhance the decorations. But more than anything else, as he had stood in the hall and sat with Gennetta, he had experienced the house's feeling of warmth and homeliness, the welcome it extended to anyone who entered.

He found himself comparing it with his own home with its sombre panelling, dark varnish, heavy furniture, and curtains so weighty they hung halfway across the windows even in daylight. It was only now, after this brief interlude of visiting his daughter, that he realised how lacking in comfort his own home was. If only Eliza had lived, she would have made it just as attractive as Edith Briggs had made hers.

Maybe then Gennetta would never have left home. Maybe she would have been set to marry Cyrus Sleightholme.

Jeremiah wondered if he could retrieve the situation by offering his daughter the chance to remodel the house, make it a home for them both. He had plenty of money to pay for the work and if she was put in charge maybe she would see what she was throwing away by marrying Reuben Briggs instead of Cyrus Sleightholme. It was worth a try. Anything was if it led to his achieving the power he craved.

The day was grey with clouds which threatened rain but might be driven away by the freshening wind. It brought waves tumbling in towards the beach below the West Cliff and drove the spray high as they broke with a crash and a roar, to send water hissing and foaming across the beach.

Cyrus bent his head against the wind as he hurried towards New Buildings. His tall, lean frame held his clothes to perfection. The cravat at his throat was neatly tied, drawing attention to his face, which was long and intelligent but frequently assumed a languid expression, as if he did not really care for anything or anybody. That attitude hid an astute sense of what was best for him. Now it was from purely selfish motives that his long legs took him through Whitby, though his father thought it was in obedience to his instructions.

Cyrus knew the advantages to himself of marrying Gennetta Turner, and if it was true that she was intent on marrying Reuben Briggs then there was no time to be lost, especially when Jeremiah's attempt had failed. He gave a wry smile as he thought of bedding this girl who was five years his junior. No experience, but he would teach her things gleaned from liaisons in Whitby society and beyond. Though he liked a life of ease and pleasure, Cyrus was shrewd enough to know that it had to be paid for and could be financed out of the jet industry. For this reason, though not wildly excited about it, he paid sufficient interest to his father's business to ensure it would be passed on to him, and knew that marrying Gennetta would bring fresh wealth along with her portion of the Turners' business.

'Mr Cyrus Sleightholme to see Miss Gennetta Turner,' he announced when the door was opened by Rose.

'Step inside, sir. I'll see if Miss Turner is receiving visitors.' Rose's voice was expressionless. She knew Cyrus by sight and reputation, and disapproved of him. Besides she didn't like 'dandified men', as she termed those with a taste for excessively fine clothes and flamboyant manners. She closed the door behind him and hurried away, to return a few moments later to show him into the drawing room after she had taken his top hat and cane.

He swept into the room with a flourish to find Gennetta sitting on a chair beside the window.

'My dear Gennetta.' He made an elaborate bow before continuing towards her.

'Cyrus,' she acknowledged with a slight nod of her head. She indicated a chair and he sat down opposite her, adjusting the fall of his coat as he did so. She saw that a sharp gleam in his grey eyes had driven away the usual dreamy expression. She guessed he was here to make another attempt to get her to return home and marry him and smiled to herself. What would their fathers dream up next?

'I trust you are well?' His words flowed smoothly, almost in a drawl.

'Yes, thank you, Cyrus,' replied Gennetta. Amusement twitched the corners of her mouth and there was laughter in her eyes as she went on, 'But I don't think you are here to enquire after my health.'

He raised his brows. 'How perceptive of you, my dear. You are right. I am here to ask you to marry me.'

The directness of his statement took Gennetta aback but she quickly regained her composure. Before she could reply he went on, 'We have known each other since childhood. Our families have been friends for years. Both are in the jet trade. We have a lot in common. It was always expected we would marry one day.'

Gennetta drew herself up straight and looked haughtily at him. 'People should not expect such things.'

'But ...'

'No buts, Cyrus. This is all a ploy. You've been sent here by your father and probably mine as well, but they cannot get round me this way.' Her eyes kindled. 'Nor any other way, for that matter. Oh, I've known the way people were thinking. We've been good friends, but nothing more.'

'Love can grow from such relationships, especially after marriage.'

'Not in my case, Cyrus. I already love Reuben Briggs and I am going to marry him. It is no good your coming here with your proposal – you've never expressed any love for me before. Our fathers are using you, just as they would use me, to further their own ends.'

'Maybe they are but it could work to our advantage. And to say I don't love you is not strictly correct. I have always admired you.'

'That is not the same as love,' she put in hotly.

'But where there is admiration love will follow. Marry me and you'll want for nothing. Whatever our fathers plan regarding the two firms, we will benefit.'

29

'Stop it, Cyrus.' Her words came out sharply. 'This interview must end here and now. Nothing is going to make me change my mind. I care nothing for our fathers' schemes. I want to marry, and will marry, the man I love – Reuben Briggs.' She held up her hand to stem the protestations she saw springing to his lips. 'There is nothing more to be said. I would be grateful if you would leave now.'

His eyes darkened with anger. It was obviously no use his saying any more. He rose to his feet and looked down at her, hissing like a snake: 'You'll regret this, Gennetta. You'll wish you'd never rejected me.' Then, without any farewell, he hurried to the door.

Shaken by the venom in his voice she stared at his back. Startled by the slam of the door, she shivered. The unexpected threat had left a chill in this cosy room.

'Now let's get down to the invitations, Gennetta. It will take your mind off Cyrus. I'm sure he meant nothing by it.' Edith gave a little shrug of her shoulders and pursed her lips. 'What can he do after all? You rejected him. It was only his pride and anger speaking.'

They busied themselves with pen and paper, a task which did not take long for it had been decided to have a small wedding. Neither Gennetta nor Reuben had formed any deep friendships with their contemporaries. Reuben had named three crew members he wanted to ask, apart from Captain Barrick, and both had agreed to ask Archibald Cooper, the drawing tutor through whom they had met when children. Edith had six friends she wanted to invite besides her solicitor, Cornelius Mitchell, who had been a friend as well as legal adviser ever since her parents had died when she was twenty.

'I would like to invite Mrs Bates and Mrs Peters. They were kind to me when I had no mother,' said Gennetta, seeking Edith's approval.

'That's a kind thought. They should be asked,' she agreed, and eyed the girl. 'What about your father, and your brother and his wife?'

Gennetta stiffened. 'After their attitude? Never!'

'They ought to be asked,' said Edith, adopting a conciliatory tone.

'They wouldn't come.'

'You don't know. They might accept the olive branch you would be offering, and if they did life would be considerably easier for you. I think you should ask them.'

Gennetta stared thoughtfully at her pen. Knowing it was wisest to say no more, Edith awaited her decision. The girl looked up slowly and met her solemn gaze.

'Very well,' she said quietly.

A smile lightened Edith's face. 'Good.'

The invitations were despatched the next day and Gennetta waited with some trepidation for her father's reaction.

It came two days later.

Jeremiah did not wait to be announced once he had been admitted to the house but stormed past Rose and burst into the drawing room. His eyes went immediately to his daughter, standing to face him in front of the fireplace.

She had shared little of Edith's hope that he would be reconciled by the invitation and, anticipating a stormy confrontation, felt it was better to deal with it standing. She stiffened her back, resolved not to be brow-beaten by him.

'So thee's ganning through with this marriage, in spite of my disapproval!' The colour was rising in his neck.

'Yes, Father. I am marrying the man I love.'

He gave a snort of derision. 'Well, don't expect me to be there. Nor Jack, nor Grace. And I have forbidden Mrs Bates and Mrs Peters to attend, on pain of instant dismissal.'

'You'd deny me any happiness and pleasure on that day?'

'Aye. And thee'll be cutting thyself off from the family. There'll be not one penny from me, ever. Think on these things.'

'I have since your last visit. But I count them as nothing where Reuben is concerned.'

Jeremiah's lips tightened. Maybe threats had been the wrong approach. Was it too late to adopt another? His voice softened a little though his eyes still burned with anger at her defiance. 'I'm prepared to let thee change the house, brighten it up and run it as thee wish, if thee'll forget this marriage ...'

'... and marry Cyrus Sleightholme,' she finished for him, looking at him with contempt. 'Bribes won't win me over. They are as contemptible as sending Cyrus here.'

'He wanted to come.'

'I could see you and his father behind it. Maybe there was something genuine in his proposal, maybe a little spark of interest in me, but I had none in him, and any respect I once had died as soon as he began to threaten me. Now, if you've nothing agreeable to say, please leave.' Her voice was cold. 'And remember this, Father. You killed my feeling for you when you blamed me for Mother's death and became so obsessed with your business that you had no time to spare for me. But maybe I could yet forgive that if you could bring yourself to approve my marriage to Reuben?'

His face reddened with anger as the truth hit home. He glared at her. 'Don't come running to me when things go wrong. Thee's

31

destroyed any connection with me and with Jack.'

His eyes bored deep into hers but she held his gaze until he turned and hurried from the room. As the door banged shut the tension drained from her and she sank wearily on to a chair.

'Rose, you can recognise the *Diana*?' Edith asked on the day of Reuben's homecoming.

'Oh, yes, ma'am,' replied Rose, who had been orphaned when her mother drowned herself after Rose's father, an ordinary seaman, had been lost at sea. The only legacy he had left his daughter was an interest in ships. She had grown up watching them about their trade in Whitby and soon came to recognise them as individuals.

'Then away to the cliff top,' urged Edith.

'And let us know the moment you see her,' added Gennetta. Excitement rang her voice. Reuben would soon be home and they would be married in two days' time.

'Yes, miss.' And Rose scuttled from the room.

Time dragged. Gennetta could not settle. She tried following Edith's example by calmly embroidering but concentration was beyond her. A glimmer of amusement crossed Edith's face when Gennetta rose from her chair for the twelfth time to look out of the window, but she made no comment. Gennetta saw nothing, her mind too occupied with thoughts of Reuben.

An hour had passed when Rose burst into the room. 'The *Diana*'s 'ere!' she cried.

'Off with you,' Edith told Gennetta.

Already halfway to the door, she stopped and turned. 'But you're coming too?'

Edith smiled. 'No. This time Reuben's homecoming is a moment for you two to savour without me.'

'But ...'

'No buts.' Edith gave a dismissive wave of her hand.

Gennetta hurried into the hall. She slipped her high-waisted green velvet pelisse over a pale blue muslin dress which fell straight from the high waist to two small scalloped flounces above the hem. She quickly smoothed the wide Vandyke collar over her shoulders and slid a straw hat trimmed with blue ribbon on to her head. She was running out of the house in a matter of moments, in her haste forgetting her gloves and bag. But she did not care. All that mattered was that Reuben was coming home.

The sound of the front door closing reached Edith. She stiffened, lips tightening as she gave a tiny grunt of disapproval at her own forgetfulness. She should be with Gennetta. She had always accompanied the girl whenever she had gone out for she was sure that there were times when they were followed. Now, in the excitement, she had let her caution drop. She put down her sewing and hurried into the hall. There was no time to change. She threw her waist-length cape over her shoulders, covering the embroidery of the wide white lace pelerine topping her dress. She tied the yellow ribbons of her wide-brimmed bonnet beneath her chin, pulled on her gloves, grabbed her silver-topped walking stick and swung out of the house.

She breathed a sigh of relief when she saw Gennetta ahead and matched her haste to that of the younger woman. She was determined to keep her in sight but not be seen. If there was a threat to Gennetta it must not materialise now.

Her heart as light as her feet, which barely touched the ground, Gennetta was soon nearing the bridge which spanned the river between the east and west banks, joining the crowded confines of the old town to the newer development on the West Cliff. Red-roofed houses, with smoke curling from their forest of chimneys reached up, one seemingly on top of another, towards the old parish church and ruined abbey high on the East Cliff. But Gennetta had no eyes for them. She glanced towards the sea. The *Diana* had not yet reached the piers at the mouth of the river. Gennetta would cross the bridge before it was swivelled back to allow the ship to move upstream to a quay beside the east bank.

Her progress was slowed by the mass of people going to and fro across the bridge as they hurried about their business: housewives with their shopping, carpenters from the shipyards, fishermen heading for their boats, sailors making for the inns – some of them, stirred by the drink they had already consumed, calling raucously to pretty girls, who ignored them or gave as good as they got. She reached the east side and turned down Grape Lane, unaware that Edith was starting to cross the bridge or that there were other eyes watching her.

Gennetta slipped through the throng of people in Grape Lane and came out on to Church Street where she turned alongside the river in the direction of the wharves. Three merchantmen were already at their berths rising and falling with the gentle motion of the water. Lines of men, shirts open at the neck, were unloading two vessels containing spices from Africa and wines from Portugal, while the third ship was being loaded with butter, flour, eggs, hams, pickled fish and tallow candles, destined for London. Further along, a fishing vessel unloaded its catch and ten women, mob-caps tight to their heads to keep their hair from falling into their eyes, sleeves rolled above their elbows, deftly gutted fish with sharp knives. Gulls screeched and wheeled to dive and snatch a tasty morsel from the guts among the glistening fishscales on the quayside.

All the activity added to Gennetta's excitement as she reached the quay where the *Diana* would berth. Knots of people were already there and others were joining them or forming their own groups as they eagerly awaited the return of their loved ones. Other onlookers positioned themselves further back, wanting to leave space for the crew's relations. Gennetta pushed her way to the front of them and moved close to the edge of the quay.

Edith stayed on the periphery of the crowd which was swelling with every minute as the *Diana* was manoeuvred past the bridge. She looked around and a tremor ran through her. Cyrus Sleightholme! Her heart fluttered. What was he doing here? He had no interest in the ship nor its cargo. His trade was jet. Edith took a grip on herself. He had a right to be here just as everyone else had. Why should she think he was here for another purpose? Was she being suspicious and mistrustful for no reason? She thought back. Was she really sure she and Gennetta had been followed when they went out? Was it not just a suspicion?

Cyrus moved a couple of paces to his right and it put his face into full view. A cold dread filled her when she saw his eyes, wide with malevolence, fixed on Gennetta. He meant her harm, Edith was sure of it. She must do something!

He started to push his way through the crowd. Edith moved quickly, ignoring the muttered protests and annoyed looks as she elbowed her way towards him. He had almost reached the front of the crowd, directly in line with Gennetta, when Edith reached out and touched his arm.

'Good day, Cyrus, I'm surprised to see you here,' she said as pleasantly as she could.

He started and glanced round. Shocked to see Edith Briggs, he glared at her for a moment then, without a word, pushed his way back through the crowd and was gone.

The tension drained from her. What had he intended? An 'accidental' push? The act of a jealous man, a thwarted lover or a man whose ambitions had been dashed? Whatever, Edith was relieved that she had been here for she was sure that he had meant to harm Gennetta. She would be glad when the wedding was over and the girl was beyond revenge. Or at least that was how she saw it. She waited and watched until she saw the two lovers united, then made her way home.

* * *

Reuben was one of the first ashore when the gangway was run out. It was always a thrilling experience to return to his home port. The ruined abbey was the first thing to be glimpsed, a promise of home and those he loved: Great-aunt Edith and Gennetta. Today it had held a greater significance; it marked his return to a wife. He had spotted Gennetta close to the quayside and excitement surged through him when his wave was answered.

Now, with eyes for no one else, he ran into her open arms. There was no need for words. Their looks said everything and the tears which ran down her cheeks were those of joy and happiness. Their lips met and sealed their love, and when they stepped back they still held hands and kept their eyes fixed on one another. His sparkled with the thrill of having her for his sweetheart; hers were filled with admiration and adoration which she would give to no one else.

'I love you.' He mouthed the words silently.

She laughed with a joy which knew no bounds. 'And I you.'

They came into each other's arms again and held each other tightly.

'Let's go home,' he whispered close to her ear.

She eased her embrace so she could look at him. 'Haven't you work to do?'

'Knowing we are to be married, Captain Barrick released me.'

'Good.' She took his hand and they started for the west side of the river.

The rest of the day and that following were hectic as Reuben was briefed on the arrangements and the ceremony, which was to take place in the old parish church on the cliff top.

There was an autumnal nip to the air when the smiling bride and groom came out of the church. The day had been overcast with grey clouds but without the threat of rain when they had entered the Norman building.

To Reuben the dull day meant nothing for it only helped to make Gennetta a more sparkling bride in her dress of white net worn over a white satin underdress. Embroidered with a motif of bunches of flowers interspersed with falling oak leaves, it was trimmed with her favourite colour, blue, which matched the delicate silk shawl thrown casually round her shoulders and over the puff sleeves of her dress. She wore a white bonnet with a blue ribbon tied below her chin. Instead of a bouquet she had decided to carry a prayer book covered in white satin on which was mounted a plain jet cross.

Beside her Reuben's morning coat was cut away at the waist, plunging at the back into square-cut tails. His yellow shawl-collared waistcoat, embroidered with red floral sprays, revealed a plain high-collared shirt and pale blue cravat tied in the waterfall style. His trousers, matching the dark blue of his coat, narrowed towards the ankles and were held by instep straps around his highly polished black shoes.

They paused outside the church where sightseers had gathered to see the bride and groom. Laughing joyously, they greeted their guests as they came from the church. Carriages, each drawn by two horses, waited beyond the churchyard to take them to the reception Aunt Edith had insisted be held ceremoniously in the Assembly Room at the Angel Inn.

Gennetta shivered. There was an undeniable chill in the air. She glanced to the north. The sky was darkening out to sea. For the first time she thought, Why couldn't it be sunny for my wedding? Her eyes strayed across the silent graveyard, with its tombstones greening with age or at ungainly angles where land had slipped near the edge of the cliff. Suddenly she started. A bleak, silent figure in black stood among the stones. He wore a long coat with a black velvet collar and carried a cane. His top hat was pulled down at the front so that she could not distinguish his face at this distance, but she felt he was staring purely at her and not taking in the rest of the scene.

She glanced at Reuben for reassurance and saw laughter in his eyes as he spoke to Captain Barrick. No one else appeared to have noticed the man. She looked back across the graveyard. The figure had gone. Gennetta started. She looked around quickly but there was no sign of him. She felt panic grip her. Had she been mistaken? Had he been a figment of her imagination, or was this graveyard truly haunted?

'Something wrong, my dear?' Aunt Edith's query startled her.

'No,' she hastened to reassure her, and took hold of Reuben's arm.

He turned to her and smiled. 'Shall we go?'

'Please.'

They started across the graveyard towards the waiting carriages.

A flash streaked through the black sky far out to sea and a few moments later thunder rumbled, leaving behind an uncanny stillness. The breeze which always seemed to curl around the cliff top had subsided. There was no movement to stir the grass. An oppressive silence hung over the churchyard.

Feeling the need to be away, the party quickened their steps, only to stop as one when a high-pitched sound like the eerie baying of hounds broke the silence. It came from the sky and all eyes turned to the north-east. Against a lighter patch of sky, birds flew in a V-formation towards the land.

'The Gabriel Hounds!' someone whispered, in a voice charged with horror.

The uncanny screeching went on as the geese flew nearer and nearer.

'Don't look,' cried someone else.

Fear in their faces, guests turned their backs to the oncoming birds, covering their eyes with their hands or pressing their face against the nearest gravestone.

'Oh, no, not on my wedding day!' Gennetta gasped. Transfixed, she stared at the sky, unable to tear her gaze away from the birds flying unerringly towards her. The Gabriel Hounds, harbingers of ill-omen and death. She shivered, mesmerised by the symmetry of the formation, the swish of their wings in unison and the cries which were commonly believed to herald dreadful misfortune.

They flew nearer and nearer, their screeches growing louder and louder until they almost deafened her. They passed overhead and on beyond the gaunt black outline of the ruined abbey, vanishing just as the figure in black had done from the graveyard.

Chapter Four

Edith Briggs, sitting on the sofa in her drawing room, arm round two-year-old Nathaniel, looked solemn. Worry seemed to have made her cheeks sag even more, adding a doleful quality to her expression. She hugged Nathaniel closer, as if drawing comfort and reassurance from him. The door of the room stood open to allow noises from the rest of the house to reach her. At the moment all was quiet and the silence charged the atmosphere with uncertainty. Edith fidgeted and then rebuked herself for getting agitated.

'Soon, Nathan, soon.' She spoke quietly, more to calm her own anxiety than anything else. 'A little sister or brother for you.'

At the sound of her voice the child looked up, his light blue eyes wide, mouth turned up in a fetching smile.

She gave him a loving squeeze and thought how much happiness Gennetta, Reuben and their child had brought her. The house had come alive. They had shaken her out of her hermit's existence and though at first the upheaval had had its drawbacks, she liked it. Now there would be another to bring joy to her.

She focused her mind, wondering what name Gennetta and Reuben had chosen. Before Nathaniel was born they had picked his name, with a female alternative should the baby be a girl.

Edith's speculation stopped as the piercing cry of a newborn penetrated the house.

At almost the same second Rose came round the door from the post in the hall which she had taken up when Gennetta had gone into labour. She had been waiting for this moment. She held out her arms and took Nathan from Edith with a smile of reassurance for the boy. There was no need of it. He was used to Rose whom Miss Briggs has assigned to Gennetta especially to help with him. Soon she would have a second child to look after too.

Edith, her heart beating faster, hurried to the stairs and climbed

38

them quickly. Her doleful look had been replaced by an eagerness for news, while anxiety tightened her chest in case all was not well with mother and baby.

As she reached the top of the stairs the midwife's assistant hurried past her carrying a pail. Edith pushed the bedroom door open and took in the situation at a glance. The doctor, his shirt sleeves rolled high above his elbows, was standing at the bottom of the bed drying his hands, having washed in a bowl of steaming water. The full-bosomed midwife, face wreathed in smiles, was holding a baby towards Gennetta whose pale face against the rumpled pillows showed relief that it was all over.

Edith paused and watched her take the baby, cradling it close to her as she gazed at it with adoring eyes.

'Well?' Edith asked, happy that the birth appeared to have been normal.

There was a contented smile on Gennetta's face as she answered, 'Aunt, meet your niece.'

'A girl! Splendid, splendid!' she cried, stepping towards the bed. She exchanged reassuring smiles with the doctor and the midwife.

'A fine healthy bairn, ma'am,' said the midwife, then went about her business of tidying up.

Edith reassured herself that Gennetta looked well and then turned her eyes to the baby.

She smiled with pleasure when the child snuffled and rubbed one chubby clenched hand across its nose. Unlike many newborn babies, who at first sight appeared wrinkled and unappealing, Edith found this one plump and bonny.

'She's beautiful,' she said, gently touching the baby's hand. 'What are you going to call her?'

Gennetta, delighted at the pleasure on Edith's face, smiled at her. 'Before he sailed, Reuben and I decided that if it was a girl we would call her Flora.'

'Ah, "beautiful offspring". How appropriate,' replied Edith. She sensed the midwife hovering behind her and took the hint. 'Now you get some rest and sleep. Everything is taken care of.'

Gennetta's smile was appreciative. 'You are so good to us.'

Edith pursed her lips in irritation. 'It's nothing, my dear child, nothing. You've brought new life to me.' She stepped out of the way and the midwife took charge of Flora, laying her gently in the cot beside the bed.

Edith accompanied the doctor downstairs. 'Everything went well? No complications?' she asked.

'None at all. Gennetta just needs rest. I've never seen a healthier baby.'

His reassurance drove out any last anxiety. 'Thank you, Isaac, I'm grateful for all you have done.'

'I've done nothing, Edith, only helped Gennetta. She did all the hard work. I'll look in tomorrow.'

Edith saw him out and returned to tell Nathaniel that he had a little sister, Flora.

Gennetta woke and immediately a feeling of happiness permeated her whole being. She turned her head to look at the baby sleeping contentedly in the cot beside her. How fortunate she was.

These last two years had been steeped in happiness, marred only when Reuben left Whitby on the *Diana*. But at least he was happy and getting on well. Promotion was certain, and with his ability and determination no doubt one day he would be master of a merchantman. She was happy because he was happy, and both felt blessed when Nathaniel was born a year after their marriage. Now, Gennetta felt life was being almost too good to them with the birth of Flora. Miss Briggs had been so kind and in the contented atmosphere of her home Gennetta found peace, tranquillity and the love which had been missing from her life with her father and brother.

For a while after her wedding day she had worried about the appearance of the Gabriel Hounds, but when the doom they were supposed to presage did not materialise they receded from her mind until they were almost forgotten. In those early days of marriage it was the appearance of the figure in the churchyard that worried her more, for she saw in that figure the embodiment of Cyrus's malice towards her. Had he come merely to witness the wedding? If so, why remain distant? Why appear so mysteriously and disappear the same way? There one moment, gone the next. Why did the mere memory conjure up a shivery feeling of doom? Was she just linking him with the appearance of the Gabriel Hounds or was it something to do with his final words the last time she had spoken with him: 'You'll wish you'd never rejected me?'

The threat still seemed to hover over her. On two occasions the figure had materialised at unexpected moments: on the quay the first time she had seen Reuben sail after they were married, and again across the churchyard after Nathaniel's christening. Each time Gennetta had worried for a while but said nothing to anyone. She had thought of visiting Cyrus and tackling him about it but realised she would only look foolish when he denied that he was the figure, as he surely would. So she had let the matter lie and with the passing of this last year when she had not seen him again she had all but forgotten the incidents.

* * *

40

'We couldn't have had a more beautiful day for a christening.' Gennetta's smile was broad, her voice tinged with joy as she stepped out into the bright sunshine. 'I only wish Reuben could be here.'

'Only another three weeks,' comforted Edith, and half turned. 'Careful with that bairn.' Her voice was sharp, her eyes piercing, but the nurse carrying the child did not take this as a slur on her efficiency. She knew it was only Miss Briggs's way of showing concern for Flora's welfare. Besides she would be leaving in two weeks and handing over her responsibilities to Rose, now carrying Nathaniel to the coach which would take them to the church on the East Cliff.

They clambered in, settled themselves, and then the coachman was away. He guided the two horses carefully down the curving road to the bridge. Pedestrians pressed back to either side to allow the coach to pass, some staring curiously, others cursing at having their progress momentarily halted. The coachman turned his horses along the lower reaches of Church Street, passing the quays which lined this bank of the river until he turned into Green Lane. He urged on the horses with harsh tones as the way steepened. The animals responded to his commands and soon they reached the top of the bank. They passed the ruined abbey and trotted beyond it to the old church.

The parson, smiling and welcoming them effusively, greeted the party and ushered them through the porch to the font which stood at the top of the nave. He performed the short service with due solemnity.

As they emerged from the church, with everyone's attention now on the child held in her mother's arms, Gennetta shivered in spite of the warm sunshine. She was feeling uneasy, just as she had done when ... She glanced across the churchyard and started. There he stood among the gravestones, a sombre figure in black trousers and waist-length jacket, cut away to knee-length tails. He wore a black top hat and carried a black cane. Gennetta felt her colour drain away. Cyrus? She glanced at her small party, hoping that someone else had seen him, but they were all intent on fussing over the baby. She tried to speak, to draw someone else's attention to him, but she was tongue-tied. Her gaze was drawn back across the space separating them. There was no one there! She shivered and clutched Flora more tightly, as if protecting her from some unexplained threat. She glanced skywards, half expecting to see a flight of geese heading towards them, but there was nothing.

'Come along now, it's time we were getting to the coach.' Aunt Edith was marshalling everyone.

41

Gennetta started. The nurse was reaching out for Flora. 'I'll carry her!' The sharpness in her voice startled the nurse who was surprised to see her hug her daughter more closely to her and hurry away as if seeking protection in the coach.

Gennetta sank back on the seat, pleased when the others were around her and the coach was in motion. She tried to drive thoughts of the strange appearance from her mind, telling herself that whoever it was had a perfect right to be there and was not interested in them. But still a nagging doubt remained. She looked down at the baby, sleeping contentedly in her arms. Surely no one could intend to harm such innocent beauty? 'No one shall, my love,' she whispered softly to herself, and glanced up to see the nurse staring at her with curiosity and concern. She held out Flora. 'You take her.' Gennetta smiled and saw the nurse relax visibly. Her job had not been usurped.

Gennetta vowed to tell Reuben about the figure in black but, immersed in the joy of her children and Aunt Edith's companionship and love, the disturbance began to recede from her mind. As Reuben's homecoming drew near she realised there would be no point in telling him. He would listen sympathetically and then, with reason, say she was imagining a threat. People had a perfect right to visit the churchyard and geese could bring no evil. No doubt he would be right.

Her fears allayed, she was on the quay to watch the *Diana* manoeuvre upstream, pass the bridge and tie up at her berth on her latest return. Clusters of people – relatives of the crew, businessmen interested in her cargo, and folk who drew pleasure from watching one of Whitby's fleet of merchantmen arrive home – were scattered along the quay. Once the gangplank was run out, sailors swarmed ashore to greet their loved ones.

'Gennetta!' Reuben swept her into his arms and she thrilled to feel his strength encompass her.

'Reuben!' His name came in a long drawn-out whisper, charged with joy and excitement.

Their lips met, eager to bridge their separation.

'All go well?' he asked.

'Yes.' She leaned back in his arms so that she could watch his expression. 'And you'll just love your daughter.'

'A girl!' Intoxicated with the news, he lifted his wife off her feet and whirled her round in joyous abandon. Her laughter floated across the quay, turning a few heads. 'I love you so,' he cried, and as her feet touched the ground, kissed her again, expressing all the feelings he had for her as a husband and lover. 'Come on, I must see her.' Grasping her hand, he started to hurry away.

42

'Haven't you work to do?' cried Gennetta, trying to keep pace with him.

'No. Captain Barrick gave me immediate shore leave to see the new bairn.'

Gennetta matched her pace to his and, hand in hand, they hurried to Aunt Edith's house, chattering and exchanging news with all the animation of lovers reunited.

'You do like her?' asked Gennetta as she lay in his arms later that evening.

Moonlight filtered through the net curtains and bathed the room in a silvery glow.

'Mmm.' Reuben sounded doubtful.

Gennetta twisted round and propped herself on her elbows so that she could scrutinise his expression.

'Well?' she prompted, her face serious.

'I'm not sure ...' he started, then burst out laughing. 'You should see your face!'

'You ...' She gave him a playful tap on the shoulder, admonishing him for his teasing, and then collapsed on top of him in laughter.

He hugged her tight, thrilling to the feel of her warm naked body. 'Of course I like her. I love her as well – almost as much as I love her mother.'

She smiled, encouraging him with her eyes, trailing her fingers down his bare chest. He drew her to him and in the passion of the moment their separation was forgotten.

'I'll be back as soon as possible,' Reuben reassured his wife as he opened the front door.

She watched him hurry down the path, his stride so full of confidence. She was so proud of him! His prospects were good, and with them in mind he had willingly accepted Captain Barrick's offer to teach him navigation, something he continued ashore as well as at sea.

Gennetta closed the door and turned idly towards the parlour. The house was quiet. Aunt Edith was out visiting a friend, the children were having their afternoon nap, the two housemaids, Barbara and Helen, had the afternoon free and had gone to visit their mother. Reaching the parlour door, Gennetta changed her mind about doing some embroidery. She felt like some company. She knew Mrs Shaw would be preparing the evening meal, so decided to go to the kitchen and ask for a cup of tea which would also enable her to have a chat.

She crossed the hall and pushed open the door to the kitchen – to freeze in horror.

Rose was on a stool, reaching up for some clothes that were hanging on a line strung from the ceiling above the large black cooking range with its central coal fire. She had stretched too far forward. The hem of her dress caught the hot embers and before she could fully recover her balance, flames flared upwards.

Mrs Shaw, busy at a table on the opposite side of the room, had her back to the scene.

'Rose!' yelled Gennetta, loudly and urgently.

Mrs Shaw, startled by this outburst which had shattered the tranquillity of her kitchen, swung round with a bowl in each hand. The sight of Rose's dress on fire sent the bowls crashing to the floor, to disintegrate into hundreds of pieces and splash their contents across the kitchen. She rushed around the table in the centre of the room but Gennetta was already grabbing Rose.

The maid's piercing screams resounded from the walls as she jumped off the stool. In her panic she started to run for the door but Gennetta had a grip on her shoulders. Ignoring the flames, she thrust her body hard against Rose's, sending her stumbling across the room. Gennetta followed and used all her weight to bring her crashing down to the floor beside a clip-rug. Gennetta swooped and, in one movement, rolled Rose in the rug, beating out the flames. Mrs Shaw dropped to her knees beside her and in a matter of moments the flames were out.

Rose, trembling with shock, was still screaming, eyes wide with terror.

'You're all right, Rose. All right!' Mrs Shaw's voice was firm, trying to cut through the hysteria which was mounting in the girl.

'Rose! Rose!' Gennetta lent her weight to Mrs Shaw's efforts to bring some calm to the victim. 'The fire's out. You'll be all right. Come on, try and stand up.'

The screaming subsided but as Gennetta and Mrs Shaw helped her to her feet, great sobs racked Rose's body.

'You'll be all right,' Gennetta said reassuringly.

The rug dropped to the floor to reveal a badly burned dress and unsightly burns on the calves of her legs.

They helped Rose to a chair and Mrs Shaw immediately started to treat the burns while Gennetta went off to find some more clothes for Rose.

When she returned the cook had removed the burned clothing and was applying some of her home-made salve. Rose still sobbed and winced every time Mrs Shaw touched her.

'She'll be all right but I think we'd better have the doctor. I'll go for him, you get her dressed,' said the cook.

By the time the doctor had carried out his examination and was satisfied that he could do little more than had already been done, Rose was calm again, though still in some pain. When Gennetta returned to the kitchen after seeing the doctor out, Rose had tears in her eyes. 'Oh, Mrs Briggs, you saved my life. How can I ever thank you?'

'There's no need, Rose. Just you get better quickly,' Gennetta replied sympathetically.

'What a blessing you came in when you did, Mrs Briggs,' said Mrs Shaw. 'I might have been too late. Thank goodness you were so quick in thinking of the rug.'

Admiration for Gennetta shone in her eyes. She had liked her from their first meeting and enjoyed having her in the house, finding her thoughtful and considerate, without any false pride. The girl had given the young master two fine children and Mrs Shaw had visualised her future as that of a good wife and mother, but now she saw more – a quick-thinking person who could size up a situation and act upon it quickly. Her admiration grew and she knew Rose would consider herself forever in Gennetta's debt.

The day before Reuben was due back at sea, Edith slipped on a crimson redingote over a pale yellow delaine dress patterned with a tiny red rose motif. She tied the dark green ribbons of her silk bonnet in a huge bow beneath her chin. They emphasised her long face and sagging cheeks. She glanced in the mirror and, satisfied that her bonnet sat neatly on her delicate lace cap, picked up her parasol, gave it a twirl, and smiled at herself in the long mirror in her bedroom. She knew deep down that the smile was really to reassure herself, to try to allay the fears which had begun to nag at her. Her suspicions, later upheld by her doctor, had made her decide to do something about a certain situation before it was too late. There were now two babes to think about as well as Reuben and Gennetta.

She left the house determined to carry through her resolve. Twenty minutes later, after a pleasant walk in the morning sunshine, she was being admitted to the office of Cornelius Mitchell, Solicitor.

'Ah, my dear Edith, it is good to see you.' Cornelius, a small dapper man, came from behind his desk to greet her. The slight stoop to his shoulders made him seem even smaller than he was.

'Time you got yourself fattened up, Cornelius.' She gave him a friendly tap on his arm with her parasol.

45

'I try, Edith.' He threw up his hands in a hopeless gesture. 'But no matter how much I eat, and I like my food, I never put on weight. Still, it keeps me sprightly.'

She knew that was true for in spite of his fifty-six years he was an active walker who loved to roam the cliff paths.

'Do sit down.' He fussed around, pulling a high-backed leather armchair closer to the desk.

They had known each other a long time and had become friends. Edith drew comfort from the fact that her affairs were in good hands, and that Cornelius could be relied upon to be discreet in all their dealings.

'Will you take a glass of Madeira?' He cocked his head like a sparrow looking for pickings. His brown eyes danced with curiosity.

Edith pursed her lips for a moment then nodded and said, 'Why not, Cornelius? Why not?'

He moved across the office in short quick steps to a mahogany press, the glass doors of which were draped in green baize on the inside. His long thin fingers turned the key and he swung the door open. He poured two glasses of wine, taking care that they were filled in equal measure. It was a ritual which always amused Edith but she knew from previous experience that it was wise not to speak while it was being carried out.

He brought one glass and placed it on his oak desk in front of Edith, who acknowledged it with a nod. He brought the second glass round behind the desk, placed it dead centre in front of his chair and sat down. He paused for a moment then reached out, curled his fingers round the stem, raised the glass and said, 'To you, Edith.' His thin face was solemn and his sunken cheeks seemed to recede even further when he spoke.

Edith raised her glass. 'And you, Cornelius.' She sipped the wine, savoured it and said, 'An admirable Madeira, Cornelius.' She sipped again. 'Yes, admirable.'

He smiled, pleased that his knowledge of wines had been acknowledged. 'Gennetta and the children well?' he asked.

'Very,' she replied. 'Little Flora is a real darling.'

'Reuben will miss them when he sails tomorrow.'

'Certain to. He dotes on her and on Nathan.'

'So he should. And I hear that he's highly thought of by Captain Barrick?'

'So I believe. He always said he would do well if I let him go to sea.'

Cornelius leaned back in his chair and eyed her shrewdly. 'Now, Edith, I can tell from your demeanour that this isn't a social call, though I would be pleased if it was and we could go on chatting.'

She gave a little smile. 'You're astute, Cornelius, always were. Nobody could pull the wool over your eyes.' He smiled at the praise. 'I suppose that's why I have you as my solicitor. Well, I'll come straight to the point.' Edith met his gaze. 'I want to alter my will,' she said firmly.

Something inside Cornelius protested but outwardly he remained calm. 'This is a sudden decision.'

'No. It has been in my mind for some time but I never got round to coming to see you. Flora's birth has pricked me into action. I really must think of Reuben and his two children, and Gennetta of course.'

Cornelius knitted his brows thoughtfully, but before he made any comment Edith went on.

'You see, and this is strictly between you and me, I am dying.'

'What?' Cornelius sat bolt upright, his face expressing disbelief. 'Never! You look so healthy.'

Edith gave a wan smile. 'Yes, I do, but that may not be for long. I have this pain ... it is becoming more frequent.'

'Your doctor?'

'He says nothing can be done. He's given me something to deaden the pain, so I'll last a little while longer.'

'Does Reuben know?'

'No. Nor Gennetta. And they mustn't until I deem it the right time. Now I want your promise on this?'

Cornelius spread his hands. 'My dear Edith, I'll not say a word, you know that.' His expression changed to one of sympathy and concern. 'I am so sorry ... what more can I say? Except that I hope you are wrong.'

Edith dismissed the suggestion with a wave of her hand. 'I wish I were but ...' She gave a little shrug of her shoulders, then stiffened her spine. 'Let's not be maudlin about this, it comes to us all sooner or later. I've had a good life and lived in the way I chose to. My only regret is that I'll not see those two bonny bairns grow up. Now for my will.'

'You want me to add a codicil leaving something to Reuben and his family?' Cornelius drew a sheet of paper in front of him and picked up a pencil as he was speaking.

'No, I want a completely new will.'

His eyes widened in surprise. 'But the previous beneficiary ...' Disturbing thoughts were running through his mind.

'Doesn't need anything from me now. But Reuben, as yet only on low pay, needs some security for the future and I can provide it.'

Cornelius pursed his lips thoughtfully. 'That's true,' he commented,

47

but there was an edge of disquiet in his voice.

'You foresee snags?' she asked doubtfully.

Cornelius gave a little start. 'No, no.'

Edith relaxed. 'Good. I want everything to go to Reuben, and in the event of his dying before me, God forbid, it is to go to Gennetta.'

Cornelius made notes to this effect on the sheet of paper then read them out to Edith. He looked up at her. 'That is what you want?'

She nodded. 'Precisely.'

Cornelius wrote the date, June 1, 1848, on the sheet of paper, an automatic action which he always performed whenever he made a record of any importance. When he raised his eyes his doubtful expression was unmistakable. 'You are absolutely certain about this?'

'Yes.'

'It's a big change you're making.'

'I know, but that's how I want it.'

'Very well, I'll draw up the necessary documents in due course. When you've signed them they will be binding. The old one will then be rescinded.'

'Good. No one need ever know that there has been a previous will. You must destroy it. The secret we hold must remain that way.'

'Very well.'

Edith relaxed. She felt more at ease now that the future was assured for Reuben and Gennetta. She sipped her wine and for ten minutes she and Cornelius chatted about the changing way of life in Whitby, of the decline of the whaling trade and the rise of jet.

'You were astute in advising me to switch my investments, Cornelius, and I'm grateful. It meant greater resources were available for Reuben. I hope you will continue to advise him when I'm gone.'

'Of course I will, but we won't talk of such things. You'll probably outlive us all.'

Edith gave a wry smile as she stood up. 'I think not, Cornelius.'

He rose and walked with her to the door. 'I'm sorry to hear about Gennetta's father. Give her my condolences.'

'Her father?' Edith looked at him askance.

'Did you not know he is seriously ill? Not expected to live more than a few days.'

'Oh, no.' She gave a little gasp. 'You are sure?'

'I heard it yesterday from his son Jack. He was here to clear up some matter relating to the estate.'

'Then Gennetta should know.' Edith patted Cornelius's arm. 'See that my request is taken care of quickly,' she said on parting, looking closely at Cornelius, dark eyes solemn, cheeks seeming to sag just a little bit more.

As he closed the door and turned back into the room, Cornelius gave a little sigh of annoyance. His thoughts were troubled as he crossed the floor to his desk. He sat down and stared at the piece of paper on which he had made the notes regarding Edith's will. Two names stood out and burned into his mind: Reuben and Gennetta.

He opened a drawer to his right and slid the sheet of paper inside. It lay there, seeming to stare up at him. He bit his lip in irritation. With sharp, fractious gestures, he shuffled some papers from lower down in the drawer to cover the one he had just placed there then snapped it shut. Then he picked up the small hand-bell on his desk and rang it vigorously.

A moment later there was a knock on his door and a thin-faced young man, high collar chafing his neck, a cravat tied untidily at his throat, walked in. Hollow cheeks accentuated his long thin nose and dull eyes looked back at Cornelius without expression.

'Benjamin, I will be going to Scarborough tomorrow, so you will be in charge,' Cornelius announced.

'Yes, sir. I'll just deal with everyday matters and leave important items for your return. Shall I tell callers you will be back on Wednesday?' The reply betrayed no enthusiasm for his tasks.

'Yes,' snapped Cornelius. There was something about Benjamin Cook that always irritated him, but he put up with him because he was efficient and cheap. Benjamin turned to go. Cornelius stopped him. 'And, Benjamin, do get yourself tidied up. At least brush that suit.' He waved his hand in the direction of the worn tails of the short jacket, the stained waistcoat and marked trousers.

'Yes, Mr Cornelius,' intoned Benjamin, and left the office muttering to himself, 'Might be able to buy something new if you'd pay me a bit more, you old skinflint.'

Edith regretted that she was the bearer of bad tidings to the girl who had brought her so much pleasure, but there could be no putting them off.

Entering the house, she quickly shed her redingote and bonnet, leaving them with her parasol on a chair in the hall. She entered the drawing room where Gennetta sat embroidering a child's frock in anticipation of the day when Flora would be big enough to wear it. Nathaniel was playing happily on the floor with a wooden horse and carriage.

49

Gennetta's smile faded when she saw Edith's solemn expression. 'Something wrong?' she asked.

Edith sat down opposite her. 'Did you not hear about your father?'

'Father?' Her brow creased. He had never been mentioned since his last visit before her wedding. That was the way she wanted it, and Edith, though she would have healed the rift if she could, respected Gennetta's wish.

'I hear that he is dying.'

The announcement startled Gennetta. A hollow feeling gripped her stomach. Her mind whirled with a confusion of emotions and her face drained of its colour.

She had cut herself off from her father when she married Reuben, always regarding his attitude as unreasonable. If he wanted nothing more to do with his daughter then so be it. She had lived her life since then as if he did not exist. There had been moments when she'd wanted to show him his grandson, but she had held back, knowing he would see it as an attempt to ingratiate herself and claim an inheritance for Nathaniel, especially as James and Grace seemed unable to produce a heir. He must have heard of the child and if he had been interested could have sought him out.

'You'll go to see him?' Edith's even tone broke into her thoughts.

Gennetta tilted her head in an attitude of resistance. 'No.'

'But he's your father!' Edith's statement had a touch of reproof to it.

'He stopped being that when he opposed my marriage.' She held up her hand, preventing Edith from chiding her. 'I'm sorry that he's dying but he has never made any attempt at reconciliation, never attempted to see his grandson. I have never told you this, but on three or four occasions when I have seen him in the street he has crossed to the other side or turned away to avoid me. Please say no more, Aunt, my mind is made up.'

The following morning, wrapped up against the inclement weather, Cornelius boarded the Diligence for Scarborough, paying nine shillings including the extra to travel inside. He ignored the other passengers, making only desultory remarks as they tried to draw him into the conversation, until at last they chose to ignore him and leave him to his own thoughts. His brother wouldn't like the situation any more than he did. Agitated by Edith's instructions, Cornelius turned over possible courses of action and their consequences but was no nearer a solution by the time the coach reached the Bell Inn, close to the top of Bland's Cliff in Scarborough. He would leave the final decision to his brother.

Cornelius turned up the collar of his long and heavy garrick against the chill wind which blew from the sea, and set out at a brisk pace in short little steps. He hoped the bite in the air would clear his head after the rocking motion of the coach which had left him with a headache.

By the time he came to the engraved brass plate announcing 'Thornton Mitchell, Solicitor' in copperplate writing, his head was clearer. The clerk, wondering why Mr Cornelius should be visiting, announced him immediately and showed him into his brother's office.

Thornton, looking over the top of his spectacles before removing them, came out from behind a large mahogany desk stacked with papers.

'Now what brings you here, Cornelius?' he asked, giving his brother's hand a perfunctory shake. He looked down at him for he was tall, in marked contrast to Cornelius. His patrician features were dominated by a long thin nose and his brown eyes were ever alert, wanting to miss nothing. His greying hair was neatly cut and brushed to hide any thinning.

'Trouble, Thornton, trouble,' spluttered Cornelius as he shook himself out of his coat and threw it on to a chair beside the door. His action made Thornton wince for he, like his brother, was a meticulous man and this was so out of character. He frowned to himself – something was seriously wrong. Cornelius fussed his way to the chair on the opposite side of the desk to Thornton who had returned to his own seat.

'Trouble? It must be serious to have brought you here without writing first,' he observed.

Cornelius nodded his head vigorously. 'It is, it is. It *couldn't* be committed to paper.' Thornton raised his eyebrows in surprise. His brother was certainly making this sound dramatic. 'Edith Briggs wants to change her will!'

The announcement made Thornton sit upright. 'What?' His eyes sharpened, then he resumed his outward calm. He deemed it unwise to show emotion in his profession but this news was shattering. 'Well, she is entitled to.' He tried to play down the implications.

'Yes,' agreed his brother, wide-eyed at Thornton's attitude, 'but she wants to leave everything to Reuben.' He went on to inform his brother of the details of Edith's request. 'And she wants it done quickly. She says she is dying.'

'What?' Once again Thornton was startled by the news. 'How long has she?'

'She didn't say.'

51

Thornton's lips narrowed into a thin line. He was irritated by this unexpected development which presented real problems.

'What are we going to do, Thornton?' There was a plea in Cornelius's voice. He always turned to his brother when important decisions were required and Thornton always felt flattered on those occasions, but this was one time when he wished it hadn't been necessary for his brother to come to him.

'Put her off,' he advised.

'I tried but she was adamant in her request.' Cornelius looked miserable at the memory.

Thornton pursed his lips. 'Then all you can do is delay writing the new will.'

'But how?' Cornelius moaned, seeing that he was going to have to bear the brunt of this deception. 'She's very shrewd.'

'You'll think of something – like the fact that you've had more important things to see to. If she presses you and brings up the likelihood of her dying, you can reassure her that you will see everything is carried out according to her wishes. She has faith in you – must have after what you did for her.'

'Yes, but ...'

Thornton smiled, not something he did often. 'You can come here for a few weeks, say there's some important work I want help with. Your clerk has taken charge before and can do so again. Edith won't reveal her affairs to him.'

Cornelius brightened at this idea. 'Hannah won't mind?'

'No.' His intonation implied that what he said was law, though Cornelius knew that Thornton's wife would be consulted. They were a couple who shared everything, even decisions, and away from the office Thornton was not the implacable man he appeared between these four walls. 'Had you planned to return to Whitby today?'

'Yes, on this afternoon's Diligence.'

'Take it, and return on the next coach in two days' time. I take it you were to let Edith know when the new will was ready?'

'Yes.'

'Then it is unlikely she'll trouble you before you return here. Leave word with your clerk that you have been called away.'

'Splendid.' Cornelius felt greatly relieved, but lurking in the back of his mind was the nagging question: how long could he delay drawing up a new will?

There was a knock on the door which opened after Thornton's call of: 'Come in.'

A young man strode in. His waist-length plain grey coat was cut away to knee-length tails and covered a yellow waistcoat, the only

52

concession to frippery Thornton allowed in the office, he himself always dressing in sombre black. The young man's white shirt and cravat emphasised the blackness of his hair and eyes. The eyes filled with pleasure when he saw Cornelius.

'Uncle, how nice to see you.' He held out his hand in respect and friendliness.

'And a pleasure to see you too, James.' Cornelius had watched him grow over the years and taken satisfaction in seeing him develop into a fine young man. At the same age, twenty-six, he would have envied James's athletic figure, always enhanced by well-fitting clothes.

Thornton watched the exchange with pride. An only child, James had brought him great pleasure as he'd watched him grow up. The boy had taken every chance of education he had been given and then joined Thornton in the firm which one day would be his. And, with a bachelor uncle, James was set to inherit Cornelius's practice as well. There were no worries about James's future. Thornton's only wish was that he might find himself an attractive young lady, marry and settle down. James, the eligible bachelor, was much sought after on the Scarborough social scene as mothers attempted to bring their daughters to his notice. But he had found no one as yet and was content to wait until the right girl came along.

'Uncle Cornelius is coming to stay with us for a week or two. He's been feeling a little peakish, needs a change for a while,' Thornton informed him.

'Splendid.' James's broad smile of pleasure showed perfect white teeth. Then his face adopted a look of concern. 'Uncle, I didn't mean it was splendid you were ill,' he went on hastily. 'I'm sorry about that.'

Cornelius laughed. 'I didn't think you did.'

'Good.' James smiled again. 'I'll get the chess set ready.'

'I hope you haven't improved. You were too good for me last time.'

'Are you staying now?'

'No, I have to go back to Whitby today, but I'll be here again in two days.'

'Right. I look forward to it.' James turned to Thornton and placed a sheaf of papers in front of him. 'For your signature, Father.'

Thornton eyed him. 'I think it's about time you took on that responsibility. You can keep me informed about the important ones, but it will save time if you do it.'

'Yes, sir.' James was pleased at the added responsibility for this would mean making decisions without having always to refer them to his father. Now he felt he would be influencing the future of the firm,

53

if only in a small way. He picked up the papers and turned for the door.

'Look forward to seeing you again, Uncle.'

'What a fine young man he's turned out to be,' observed Cornelius when the door clicked shut.

Thornton nodded his agreement. 'Yes, and one who deserves everything he can get.'

Chapter Five

'I'm going out for a while this afternoon, Aunt,' said Gennetta when they had finished their midday meal.

'Very well, my dear.'

Gennetta hurried from the room and Edith gave a little nod of satisfaction to herself.

Her suspicions were confirmed twenty minutes later when, after hearing the front door close, she went to the window and saw Gennetta, dressed sombrely, hurrying down the garden path. Edith found some relief in what she saw.

While not in mourning black Gennetta had put on an untrimmed waist-length cloak over her plain woollen dress of deep purple. Her bonnet was of a simple design with no frills and she wore black gloves.

She walked quickly to the bridge. With her mind on her destination, she was almost oblivious to the people going about their daily business as she crossed to the east side of the river. She did not even give the ships and the bustling harbour a second glance. She hurried along Church Street and, reaching the Church Stairs, started up the one hundred and ninety-nine well trodden steps. Her breathing quickened as she climbed but she did not pause. She knew she was a little late.

Reaching the top of the stairs she slowed her pace. A group of mourners stood around a grave beside which rested a coffin. She stood and watched from a distance. All were dressed in the deepest black without a hint of decoration to relieve this symbol of mourning. Black made her brother Jack look older, or was it the fact that she always remembered him wearing colourful clothes? He stood erect and even from this distance she could sense the steel in him, a quality which had hardened in the face of his new responsibilities. Beside him Grace looked diminutive, her head bowed, her face almost hidden by the exaggerated brim of her bonnet, as if in these moments of sorrow she should hide from the world. Even her handkerchief was black as she raised it to dab her eyes.

Gennetta's eyes drifted across the other mourners: Robert Sleightholme, here to pay his last respects to his friendly rival, no doubt wondering how Jack would face up to being in charge, and beside him Cyrus. Gennetta stiffened. The sight of him recalled that mysterious figure in black which had appeared and vanished on her wedding day and after Flora's christening. Could it have been Cyrus? He was certainly dressed the same, but mourning suits such as his were commonplace at funerals. The mysterious figure could have been anyone. Or had her imagination played tricks on her? No one else had seen him. She tore her eyes away from the tall figure of Cyrus.

Friends, men from Whitby's thriving business world and representatives of Jeremiah's employees, all stood respectfully silent as the parson intoned the graveside prayers.

A lump came to Gennetta's throat and her eyes dampened when the coffin was picked up then lowered slowly into the grave. A low thud signalled it had reached its resting place and ropes scored the wood as they were withdrawn.

The cleric continued his final prayers and then, one by one, the mourners paid their last respects, sprinkling earth on to the coffin.

Jack, his hand lightly on Grace's elbow, moved away from the graveside to take up a position from which they could thank people for attending the funeral.

Gennetta offered a silent prayer and turned away. She wanted contact with no one. But for the briefest of moments, across the gravestones, her eyes met Jack's. Only from the upward tilt of his chin, expressing haughtiness and disdain, did she know her presence had been noted.

She hurried away, unaware that someone else had seen her. Cyrus's eyes narrowed as he recalled the refusal which had destroyed his expectations of a useful alliance and denied him an entrée to Turner's jet workshops.

'Now, my dear, stop that sniffling, wipe those eyes and compose yourself.' Jack Turner's tone was sharp as he eyed his wife, sitting perched on the edge of the easy chair to the right of the fireplace.

He stood with his back to the grate, feet apart, his hands clasped behind his back under the tails of his mourning suit. He stretched his neck, longing to be out of the high stiff collar around which was tied a black silk cravat, but decorum dictated that he could not do that until those who would be arriving any minute to offer sympathy and condolences had departed. And that would not be for some time, if he judged their friends and business acquaintances correctly. They would make their dutiful murmurs, praising his father's so-called virtues without really knowing the inner man, and would gorge themselves on the spread set out in the dining room. He had ordered cold ham, cold beef, sausages and pork pies, all with their appropriate accompaniments, to be followed by apple pie, fruit, sweetmeats and jellies. There was a choice of drinks: Madeira, claret, whisky, tea or coffee. He was not going to let it be said that he had stinted on his father's 'send off'. He'd trusted Mrs Bates and Mrs Peters to have everything ready but had glanced in the dining room immediately on his return just to make sure.

Grace dabbed her eyes and then folded her hands on her lap to await the first arrival. She had removed her bonnet to reveal straight, silky hair, drawn back tightly into a bun in the nape of her neck. Her black silk dress fell wide from its tight waist and had a close-fitting bodice, long sleeves and high neck trimmed with the merest hint of black lace. Its severity emphasised her pointed nose and thin lips.

'Well, my dear, this is all ours now.' Jack's glance was filled with satisfaction. 'We shall sell our house and move in here immediately. We'll keep the same staff. They know the running of the place, and it will be easier for you to start entertaining people. I want to build up the business now it is all mine.'

The satisfaction in her husband's voice was not lost on Grace but she made no comment and merely said, 'Yes, Jack.' She knew it was useless to express her opinion or to oppose his ideas. She did not look forward to entertaining, especially anyone who might bring up business questions, for she had no knowledge of the workings of the jet trade and was not privy to any matters relating to the Turner business. All she knew was that it was thriving on the increased market for jet ornaments and jetware and looked like continuing to do so.

Now she waited to receive the 'mourners', would listen to their platitudes and then watch them move on to resume their lives as if Jeremiah Turner had never existed. She realised her husband was already doing that as he intoned, 'It was very much in our favour when Gennetta walked out. Now everything is ours. By the way, did you see her today?'

'Gennetta? No.' Grace looked up in surprise.

'Oh, she was there in the distance. I caught a glimpse of her walking away. I suppose her conscience pricked her at the last minute. She certainly wasn't there when we came out of church. Well, she needn't think she can come back into favour, now Father's gone.'

Any further comment was cut short as the maid announced the first arrivals.

With greetings exchanged, condolences given, and praises for the deceased sung, everyone moved into the dining room to express surprise and pleasure at the sight of the laden tables. It was as if they were a demarcation line. Food was needed to sustain life. The past had been duly recognised. Life went on.

'Now, Jack, I expect thee inherits t'lot.' Robert Sleightholme, having charged a glass with whisky before turning his thoughts to food, had sought out his host.

'Aye,' replied Jack cautiously.

'I hope I'll have as good a relationship wi' thee as I had wi' thy father,' Robert went on, puffing out his chest. 'Rivals, but friendly rivals.'

'No reason why you shouldn't,' said Jack curtly.

Robert sipped his whisky and, enjoying the taste, smacked his lips. With a knowing smile, he leaned closer to Jack. 'A pity thee and Grace don't seem able to have children,' he said in a low voice. 'No heir for the business, so if ever thee feels like selling, let me know.' He straightened and glanced around at the people helping themselves at the tables. 'Now for some of this delicious-looking food,' he said, and left Jack to his disturbing thoughts.

He had some pride in his firm and shuddered at the idea of its ever falling into the hands of the Sleightholmes, whether it be in Robert's day or Cyrus's. His lack of a son and heir tormented Jack for the rest of the day. He became more and more morose and drank too much whisky to try to eradicate the thought. By the time he and Grace reached their own home he was in a foul mood. He threw down his coat and hat in the hall and went immediately to his study. He flung the door open and strode to a small table on which stood a decanter and glasses. He splashed whisky into one of the glasses.

'Don't you think you've had enough?' Grace said quietly from the doorway.

Jack swung round, eyes blazing with fury that she had dared to admonish him. 'Don't you tell me when I've had enough, woman. Get yourself upstairs! I want a son!'

She stared at him. Fear rose in her at the sight of the lust in the eyes. She turned and fled, running quickly to the next floor where she hurried to her bedroom, slammed the door and locked it. She glanced desperately round the room as she leaned against the door, breathing deeply from the exertion. She would have left the house there and then but where could she go? Her parents were dead, she had no brothers or sisters, no one. To go to friends would raise a scandal which she did not want for she could not bear to think of fingers pointing at her.

She started at the sound of shattering glass from the room below. She heard the door bang followed by the thud of Jack's shoes as he clumped drunkenly up the stairs. She moved as far away as she could get from the door, anxiously searching for some way out of the crisis about to erupt but she could find none. Her only hope was that the locked door would make Jack realise his condition.

The footsteps stopped outside. The knob was turned and a thrust made at the door. When it did not yield, she heard a curse.

'Damn you, woman, open this door!' It shook violently.

Grace cringed but managed to muster up enough courage to answer him. 'No, Jack, you're too drunk.'

'Drunk or not, I'm coming in.'

'Jack, please, when you've sobered up.'

'No, now!'

There was a pause followed by a shattering kick which burst the door off its hinges.

He stood there, feet apart. The cravat had been torn from his neck and his shirt was open at the front relieving the restriction around his throat. His chest heaved, his eyes narrowed and his lips held a disdainful sneer of contempt.

'Now!' he snarled, and strode into the room slamming the door behind him.

'No, Jack, no! Not like this. When you're sober. I've never denied you!' she pleaded.

'Now! I want a son now. I'll not have the Sleightholmes laughing at me, not have that bastard Robert mocking me, implying Cyrus could do what I can't.' He grabbed at her. She twisted away but his hand closed on the neck of her dress, ripping it open, while in the same movement he flung her on to the bed. He was quickly over her, tearing the clothes from her body with a viciousness which hurt. She tried to fight him off but her blows were weak against the strength which overpowered her and she knew it was useless to struggle.

Grace lay immobile, exhausted by the lust that had been born in drink. She felt unclean even though it had been her husband who had taken her. He was breathing heavily beside her. She shuddered at the thought that he might do it again. She turned her head slowly and found a tiny measure of relief that he was asleep.

Moving slowly and carefully so as not to wake him, she slid from the bed and discarded the remains of her torn clothes. She stepped to the ewer and basin standing on a small table beside the door and

59

eased the feeling of defilement as she washed her whole body.

She found some fresh clothes and dressed, then stood staring at her drunken husband sprawled on the bed. In those moments a feeling of resentment towards him was born.

She left the room and did not see him until morning. He had washed and had finished dressing when she came into the bedroom. She could tell immediately that his mood was sour from the hangover which had no doubt left him with a bad headache.

'You were odious.' Her lips curled with disgust, her eyes narrowed. 'Don't ever do that again.'

'No need if a son comes from it.'

'You know what we've been told.'

'Doctors can be wrong.'

'True. They might be wrong about me. It might be *you* who can't make children.'

Her statement taunted him. He swung round, his eyes blazing with fury. 'Rubbish. Me? Never!'

She shrugged her shoulders. 'Believe what you wish.' Her voice hardened. 'But if ever you take me that way again, I'll reveal just what you are.' He had never seen her so determined and realised his action had swollen a hidden strength within her he'd never known existed.

'I'll divorce you to get the son I want,' he spat defiantly.

'Divorce? And suffer all the scandal that will bring? You'd be the laughing stock of Whitby by the time we were finished.' There was contempt in her regard. 'I may be meek and humble, mousy and sat upon in some people's eyes, but in this matter I am resolute. You'll not divorce me – never.' She swung round and left the room.

Grace was determined not to surrender her position, she had too much to lose: a comfortable life, never going short of anything for Jack liked to keep up appearances. She had been more than pleased when Jack Turner, heir to a promising jet manufactory, had proposed and had decided then that her stoical nature would fit her for the role of dutiful wife, and so it had. She was content and happy with her lot and resolved that it should continue that way in spite of Jack's action.

Gennetta watched the *Diana* dock safely under a threatening sky and strong wind. She had wrapped up well to come to the quay. Over her slender-waisted green woollen dress with its high neck-line she wore a three-quarter-length coat of darker green with wide collar and cuffed sleeves. She was glad of it for the wind tore along the river between the cliffs, warning people not to tarry as they crossed the bridge.

Reuben was down the gangplank as soon as it was run out, his smile was filled with joy at seeing his wife. He took her in his arms and hugged her tight.

'A sailor's most precious moment,' he whispered close to her ear. 'I love you more each time I see you waiting on the quay.'

'I'll always be here for you, my love,' she returned, expressing a love she felt would last for all time. They kissed and as their lips parted she asked, 'Coming home now?'

Reuben frowned regretfully. 'Sorry, love, I'll be about an hour.'

Disappointment flashed in Gennetta's eyes but she knew this was the lot of a sailor's wife. 'Two things before you go.' Her face had filled with concern.

'Not the children?' He experienced dread, cold and heavy.

'No, they're in good health,' Gennetta hastened to tell him. 'But my father died.'

'Oh, my love, I'm sorry.'

She gave a quirk of her mouth which told him there had been no reconciliation between father and daughter. 'It's Aunt Edith who concerns me,' she went on.

'What's the matter?' It was as if an icy hand clutched at Reuben's heart. His face drained of colour and his eyes held the expression of one expecting the worst.

'Nothing serious so far as I know. It's little things. There are days when she is off her food, and you know she's normally a good eater. I've asked her if she's all right and she says she is. But at odd times, when she hasn't known I've been there, I've seen her holding her side. She stops as soon as she is aware of me. And she doesn't seem as lively as she used to be.' Gennetta gave a little shrug of her shoulders. 'Maybe I'm mistaken, but see what you think. You're everything to her so she may put on a brave face and disguise her feelings. Don't say I've told you.'

'I won't. I'll have time to see how she is. The *Diana* needs some repairs so I'll be home for three weeks.'

'Oh, good.' Gennetta was relieved. The responsibility for Edith's welfare would be shared.

'I must go. I'll be as quick as possible.' He kissed her.

She waited until he was back on board, gave him a final wave and turned for home.

With their yearning for love satisfied Gennetta lay in Reuben's arms, relaxed and content. She thought how lucky she was and, overwhelmed by this feeling, turned over so she could look into his deep brown eyes.

'Oh, I love you so, Reuben Briggs.' Her words went far beyond that moment. 'Thank you for marrying me.'

He smiled, enveloping her in warmth. 'I was the lucky one.' His arms came round her shoulders and drew her to him. Their lips met gently, brushing each other tantalisingly, then moved in a consuming passion which revealed that the strain of their separation had not yet fully been appeased.

Gennetta broke the silence which followed. 'What did you think to Aunt Edith?'

'Saw nothing wrong,' he replied.

She gave a small smile. 'I thought not. She was like her old self. Or was it put on for your benefit?'

'We'll see. I'll keep an eye on her.'

Reuben's homecoming had sharpened Edith's concern over her will. A month had passed since she had visited Cornelius Mitchell and she had heard nothing from him. Her two visits to his office to pursue the matter had brought the same reply from his clerk: 'Mr Mitchell is still in Scarborough with his brother. I don't know when he'll be back.'

Edith was beginning to feel that she needed to get the matter settled quickly.

She left the house without saying a word to anyone and hurried in a state of considerable disquiet to Cornelius's office.

'Now, my man, is your master back yet?' she demanded, confronting Benjamin.

'No, ma'am, he's not,' came the crisp reply. Would this woman never stop pestering him?

She tapped the ferrule of her parasol impatiently on the floor. 'Really, this is too much.' How could Cornelius run an office efficiently when he was away so long? 'Have you had word from him?'

'Just an acknowledgement of some documents I sent him.'

'So he's still attending to his work?'

'Oh, yes, ma'am. I have instructions to send him anything which needs his attention. He deals with it as well as the work he and his brother are doing together.'

'You get work back from him?'

'Of course, ma'am.'

'No document for me?'

'No, ma'am.' When was this woman going to stop asking questions?

'When do you expect him back?' The agitation in her voice increased.

Benjamin raised his eyebrows and spread his hands. 'I don't know, ma'am.'

Edith's lips tightened in a thin line, emphasising the sagging of her cheeks. Her arched eyebrows seemed to bristle with annoyance. 'Confound the man! He has important work for me and seems to be doing nothing about it.'

'I'm sure he'll have it in hand, ma'am,' replied Benjamin in an attempt to placate and hopefully get rid of her. There was nothing he could do about her dilemma. Besides, she was interrupting his peaceful morning. He liked these times when his superior was away and wished they were more frequent, though he couldn't grumble at this one for Mr Cornelius had been absent longer than usual.

'He'd better be quick,' snapped Edith, clearly growing more agitated. 'You send him word that Miss Briggs is waiting for her document.'

'Yes, ma'am.' That was the easiest answer. He raised his eyes heavenwards as she turned towards the door, but was quick to turn himself back into the meek and humble servant as she stopped and glanced round.

She pointed her parasol at him. 'Don't forget.'

'No, ma'am.'

'And do it now!' She drew herself up and looked at him with an air of command.

'I will, ma'am.' He skittered across the office and opened the door for her so that she would not stay a moment longer. 'Good day, ma'am,' he offered with a slight bow as she swept through the doorway.

He shut the door, sank back against it with a sigh of relief, turned the key and went to the chair normally occupied by his master. Putting his feet up on the desk, he cradled his hands on his chest and closed his eyes.

Edith muttered to herself as she hurried through the streets. The pace matched her mood of agitation. 'What's got into the man? He's never been as incompetent as this before. Always seen to my affairs promptly. He's letting things slip, leaving that "yes, ma'aming" Benjamin in charge.' Her parasol beat a tattoo to match her rapid footsteps which did not slow as she climbed the hill to New Buildings.

She was breathing heavily and her face was flushed when she entered the house.

The pain struck suddenly, sharp and deep. She gasped and clutched at her chest, her face contorted with its severity. Strength drained from her. Her legs gave way and she slumped to the floor. The parasol slipped from her grasp and rattled on to the tiled floor.

Five minutes passed before anyone came into the hall. Reuben, coming out of the drawing room, stopped in full stride. 'Aunt Edith!' Seeing the prone figure sent a wave of shock through him. He was beside her in four steps, shouting, 'Gennetta!'

His cries, sharp with distress, brought her running into the hall, closely followed by Rose who was carrying Flora and had Nathaniel at her side. Mrs Shaw and the maids appeared from the kitchen.

Anguish gripped Gennetta as she flew across the hall and dropped to her knees beside Edith. She looked enquiringly at Reuben who was feeling for her pulse.

'Barbara, get Doctor Potter, quick!'

The maid reacted immediately.

'Rose, take the children upstairs.'

She had already sized up the gravity of the situation and, with a nod of her head, indicated to Helen to help her. Together they ushered the children up the stairs to the nursery.

'Is she ...?' The word she feared to say was in Gennetta's tone as she looked anxiously at Reuben.

'Her pulse is extremely weak.' His eyes expressed his worry. The woman who had befriended him when he needed someone, who had taken him in even though it meant turning her life upside down, and who had resented his intrusion but little and given him all her love when they had come to terms with each other, was in distress and he was powerless to aid her.

'Should we get her upstairs?' Gennetta asked.

'Better leave her until Doctor Potter comes. He shouldn't be long. Let's hope he's in.' He glanced up at the cook who was hovering beside them. 'Mrs Shaw, a blanket and a pillow.'

She hurried away, to return a few moments later with the two items. Removing Edith's bonnet, they rested her head comfortably on the pillow and covered her with the blanket.

Gennetta brushed the hair from Edith's forehead, then took her hand in hers. She had no idea if Edith was aware of this but hoped that it would soothe her.

'Where had she been?' asked Gennetta.

'I didn't even know she was out,' replied Reuben.

The minutes were interminable, the ticking of the grandfather clock making them seem longer and more ominous with every stroke.

The front door burst open and the doctor and Barbara rushed in. He took in the scene at a glance and was on his knees beside Edith in an instant. But even as he made his examination she heaved in spasm, gasped and collapsed back on the floor. He felt her pulse and listened to her heart then straightened on his knees slowly. Reuben and Gennetta, their thoughts racing, gazed at him, willing him to tell them what they wanted to know. But their hearts froze and their minds went numb when they saw him shake his head.

'I'm sorry, she's gone.'

'Oh, no!' Gennetta's cry was a gasp of disbelief.

Stunned, Reuben stared at his aunt. It couldn't be true. That vibrant woman so full of life just couldn't be dead. He bit his lip and silent tears flowed down his cheeks.

The doctor respected their grief for a moment before saying, 'Could we get her upstairs, Reuben?'

He nodded and stood up. Mrs Shaw, tears in her eyes, moved to relieve him of the unpleasant task.

'It's all right, Mrs Shaw, I'll manage. You look after Barbara.'

Mrs Shaw nodded and escorted the weeping maid to the kitchen.

Once they had laid Edith in her room and had returned downstairs the doctor asked, 'Where had she been this morning?'

'We don't know,' said Reuben. 'We didn't know she was out.'

'I would say she overexerted herself coming back here and was probably upset about something. The combination of that on top of the worry she has had lately led to the heart attack which killed her.'

'Worry? What worry, Doctor?' asked Gennetta puzzled by his statement.

'Didn't you know she had been seeing me?'

'No.' Gennetta sounded amazed. Reuben looked questioningly at her.

'Why had she been seeing you?' he asked, turning to the doctor.

'She had a suspicious lump. I examined her. There was nothing we could do. She would have died later this year.'

'Oh, no! Why didn't she tell me?' said Gennetta full of regret. 'I could have been a comfort to her.'

'You were, you and the children. She took great pleasure in you all. That was a comfort to her. She wanted no one to know. If you had, you would have treated her differently and she didn't want that. As it is this heart attack has spared her suffering. Be thankful for that.'

As they saw the doctor from the house, Gennetta shuddered. She could have sworn she heard the distant cry of geese.

Chapter Six

Neither Gennetta nor Reuben was aware of the warm sun on their backs as they watched the coffin lowered into the grave. The parson spoke the usual words with soft clarity then stepped back and waited while the two chief mourners sprinkled soil on the coffin. Not wanting to leave just yet, they moved to one side to allow the rest of the gathering to pay their final respects to Edith Briggs. When the last one had done so and had had another word of sympathy with them, they stepped to the edge of the grave and, holding hands, gazed on the coffin of their dearly loved benefactor. At different times she had given both of them a chance when life seemed to have delivered an insurmountable blow. They would be ever grateful to her and she would be held in their minds with the fondest of memories.

With tears in their eyes they reluctantly turned away, had a word with the parson and walked to the coach awaiting them. As they neared it they saw Cornelius Mitchell standing nearby.

He removed his black top hat and made a slight bow. He expressed his sympathies again then added, 'Your great-aunt left a will in my care. I would be grateful if you could come to my office in the morning, say ten o'clock, if that is suitable to you?'

'Certainly,' replied Reuben.

'Good.' He bowed to Gennetta and, replacing his hat, hurried away, short steps beating crisply on the paved path through the churchyard.

Whitby basked under a gentle sun as Gennetta and Reuben walked to Mitchell's office. She wore a black woollen dress, with nothing to relieve its simplicity. Her black bonnet was plain with no frills and she wore a black silk fringed mantle and matching gloves. Reuben's tailed suit was dark grey, his top hat black to match his frock coat.

Immediately they arrived at the office, Benjamin, who had been warned of their appointment, showed them straight into the room occupied by Cornelius.

He came from behind his desk to greet them and usher them to the two chairs placed ready for their arrival. When they had settled, he resumed his own seat.

He glanced from one to the other, cleared his throat and picked up the paper laid on the desk in front of him. 'I have here the last will and testament of Edith Briggs and before making any comments I should read it to you.'

Gennetta and Reuben exchanged a quick glance and waited for him to go on.

He looked down at the paper and started to read. '"I, Edith Briggs, being of sound mind and body, do here bequeath all my wealth to a person who shall not be named in this will but who is known to my solicitor, Cornelius Mitchell. He is under oath that he will not disclose this person's name to anyone before or after my death. Furthermore he will reveal to the recipient only my name and shall not give any reason for my bequest.

'"In case of his death before mine a copy of this will and the name of the recipient has been lodged in a sealed envelope with his brother, Thornton Mitchell, solicitor in Scarborough, and will be held by him until I die.

'"If I die before Cornelius Mitchell that envelope in the possession of Thornton Mitchell will be destroyed unopened."' He paused a moment then added, '"Signed and sealed by me, Edith Briggs, and dated first day of August 1823."'

Reuben gasped. 'Before I was born!' He glanced at Gennetta who frowned, puzzled by the meaning of the will. Reuben's eyes switched quickly to Cornelius. 'She never altered the will, never made another?'

He shook his head slowly. 'No, I'm afraid not.'

'Then there is ...' Reuben hesitated to say what would sound so mercenary.

'Nothing for you,' the solicitor completed his thoughts.

Reuben bit his lip, his emotions a mass of hurt and regret, while anger lay just below the surface. He had never encouraged thoughts about his aunt's wealth. She had been a generous benefactor ever since she had taken him in and he had won her heart but he had never entertained thoughts that he had a right to any of her money. Yet when she had died he had automatically expected that he would inherit. After all, he was her only relation. Now to learn of a will made before he was born, depriving him and therefore his family of any prospect of security, had come as a terrible shock. He just could not believe, after all he and his aunt had meant to each other, that she had intended it this way.

'You are certain that she did not make another will?' he demanded.

'This is the only will your aunt made.'

'So everything goes to an unknown person?' put in Gennetta quietly.

'Someone known only to me,' replied Cornelius.

She nodded. Following the initial shock after Cornelius had read the will her mind had focused sharply on the implications. 'Can you tell us where this person lives?'

Cornelius gave a small smile and a slight shake of his head. 'I'm afraid I cannot divulge that. If I did you could find out who it is, and, as you heard, I am sworn to secrecy on the matter.'

'But why the need for this secrecy?'

'Only Miss Briggs knew that.'

'You don't?'

'No.'

'But this is ridiculous!' burst out Reuben.

Gennetta laid a hand on his arm to calm him. 'Aunt Edith had every right to make a will as she liked,' she pointed out in a quiet voice. 'There is nothing we can do about it.' The look she gave him pleaded with him to curb any hasty reaction. She saw him respond and knew that he had realised that any mercenary thoughts would only mar his memories and love for his aunt. Gennetta looked back at Cornelius. 'If everything goes to this unknown person then I suppose we must leave the house?' Her statement posed a question.

'Well, I feel sure I can persuade the new owner to allow you to go on living in the house at the same rent as Miss Briggs paid.'

'What about the furnishings?'

'I don't think he will want to remove anything.'

Gennetta felt relieved. The situation was not as bad as it had first seemed. 'Very well, Mr Mitchell, if you would see to that for us we would be very grateful. But tell the beneficiary that if there is anything he wants, he is at liberty to take it.'

'That is generous of you, ma'am, but I don't think it will come to that.'

'It seems you know this person well,' put in Reuben.

Cornelius pursed his lips and gave a little nod. 'Yes, I do.'

As they walked home, Reuben was the first to speak. 'I wonder why Aunt Edith never rescinded that will? After all, it was made before she knew me and we became close.'

'Maybe she intended to and never got around to it. But let's be thankful we can still have the house.'

'We'll have to economise. My wages plus what I have saved from the allowance she made me while she was alive cannot match her generosity.'

'I've already been thinking of that,' said Gennetta, her voice filled with determination. 'The maids will have to go. I'll try and persuade Mrs Shaw and Rose to take on some other duties and I'll work with them. I think they'll agree, they're fond of the children.'

'This is going to alter the life we have become accustomed to,' warned Reuben.

'I know, I'm prepared for that. Let's look on the bright side. It might only be for a year or two. You are bound to get promotion, then on to captain.'

Reuben laughed. 'You *are* rushing things! Promotion won't come that quickly.' His voice hardened with determination. 'But it will come, I'll see it does, and then you'll have the life you deserve.'

Cornelius made only the odd contribution to the conversation between the other coach passengers on the journey to Scarborough. He had settled in the corner seat, smug with satisfaction at the way things had turned out. His manoeuvring had paid off and his mind was occupied with the outcome.

Once he had alighted from the coach he lost no time in reaching his brother's office.

Thornton greeted him with a smile. Knowing of Edith Briggs's death, he anticipated a satisfactory conclusion. 'All went well?' he asked as his brother took off his coat and hung it on the stand near the door.

Cornelius turned round with a smile. 'Of course. What did you expect?'

'Young Mr Reuben made no protest?'

'How could he? It was all down in the will. He had no grounds to question or contest it.' Cornelius sat down in front of the large desk and gave a satisfied nod at his brother.

Thornton rose from his chair and crossed to a cabinet. 'Cause for a celebratory drink before we break the news to James.' He opened the glass doors and took out a decanter and two wine glasses. He poured the Madeira and passed a glass to Cornelius, who studied the rich liquid until his brother had returned to his seat.

Thornton raised his glass. 'To us and the coup we brought off to great effect.'

Cornelius smiled and raised his glass in reply. 'I have told Reuben and his wife that I can arrange for them to stay in the house. They accepted.'

'Good. At the same rent Miss Briggs was paying?'

'Of course, nothing less.'

'They agreed?'

'Yes.'

'Then that shall be yours in payment for what you have done to secure the inheritance for James.'

'Generous, dear brother, generous,' replied Cornelius in a satisfied voice.

'And from time to time there could be a gift from the interest on the money we shall invest on James's behalf.' Thornton gave a little chuckle.

Cornelius gave a graceful gesture with his hands. 'Oh, my thoughtful brother, even more generous.'

Leaning forward they clinked their glasses then sank back in their chairs, pleased with the fulfilment of their plans and savouring the tang of the wine.

With the glasses drained and returned to the cabinet, Thornton went to the door and crossed the corridor to the office opposite. A few moments later he returned with James.

'Uncle Cornelius! Father didn't say you were here.' His face broke into a wide smile as he crossed the room and shook his uncle's hand.

'Bring up a chair, my boy. Your uncle has something important to divulge to you.'

James brought a chair from beside the door and placed it so that he could view both men. He was curious. What had his uncle to tell him? He sensed from their expressions that it must be something good.

Cornelius fished in his inside pocket and drew out an envelope. 'This, my dear James, contains the last will and testament of one Edith Briggs.' He handed it to James. 'You must read it.'

Puzzled, he opened the envelope and withdrew a sheet of paper. What had this to do with him? He knew no one called Edith Briggs. He unfolded the paper and began to read.

The two brothers watched in silence, deriving great satisfaction from the changes of expression in the young man's face.

When he had finished reading he stared at the paper a moment longer then looked at the two older men in turn. 'What does it mean? What has this to do with me?'

'You are the unnamed recipient,' replied Cornelius, with a twinkle of pleasure in his eyes at imparting this surprise.

'What!' James glanced disbelievingly at his father. 'Why me? Who is this Edith Briggs?'

'Was, my dear boy, was. Sadly, Miss Briggs has died and her will now comes into force,' explained Cornelius.

70

'But who was she?'

'Ah, I am not at liberty to say, as you see from the wording of the will.'

'But why me? I never met her.'

'She had no one of her own and had heard your uncle talk a lot about you,' said Thornton.

Cornelius nodded. 'That's it. And so you are now a rich man. Miss Briggs inherited wealth from her father who made his fortune in the whaling trade. She, taking my advice, invested wisely and her fortune grew. Now it is yours.'

'I still don't understand. I wish I had met her,' said James with regret.

'I suggested it on two or three occasions,' said Cornelius, 'but she wouldn't agree. She wanted to remain anonymous.'

'I don't know what to say.' James was feeling bewildered, now that the whole situation was beginning to sink in.

'Say nothing,' said Thornton, rising from his chair. 'Best leave the money invested. It will bring you in a tidy sum. Uncle Cornelius will see to that.' He gave his brother a knowing look which implied that the interest could be split three ways.

Cornelius gave Thornton an almost indiscernible nod of understanding.

'I think, my boy, this deserves a toast.' Thornton went to the cabinet, removed the same former glasses and added a third. This time they were raised on a sombre note to: 'Miss Edith Briggs, may she rest in peace.'

Two days after the interview with Cornelius, Reuben was summoned to attend Captain Barrick on board the *Diana*. While he was gone Gennetta set about making the necessary rearrangements within the household. Regretfully she gave the maids their notice, thanking them profusely for all they had done and promising them that, should circumstances change, she would consider employing them again.

Realising the situation, Mrs Shaw and Rose sought an interview with her, the cook acting as spokeswoman for them both.

'Ma'am, we gather that the maids have had to leave because of money problems,' she said tentatively, feeling embarrassed at having to make such an observation.

'That's right, Mrs Shaw. We have lost a good friend in Miss Edith, but we must be thankful that we can stay in the house,' said Gennetta.

'Well, ma'am,' went on Mrs Shaw, still a little nervously, 'I'm happy working here and I love the bairns, and I know Rose feels the

71

same. With mine all grown up and gone, I would like to stay on here. I've talked it over with my husband. He's fully employed at the ropery, and although extra money always helps, he's agreeable to me earning less so that I can stay working for you.'

'Ma'am, I'm willing to do the same,' put in Rose when Mrs Shaw paused for breath. 'It would break my heart to leave the bairns. Please let us stay, ma'am, please.'

Relief swept over Gennetta as she leaned back in her chair. After the trauma of having to dispense with the services of the maids, this suggestion eased her mind. 'Of course you can both stay though I can only afford half of what you are getting now. But once things get better we will return to our present arrangement.'

'That'll do for me, ma'am,' agreed Mrs Shaw.

'And me, ma'am,' put in Rose quickly, as if she was afraid the offer might vanish.

'Good. That's settled. I'm sure we three can work well together.'

Mrs Shaw and Rose expressed their thanks and left the room.

Gennetta's mood was matched by that of Reuben when he returned from the meeting with Captain Barrick.

She turned from the curtains she was adjusting when the door burst open and Reuben strode in with a purposeful stride. 'You look cock-a-hoop,' she observed when she saw his wide smile.

He grasped her in his arms and swung her round. 'And you look pleased with yourself. What have you to tell me?'

'You first.' Laughter spilled from her lips as he whirled her around the room before putting her down.

'Gen, I'm promoted to Second Mate!'

'Reuben, that's wonderful! You deserve it.' Her delight matched that in his eyes. She hugged him tightly.

'Now you,' he pressed.

She laughed at his eagerness to hear her news, taking his hand and leading him to the sofa. 'Well, the nurse and the maids took their dismissal very well. They understood, and I promised them that I would have them back in the future if at all possible. But the great news is that Mrs Shaw and Rose expressed a desire to stay and said they would take a cut in wages to do so. I told them it would have to be half what they are getting now and they agreed.'

'Marvellous!' cried Reuben, squeezing his wife's hands. 'With the savings you're making and the extra money my promotion will bring we should be able to manage. And with my foot well on the ladder a captaincy is not impossible.'

'It's a certainty, or I don't know my Reuben.' She leaned forward and kissed him.

His hands grasped her shoulders to draw her to him. 'I hope I can always fulfil your dreams.'

'Just be you, and you will,' she whispered in a husky voice.

He kissed her gently. She held him and enticed him with the brush of her lips until he could resist no longer. Their kiss held a promise of passion to come.

'Cyrus, keep an eye on the Turner business, I reckon Jack hasn't the ability of his father.' Robert Sleightholme looked across the breakfast table at his son. He dabbed his lips with a white table napkin and, already savouring the succulent taste, glanced down at his plate which contained two eggs, three rashers of bacon and two pieces of fried bread.

He had worked hard to rise above the mediocrity and poverty around him, pinning his faith in the jet trade. It had paid off. He moved from the east side of the river at the first opportunity, to the opulence of the newer houses in Bagdale. He matched that with his style of living and was determined to go on enjoying it, backed by a determination to expand the business which had brought him his wealth.

'You think Turner's will run down?' asked Cyrus, spooning sugar into his tea.

'Could do. Jack's not as astute as his father. And he has no heir, so he just might want to sell sometime and then I'll have it. If I'm gone by then thee get it, fulfil my ambition for me. Promise me that?'

'You'll have it before that happens,' said Cyrus with conviction. 'I'll see you do.'

'Aye, well, maybe. It would be a fine thing.' A faraway look came into Robert's eyes as he visualised achieving his desire. He gave a little start and looked at his son with a serious expression. 'But I want t'business to remain Sleightholme's. So get thissen wed, lad, and bring me a grandson.'

'In good time, Father.'

'Stop playing around. I know your reputation in and around Whitby. All right, I don't mind you having your fling, but find a lass to give me a grandson.'

'Gen, will you be all right? I'll not sail if you'd rather I stayed at home?'

She twisted out of Reuben's arms and turned in the bed so she could look into his eyes. 'Of course I'll be all right, and I don't ever want to hear you make that suggestion again. I married a sailor and that means I'm prepared for separations. It's your life, it's what you want to do and you do it well. I'm proud of you.'

His arms came round her bare shoulders. 'You're the sweetest thing I know. Thank you for marrying me and being so understanding. I'll miss you when I'm gone.'

'And I'll miss you too.' Her voice was dreamy. 'Just now I gave you something to remember me by. Well, now I'll make it doubly memorable.' She sank towards him and as their lips met he accepted her offer willingly.

The following morning, as the *Diana* widened the distance between them and she held Flora high while Nathaniel waved, Gennetta felt she loved him all the more.

'God speed and bring you back safely,' she whispered to herself.

She stood watching the ship grow smaller and smaller.

'If you'd married me, you wouldn't have had such partings.' A voice, soft in her ear, startled her.

She glanced round sharply to find Cyrus doffing his top hat. A tremor ran through her when she saw he was dressed all in black with only a white shirt and blue cravat to detract from the threatening image of her previous encounters.

'And I would never have known love,' she snapped testily. Then turned, and with her head held high walked briskly away, Nathaniel running beside her.

Cyrus watched her through narrow lustful eyes for a few moments then turned to glance at the tiny speck on the ocean. He gave a little chuckle and walked towards the bridge to cross the river to the Sleightholme jet works.

Life in the Turner household was back to normal. Grace had been determined that it should be so. Nothing was going to spoil her comfortable life. She cared not a jot for the jet trade except for the comforts it brought her. She had scotched Jack's threat of divorce. If he wanted an heir, he had better make peace with his sister and appoint Nathaniel, as his nearest relation, to that role.

A month later, when there was still no sign that she was pregnant, he greeted this suggestion with icy contempt. 'Never! Gennetta relinquished all her rights and those of her family when she walked out of this house.'

'I hear things are not easy for her since Miss Briggs died and left Reuben nothing. It would be a generous gesture to help her.'

'Father would turn in his grave if I was to welcome her back.'

'But you would have the heir you want.'

'One who does not bear the Turner name.'

'What does that matter so long as he's from the same stock?'

Contemptuous of the suggestion, he fixed his gaze on his wife across the dining table. His hand fingered the stem of his wine glass. 'I want my own son to inherit the business. I want him to learn the trade so thoroughly that he'll be more knowledgeable than any brat Cyrus Sleightholme may sire, and able to outmanoeuvre any attempt by the Sleightholmes to get our business. I know full well that they would like to do that.' His voice and eyes hardened. 'And they're not going to. You'd better get yourself to Doctor Potter and see if anything can be done.'

'We've been through all this before,' replied Grace wearily. 'Will you never accept that fact that it looks as if, for whatever reason, we won't have a child?'

Jack's lips tightened. 'See another doctor,' he hissed. 'That old fuddy-duddy Potter could be wrong.'

Grace saved the moment until, dressed for bed, she was seated in front of the dressing-table mirror, combing out her hair. She paused and focused her eyes on her husband. She watched him for a moment as he slipped out of his jacket and unfastened the collar of his shirt. He was a handsome man. She loved him and wanted the security and good living he could provide so she would forgive him for his actions that night, but she would never forget.

'Jack.' She drew his attention and their eyes met through the mirror. 'I went to see Dr Witham today.'

'And?' he prompted as she hesitated.

She swung round on her stool to face him. 'He can see no reason why I should not have a child.' For a moment Jack stared disbelievingly at her, then heard her going on, 'He says I have been too anxious to conceive. I should relax and forget about wanting one so I am ...'

'Why didn't you tell me before?' he cut in.

'I wanted to save it for this moment.'

She saw the light in his eyes change to that of the loving considerate man she had married. The thought of never having a heir had changed him but now she saw that their relationship could resume its former warmth.

He came to her, seeing the passionate young woman he had married. She had loved him whenever he wanted, and, remembering, he was filled with remorse at his drunken defilement of her body.

His eyes brimmed with love as he reached out and took her hands in his, pulling her slowly to her feet. His eyes never left hers as he unfastened the silk bow which held the neck of her nightdress closed. His fingers brushed her skin as he drew it open and slid it from her shoulders, to let it fall to the floor at her feet.

'Can we go back in time?' he said huskily, with a note of pleading to be forgiven for the wrong he had done her.

She nodded. He drew her to him, relishing the softness of her body as their lips met in a kiss which quickly changed into one of yearning passion.

He swung her off her feet and as he carried her to the bed her hands were eagerly unfastening his shirt.

Chapter Seven

The moon shone brightly from a frosty sky. There had been only a hint of snow along the coast, unlike the moors a few miles inland where it lay deep, making Whitby even more isolated. The people of the town faced Christmas of 1849 in their own individual ways. Some, bowed down in poverty, wondered where the joy of this festive time had gone but put on a brave face for the sake of their children, scrimping to make the Christmas meal a little different, frugal though it was, and to provide some little gift for their stockings. Others faced it with joy and laughter, with gaily wrapped presents and laden tables. But even among those there were some who found no pleasure in it.

Jack Turner sat morosely staring at the fire, hardly aware of the dancing flames which reflected in the coloured baubles hanging on the Christmas tree, bringing it alive in myriad hues.

He had tried to persuade Grace to forget the tree this year. Trees and baubles were for children. But she had insisted that a tree was essential to any festivities since Prince Albert had introduced it as part of the Christmas scene. It wouldn't be the same without one. Jack had given way as he had been doing over most things for the past year, trying to salve his conscience but most of all attempting to pamper her and make her relax in the hope that it would enable her to have a baby. But there was no sign as yet of her fulfilling his wish.

He felt a pang of jealousy as a vision of his sister, excitedly opening presents around a tree with her children, filled his mind. He cursed to himself. Why had she sprung to mind when he had never given her a thought since he had noticed her at their father's funeral? His lips set tightly for a moment then he drained the rest of the whisky from his glass and sprang from his chair to get another. As he poured the liquid from a decanter the door opened and Grace came into the room, closing the door quietly behind her.

'Hello, love,' she greeted him as she walked towards the tree, admiring its flashes of colour.

He looked up, and as he studied her he put the decanter slowly down. Her hair was different. Gone was the severe style, pulled back tightly and tied in a bun. Now it was brought more to the crown of the head and clasped by a string of pearls. Side curls fell away on either side from the central parting and the fine silkiness of her hair gave the whole a gossamer effect. She wore a white embroidered muslin dress, the neckline low on her shoulders, the puffed sleeves narrowing from the elbows to frills around the tight wrists. A belt of figured silk ribbon in red and blue held the waist tight and allowed the dress to flounce from the waist to the tops of her blue cloth shoes. Two rows of silk threaded through the dress below the knees matched the colours of her belt. A red silk scarf, with floral patterns in green and blue at each end, was slung casually around her shoulders.

'You look exquisite, my dear,' he said gently, all moroseness gone at the sight of his wife so beautifully presented. He felt desire surge through him and crossed the room slowly, his eyes devouring her.

She smiled, knowing the effect she was having. Though she was still the same unassuming person in her attitude to anything to do with Jack's business, taking no interest whatsoever, she had altered many other aspects of their relationship. Yet there were times such as this when she could be a temptress.

She took the glass from his hand and placed it on the table beside the tree. He let it go without protest.

'Our presents are all here,' she said quietly, 'but there is one I want to give you now.'

'But we don't open them until tomorrow, Christmas Day,' he protested.

'You must have this one now,' she insisted, her lips twitching with amusement.

He cocked his head curiously. 'What are you up to?' He eyed her with suspicion.

'I'm going to have a baby.'

For a moment the words did not sink in. Then they did. His eyes widened and his mouth opened in a gasp.

'You're ...' He swallowed hard.

She trilled with laughter at the sight of Jack Turner, dumbstruck. 'Yes, I'm going to have a baby.'

'Grace!' His ill-humour was banished by the news and his face broadened into smile which betrayed his excitement. He hugged her. 'A boy! Someone who'll take over from me. The Turner business assured!'

She laughed even louder, amused at his reaction. 'It may be a girl,' she warned.

Still holding her, he moved back so that he could look at her. 'No, it'll be a boy. The name Turner must never disappear. We've done it! This will make the Sleightholmes jealous. They've always hankered after my business. Thought I would slip up, prove not worthy to follow Father, but I've shown 'em and I'll go on doing so now I've someone to work for.' He glanced at the presents at the foot of the tree. 'The best present isn't there, you take care of that for me.' He bent and kissed his wife.

She felt in his touch all the love that had been there when they first married. It had waned with what they thought was her inability to have a child, but now that was over. The old loving, kind Jack she had known was back. She knew harshness lay below the surface but it was not for her. That was part of the strong-willed businessman cultivated by his father so that the jet firm of Turner's would always have a powerful master. Sometimes he could still play the fop and she realised that the Sleightholmes had been taken in by this outward façade. She hoped for Jack's sake that the baby would be a boy.

'Come and sit down, Grace. You must take care. Pamper yourself. Anything you want, let me know. More help? Someone to watch over you?'

She laughed. 'Stop, Jack, stop. I'm all right. Don't fuss.'

'Nothing must go wrong. Take care,' he urged.

'I will.'

'And next year we'll have a bigger tree, more presents.' He looked around him, filled with enthusiasm for the years ahead. The baubles seemed to shine brighter in the flames which danced a merry jig in tune with his upsurge of joy. The future was assured.

Christmas peace had settled on seven New Buildings. The grandfather clock ticked with soothing regularity, moving its hands closer to the first minute of Christmas Day.

Gennetta lay in Reuben's arms on the sofa, her toes curled towards the warmth of the fire. The flames twisted brightly, curling round the remains of the Yule log and sending light and shadow chasing each other around the walls and across the furniture, playfully bringing the room alive. The decorations on the tree shimmered with colour enhanced by the firelight.

Gennetta sighed contentedly. The children, excited by the thought of a visit from Father Christmas, had finally settled down. Rose was in bed across the corridor from them. Stockings were filled with fruit, sweetmeats and tiny toys ready to be placed at the foot of each child's bed. Now Reuben and Gennetta seized their moment to be alone, to share the cosy comfort of this room which had been a favourite of Aunt Edith whom they knew would have enjoyed being with them for she had had a special liking for Christmas.

'Tired, darling?' Reuben asked quietly, brushing his lips against her neck.

'Mmm, but let's enjoy this for a little while longer.' Gennetta snuggled closer into his arms. 'It's so peaceful and I'm so happy.' She squeezed him. 'Thank you for being you.'

'And you for loving me.'

'We're so lucky.'

'Ever have any regrets at walking out on your father and Jack?'

'None,' she replied firmly. 'Though I sometimes wish we had been closer. But he was always Father's favourite, could do no wrong however much he played Father up.'

'You might have been better off – had a share of the jet business, with which I hear Jack is doing well.'

'So I'm told, but I'd rather have you and the children. Wonder what Jack's doing this Christmas?'

'It'll be a staid going on, just him and Grace.'

'They miss out with no children. But they could have been a favourite aunt and uncle and enjoyed Nathan and Flora.' She gave a little shrug of her shoulders. 'However, if that's the way they want it.'

The clock started its midnight chimes, breaking into their conversation. They listened in silence, counting the strokes to themselves. As the last one died away, Gennetta twisted round. 'Happy Christmas, darling.' Her eyes were full of devotion and when her lips met his there was no need for words to express the deep love between them.

She stood up and held out her hand. 'Bed, darling,' she said huskily.

He pushed himself from the sofa, checked the fire and placed the guard around it, picked up the two stockings stretched with their contents, handed one to her and took her other hand in his. When they came into the hall he picked up the lighted lamp from the small table and, hand in hand, they walked up the stairs.

Quietly they entered the children's room and laid a stocking at the foot of each bed. They paused and looked down adoringly at the innocent peace of childhood asleep on pillows so white they matched the snow which was beginning to fall gently outside.

'Thank you for them,' Reuben whispered.

'I needed you.'

With fingers entwined, they tip-toed on to the landing and beyond the top of the stairs to their own room.

Cyrus Sleightholme hurried into the house, dropped his hat and gloves on a chair in the hall and, shrugging himself quickly out of his topcoat, flung it across the back of the chair and strode into the drawing room where his father, feeling comfortably full after an enjoyable meal, was reading the latest issue of the *Whitby Gazette* and enjoying a cigar, a glass of port on a small table at his elbow. His wife, in a high-backed armchair placed on the opposite side of the fireplace, was engrossed in *Vanity Fair* borrowed from the subscription library on Pier Road.

They both looked up at this sudden intrusion to their peaceful evening and saw immediately that their son was bursting to tell them something.

Cyrus made no preamble. 'The Turners are going to have a baby!'

'What?' Robert almost choked at the unexpected information.

'Splendid!' smiled Mrs Sleightholme.

'Rot, Maud, rot!' spluttered Robert.

'But ...'

'Thee wouldn't understand,' cut in Robert sharply, dismissing her protest with a wave of his hand. He turned to his son. 'How does thee know?' he queried with a touch of doubt about the validity of the information.

'It's true all right,' went on Cyrus. 'I've been at the Angel and Jack came in all puffed up with self-importance, full of good cheer that had nothing to do with Christmas. He made the announcement that he was going to be a father and started throwing his money around, drinks for all.' He paused momentarily and added with a touch of scorn, 'Jack Turner, tight with his brass, wouldn't be doing that if it weren't true.'

'Damn!' Robert's lips were tight with annoyance. 'He'll never sell now.'

Gennetta watched the *Diana* sail the second week in January. It was a cold, bleak day with grey clouds driven by a freshening north-easter. She hoped it would strengthen no further for the sake of the *Diana* and all those on board her.

The light fall of Christmas snow in Whitby had gone. Gennetta turned up the collar of her redingote, snuggled into its protective warmth and headed for the bridge and home.

Her thoughts turned to Reuben. He would miss the comforts of home, though conditions on board ship had improved a little for him since his promotion. They should continue to do so because, just before sailing, he had informed her that Captain Barrick had told him that the First Mate was leaving after the return voyage and it was more than likely Reuben would get the job. The owners would have to be consulted but they very rarely opposed any recommendation of the captain's. She was pleased. Reuben deserved it.

Things were going well for them. The past year had been a good one. They were managing on his wages with a little taken from his savings. Further promotion would help even more. They were lucky to have the house and she was thankful for Cornelius's advice and negotiation with the owner on their behalf. The children were healthy and Rose and Mrs Shaw eager to please, and delighted at the way Gennetta had settled in to run the household without any airs and graces. The future seemed rosy. She had forgotten the Gabriel Hounds and now believed the figure in black to have been a figment of her imagination.

'Don't bother to come to see me sail, there's a raw February wind blowing off the sea.' Reuben tried to dissuade his wife before he left to join his ship.

'It's no colder than when you sailed in January, and I've never missed a sailing yet, nor a homecoming. I'm not going to start now,' she had replied firmly. 'I'll be there.'

'Then wrap up well, my love. I don't want you catching a chill because of me.' He took her in his arms. 'You're very precious.'

'So are you.' She snuggled close and turned her face upwards to meet his kiss. They lingered for a while.

'I must be away, love.' His words came regretfully as he finally broke their embrace. His farewells to the children had already been made and Rose was keeping them occupied upstairs. He picked up his bag and she accompanied him to the front door. A chill wind funnelled into the hall when he opened it. He kissed her quickly and was gone. She closed the door and ran to the room from which she could watch him stride down the path. Knowing where she would be, he turned at the gate and waved.

Ten minutes before sailing Reuben came back to the quay to join his wife. In the quickness of his step, in the tension she could sense before he reached her and more especially from the excitement in his eyes, she knew he had something to tell her.

'My position as Mate has been confirmed,' he announced.

'Oh, I'm so pleased for you,' cried Gennetta as she hugged him. 'It's what you deserve.'

Around them families and sweethearts, huddled into thick coats and jackets, backs to the biting wind, making their last goodbyes. People about their business hurried along the quay, anxious to be out of the cold as soon as possible. Others, always fascinated by sailing time, lingered, ignoring the sharp air, their attention held by the activity on board ship. Further along the river at another quay bordering the roadway two ships were taking last-minute goods on board, their crews eager to sail on the tide.

But Reuben and Gennetta were oblivious to it all, lost in each other's presence.

'I'll miss you, love,' said Gennetta, her eyes revealing sadness at parting from her husband.

'You'll always be in my thoughts,' he said, gently brushing her cheek with his fingers.

'Hope it's not going to be too rough for you,' she commented, endeavouring to turn her mind away from the parting.

'We'll be all right. *Diana*'s a stout ship and we've a good crew.' Reuben tried to sound confident. He knew how Gennetta worried about what the sea could do.

But never once had she voiced her fears or complained. This was the job he wanted to do and she knew he would do it well. Work ashore would break his heart and if she pressured him to leave the sea she knew their love would suffer. As it was, parting and coming together again heightened their desire into renewed expression of the boundless love which held them so strongly together.

These final moments on the quay were very precious to them. Lost to the world around them, their love needed no words.

'All aboard! All aboard!' The cry cut through the wind.

'Reuben!'

'Gen!'

They kissed. Love was expressed in the last touch of their lips. They parted. He moved away. Their fingers trailed apart from one final touch. Their eyes held each other.

'God go with you.' She mouthed the words silently.

He read them and responded, 'God keep you safe.'

The last sailor scrambled aboard. The gangway was withdrawn. The deck of the *Diana* was a scene of frenzied activity as men went about their jobs with the efficiency expected by their captain.

'Get singled up!'

'Loosen fore tops'l.'

'Hoist it!'

Backs bent and muscles strained in answer to Reuben's orders. With eyes moving constantly, watching, assessing, he kept a sharp watch over them.

'Let go fore and aft!'

The ropes were cast off. The *Diana* slipped away from the quay, slid steadily through the narrow open bridge and, with the wind catching the top sail, headed downstream towards the piers which gave their final protection before releasing the ship to the ocean.

'Get aloft!'

Men awaiting the order sprang into action and climbed the rigging to loosen the main topsail. The *Diana* dipped into the strong-running sea. Water sprayed over her bow and swished along her sides to leave a foaming trail. She rode the incoming waves with ease. The sea was her element. She was home. The crew had faith in her, Whitby-built as she was.

As the *Diana* moved downstream the crowds on the quay began to disperse. Gennetta pulled her coat more tightly around her, thankful she had chosen the one with the large collar, and with a sad heart walked slowly towards the bridge.

She started, her heart racing. Ahead, among the press of people, was a figure in black. She blinked. Shook her head in disbelief. It had gone. Had she imagined it? She had almost forgotten its appearance. It had been over a year ... She searched ahead, eyes moving swiftly across the crowd. No one. She must have been mistaken. Imagination was a strange thing. But why had she imagined it now, after all this time? She shuddered and quickened her step. Try as she might to forget, the figure still dwelt in her mind as she approached the bridge. She moved on above the water, then paused and turned her gaze seaward. She stood catching a last glimpse of the *Diana*.

Oh, no! The words rang silently in her mind as the call of wild geese assailed her ears. She swung round, eyes wide with disbelief, searching the sky. She turned and turned, her gaze turned ever upwards. Nothing. There must be. She could hear them. Others must have done so. She looked wildly around her. People were still moving across the bridge with the normal hustle and bustle. No one had stopped. No one was looking skywards.

She looked round desperately, wanting to stop everyone, tell them the portent of doom was in the air. But people hurried on, only the odd one casting her a glance of curiosity, wondering why she appeared to be searching for someone.

Gennetta's mind rang with the cries of the geese. Then they faded and were gone. She held her head, overwhelmed by the experience. Had she really heard them? Was it her imagination again, linking the apparition of the figure in black with the Gabriel Hounds? Was it an association of ideas brought on by tricks of the mind? What did it all mean? The manifestation had only made itself felt when the *Diana* had sailed. Was Reuben in danger?

She felt weak at the thought, grasping the rail on the bridge where she steadied herself and breathed deeply, trying to bring peace to a tortured mind. Slowly she took a grip on her feelings and became more aware of her surroundings. She shivered as the chill wind drove into her bones, then turned and walked home. With her thoughts dwelling on Reuben, she prayed hard for his safety.

Sleep did not come easily that night and when it did was fraught with nightmares. A figure in black, whose face she could not see, laughed with mockery and delight as he walked across the sea, drawing nearer and nearer to a ship on which the crew cowered in terror as the figure towered over it and, with outstretched hands, created a maelstrom in which the ship whirled and whirled until it was dragged down beneath the waves, leaving Reuben crying out for help.

The nightmare changed to one of evil birds, hybrids of goose and black eagle, sweeping down with talons extended to seize the ship and bear it off until she could see it no more and her grasping hands made future attempts to pull her beloved Reuben back to the safety of her arms.

To Gennetta it was a long three weeks that he was away. Her days and nights were fraught with the idea that Reuben was in danger. Mrs Shaw and Rose soon realised that something was worrying their mistress but knew it was not their place to ask questions. They saw it in the way her mind seemed to wander even while she was attending to the children. They witnessed her loss of appetite and were troubled by the occasional snap in her voice. They said nothing except to each other and hoped all would be well when Mr Reuben returned. They took heart when Gennetta brightened and was more her usual self as the day for the *Diana*'s arrival drew near.

That day, the Monday of the second week in March, dawned with a touch of spring in the air. Gennetta welcomed the change in the weather from the grey, oppressive days which had preceded it. She saw it as a sign that all would be well, and chastised herself for having allowed her imagination to overwhelm her reason.

She left the house with every intention of going straight to the quay on the east bank of the Esk as she usually did, but found herself turning away from the bridge and making for the west pier instead. From there she would get an earlier view of the *Diana* as she left the sea to make her way upstream to the quay beyond the bridge. She would see Reuben all the sooner and know he was all right.

Moving along the pier, she left the protection of the cliffs and felt the freshness in the wind. But the day was bright and she found the air invigorating. It gave her a feeling of well-being and brought a crispness to her step.

She searched the sea and her heart gave an excited flutter when she recognised the set of the *Diana*. In her mind she urged the vessel on, anxious to be sure that Reuben was all right, that the figure in black and the Gabriel Hounds meant nothing. Even as they entered her mind and she realised they must have been lurking in her subconscious, she dismissed them. The *Diana* was home.

Then she was there, so close, sweeping between the piers, leaving the running sea for the calmer waters of the river. Gennetta's eyes quickly scanned the deck. Reuben? Where was he? She could not see him. Anxiety gripped her. Her mind raced. She calmed herself, forced herself to sweep across the deck more slowly. Then she saw him towards the bow, surpervising the preparations for docking. Relief surged over her.

As he raised his head he saw her. In that moment of unexpected contact he froze. Thrilled at seeing her, he raised his arms and waved. Excited, she waved back. Across the distance their eyes locked and in the love between them space was no barrier. They waved until he turned back to his job. Gennetta hurried along the pier, her eyes hardly leaving the *Diana*. When she reached the bridge, the ship had just moved beyond it and she had to wait impatiently for it to close. Once it had done so people streamed across it, impeding her progress. She pushed her way through the crowd and by the time she reached the quay the *Diana* was tying up.

She watched as Reuben issued orders and the gangway was run out. A few moments later he was striding towards her, seeming to cleave a path through the people crowding towards the vessel to greet their loved ones. Then she was in his arms, thrilling to the feel of him. Their lips met. They were oblivious to the crowd around them. They heard none of the shouts and the laughter. This homecoming was theirs alone.

'Coming home now?' she asked when their lips parted.

'Can't, love, the voyage isn't over for me. I've to collect the money to pay off the crew.'

Disappointed, she pouted.

He smiled at her expression and flicked her lips with his fingers. 'I shan't be long, love. You go home.'

Loth to leave him, she knew it was the better than hanging around the quay waiting for him. 'Hurry,' she said.

'I will.'

As she walked home, his words 'the voyage isn't over' haunted her. She had feared that the omens of the figure in black and the Gabriel Hounds had meant tragedy on the voyage but with the arrival of the

Diana and having Reuben in her arms, she once more dismissed the fear. He was home. He was safe. Nothing had gone wrong. Tragedy had been a figment of her imagination. But now, recollecting his words, the doubts and anxieties were back. Then she chided herself severely. What could go wrong now? Reuben was safely ashore. The sea had no power over him. It could not exert its fearsome might. But ... the voyage was not over.

Back on board the *Diana* Reuben received his note of authority from Captain Barrick and immediately left the ship. He lost no time in reaching the bank in Church Street and was immediately admitted to the manager's office. His note was quickly scrutinised and approved, and the crew's pay in notes and coins made available. He left the bank with it in a black leather bag.

As he stepped out of the building he was unaware that two men, lounging against the wall on the opposite side of the street, straightened and fell into step behind him. After a few paces one of them quickened his stride. Reuben took no notice of the man in the thick high-necked jersey, a woollen cap covering all except the fringes of his dark brown hair, who hurried past him as he sidestepped two ladies deep in conversation.

Reaching an alley that ran off to the right, the man turned to see his companion was now only a yard behind Reuben. As Reuben moved to his left to pass him, the man stepped in front of him.

Startled to have his path blocked, Reuben faltered.

'Mate from the *Diana*?' the man queried.

'Yes.' He nodded, his eyes carrying a query at the intrusion.

Not another word was spoken. The man behind Reuben grabbed his right arm and turned him towards the alley. At the same moment the first man grasped his left arm, and, caught unawares and off balance, Reuben had no resistance as he was propelled into the alley. He felt a sharp blow in his kidney. Pain seared through him. Instinctively he resisted the hand which grabbed the bag. As he was slammed hard against the wall, a searing pain ripped through his stomach. He gasped, eyes wide in disbelief as the narrow alley swam before him. He was jolted upright by the force of a second blow to his stomach. His vision blurred and as his attackers stepped out of the way he pitched forward on to the rough hard ground. For one moment his hand reached out as if he would stop the two men who ran off down the alley towards the river and their boat. Then Reuben jerked and lay still.

87

Chapter Eight

By the time she arrived home Gennetta had cast all apprehension aside and was eager to prepare for the arrival of her man, home from the sea. She fussed around the kitchen supervising the meal though there was little to do for she had implicit faith in the competence of Mrs Shaw, but Gennetta wanted everything to be just right today.

The children, excited by the prospect of seeing Papa again, and at the thought of the present he must surely bring them for he always did, had been ushered away by Rose who was trying to curb their exhilaration.

Mrs Shaw smiled to herself as Gennetta scurried away for the umpteenth time to look out of the drawing-room window to see if Reuben was hurrying up the path. It was good to see the mistress so lively again.

'He's a long time,' she commented when she returned to the kitchen. 'It's been an hour since I saw him.'

'There's a lot to do at the end of a voyage, ma'am,' replied Mrs Shaw.

'But he said he only had the crew's wages to collect and he wouldn't be long.'

'Maybe Captain Barrick had summat else for him to do when he got back to the ship.'

'Maybe,' agreed Gennetta half-heartedly.

Another hour passed and worry was beginning to gnaw at her mind. She was tempted to put on her outdoor clothes and return to the ship to see what was delaying her husband but knew that would embarrass him.

The sudden jangling of the doorbell startled her. Reuben? But he would know the door would be open for him. She hurried into the hall just as Rose appeared at the top of the stairs.

'I'll get it, Rose,' she called, and crossed the tiled floor with a brisk step.

She flung the door wide. 'Reuben ...' The name faded on her lips. She was taken aback to see a serious-faced Captain Barrick standing there. Her heart fluttered and a dreadful anxiety gripped her. Something was wrong. Something had happened to Reuben! 'Captain Barrick.' Her voice was low and contained the unspoken query, Why are you here?

'Mrs Briggs, ma'am. May I come in?'

'Oh, of course.' She moved aside, trying to read his grave expression as he stepped past her and removed his peaked cap.

Gennetta's heart was beating fast as she led the way into the drawing room.

'Ma'am, I have some distressing news for you,' the kind-faced man said solemnly, wishing that he hadn't to perform this task.

'Reuben?' Her voice was filled with anxiety.

He nodded. 'He was murdered for the crew's wages. Stabbed in an alleyway and the money taken. I'm sorry to be so blunt ...' His apology was lost in her cry.

'Oh, no!' The words were agonised. The colour drained from her face. This couldn't be true! Reuben couldn't be dead. He'd be home any minute. But this was Captain Barrick. He wouldn't be here unless ... Bewildered, she sank on to a chair.

'I'm so sorry, ma'am. He was a fine young man. Conscientious, hard-working, had all the makings of a good captain,' Captain Barrick went on, but Gennetta didn't want to hear this praise. She wanted Reuben. Her mind screamed for the captain to stop. Then she heard him say, 'If there's anything I can do, please let me know. I'll see you get his things and his pay.'

Gennetta nodded weakly. 'Thank you.' Her voice was barely above a whisper.

'I must go, ma'am. Shall I call someone to be with you?'

Though she was fully aware of his question Gennetta did not speak for a moment. Then it seemed she understood. She started. 'No, I'll be all right. I want a moment on my own.'

He looked askance at her, but respected her wishes. 'No, don't move,' he said as she began to rise from her chair. 'I'll let myself out.'

'Thank you.'

She sat, stunned. How could this be true? She had seen Reuben not long ago. He was alive. He couldn't be dead now. But Captain Barrick had been here. The enormity of the situation struck home. Devastated, she sank her head into the cushions and cried.

How long she was there she never knew but with the immediate grief wept out of her, she sat up. She rested for a few moments gathering her thoughts, trying to compose herself. She stood up, stiffened her back and walked towards the door. Life must go on. There were the children to think about, things to do, the future to plan.

She hesitated at the door, drew a deep breath, turned the knob and started across the hall.

'Mama! Mama! When's Papa coming?' Nathaniel's voice, strident with excitement, burst from the top of the stairs and brought her to a sudden stop.

She looked up to see her young son racing down the stairs followed slowly by Flora who was holding Rose's hand.

She dropped to one knee and hugged him when he flung himself into her outstretched arms. It was all she could do to prevent herself from bursting into tears.

'When will he be coming, Mama?'

'He's had to go somewhere else,' she said.

'Will he be long?' Tiny furrows creased his brow as he leaned back to look at his mother.

'He might be.' Gennetta stood up as Rose and Flora reached them. 'Now, you two, run along and play, I want to talk to Rose.'

'Yes, Mama.' Nathaniel took his sister's hand and started back towards the stairs. At the bottom step he paused and looked back over his shoulder. 'Tell him to hurry, Mama.'

She nodded and watched them go. She resisted the temptation to bring them back so she could find solace in their touch, wiping away the tears which started down her cheek.

Rose sensed there was something wrong. But before she could speculate further, Gennetta's voice broke in. 'Come along, Rose.'

When they entered the kitchen Mrs Shaw, standing beside a large well-scrubbed table in the middle of the room, was busy mixing the ingredients for a cake in a large bowl. She stopped beating when she saw Gennetta's dull expression.

'I've just had some terrible news.' There was a catch in her voice as she looked from one to the other. Mrs Shaw's usually bright, smiling face took on a mask of seriousness, while Rose, mystified, stared at Gennetta with fearful eyes. 'Captain Barrick has just been to tell me that my ...' Her words caught in her throat. She leaned her hands on the table for support. She tightened her lips and controlled herself. 'He told me Mr Reuben has been murdered.'

The two women gasped. They stared at her in shock horror, their minds numbed by the news.

'Oh, ma'am.' Mrs Shaw was already moving round the table. She had seen that the effort of saying the awful words had drained her mistress and dragged a chair from under the table. 'Here, sit down, ma'am.' As Gennetta sank on to the chair, Mrs Shaw glanced at Rose who was standing with tears streaming down her cheeks. 'Mash some tea, Rose.' She put a little sharpness into her voice to jerk the maid out of her trance.

Rose scurried over to the iron kettle which was always kept on the stove and in a matter of moments was pouring the tea.

Gennetta was thankful for hers. It brought a little colour back to her cheeks. 'Rose, when you've finished yours, wash your face, hide those tears and go back to the children.'

'Yes, ma'am,' she sobbed.

'And take hold of yourself. I don't want you to breathe a word of this to them.'

'But Nathaniel was so excited about his father coming home. What have I to say if he asks me when he will be here?' wailed Rose.

'Tell him you don't know. I'll break the news to them when it's the right time.'

Gennetta closed the door behind the last of the departing sympathisers who had been at the funeral and had returned to the house to make their condolences and praise Reuben while partaking of refreshments. They had been few, Captain Barrick and some of the *Diana*'s crew, neighbours, half a dozen friends and Cornelius Mitchell. He awaited her now in the drawing room, having requested an interview after the funeral.

It had been bleak on the cliff top in the churchyard which was open to the wind from the sea. Alone by the grave, looking down on the coffin, Gennetta recalled how Reuben loved the feel of that wind for it reminded him of days at sea. In a silent prayer she hoped that from beyond the grave he would give her strength to bear the loss and cope with life without him for the sake of their children.

They had been told, and though they could hardly understand that they would never see Papa again they still possessed the gift of innocence. Tears had been shed whenever they wanted him but Rose was always there to look after them. Now she had taken them for a walk while Gennetta spoke to Cornelius.

'I am sorry to have to bring this up so soon, ma'am,' he apologised when they were alone, 'but have you thought of the future? What you will do regarding this house? I know the funeral has just taken place but realities have to be faced and, I always think, the sooner the better.'

Gennetta, who was sitting primly on the edge of a chair, smoothing her black muslin dress, looked up at the small man cocking his head sideways as if to emphasise his point.

'Mr Mitchell, obviously I have given thought to my predicament. There has been little time to reach a conclusion but it has been in the back of my mind. I have the children to think about. But, I must say, all I can see at this moment is uncertainty.' Gennetta spoke firmly. As she had walked away from the graveside she had concluded that one life was over for her and a new one had to begin. Reuben would not want her to mourn for him but be thankful for the life and love they had shared. 'Mr Mitchell, have you come here to advise me?'

'No. No. Please don't get that idea.' He raised his hands in protest. 'I have no right. Your husband made no will with me.'

'Then why did you wish to see me?'

He raised his eyebrows and looked around. 'This house, my dear madam. Will you be able to keep it?'

She eyed him for a moment and he shuffled uncomfortably under her gaze. 'I take it you are worried about the rent?' She paused but continued before he could comment, 'Mr Mitchell, I have no income. There is Reuben's pay from his last voyage and a few savings.'

'Then what are you going to do?'

'I must get work. I had thought I might take drawing classes but that would jeopardise Mr Cooper's income and I could not do that when he was so kind to me. A governess? Maybe, but who would want me with two children of my own?'

'I'm sorry, Mrs Briggs, I have no answers. It is you who will have to find a solution. All I am concerned about is this house. If you can pay the rent, all well and good, but I must have an answer within the week.'

'Mr Mitchell,' she drew herself up, 'how do you expect me to find an answer in that time?'

He shrugged his shoulders and grimaced. 'But I must have an answer and it must guarantee that you will be able to meet the rent for at least a year. I have a client who wants ...'

'Someone approached you even before poor Reuben was buried! Couldn't they have had the decency ...'

Cornelius held up his hands. 'Please, Mrs Briggs, I'm only doing my job. After all, I have the owner's interests to look after. I cannot turn away a prospective tenant without knowing your position. If you can assure me that you will take a year's tenancy, I will be satisfied.'

'You know I can't do that until I sort things out and see if I can find employment.'

'Why not ask your brother to help you?'

'Jack!' Gennetta gave a half laugh. 'He wouldn't lift a finger to help me.'

'You never know.'

'Then you don't know Jack.'

'Well, I'm sorry.' He started to rise from his chair. 'I must have your answer a week today.'

As Gennetta grappled with her problem over the next three days while getting no nearer a solution, her mind kept turning to Cornelius's suggestion of approaching her brother.

She kept dismissing the idea as preposterous. She and Jack had never been close. His father's boy, he had always sided with Jeremiah's views of her, and no doubt the day she walked out had rejoiced. Their father's business and fortune would be his and his alone. How she could do with a little of that money now! Maybe he would relent. After all, he had made an appearance at Reuben's funeral, albeit on the periphery, hastening away once the coffin had been lowered into the grave. Could there be a spark of hope in that? Maybe there was a chance that he would help. She did not want to go begging but would if it came to it, for the sake of the children. With a child of his own on the way, Jack might be more amenable, especially with the threat of losing their home hanging over them.

That evening, resolved to curb her pride, she donned her waist-length cape over her mourning dress and left for the house in Bagdale.

Nearing her old home, her step faltered. Doubt had entered her mind about the reception she would receive, but then she thought of Nathaniel and Flora and resolved to face her brother. Her heart beat a little faster when she turned up the path towards the front door, and when she rang the bell apprehension heightened the fluttering in her heart.

The door was opened by a maid whose plain black dress was relieved only by the white apron tied at her waist and a small white mob-cap.

'Mrs Briggs to see Mr Turner,' Gennetta told the girl.

'Step inside, ma'am. I'll see if Mr Turner is at home.'

As the maid crossed the hall and knocked on the door of the drawing room, Gennetta glanced around the hall. Nothing had been changed since the day she'd left and she felt a tightening in her stomach at this homecoming. It was as if the years had slipped back.

But she was brought quickly to the present when the girl reappeared and informed her that Mr Turner would see her.

Reopening the door, the maid announced, 'Mrs Briggs.'

Gennetta stepped past her to find her brother and his wife sitting in chairs to either side of the fireplace. Jack rose, dropped his newspaper on to a small table beside him and threw the remains of his cigar into the

93

fire which burned brightly. As she crossed the room, Gennetta was aware that some of the heavier furniture which she remembered had been removed and that the room bore evidence of a woman's touch which it had always lacked in her time. No doubt Grace was responsible, for the frills and flouncy curtains were typical of her taste.

Her brother's serious expression was tinged with hostility. He gave her no greeting as he watched her cross the room. It was Grace who spoke first.

'Gennetta, how nice to see you.' She held out a hand and smiled warmly.

Gennetta saw Jack frown and shoot his wife a look of disapproval. This did not augur well for the success of her visit but she determined to press on. Maybe the fact that Grace was present would have an influence, though she knew all decisions were taken by Jack.

'And you, Grace.' Gennetta took her hand and bent down to kiss her on her cheek.

'We were so sorry about Reuben. Terrible tragedy.'

She heard Jack give a little grunt of agreement.

'Thank you.'

As she straightened he spoke gruffly. 'What do you want here?'

She looked at her brother. There was no warmth in his eyes.

'I need help. I'd hoped you might ...'

'Help you? Why should I?' There was contempt in his voice and in his eyes as he turned and assumed a dominant position with his back to the fire.

'I'm your sister.'

'Sister? I think you forfeited that right when you walked out. Maybe even before, when you were born and killed my mother.'

Grace gasped at the harshness of her husband's statement. 'Jack, you can't blame Gennetta for that.'

'You keep out of it. I don't need your opinion,' he snapped, and glared at his sister. 'Why should I help you?

'I've been hit hard. I desperately need help or we will be out on the street.'

'On the street? You have the house.' Jack was taken aback by her answer.

'That's just it, we haven't. Edith Briggs left everything to a person unknown to us. The name, known to Cornelius Mitchell, was never to be disclosed.'

Jack raised his eyebrows. 'But you've met this person to negotiate the tenancy of the house?'

Gennetta shook her head. 'No. Everything was handled by Cornelius.'

'And now that old Shylock is turning the screw.'

'He wants us out in four days' time unless I can assure him that I can afford to rent the house for at least a year. He needs to know immediately because he has someone else interested in the tenancy. I'm desperate, Jack. I need your help, I've no one else to turn to.'

'And you have the gall to come to me, after cutting yourself off from the family?'

'Father insisted I marry Cyrus Sleightholme but I loved Reuben. I had to walk out.'

'And lose us the chance of taking over the Sleightholme jet works?'

'There was no certainty that would ever have happened,' she cried, desperate to make her case.

'Father had ideas of how it could be achieved, you wouldn't know about them, but you killed them when you left. No, Gennetta, you walked out to marry a sailor. You must follow the path you chose.' He delivered the words with finality, as if that was an end to the matter.

Grace stared at him in disbelief. 'Jack, you can't see Gennetta evicted with nowhere to go.'

'Then she must take employment.'

'I've tried but there's nothing and it is made more awkward with having the children to look after.'

'Put them into an orphanage.'

'Jack!' Grace was astonished by her husband's suggestion.

'Never!' cried Gennetta defiantly. She felt her flesh crawl at the thought of her children condemned to such a harsh life. She'd do anything to prevent that.

He shrugged his shoulders with the gesture of one who didn't care. 'Then you'll have to do the best you can.'

'Jack, you can't turn your sister away,' protested Grace.

'I can and I will.'

'You must help her.'

'I have no need.'

'She's your sister.'

'Only by birth. And her birth,' he nodded at Gennetta with loathing in his eyes, 'brought tragedy. I've never known a mother's love.'

'Nor have I, Jack.' She broke into the sharp exchange between husband and wife. 'And, unlike you, I never received a father's love either.'

'He provided for you but you showed how much you appreciated that when you left. He wanted nothing more to do with you after that, and nor do I.'

'Jack, please help her,' pleaded Grace.

95

'No!'

'Think of the children,' cried Grace. 'You can't ...'

'They aren't my concern,' he broke in sharply, casting her a withering look for interfering and taking sides with his sister.

'But they're your nephew and niece.' Anguish had come to Grace's voice. She knew how adamant her husband could be when he had his mind set.

'They're no relation of mine. Gennetta cut them off when she married that sailor.' There was scorn in his tone as if such a person were beneath his consideration.

Gennetta's eyes blazed. 'Reuben was a good man. He worked hard and had just been made Mate. Had every prospect of becoming a captain. You wouldn't have spoken of him in that tone then.'

Jack gave a little laugh. 'You married him, you must face the consequences.'

'Gennetta couldn't foresee Reuben's murder.' Grace's words admonished him for his attitude. 'You should be sympathising with her and helping her.'

Jack was growing annoyed with his wife's continual siding with Gennetta. 'Keep out of it, woman,' he snapped angrily. 'This has nothing to do with you.'

'It has everything to do with me when I see my husband demeaning himself over such a simple thing.'

'It's not a simple thing,' he snapped, anger clouding his eyes.

'All you have to do is to make Gennetta an allowance. You can afford to. Isn't it her right as your sister?'

'She has no rights! If I did that it would be a betrayal of what my father wanted. She forfeited all rights when she disobeyed him. He changed his will, cutting her off completely. I became the sole heir to everything he had: the business, this house, all its contents and his money. If I gave any of that to her now it would be a betrayal of his wishes. I could never live with myself if I thought I had let him down.'

'And can you live with yourself if you see Gennetta and her children on the street?' Grace pressed home her point in a quiet voice. Even as she put this question she knew what his answer would be.

'I can and I will!' he replied firmly, turning to his sister. 'There is nothing I can do.'

'Won't, you mean,' she returned.

He shrugged his shoulders and gestured with his hands. 'Look at it which way you like, the answer is the same.'

Gennetta rose from her chair. 'You have been schooled very well

96

by Father. I am sorry for you.' Her voice was low but tight, failing to disguise the opinion in which she now held her brother.

Jack drew himself up to his full height. 'And I couldn't have had a better mentor.'

Gennetta's half smile was cynical as she turned to go. She hid the deep dread of the future which lay cold and heavy upon her heart and walked with a firm step towards the door.

'Gennetta!' The cry came from Grace. She looked at her husband. 'Jack, help her!' The plea was harsh with desperation.

'No!' The word resounded from the walls, an omen of doom for Gennetta.

Grace sprang to her feet, her heart racing. She needed to do something to help her sister-in-law. 'Gennetta, wait!' she cried. But Gennetta was already crossing the hall to the front door.

Grace started after her. Jack grabbed her arm. 'Let her go,' he snarled. His grip tightened but before it could detain her, Grace had squirmed loose and was running for the door.

'Grace, come back,' yelled Jack, trembling at his wife's defiance.

But she was out of the room, heading for the front door which had swung to behind Gennetta.

'Grace!' Jack boomed across the hall but she took no notice.

She jerked open the heavy wooden door with the energy of one who must prevent a catastrophe. Anxiety creased her face when she saw Gennetta running down the path towards the gate. Grace went after her. After three paces she tripped, stumbled and, with a cry of fear, plunged headlong down the path. Pain seared through her stomach as she hit the ground. Everything swam before her. The pain tightened and her body seemed to give way under it.

Jack reached the door of the house just in time to see his wife fall. His eyes widened in horror as his mind filled with the nightmare of what could happen to his child. 'Grace!' Alarm filled his cry.

It stopped Gennetta in her tracks. She swung round to see her sister-in-law roll over, grasping her stomach, her face contorted in agony.

'Oh, my God!' She started back up the path.

By the time she reached Grace, Jack was on his knees beside his wife.

'Oh, Jack, I'm losing our baby!' Surprise, pain and sorrow were combined in her tone.

'No!' he cried as if he would stop what was happening. 'The doctor, we'll get the doctor.' He yelled for the maid.

'It's too late,' she whispered.

Jack read the truth in those words. He looked up at his sister who was stroking Grace's brow. 'You!' he hissed. 'It's *your* fault. Why did you have to come here? You've killed my son just as surely as you killed my mother!' Hatred burned in his eyes. 'Get the hell away from here. I never want to see you again!'

Chapter Nine

The following morning, sitting alone at a desk in the room which Aunt Edith had used as a library, Gennetta looked despondently at the figures she had written down. They told her that she could not buy time. There was insufficient to meet Cornelius's demand for a year's guaranteed rent. If there had been she would have met it and hoped that within that year she could have found some other source of income.

She felt weighed down by the problem. What could she do? To whom could she turn? The thought took her back to her visit the previous day. It had haunted her during the night. She could still see the hatred in her brother's eyes as he blamed her for the death of his child. Maybe he was right. If she hadn't gone, none of it would have happened. As much as she tried to cast the guilt from her mind by telling herself that if Jack had been more reasonable everything would have been all right, his words still tormented her. The one hope she had, the only chance she could see, had gone with his intransigent attitude, and in its wake had come the remorse which now lay heavily on her. If only she had not sought his help ...

Her thoughts drifted despondently. She was only half aware of the bell ringing in a distant part of the house. Sighing, she rose to answer it, knowing that Rose had taken the children for a walk. Then she heard footsteps crossing the hall and realised that Mrs Shaw was on her way to the front door.

A few moments later there was a knock on the library door and the cook appeared.

'A letter for you, ma'am.' She crossed the floor holding out the envelope, her footsteps quiet on the thick carpet. 'Mrs Turner's maid. Said she hadn't to wait for an answer.'

'Thank you. Did you ask her how Mrs Turner was?'

'After what you told us yesterday, I did, ma'am.'

'And?'

'She said that Mrs Turner lost the baby but seems to be recovering. The doctor has instructed her to stay in bed for the next week.'

Gennetta nodded. 'Thank you, Mrs Shaw.' There was a slight feeling of relief to learn that Grace was safe but Gennetta still faced the enormity of the future.

She looked down at the envelope and, recognising Jack's writing, wondered why he was corresponding with her. She picked up a letter-opener, carved from a piece of whalebone, and slit the envelope. She withdrew a sheet of paper, unfolded it and stared at the words: *Come to see me. Jack.*

Why should he want to see her? Had he relented? Hope soared but was dashed again when she recalled, with terrible clarity, the hatred on his face. *'Come to see me.'* She placed the paper on the desk and stood up.

As she walked up the path towards Jack's house she shuddered. She could still see Grace sprawled on the ground, her face ravaged by pain. Gennetta hurried past the spot.

The door was opened by the maid who had admitted her yesterday. She immediately ushered Gennetta into the room which Jack used as a study, obviously having been instructed to do so. As she sat down to await him, Gennetta glanced around her. It was little altered since her father's time and she could imagine that here her brother sensed a closeness with their father, as if Jeremiah was still there to guide him in decisions. Was that why Jack was using this room to see her rather than the drawing room, which would have been more usual? Did he need to feel his father's presence for what he had to say to her?

She heard footsteps cross the hall and judged them to have come from the stairs. A moment later the door opened and Jack came into the room, shutting the door carefully behind him. He did not speak as he took his chair at the desk. His eyes were cold as he looked at his sister.

'How is Grace?' she asked tentatively.

'She will recover,' he replied icily. 'I do not want you here, but she begged me to help you. She's been worrying about it all the time. It was bothering her and as I want nothing to mar her recovery, I agreed to see that you had a roof over your head. To her that implies that I am giving you an allowance. That I will not do, but I will see that you have employment.' There was no warmth in his gesture and he made it obvious that it was against his own wishes.

But that did not matter to Gennetta. Here was some provision for the future. She took him to mean that the employment would enable her to stay in Aunt Edith's house.

Jack offered no further explanation but stood up when Gennetta started to thank him.

'I want no thanks.' As he looked down at her the hatred had not left his eyes. He was still thinking of the son he had lost. 'Come with me,' he said curtly.

He paused in the hall to throw a cape around his shoulders, put on a top hat and pick up a walking stick.

He uttered no word as he strode down Bagdale to the bridge, seeming to cleave a path through the people who were on the streets while Gennetta found it difficult to keep up with him. He took no notice of her rapid breathing and kept to his relentless pace. As they crossed the bridge she wondered where they were going but with his face set so grimly she knew it would be useless to ask him.

Once on the east bank they turned left along Church Street. Buildings crowded in on them and towered over them as the multitude of terraces climbed the steep cliffside. These poverty-stricken yards were crammed with inhabitants who seemed to be clinging to the rockside just to survive. Conditions were harsh but the poorest of the poor clung tenaciously to their precious habitation in order to keep a roof over their heads. Beyond that, life held little hope for them.

Gennetta knew there were yards only a short distance away where sympathetic landlords took an interest in their property and housewives had some pride in their homes, keeping them clean and neat. Generally they were fortunate in having husbands in regular work.

Jack turned into one of the yards and, as they climbed some twisting broken steps, Gennetta realised this place was far from being one of the better ones. Their presence stopped the children at play. Dirty faces with running noses stared at the lady and gentleman in their fine clothes. They never saw such elegance in their yard. Word spread quickly through the warren of houses and in no time women stood at doorways, eyeing the strangers, wondering who they were until someone recognised Jack. Then the whisper of 'Mr Turner' ran before them like wildfire.

Recognition brought requests from the bolder ones.

'Roof's leaking, Mr Turner ... '

'Should have more privvies.'

'Bedroom floor's caving in.'

'Get your hand down, y'mean old bastard!'

'How'd y'like y'lady friend to live like we do?'

Jack marched on, ignoring their comments.

Gennetta was shocked at the realisation that he owned these

properties and seemed oblivious to the conditions under which his tenants were living. She could feel curious gazes directed at her and knew she was being looked up and down. She made a marked contrast to the women who stood in their doorways. Their clothes were creased, dirty, and in many cases tattered. They wore aprons which had not seen water for a long time. Their hair was lank and unkempt, only a few having made an attempt to tie it neatly back.

What on earth was Jack bringing her here for? When he stopped at a house halfway up the cliffside and produced a key, Gennetta knew.

He pressed the sneck and pushed at the door. It was reluctant to move but a stronger shove elicited the screech of rusted hinges. The door swung wide and allowed light to spill into the gloomy place which had not been penetrated by light from the dirty window.

Jack stepped to one side to allow his sister to enter.

She stopped and stared incredulously at him. 'This?'

'For you, my dear.' His voice was full of triumph. He knew he had shocked her with his offer.

'Live here?'

'Where else?'

'But I thought ...'

'You thought I was going to pay your rent and let you live where you are now?' He grinned malevolently at her. 'All I said was that I would find you employment. Your wage will pay your rent on this place, with a little left over. Take it or leave it.'

Gennetta's heart was heavy. Her body was numb with shock at her brother's offer, but could she have expected anything else? If she had stopped to think, to weigh up what his possible reaction would be, wouldn't she have realised he would try to humiliate her?

She walked into the house. The lime-washed walls were marked with damp. The flagged floor was uneven. She went through into the small room at the back which was even worse for it backed on to the cliffside and hardly any light came through the one small window which was thick with cobwebs.

'Want to go upstairs?' asked Jack, adding in a sarcastic tone, 'My dear.'

She shot him a withering look and climbed the rickety stairs to find two small rooms in a worse condition than those downstairs, for here the ceilings were showing signs of bulging and mortar was crumbling from the walls.

She bit her lips. Tears stung her eyes but she forced them back. She would not let Jack see her cowed by the thought of living in such a hovel. She came slowly down the stairs, wondering if she could bring the children to live in such conditions.

102

'Well?' he asked sharply.

'You said you would see that I had employment?'

'Yes, I will.'

'Can I know what that is before I decide whether to live here?' Gennetta wanted to maintain some pretence of dignity.

'Yes. Come with me and I'll show you. It's not far.' He strode out of the house, ignoring once again the disrespectful calls which came from the bystanders still curious as to why he and this lady were looking at the worst house in the yard.

Reaching Church Street, he turned right and after about fifty yards entered a building on the opposite side of the street.

Once again Genneta was thunderstruck. Was he going to offer her employment in his jet works? He couldn't! This was a man's world. No fit place for a woman.

She stepped into a new world for she had never been brought by her father to see the workshop in which he made his money. A wooden bench occupied the centre of the room, around which three men were seated etching on flat pieces of jet. At one end a fourth was deftly cutting at a lump of jet, obviously a man in some position of authority for he was the only one sitting at the bench who wore a bowler hat. Beyond them along one wall were the grindstones, driven by belts on shafted wheels at shoulder height. The clatter of the wheels turning at high speed and the rasping noise as they smoothed and polished the jet, at various stages of its production, filled the room with an unholy mixture of sounds. A fine brown dust rose, seeming to haze the air and settle over the whole room. Jack's only concession to keeping his employees warm in cold weather, throughout their long working day, was a solitary iron stove set at one end of the bench. Light came from windows set high on the outside walls.

As they entered the room the men looked up to see who the unexpected visitor was. Seeing their employer the engravers bent their heads over their pieces of jet as if working with more concentration and those at the lathes drove them faster, but the carver appeared to take no notice, though Gennetta felt sure he was not oblivious to their arrival.

One man who had been standing near the bench, the only other man to wear a bowler hat, keeping a watchful eye over every workman, came quickly to meet them.

'Good day, Mr Turner.' He touched the brim of his hat and glanced suspiciously at Gennetta. 'And thee, ma'am.'

She nodded and smiled.

''Morning, Young,' Jack greeted him, his voice gruff as if warning his employee to keep his place. He half turned to Gennetta. 'This is my foreman, John Young. Young, my sister, Mrs Briggs.'

103

'Good morning, John.' Gennetta held out her hand. She noticed her brother frown at her gesture but, guessing what was coming, wanted to start on friendly terms with the foreman. John Young's hesitation was momentary. The surprise on his face was gone almost before she saw it. He wiped his hand down his dark blue smock and shook her hand. She felt his warm grip and judged that behind the wariness in the lined, bearded face was a measure of friendliness.

'Young, I'm employing my sister. Give her a job.' Jack's words were sharp.

The foreman, surprised at the order, looked askance at his employer. 'Work 'ere?' He glanced at Gennetta, trying to equate this with her elegant mourning attire.

'That's what I said,' snapped Jack.

'But, sir, this is man's work,' John Young protested. There must be trouble in the family for a brother, and a rich one at that, to offer his sister work in this man's domain set in unwholesome surroundings. 'I can't be responsible for my men if Mrs Briggs works 'ere. They won't like 'aving a wo— er, a lady among 'em.'

'Then let her work in there,' said Jack gruffly as he nodded in the direction of a door just beyond the lathes. 'She can sort jet. She'll be out of the way.'

'That's rough work.' The foreman was clearly embarrassed by the situation in which he had been placed.

Doubts crept into Gennetta's mind. Could she ever survive in this enclosed atmosphere of dust and grit, of whirling grindstones and rasping tools? Her whole being cried out to reject Jack's offers but what else could she do? She had been unable to find any other form of employment and was certain Cornelius would have her evicted if she tried to stay in Aunt Edith's house. At least Jack's proposal would give her a roof over her head and an income of sorts. She could do nothing but accept.

She was determined to show no weakness. She would not give Jack the pleasure of seeing her plead. 'I'll be here tomorrow morning, John,' she said firmly, easing his predicament and deliberately using his Christian name to annoy her brother. 'What time do I start?'

'I want you to give her no privileges, Young. If I hear of any she will be dismissed immediately and you with her,' Jack interposed before the foreman could answer.

'I want none!' Gennetta's eyes flashed defiantly.

'Then thee start at seven and work 'til six, with time off for summat t'eat at twelve,' John Young answered her.

'I said no privileges, Young!' Jack's voice boomed. 'She can start at six with the apprentices.'

'But surely Mrs Briggs is not being indentured?'

'No, but she can start when the apprentices do. I'm sure you'll find plenty to keep her occupied.'

'Aye, sir.' John cast Gennetta a sympathetic glance as Jack turned to leave.

Gennetta followed him out but once in the street she did not attempt to match his stride and let him go. She made her way home, oblivious to her surroundings. Her mind was in a daze, trying to comprehend the change in her life which was about to take place.

When she arrived home she called Mrs Shaw and Rose to the drawing room, telling the children to go and play.

'I'm sorry to tell you that I will no longer require your services,' Gennetta informed them.

The sadness and weariness in her voice did not escape them. Sensing that this decision must have been forced on her, Mrs Shaw spoke up. 'But we don't want to leave.'

'As you know, I have to be out of this house in two days' time. You will not want to go where I have to.'

'But, ma'am, we'll go anywhere with you,' cried Rose.

'That's kind of you, and I thank you, but would you like to live in Hacker's Yard?'

Rose looked shocked and Mrs Shaw gasped before saying, 'You can't mean it, ma'am?'

'I'm afraid I do,' replied Gennetta.

'But that's the poorest, roughest yard on the east side. The houses are hovels and ...'

'I know,' agreed Gennetta. 'I went to my brother to see if he would help me. He finally said he would give me employment and offered me a roof over my head. He did that all right – a place in Hacker's Yard, and work in his jet workshop.'

'Ma'am, you can't!' cried Mrs Shaw.

'It's no place for you!' Shocked by the news, Rose threw her objection behind Mrs Shaw's.

'I have no choice. I'll be on the street otherwise.'

'Ma'am, what about the bairns? You can't take them to Hacker's Yard.' The prospect of the two children being subjected to such an insalubrious environment chilled the cook with horror.

'What else can I do?' Gennetta sighed in despair.

'But how will you manage if you are working?'

'I'll have to find a neighbour to keep an eye on them.'

'Wouldn't trust any of that lot to do it,' Mrs Shaw said flatly.

'Wish I could help,' murmured Rose.

105

'Ma'am, let me take the children.' Mrs Shaw was watching Gennetta intently, eager to persuade her. Seeing her mistress's curiousity roused, she went on: 'Oh, I couldn't offer them a home like this but it would be far better than Hacker's Yard and our neighbours are certainly different to those you'll encounter. You couldn't leave your poor bairns to the likes of them to look after.'

The idea gave Gennetta hope. She would miss the children but had been worried as to what would happen when she was at work. This way they would be cared for and she knew Mrs Shaw loved them as if they were her own.

Knowing Gennetta would not like parting with them Mrs Shaw pressed on, 'You could see them every day. I'm sorry I can't offer you accommodation as well but as you know we have only a small house. We'll manage something for the bairns, though. You can't let them go to Hacker's Yard even if you have to.'

Gennetta nodded, looking thoughtful.

'Oh, ma'am, I think it's a good idea.' Rose put her weight behind Mrs Shaw's proposal. 'And let me come with you.'

Startled by this suggestion, Gennetta shot a questioning look at her but saw that the girl was serious. 'You mean that, Rose?'

'Of course,' she replied.

'But what would you do? I wouldn't need a maid.'

'I know, but I've nowhere else to go. I'm alone with no one I can go to. I'd rather be with you. I could be a help. You'll be tired after a long day in the workshop. I could have your food ready. I've picked up a few tips from Mrs Shaw. And that would give you time to see the bairns.'

Gennetta's mind was awhirl with the kindness shown her by these two. Tears came to her eyes. 'What can I say? You are both so generous.'

'Then you agree, ma'am?' asked Mrs Shaw eagerly.

Gennetta replied, 'Yes,' in a voice filled with emotion.

Mrs Shaw and Rose exchanged smiles, pleased that their mistress had approved their suggestions.

'With your permission, ma'am, I'll go home now and make arrangements,' suggested Mrs Shaw. 'You come as soon as you are ready.'

Gennetta's heart was heavy as she sat down on the sofa and held out her arms to her children. They came and sat, one on either side, and she hugged them close. She looked down into their upturned eyes, her emotions mixed as she tried to find a way of explaining to them what was going to happen.

106

Nathaniel and Flora, even at so young an age, sensed the serious atmosphere and their eyes widened questioningly. Their trusting gaze almost brought tears to Gennetta's eyes but she fought them back. She must not break down in front of them.

Her voice was tight when she started. 'You remember I told you Papa has had to go away to live with Jesus?' She was thankful now that there had been nightly prayers and explanations at their bedsides.

Two little heads nodded. 'Can we go too, Mama?' There was hope in the little boy's face and Flora's expression mirrored her brother's.

Gennetta inclined her head and gave a wry smile. 'We will some day, darling, but not just yet. Papa would want us to go on doing what we have to do here. But it is going to mean some changes.'

'Nice ones, Mama?'

'Some nice, some not so nice.' She visualised the hovel she was condemned to but cast it from her mind as quickly as it had appeared. 'The first thing is that we shall have to move from this house.'

'Why, Mama? I like it here.' Alarm rang in Nathaniel's voice.

'Well,' Gennetta made her tone gentle, 'we shall not have enough money to stay here. I have found work starting tomorrow morning but the pay will not be sufficient to enable us to stay on. Your Uncle Jack has given me a house where I can live for the moment but it is not big enough for you two to be with me.'

'Mama!' Nathaniel's cry, echoed by Flora's, pierced her heart. 'We don't want you to leave us.' His mouth quivered and he sniffed, trying to hold back the tears. 'Where will we go?'

'And I don't want to leave you. All of us have to be brave about this. For the time being you are going to live with Mrs Shaw.' She sensed a lightening of their mood with the thought that they were still going to be with someone they knew. 'That will be fun, and I will see you every evening.'

Hope came to Nathaniel's face. 'Promise?'

'Of course.'

'Pwomise?' Flora followed her brother in seeking reassurance.

'I do,' replied Gennetta, giving them both a hug. 'And I promise we will all be together again as soon as possible. Now I must get your things ready to go to Mrs Shaw's. Come and help me.'

The children slid from the sofa and ran to the door, Gennetta's sadness almost overpowered her as she watched them, thankful that the ordeal to which she had not looked forward had gone better than she had expected. She admired the resilience of children and wished she was so blessed. She must not show the sadness she felt and must keep hidden her doubts about the future. She stood up, took a grip on

107

her feelings and walked to the door after them with a firm step. The children were already halfway up the stairs.

With bags packed, Gennetta, accompanied by Rose, took the children to the Shaws' modest house in Pier Lane at the end of Haggersgate. Mrs Shaw greeted them with a wide smile, and once inside they immediately felt the homely atmosphere. A bright fire burned in the grate, heating a huge black pan which hung on the reckon. A kettle stood on the hob in front of the grate, and the smell of home baking wafted from the bread oven let into the stonework beisde the fire. The room was sparsely furnished with two Windsor chairs, one on either side of the fireplace. A well-scrubbed wooden table was set in the centre of the small room and a dresser occupied one wall. A stone sink stood under the tiny window let into the back wall, and a ewer of water stood on the stone slab beside it. A door shut off the stairs at the left-hand corner of the room. Two large clip-rugs of mixed colours covered most of the flagged floor.

'This is cosy, Mrs Shaw,' observed Gennetta putting brightness into her expression for the sake of the children.

'Flora and Nathaniel will be well looked after and they'll enjoy being here.' The cook smiled broadly at the children and added affectionately, 'Won't you?' Then she held out her arms to them.

They ran to her and cuddled close, enjoying the smell of her newly washed apron which still held the tang of the sea air after being hung outside. It complemented her homeliness and there was love and reassurance in her touch as she tousled their hair.

'Want to see your bedroom?' she asked with a lifting of her eyebrows.

'Yes, yes!' They jumped up and down excitedly. Catching the look in their mother's eyes, they added, 'Please.'

'Come along then.' Mrs Shaw turned to the door and, lifting the sneck, revealed the staircase.

Used to a staircase which swept up from a large hall, it amused the children to walk through a doorway giving access to stairs narrowly enclosed by flanking walls. They climbed excitedly, following Mrs Shaw, while Gennetta, bringing up the rear, tried to calm them. But Flora and Nathaniel took no notice. This was a new adventure for them.

The top of the stairs gave on to a tiny landing with one door directly in front and a second to the left.

'That's where my husband and I sleep,' said Mrs Shaw, indicating the door immediately ahead. 'And this will be your room.' She pushed open the other door and stood to one side as the children and Gennetta entered.

Two small beds stood to the left of the door with a small table between. They were covered with patchwork quilts turned down at the top to reveal sparkling white pillowcases. The window had plain red curtains, their colour enhancing the brightness of the quilts. On the wall opposite the beds was a table with a flowered basin and matching ewer. Two towels hung on a rail beside it.

'Mr Shaw fixed those hooks so the bairns could reach them.' Mrs Shaw indicated a row of four hooks beside the chest of drawers.

But none of this held the children's attention, which was concentrated on the wooden toys and bag of sweets resting on each pillow.

They looked at Mrs Shaw, wide-eyed. She saw the expectation on their faces and nodded. 'They're for you.'

Excitedly they jumped forward, grabbed the toys and hugged them under one arm while starting on the sweets.

'I thought it would ease their coming here, ma'am,' said Mrs Shaw.

Gennetta's eyes were damp with tears. 'You are so kind. And thank you for taking care of them.'

'It will be a pleasure. I'm looking forward to having young ones in the house again now my two have gone.'

'I hope Mr Shaw doesn't mind?'

She smiled. 'He's pleased to have them, he'll spoil them if I don't watch him.' She looked back at the children. 'Now, you two, downstairs, we're going to have a cup of tea.'

Cradling their toys, the children hurried to the room below.

'Ma'am.' Mrs Shaw stopped Gennetta before she could follow. 'Mr Shaw will bring a cart tomorrow to take your belongings to Hacker's Yard.'

'Thank you.' There was a catch in her voice. 'I don't know what I'd have done without you.'

'You were always kind to me, ma'am. I only wish I had room for you. I hate to think of you living in that terrible Hacker's Yard.'

Chapter Ten

'You're clear about tomorrow, Rose?' asked Gennetta, brushing back a wisp of hair in annoyance for it persisted in being unruly. No wonder, though, with all her rushing about since returning from Mrs Shaw's.

Two bags of clothes had been packed. The bed linen which she and Reuben had bought was in a trunk along with some cutlery and pottery which they had presented to Aunt Edith as a thank you present for what she had done. Gennetta felt entitled to take this and felt sure that whoever had inherited the house would not begrudge it.

'Yes, ma'am. Don't worry about a thing. Mr Shaw and I will see to everything.'

'He'll help you take the bed down, and you know which other items are mine?'

'Yes, ma'am.'

'And ignore any comments you get when you get to Hacker's Yard. They may not be pleasant.'

'I know the sort, ma'am. I can give as good as I get,' replied Rose with a firmness that showed she was ready to stick up for herself and her mistress.

'Now, Rose, no retaliation. Remember, we have to live there.'

'Yes, ma'am,' she agreed, a little reluctantly. 'I'll expect you after work.'

'Yes. And then I must go and visit the children.'

Sleep did not come easily. Though Gennetta was certain that the children would be well cared for by Mrs Shaw, the knowledge that they were no longer in the house brought a strange sense of loneliness. This was the first time they had been parted and Gennetta's heart ached with the desire to peep into their rooms and see them deep in contented sleep.

The tragic loss of Reuben and its consequences, bringing such a sweeping change in her life-style, overwhelmed her and she wept.

She dozed in the small hours but kept coming awake with a start, for she feared sleeping in and being late for work on her first morning. She did not want that for she was certain Jack would check up on her. From what she had seen, no one dare conceal the truth from him, and there was sure to be someone who resented her there and would gladly expose any untruth.

As she dressed she heard Rose moving about and counted her blessings at having such a loyal servant. When Gennetta entered the kitchen the smell of frying bacon made her realise that she was hungry and reminded her that in the upset of yesterday she had eaten little.

''Morning, ma'am,' Rose greeted her brightly, having resolved to put on a cheery smile to try to alleviate what she knew would be a difficult day for them both. 'You'll need a good breakfast this morning.'

'Thanks, Rose. It smells good.' Gennetta pulled out a chair and sat down at the scrubbed table.

'Ma'am?' Not expecting her mistress to eat in the kitchen, Rose eyed her doubtfully.

Gennetta smiled, reading embarrassment in her tone. 'You fill your plate too and sit down there.' She indicated the chair on the opposite side of the table.

'But ... ' Rose began hesitantly.

'We start a new life today,' Gennetta pointed out. 'The way we are going to have to live, there can be no more mistress and maid. We are going to be living much more closely, so we may as well start now by enjoying this meal together.' Her voice was firm, brooking no protest.

Realising the wisdom of her words, Rose made no objection but shovelled bacon from the pan on to two plates and cut some bread.

As they ate they checked that they had not forgotten anything they needed to take to Hacker's Yard.

'I'll leave you some money so you can get some food for us,' said Gennetta later, as she rose from the table.

She turned for the door but was halted by Rose's tentative tone: 'Ma'am, if you don't mind me saying ... ' She hesitated and bit her lip, wondering if she should go on.

'Well, Rose, what is it?' Gennetta prompted.

'Well, it'll be rough, dirty work you'll be going to, wouldn't you be better in a different dress?' Rose's face reddened at the thought that she had dared to comment on her mistress's clothes. She looked shyly at the floor.

111

'You're quite right, Rose. This dress is much too good for what I will probably have to do.' Rose looked relieved that Gennetta was in agreement. 'But I am in mourning, and will be for some time yet. The fact that I am having to take up this work will not deter me from the respect I must show my husband.' As she had dressed that morning she had resolved that no matter how trying her surroundings, or how provocative the situation, she would maintain her dignity for Jack would be delighted if she succumbed to the squalor of the life to which he had condemned her. 'This dress will receive some rough treatment, no doubt, but wear it I shall.'

'I hope you didn't mind me saying ...'

'Of course not.' Gennetta smiled reassuringly and made her way to the hall.

As she was swinging her cloak around her shoulders, Rose appeared, carrying a small bundle. 'Ma'am, take this. It might help to preserve your dress a little longer.'

Gennetta took the proffered bundle, recognising it as one of Rose's hessian work aprons. 'Thank you.' She looked round the hall. 'Well, this is the last time I'll walk out of this house.' There was a catch in her voice and a wistful look in her eyes as her gaze roamed around the hall.

'Oh, don't say that, ma'am,' Rose protested. 'You might be back one day.'

Gennetta inclined her head and gave a wry smile. 'I doubt it. But I will always treasure its memory. I have known happy times here.'

There were tears in Rose's eyes as she watched her leave the house.

Gennetta walked down the path and paused at the gate to look back. Even at this early hour of the morning, with the first streaks of daylight flushing the sky, the house looked friendly and, Gennetta thought, maybe a little sad at losing the family which had treasured the home it had been.

Gennetta walked briskly to the bridge. Whitby was beginning to come alive with early morning workers hurrying to the shipyards, the sail-makers, the roperies and jet shops, but none would have guessed that this well-dressed woman was on the same errand as themselves.

No breeze disturbed the river's gentle flow to the sea. The quays were as yet silent, the ships still, barely hinting at the bustle of activity which would soon begin.

Gennetta turned into Church Street, and without so much as a glance at Hacker's Yard, hurried on to the workshop.

She reached the door at the same time as a tall, well-built man

112

wearing a thick dark blue jersey, which came high to the neck and below the hips. A bowler hat sat at a slight angle on his head, revealing dark brown hair with a natural wave. His features were clean-cut, his chin firm, and a thin moustache added charm to his handsome face. But it was his eyes which held Gennetta. They were pale blue and she guessed they could sparkle with a joy for life though now there was a hint of sadness behind them. She found herself wanting to know why.

'Good day, ma'am.' He touched the brim of his hat and then let his hand fall on to the shoulder of the young boy beside him in a gesture of reassurance and protection. 'Tom Unwin.'

'Good morning.' Gennetta returned his greeting with a smile. She recognised him from her brief visit yesterday as the man who had been carving.

'I'm sorry about your husband and the consequences.' He nodded towards the workshop. 'If there's anything I can do ...' His voice was gentle with no hint of roughness to it.

'Thank you kindly but I don't want you to jeopardise your position. I know my brother and if word got back to him that you had shown me any favours, you could lose your job. I wouldn't want to be the cause of that.'

'Thank you for your consideration, ma'am.' He looked down at the boy by his side and Gennetta saw a hint of pride in his eyes. 'Davey, this here's Mrs Briggs. She'll probably be working alongside you, so you show her respect.'

He looked wide-eyed at the lady who was so nicely dressed, wondering why she should be working alongside him.

'Yes, Pa.'

Gennetta glanced sharply at Tom, a query in her eyes. 'Davey works here?'

'Thirteen so he starts today, ma'am. Just like you.'

'But so young?' She was shocked at the thought of her Nathaniel having to start work at this age.

'Oh, I'm pleased. I'll be able to keep an eye on him and he won't get into bad company and run wild,' said Tom.

'But couldn't his mother ...'

'She died of the fever a year ago.'

'Oh, I'm sorry.' Dismayed that she might have brought pain to this man, Gennetta quickly turned her attention to the boy who was very like his father and had a winning innocence about his friendly face. 'I'm pleased to know you, Davey, and if we are working together I'm sure we'll be good friends and help each other.' She extended her hand to him.

113

Never having experienced such treatment from so elegant a lady before, he was unsure what to do. He glanced up at his father who smiled and nodded. Davey looked back at Gennetta and took her hand. From her smile, he knew he was going to like her.

'I think we'd better get along in, ma'am. Mr Young will be after us if we're late.'

'And we don't want to get off on the wrong foot on our first day, do we, Davey?' She smiled at the youngster.

When they entered the workshop most of the workers were already there. The chatter subsided at the sight of a woman entering a man's place. There were those who glanced at her with curiosity, already wondering how she would cope. From some she sensed hostility. Why should a woman invade their province?

Others eyed her with disdain and then turned their attention elsewhere, preferring to ignore her. The lust in the eyes of a few sent a shiver down her spine and she knew she would have to be on her guard, especially when they found out that she was living in Hacker's Yard where no one would worry what happened to her.

'All right, stop gawking and get to work.' John Young's voice rapped authoritatively round the room as he stepped towards Gennetta. 'Good day, ma'am.' He touched his hat.

Though her eyes were on him, she was aware of a well-built, bareheaded man across the room mimicking John Young's gesture. The grin on his face had no warmth in it, only mockery, and his eyes were as cold as any she had ever seen. He made an aside to the two men beside him. She could only guess what had been said but it brought salacious grins in her direction.

Tom had noticed the reactions of the three men. 'To your work, Harrison,' he barked sharply, conveying a warning that he would stand no nonsense from these men, now or in the future.

The foreman gave him a nod of approval for he could guess what Harrison had been up to even though he had his back to him.

'I see you've met Tom Unwin, our head carver, a real craftsman and my deputy.' He turned to Tom after giving Davey a wink. 'Thee'd better show our new apprentices what t'do.' He glanced at Gennetta. 'Ma'am, that dress is too good for the work thee'll be doing. Wouldn't you be better ganning home to get summat more suitable?'

She smiled. 'I know, but I am still in mourning. I have some protection.' She took out the apron. 'And another thing – you can't go on calling me "ma'am". If you're used to using surnames then call me Briggs. If Christian names, then I'm Gennetta, though it's probably better if you call me Gen.'

114

'Very well, ma'am ... Gen,' replied John, relieved by her attitude. As he watched her and Davey follow Tom through the workshop to a room at the back, he could not help admiring her tenacity. This was an alien world and yet she was not flinching from it. He only hoped she could survive.

When they entered the room at the back of the workshop Gennetta was faced with a huge pile of pieces of jet, with several smaller piles around the room. A youngster examining pieces of jet from the main pile stopped to see who had come in. His face was grimy, hair unkempt and his clothes little more than rags.

'Joey, two new sorters.' Tom's voice was firm but friendly. 'Mrs Briggs, and you know Davey.'

'Blimey!' gasped Joey at the sight of a beautifully dressed lady in their dusty, grimy workplace. 'It's true!' he gulped. Yesterday he had overheard the men talking about a woman coming to work here but hadn't believed it. It still took some believing. Not this person in her fine clothes? Mr Unwin was surely having him on.

'It's true, Joey.' Gennetta smiled at the boy. 'I need work just like you. I'm sure we'll get on.'

Tom laughed at the astonishment on his face. 'It's right enough, lad,' he confirmed, and went on, 'Mrs Briggs, Joey is fifteen, been here two years. He'll keep you right after I've explained what we do here.'

'I'll do that, missus,' said the lad brightly.

Gennetta smiled to herself. No doubt he would. She could sense that Joey was king in this room. She must fall in with his ways and not cross him. He could be a good ally.

'Thanks, Joey.' Her voice was warm, her smile friendly. She liked the lad's open face. His eyes sparkled with the lively curiosity that had replaced his initial suspicion. He was thin, just past the gangling stage, but he would fill out. His jawline indicated determination but did not detract from his attractive high cheekbones, thin arched eyebrows, and most of all his bright, unusually clear grey eyes with their long lashes. He had the look of self-assurance usually gained by having to fend for oneself. Gennetta's curiosity was roused. She must get to know more.

Her musing was interrupted by Tom. 'This big pile of jet has to be sorted,' he explained. 'Mr Turner buys direct from the miners, chiefly from around Staithes, Ruswick, Hinderwell and Kettleness. There's some useful jet holes around there.'

'I thought the jet came from the seashore?' she said.

'Aye, some of it does. Mr Turner will buy any that's found there. It's generally of good quality, and if it's been in the sea for some time, it will have had its outer skin worn off by the action of the waves and will be easier to work. There are folk who scour the shore and falls of rock for what they can find. Others will dig into the cliff face. The best jet is what we call "rough" jet. It's hard, easier to work, and gives the best results. Soft jet, so called to distinguish it from the better jet, though still hard, is brittle and breaks easily.'

Tom paused, looking embarrased. He was generally a man of few words, but for some reason he felt at ease with this woman who had so unexpectedly come into his life. 'I'm yapping on instead of telling you what you have to do. There's a first sorting from the main pile. If Mr Turner bought from folk known as rough jet dealers it would have been done for us, but he prefers to buy direct from the miners and have the sorting done here.'

'So these smaller piles are the different grades?' queried Gennetta.

'Well, sizes really. Large ones, smaller stunted pieces, thin ones which are not often used, and finally the rubbish.' He glanced at her. 'Think you can manage, 'cos I'll have to go?'

'I'm sure we will, won't we, Davey?' She gave the youngster a reassuring smile.

'Yes,' he murmured doubtfully.

'Joey will look after us.'

'I will,' he called, full of self-importance as he dropped a large piece of jet on to the biggest pile.

Tom nodded and headed for the workshop. Gennetta caught Davey looking after him wistfully. She placed a comforting hand on his shoulder and said, 'Let's get started, Davey,' then unrolled her apron and fastened it round her waist.

As he showed them the different sizes of jet, Joey began to wonder about Gennetta. He had not been prepared for someone like her. Such elegant clothes, such an attractive face, smooth skin with hardly a line and a pleasant friendly smile which came not only from the lips but from her pale blue eyes. He could detect a touch of sadness dwelling in them, but that was only to be expected in a woman whose husband had recently been murdered. He had expected a grumbling old harridan who would make life awkward for him, someone wanting to be boss because she was an adult. But this lady was none of those things. She seemed willing to let him be in command, accepting the position she was in and prepared to face whatever it brought. Maybe they could get along.

Gennetta found selecting easy enough but the jet was rough on hands that had never been used to such work, and before long the reaching, bending and straightening began to tell on muscles which had never been used much before. Her hands had become tinged with

116

brown from the jet and her face streaked with it where she had brushed back her hair.

After an hour she straightened, easing her back with her hands.

'Tired, missus?' asked Joey. 'Thee's still a long day ahead.'

Gennetta nodded, tightening her mouth. 'I know, Joey. I'm just not used to this sort of work.'

'Then why is thee here? And thee Mr Turner's sister. I heard the men talking after he brought thee here yesterday.' He was forthright in his questions and observations.

She gave a wry smile. 'It's a long story, Joey, but I need work and my brother offered me this.'

'Old skinflint! With all t'money he must have.' There was venom in his voice and he must have realised it for he put his hand over his mouth as if he would suppress the words. His eyes widened. 'Eh, missus, thee won't tell him I said that?'

Gennetta laughed at the alarm on his face. 'No, Joey, I won't tell him. As you might guess, my brother and I don't get on.'

'Eh, who couldn't get on wi' thee?' As they had worked and chatted Joey had summed her up and now there was open admiration in his tone. Gennetta knew she had made a friend. 'Missus, have a rest. Here, I'll show thee.' He gave a nod of his head and started towards a gloomy corner of the room. Out of sight behind a pile of jet were a couple of old rugs and some worn blankets. 'Ain't very clean,' he offered in apology. 'But thee can have a rest here, like I do.'

'Don't the men check on you?'

'Nay. They come t'get t'jet but don't bother me. If gaffer comes he thinks I've gone to t'privy. I can cover for thee.'

Gennetta smiled to herself. She was pleased she had found a friend where she might have found hostility. She hoped it would be the same from the men but, recalling the salacious looks of Harrison and his cronies, doubted if everyone would be as friendly as Joey.

'Mr Unwin said you've been here two years?'

'Aye. I hope Mr Young will take me into t'workshop one day. Here, can I show thee?' A note of enthusiasm had come into his voice and he bent down to remove a stone from the wall. He reached into a gap behind it and pulled out a rag. Straightening, he unrolled it to reveal a piece of jet and a carving tool made from an old file on to which a wooden handle had been fixed. He handed the piece of jet to Gennetta with some pride. It was a flat piece, thin, like those he had told her were only used for engraving.

Gennetta was amazed to see the delicate use of lines to create an impression of the west front of the abbey. She looked at Joey. 'You did this?'

'Aye.'

'It's beautiful. Where did you learn?'

'Davey's pa showed me, unknown to anyone else. Then it just seemed to come. He gave me that tool.'

'Have you done others?'

'Some. They're hidden behind another stone. Going to sell them one day.'

'You'll give one to your mother?'

'Ain't got a ma. No pa neither. He was lost at sea five years ago and Ma died of the fever three years since.'

'I'm sorry,' sympathised Gennetta. 'You're at the orphanage?'

'Nay. Kept out of that place. Ran off when Ma died. Lived rough till I came here.'

'And now?'

'Live here.'

'What? My brother lets you?'

'Nay. Wouldn't let him know. Nobody knows, only Mr Unwin and he'll tell no one.'

'You're locked in all night?'

Joey gave a grin. 'I have a way in and out. No one knows it, and I ain't showing thee.'

'Quite right, Joey. It must be your secret.' All the time Gennetta kept glancing at the etching with critical eyes. She recognised faults, particularly in the perspective, but these were outshone by the basic talent. There was nothing that could not be put right with tuition. She saw a gift here which should be nurtured. 'Joey, have you ever been shown how to draw?' she asked.

'Nay, missus, who was there t'teach me?'

'You should have lessons. From what I've heard, all the best workers of jet have been encouraged to draw.'

'That's right, missus, but who'd show me?' he said with a resigned note in his voice and a dismissive shrug of his shoulders.

'I could.'

Joey stared at her. 'Thee?'

Gennetta smiled. 'Yes, me. I've had a lot of lessons and I could teach you.'

'Would thee?' He bristled with excitement.

'Yes, of course I would.'

'Then I could move into t'workshop all the sooner and become more than a mere grinder. I could actually work the jet. Maybe escape t'first grindstone. They put youngsters on that, missus, 'cos they can easily be replaced – older skilled workers can't. Most dangerous job in t'shop. Solid sandstone that wheel. It can shatter, and flying sandstone can kill.'

118

His voice brightened after this sombre note. 'And if thee can draw, thee could do etching too and move into the workshop wi' me, out of all this.' His glance took in the gloomy, dusty room.

'Well, we shall see, but now I think we'd better get back to that pile of jet.'

Once Gennetta had left the house, Rose busied herself packing the bedclothes and the few remaining items into boxes ready for the arrival of Mr Shaw.

He arrived at eight and she was surprised to see that he had a young man with him.

''Morning, Rose.' Seth Shaw gave a slight shake of his head. 'Sad day this. Never thought Mr Turner would let it happen.'

'Bad lot, that man.' Rose screwed up her face in disgust. 'Hasn't a care for his sister, nor his niece and nephew. But we'll not let him get us down. We'll make the best of it. How are the bairns?'

'Right as rain,' he replied, his smile expressing the pleasure he found in them. 'You've got the right spirit. We'll get the place in Hacker's Yard in shape before Mrs Briggs arrives.' He saw her eyeing the young man beside him. 'I've brought Caleb Smailes along to help.'

He looks a likely lad to help, thought Rose. He was tall, over six feet, and broad-shouldered with it so that he gave the impression of power in his large frame. She could almost sense the muscles in his arms and back. His neck was short and thickset, his jaw angular, hair short. His dark brown eyes were friendly, though, and he smiled readily.

'Glad to know you, Rose.' His voice was deep sending a shiver down her spine. The wink he gave her had a hint of mischief in it.

'And you,' she answered, as she took his proffered hand, feeling his strong fingers wrap round hers.

'Caleb's a fisherman but he isn't putting to sea until day after tomorrow so he said he would give me a hand today,' explained Mr Shaw.

'And tomorrow if necessary,' said Caleb, not one to miss an opportunity where a pretty girl was concerned.

'Thank you,' replied Rose. 'Both of you.'

The two men quickly assessed the items to be removed and decided they would have to make three journeys with the cart.

'Bed first,' said Mr Shaw.

'Right, this way.' Rose bustled up the stairs.

She stood to one side while the men quickly dismantled the bed. When the first load was ready, she threw a cape around her shoulders and draped a shawl over her head. She led the way to Hacker's Yard, prepared for the curiosity of neighbours when they arrived there. Word soon swept along the narrow street and then there were women at every doorway, inquisitive to know what the new occupants were bringing. Children scooted around the cart in chase as the two men heaved and pushed it upwards over the rough ground.

Rose, ignoring the squalor around her, flung the door of their house open wide, hoping the breeze might reach the house and blow some air through it. She glanced quickly round the room, pulling a face which expressed her opinion of the place. 'How could Mr Turner commit his sister to this?' she muttered in disgust as she went through to the back room and opened its door wide. She glanced out and saw a small yard backing into a hollow in the cliff face. 'Well, that's something,' she commented to herself when she saw they were separated from the next house by a high wall and that they had their own privy, not one which was shared as she knew some of them were. She ran quickly up the rickety stairs and in a moment summed up what should be done to try to bring some comfort to the place before Gennetta arrived that evening.

When she reached the front door the men were already unloading the bed.

'Like to try me in that, big 'un?'

'Thee couldn't cope, Maggie. He'd do better with me.'

Embarrassed, Rose was pleased to see that Caleb ignored the remarks directed at him.

Once inside the house the two men paused. Seth looked around and then back to Rose.

'This is no place for Mrs Briggs,' he remarked with a shake of his head.

'I know,' replied Rose, 'but she's nowhere else to go so we'll just make the best of it. Get the bed upstairs and before you go back we'll have some jobs done.' Her words came crisply. She was in command. She had never been in such a position before, always having had Mrs Shaw taking the responsibility, but she had noted and learned and now would put it to good use.

While the men manoeuvred the bed up the narrow stairs and erected it, Rose got the bucket and cloths she had put on the cart. She filled the bucket from the pump in the street and started to remove the grime from the front window. She broke off when the two men had finished their task.

'Right, Caleb, can you get some clean dry straw and we'll have some on the floor?'

He nodded. As he strode through the door he heard Rose giving further orders.

'Mr Shaw, could you light a fire, please? I see there's some wood and some coal out the back. Must have been left by the last tenants, whoever they were.'

'I'll see to it,' replied Seth.

When Caleb returned the fire was burning brightly and Rose and Seth were liming the walls.

'What a change already,' he commented, admiring the transformation which was being wrought.

'We've got a third brush, Caleb,' she hinted.

They worked quickly and cheerfully and by midday had done every wall in the house. With the final brush stroke, Rose stepped back, pleased with the work. It was by no means first class but it was an improvement.

She expressed her thanks to the two men.

'Only too pleased to help,' said Caleb brightly.

'Aye,' agreed Seth. 'It'll be better for Mrs Briggs coming in. We'll away and bring the rest of the things.'

'Hold on, Seth, I've a cartload out there,' Caleb reminded him.

'Forgot, lad.' Seth headed for the door.

'What have we got here?' asked Rose in surprise when the two men returned carrying some carpets.

'Well, it ain't straw,' grinned Caleb teasingly.

'I can see that. But where did they come from?'

'I knew Ma had some old carpets stacked away. She's always reluctant to throw things out. "Never know when things might come in useful," she says. Well, here we are, and she was only too pleased to have her words proved right. They're worn in places but we'll get them laid right.'

'Oh, thank you,' cried Rose as the carpets were unrolled. 'These will make a big difference to the look of the place and be warmer than the flagged floor.'

They sorted the carpets out and when the men returned with the next load were able to cover all the floors.

By late afternoon the furniture had all been brought in and the house made as cosy as possible. The neighbours' curiosity had been aroused with each new arrival of goods and some had even had the audacity to peep through the door on the excuse of seeing if they could help. But Rose was aware of their motive and fended off every intrusion.

Caleb admired her industry, the way she knew exactly what she wanted and her obvious affection for her employer. But more than anything, he admired her breezy manner and ability to take a joke.

'I'll be round tomorrow,' he said as he was leaving. 'I noticed a few broken tiles that'll let rain in. I'll fix 'em.'

Six o'clock that evening could not come quick enough. Though Joey encouraged Gennetta to take more frequent rests she felt she was letting the team down if she did so. She battled on against the ever-increasing aches and pains which attacked muscles and bones she'd never known existed.

'Did you manage?' Tom asked her with some concern when he came for his son.

She saw him eyeing the dust on her clothes, the brown grime on her hands, and tried to brush away the streaks on her face, only to stop when she realised that she was making them worse.

'Yes, Joey looked after us, didn't he, Davey?'

'Yes, Pa, he did.'

'Good. Come on then, we'd best be off.' Tom glanced back at Gennetta. 'Good night.'

'Good night. See you in the morning, Davey.'

He smiled at her and followed his father.

'Good night, Joey.'

'Missus, the drawing lessons?' he asked with a note of eagerness.

'We'll see about them tomorrow,' she promised.

Passing through the workshop she felt the eyes of the men on her. Gennetta walked steadily, though each step tried her aching muscles. She kept her face serene and dignified when she wanted to wince from the pain that stung her legs, arms and back. There was whispering amongst some of the men and though she caught no words she could guess what was said.

Once outside, she breathed deeply. After the dust and grime she welcomed the salty freshness, even though the air was tainted with the smell of rotting rubbish strewn along the street and the inevitable odour of fish. Having been inside since six o'clock that morning, she was glad to see the sky even though it was only a thin strip, with the buildings lining the narrow street threatening to blank it out.

She was free! Her time was her own. The urge to rush to her children was overwhelming but Gennetta could not let them see her like this. They had been used to seeing her clean, her clothes immaculate, hands unsoiled, not like this with fingers and face marked with dirt, her dress grimy and hair straggling in spite of all her efforts to try to keep it pinned into place. She must get to the house in Hacker's Yard and tidy herself up before going to see Nathaniel and Flora.

House? She gave a derisive laugh. Hovel more like. What could she hope to find there in the way of comfort and cleanliness after

122

what she had been used to? She steadied herself. Such thoughts could destroy her if she succumbed to them. She must not allow that. She must rise above them and find a way to better herself and escape from the squalor which faced her.

'How d'ya like workin' for a livin'?'

'Nice white hands, lady.' Sarcasm rang in the last word.

'Thee's torn thy dress.' The chuckle which accompanied the observation was tinged with glee.

'Did thee work or keep the men happy?'

'Would she know how?'

Laughter rang from house to house. The women of Hacker's Yard, knowing what time Gennetta would be leaving work, were waiting on their doorsteps to have their bit of fun with her.

She walked on, hiding her feelings, ignoring the dirty childen who ran around her making snide remarks, encouraged by their mothers' barbs.

Hearing the catcalls, Rose came to the door of the house, a white apron tied around the waist of her clean black dress, in marked contrast to the garb of the women who mocked her mistress. She saw Gennetta stumble and ran to steady her.

'Whoops! Called at the Black Bull?' someone shouted.

'Find out what it's all about if she had.' The remark sent knowing laughter sweeping along the narrow street.

'Take no notice, ma'am,' said Rose as she took Gennetta's arm. 'They're an ignorant lot.'

'Thanks, Rose.' There was a catch in Gennetta's voice, and tears welled in her eyes. The remarks were getting to her. She must not let them. She fought back the tears.

They were banished once and for all when she entered the house. She just stood, unable to believe the transformation from what she had seen yesterday.

The walls were bright with fresh lime, the carpeted floor seemed luxurious even though it was worn and could not disguise the uneven flagstones. A fire burned in the grate, bringing life to what she had seen as a dank unfriendly hovel. A chair was set to either side of the grate and a small table stood by one wall.

'How do you like it, ma'am?' Rose's question broke the spell.

'It's ... It's ... I can't believe it!'

'It's not like we're used to but ...'

'Rose,' Gennetta turned wide eyes on her, 'how did you manage it?'

'I had good helpers.'

'Mr Shaw?'

'Yes.'

'You said helpers. You had more than one? Not some of them out there?'

Rose gave a little laugh. 'Not likely! They were nosy but I kept them out. Mr Shaw brought Caleb with him.'

'Caleb?'

'Caleb Smailes, he's a friend of Mr Shaw's. He was a great help, got these carpets from his mother.'

'You paid him for them?'

'No, ma'am. They weren't in use. Some old ones his mother had kept. She said he could take them when he told her what they were for. And he got me a bed. Come upstairs and see.'

Excited at Gennetta's reaction, Rose led the way upstairs. There was a bed in each room and a chair beside each one. They were made up and Gennetta's looked so inviting she wished for nothing more than to roll into it and ease her aching limbs.

'Rose, you've done wonders. I'd been dreading coming to such a place as I saw but you've made it welcoming.'

'It'll do until you can get somewhere better and I'm sure that won't be long.'

Gennetta gave a wistful smile. 'I hope so, Rose, I do hope so. Now I must get ready to go to see the children.'

Chapter Eleven

'Ma'am, ma'am ... it's time to be up.' The distant voice came hazily to Gennetta, still befuddled by sleep. She wanted the sound to go away and allow her to be dragged back down to the peaceful depths of slumber where there were no problems, no upheavals, no sadness. But the voice was insistent. 'Ma'am, you mustn't be late for work.'

As she turned over, her whole body cried out against its unbearable stiffness.

'Yes, Rose. I'll soon be up,' she said drowsily, feeling she would surely not be expected to get up for a fortnight, not while she ached so much. But she had to get up. She was sure Jack would check her time of arrival and there would be no brotherly forgiveness if she was late. She swung out of bed, determined not to give him one reason to criticise.

Gennetta winced as her feet missed the narrow strip of carpet beside the bed and touched cold wooden boards instead. She stretched. When she picked up her dress she found that Rose had brushed it clean and mended the tear in the sleeve. By the time she had put her clothes on, movement had brought some relief to her aching back.

Her mind turned to her children and she pictured them sleeping the sleep of the innocent, their faces rosy against snow-white pillows. Gennetta recalled with pleasure their excitement at seeing her yesterday evening. She had made sure they would see her as they knew her so had abandoned the torn grimy dress she had worn at work. Not having another mourning dress, she had put on the deep purple one with high neck and long sleeves with only a small flare from the close-fitting waist. She knew it was a dress they liked.

She was delighted that they had settled so well with Mr and Mrs Shaw, who seemed glad to have them. When she saw them into bed, the sadness of parting was alleviated by her promise to visit them at the same time the next day. Now, as she negotiated the rickety stairs, she looked forward to seeing them again.

Rose had brewed tea, buttered some bread and was frying bacon on the open fire.

'You're a gem,' said Gennetta, savouring the aroma of the sputtering bacon. 'And thank you for doing this dress so beautifully.'

Pleased at the praise, Rose gave a little smile of embarrassment. 'Now sit you down and get a good breakfast into you before you go to that awful work.' As they both started their meal, she added, 'Caleb said he would come this morning to mend the broken tiles.'

Gennetta noticed a special timbre to her voice when she mentioned Caleb. 'That's kind of him,' she replied. 'Mr Shaw tells me he's a nice young man, a fisherman, and lives on Henrietta Street. I wonder if Tom Unwin knows him?'

'Yes, he does. Lives a couple of doors away. Caleb mentioned Tom when I told him where you were working. Thinks highly of him and his boy Davey.'

'I'd like to meet him sometime to thank him for his help.'

'I'll tell him, ma'am. He's away fishing later today, but next opportunity I'll see he's here.' Rose tried to hide her enthusiasm but it did not escape Gennetta. Rose was obviously smitten.

Gennetta pulled her shawl closer around her shoulders against the nip in the air. The early morning light was only just beginning to filter into the close warren of streets on Whitby's east side. Her footsteps sent cats scurrying to their dark hiding places. She almost slipped on some rotting cabbage leaves flung by some uncaring person from their front door. She put her hand to her nose to try to shut out the stench from an overflowing open drain. She shuddered at the thought of what she was living among and felt sure that Aunt Edith would turn in her grave if she knew.

Although faced with another long, hard day she was almost thankful to reach the workshop. No greetings were given to her. She still sensed curiosity in many of the men, hostility in some, and caught lewd glances from Matt Harrison and his cronies, Jake and Tully. In Tom's eyes alone was a welcome and she exchanged greetings with him as she rested her hand on his son's shoulder and said, 'We'll start together, Davey.'

By mid-morning Joey had said little. It was as if he was waiting for something. Gennetta guessed what it was and saw relief cross his face when she said, 'I've been thinking about those lessons ...'

'Yes, missus?' He was all attention.

'You come to my house each night at eight o'clock, starting tomorrow.'

'Yes, missus.' His eyes were bright. 'Where do you live?'

'Hacker's Yard.'

'Hacker's Yard! Not thee, missus?' Joey was having difficulty in associating this with the refined lady, the widow of the Mr Briggs who had been murdered ... Hacker's Yard!

Gennetta smiled at his expression. 'When needs must, you have to take what you can.'

'But, missus, that's the roughest street in Whitby.'

'I know, but I'll have to make the best of it for the time being.' Before he pressed her in his curiosity she added quickly, 'So, tomorrow night at eight?'

'Yes, missus, I'll be there.'

Most of the men had left the workshop when Gennetta was ready to leave a little after six that evening. Tom was still at his bench putting the final touches to a carving of a jet cross. Each extremity had been exquisitely carved with intertwining vines while the crosspiece consisted of the interwoven letters IHS.

'Nearly finished, Pa?' asked Davey.

'A moment, son,' said Tom without breaking his concentration on his work.

'Stand still a minute, Davey,' Gennetta instructed quietly, knowing how important it was for a craftsman not to have his attention diverted.

She watched Tom's long fingers handle his carving tool with an expertise which made it seem like an extension of his own hand. Carefully he shaped the final leaf then straightened and leaned slightly back on his stool, viewing his work with a critical eye.

He gave a little grunt of satisfaction and then looked up. 'Mrs Briggs.' He jumped to his feet. 'I'm sorry, I was concentrating so much ...'

'Quite right. I didn't want to interrupt you.' She looked at the cross. 'That's beautiful. You are a wonderful carver. Where did you learn?'

'Self-taught.' He was pleased by her interest. 'Watching when I was a lad, and then finding I had a flair for it.'

'Ever had any drawing lessons?'

Tom gave a small laugh. 'Who, me? No one to teach me. Besides, I never felt I needed them.'

Gennetta pursed her lips doubtfully for a moment, then agreed. 'Most likely not with the talent I see here.' She indicated the cross.

'Mind you,' went on Tom, 'I couldn't etch like some of the men here.'

127

'Davey going to take after you?'

'He might.' He smiled at the boy and Gennetta saw in his eyes not only a deep love but pleasure in the boy's companionship. 'But I'd like him to be able to etch as well.'

'Drawing lessons would help.'

'Aye, they would that.'

'I'll teach him.'

'You?' Tom could not hide his astonishment.

'Yes. I was given lessons for a number of years. I could teach Davey.' She paused then added quickly, 'That is, if you agree and he would like to learn?'

Tom looked at his son. 'Would you?' he asked.

Davey's eyes were wide with excitement. 'Can I, Pa?'

Tom didn't want to dampen such obvious enthusiasm but doubt clouded his face as he looked at Gennetta. 'How much would it cost?' he asked tentatively.

'Nothing, Tom.'

'But I couldn't let you ...'

'Nonsense. It will be a pleasure. Davey and I get on well. Don't we, Davey?' she added with a smile at him.

'Yes, ma'am, I like working with you.'

She looked back at Tom. 'Well?'

He spread his hands in a gesture of capitulation. 'Very well.'

Davey gave a whoop. 'Thanks, Pa.'

'Quieten down, lad.'

'I've already offered to give Joey lessons ...'

'So he's shown you his etchings?' Gennetta noticed that Tom had lowered his voice and had glanced round to see that there was no one in earshot. 'You're privileged. I'm the only one here who knows about them. He's frightened he'll get the sack for taking pieces of jet. I caught him one day. He was scared to death I would tell the foreman. Instead I gave him a carving tool – he'd been using a nail.'

'And you nurtured his talent,' said Gennetta with approval. 'Well, now I hope to take it further. Joey is starting tomorrow night at eight o'clock at my house.'

'In Hacker's Yard?' Tom's voice combined statement and question.

Gennetta raised her eyebrows in surprise. 'You've made enquiries?'

'I'm sorry, I shouldn't have pried.' There was genuine apology in his tone. 'Forgive me?'

Gennetta smiled. 'Nothing to forgive. It would have become general knowledge before long.' She changed tack to dispel his embarrassment. 'Is eight too late for Davey?'

'No. It will be all right.' Tom was quick to banish any doubt.

'He won't have to come far. You live in Henrietta Street, I believe?'

There was an impish sparkle in Tom's eyes as he replied, 'So you've been enquiring too?'

Gennetta, looking a little embarrassed, hastened to say, 'No, no. I learned it accidentally, through Rose my maid who insisted on coming to live with me. She heard it from Caleb Smailes.'

'Ah, Caleb.' Tom nodded his understanding.

'So it's all settled?' Gennetta diverted the conversation to the matter in hand. 'Tomorrow night at eight. Good night, Tom. Good night, Davey.'

Tom watched her walk from the workshop, admiring her poise. He felt this friendship would be good for Davey who lacked a mother's love. And he suspected that Gennetta too had need of a friend.

The following evening, as Gennetta hurried home after seeing her children, she had to admit that she was looking forward to giving the drawing lessons.

Promptly at eight Joey and Davey arrived. Gennetta was surprised to find herself feeling disappointed that Tom had not brought Davey. She chided herself severely. Recently widowed, she shouldn't have such feelings, but she told herself that he was only a friend, and she needed friendship in her present circumstances.

Joey gaped at the room he found himself in. He had expected a hovel, as were all the other habitations in Hacker's Yard, but here something had been done to overcome the squalid conditions. The meagre trappings of comfort seemed luxurious to him.

Davey showed no reaction to his surroundings and Gennetta had not expected any for she knew that the respectability of Henrietta Street must mean that Tom would have a decent home.

She allowed the two boys to draw as they wished so that she could assess their dexterity with a pencil, their latent ability and the way their minds worked.

Joey's lines were delicate, wavering between detail and broad impression. She saw that he had a keen eye for observation when he produced a drawing of Whitby's bridge and then one of a seagull. They left something to be desired in their final execution but she realised that here was a gift which could be nurtured and directed without overwhelming the natural talent.

Davey's drawings had the crudity of execution of one much younger than Joey. His lines were bold but they imparted a sense of motion in his drawing of a ship. Gennetta could feel the sea sweeping

129

along its side. Though the bodies were out of proportion, his flowing lines easily portrayed protagonists in vicious combat. With guidance at this early age, she felt sure that he could become an expert craftsman. She looked forward to their continuing lessons, not only so that she could do something worthwhile, but also because in them she found an escape from her workplace and from the dubious surroundings of Hacker's Yard.

But the Yard was not going to allow her to escape so easily.

Returning home for the fourth lesson, after visiting Nathaniel and Flora, Gennetta saw nothing unusual in the fact that gossiping women with dirty-faced children clinging to their skirts occupied most doorsteps. Barefooted youngsters, clothes in tatters, chased each other, slipping and sliding in the refuse strewn among the paving stones and rough ground. Gennetta hurried past as she always did, ignoring the remarks thrown at her, allowing them to go in one ear and out the other. But this evening it was different. Their taunts shocked her with their implication.

'Call thissen a woman?' There was mockery in the voice.

'Can't thee get a man?'

'Maybe thee hasn't the talent for that.' Laughter swept along the yard.

'Can only manage little boys ...'

'Every night ...'

Gennetta froze. Her mind was numb. This was something she had never thought of – that the visits of Joey and Davey would be seized upon by the evil minds of Hacker's Yard for all the wrong reasons.

She swallowed hard. She wanted to retaliate but had sworn she would never get into a slanging match with her neighbours. She would have nothing to do with them. With her gaze fixed ahead, she hurried on.

'Ganning to get ready for 'em?'

'Does yon lass with you have 'em as well?'

'Or maybe she's waiting for the big 'un when he gets back from his fishing.'

'Now there's a man. Can't thee get him, lady?'

''Course not. That why she has boys!'

Gennetta tore into the house and slammed the door behind her. Breathing heavily, she sank back against it, trying to drive from her mind the accusations which had been flung at her.

'Ma'am, what's the matter?' Rose hurried to her side.

'Oh, Rose, those horrible folk,' Gennetta sobbed. 'They think the boys are coming here for ...' Her voice faltered. 'For reasons other than drawing lessons.'

'Here, come and sit down, kettle's boiling, I'll get you a cup of tea. Take no notice of them. They're not worth bothering about.'

'But they think ...'

'Never mind them. Look, the boys will soon be here. Don't let them see you're upset.'

Gennetta blessed Rose's commonsense. It wouldn't do to let the boys think that things were anything but normal.

She had only just taken her first sip of tea when there was a knock at the door.

'The boys! I hope they didn't hear any of that.' The alarm in her voice matched the fear in her eyes.

Rose opened the door.

'Where's Davey?' Gennetta asked when only Joey entered the house.

'He's sick, missus,' he replied.

Gennetta felt relieved. Joey alone could have heard the crude remarks she had just endured. If he had, she was sure he could cope with them for, thrown on his own resources from an early age, he was much more mature and worldly than Davey.

Younger, protected from the harsher aspects of Whitby life by a loving respectable father, Davey would not have understood what had been said but his curiosity would have been roused. At his age she did not want that.

This evening's lesson did not go with its customary ease and light-heartedness. The latter was missing. Gennetta tried to put her usual enthusiasm into her teaching but lacked her customary sparkle. Joey, though he showed increased understanding of perspective, seemed preoccupied and Gennetta began to wonder if he had been bothered by her neighbours' comments.

It was something of a relief when Rose went to the back room to prepare him a meal before he left and Joey looked up to meet Gennetta's eyes with the seriousness of an adult. She knew something was troubling him.

'Missus, I heard what they were shouting at thee.' His voice was quiet, as if he was embarrassed to mention it.

'I'm sorry you did, Joey.'

'Tak no notice of 'em, missus. We know why we come here and it's not what they were thinking.'

'But they'll still think it. It's made me wonder if I should go on exposing you boys to such malicious remarks. There's no telling what it might lead to.'

'Oh, don't stop t'lessons, missus. Please don't.' The alarm in his voice was plain.

131

She did not want to deny them the chance to develop the talents she had discovered, but wanted so much to help them. In doing so she knew she would also be helping herself to get over the loss of Reuben. It was not long since that terrible day but in some ways seemed a lifetime ago.

Under normal circumstances, following the usual expected code of mourning for her level of society, time would have dragged. She would have been sitting at home in widow's weeds, politely receiving visitors and quietly tending the needs of her children.

As it was she had been pitched quickly into a different environment, into a way of life that was foreign to her, harsh and unrelenting, and to survive she had to look out for herself. She had been propelled into a world of suspicious strangers, knowing no one, yet among them she had found friends. She couldn't let the boys down ...

Her thoughts were interrupted by Joey. 'See what Mr Tom has to say.'

'Oh, I couldn't. It would be embarrassing to tell him what happened.'

'He'd understand. Besides, it will have to be his decision whether Davey can still come here.'

Gennetta looked thoughtful. Joey was wise beyond his years.

'Thee'll have t'do summat, missus, and that might be t'best thing.'

Gennetta was pleased to see Davey arriving for work the next morning.

'Something he ate,' Tom explained.

'I'd like a word with you,' she said as they passed in the workshop.

Tom took his opportunity during the midday break when the boys had gone to skim stones in the river.

'Is it about Davey?' he asked with a little concern.

'In a way,' replied Gennetta. Trying to hide her embarrassment, she went on to tell him what had happened.

'Only to be expected from that lot in Hacker's Yard,' he said with disgust. 'Do you have to live there?'

'House and job go together. Leave one and I lose the other. My brother's stipulation.'

Tom's lips tightened. He held back his opinion of a brother who could subject his own sister to such conditions. It was not his place.

She gave a wry smile. 'I know what you're thinking. It's a long story, Tom. I can leave neither job nor house. This is my only source of income and I need the money, meagre though it is.'

'But didn't Miss Briggs ...'

'No, Tom. And that's another story.'

'So you're stuck.'

'Yes, until I can find some way out of my dilemma. In the meantime, what am I to do about these lessons? I want to carry on but is it fit for the boys, especially Davey, to be coming to Hacker's Yard?'

Tom frowned thoughtfully. 'I'd rather he was protected from such folk, but I want him to carry on with the lessons. He enjoys them and I know he likes you.' He paused momentarily then added, 'And, if you don't mind my saying so, you are good for him. He misses his mother's influence.'

Gennetta was flustered by this praise she had not expected. She felt his pale blue eyes, filled with thanks and appreciation, intent upon her.

'Then I'll carry on.'

'But not in Hacker's Yard.' The statement was firm and Gennetta looked at him with curiosity. Catching her gaze, he explained, 'What I mean is – I have a suggestion. I will understand if you don't agree, and hope you will not take offence at what I am to say.' He hesitated but when she made no remark, went on, 'Hold the lessons at my house in Henrietta Street.' His voice quickened. 'I know it may not look right for a recently bereaved widow to be making regular calls at a widower's house, but I don't mind if you don't?'

Gennetta stared at him for a moment. Here was a way to continue the lessons. 'Your neighbours?'

'Oh, no doubt they'll gossip among themselves and speculate but they are different from the folk in Hacker's Yard. There'll be no abuse thrown at you. We may get curious glances but they'll stop in time.'

Gennetta looked thoughtful. She hadn't dismissed his suggestion and it encouraged him to go on. 'But you must want to come. If you see any reason why you shouldn't, if you think it disrespectful at this stage of your mourning ...'

'Tom,' she stopped him in full flow, 'you're a very considerate person. My mourning is not being conducted as usual, you must realise that. If I have been thrown into situations which would not normally have occurred, then I need to deal with them differently. Yes, if you agree, if you are certain, we'll continue the lessons at your house, starting tonight.'

'Good, then it's settled,' he approved brightly. 'You tell the boys. Now I think I'd better be getting back, I can hear the men returning.' He glanced in the direction of the workshop and pushed himself to his feet.

As Gennetta watched him go she felt a sense of security. There was

133

confidence in his step and a determined set to his body. Tom would face any challenge that came his way.

It did not take the inhabitants of Hacker's Yard long to see that something different was taking place. After a week of observing that no boys came to Mrs Briggs's, but that she left her house every night at a few minutes to eight, their curiosity was roused and had to be satisfied.

On the seventh evening she was followed, with the consequence that on the eighth comments flew as she left her house.

'Got yer little boys tucked away, 'ave yer?'

'Does thee entertain the widowman after them?'

'Or before 'em?'

'What would thy husband think?'

'Turn in his grave, he would.'

The words pounded at her in spite of her effort to ignore them. They thundered in her mind until it felt it would burst. Gennetta swallowed hard. Tears filled her eyes and she started to run. She heard laughter, louder and louder, flowing along the street in a wave that threatened to drown her.

'Running! Can't get to it quick enough.'

'Must be desperate.'

'How much does he pay thee?'

She stumbled on the uneven flagstones in her desperation to get away.

'Whoops!'

'Careful. He won't like scrubbed knees.'

Gennetta managed to save herself from falling and burst into Church Street with derisive laughter still ringing in her ears. She steadied herself to walk when she saw curious glances cast at her by passersby.

As soon as he opened the door in answer to her knock, Tom realised that something was the matter. He could see there had been tears and that she was still in a state of agitation.

As he ushered her into the room with its cosy, comforting warmth, he fished in his pocket and flicked a coin to the boys. 'Go and get some sweets.'

Joey caught the coin deftly as Davey sang out, 'Thanks, Pa. Come on, Joey.' They raced for the door.

'What's wrong?' Tom asked gently as he took Gennetta's shawl and coat.

'They said some awful things as I came out this evening. They know where I come.' There was a catch in her voice. Tears stood in

134

her eyes. 'Why can't they leave us alone?' she cried in desperation. 'Why do they have to spoil everything?' Her eyes were wide as she looked at him. They were seeking help, craving sympathy and understanding.

Tom's gaze held more than sympathy. He wanted to reach out and take her in his arms so that she could draw strength from him and feel safe. But he held back for fear that she would misinterpret his action, and in doing so think he had had an ulterior motive for suggesting the lessons be held at his house.

'Would you prefer to stop coming?'

This suggestion was the one she had feared. A heavy feeling of dread seemed to weigh down her body. She had to fight it to survive. Give way now and Hacker's Yard and Jack had won. She stiffened and said, 'No!'

'Then don't.'

'But what about you? I don't want you getting a bad name.' Her thoughts were in confusion. She saw before her a good man, one to admire. It was not right that he should be stigmatised because of her. She dearly wanted to go on coming here to teach the boys, but was that still her main reason? She tried to tell herself it was, but knew she had found a welcome in this house and was stimulated by the conversation she had shared with Tom. She had found him a man of intelligence, a reader with a studious mind, and wanted to know more about him.

He gave a wry smile. 'Don't worry about me.'

'But I do. What will people say and think?'

'I told you before, people in this street will gossip and then think no more about it. It's what you might get thrown at you in Hacker's Yard that counts. But if you have the strength to ignore it, then they will get tired of baiting you. Take no notice of what they say about me.' He looked at her closely. 'Say you'll still come?' he added.

Gennetta felt certain his voice was laced with hope. Should she refuse? If she kept coming here, was she lighting a fuse which might catch fire and overwhelm them? Should she ignore the stirrings she was feeling? Was this a betrayal of Reuben? What would he have wanted her to do? Would he really have wanted her to live the rest of her life on memories of him? Hadn't he always wanted her happiness? Would he still want that from beyond the grave? She was still young. There was a lifetime ahead.

'Yes, I'll still come,' she said quietly, and saw the relief in Tom's face.

Over the next week Gennetta still had to endure the catcalls and ribald

135

comments of the women of Hacker's Yard and was scared by the glances their menfolk cast her. She was sorry that they also targeted Rose and Caleb, and even considered forsaking her job and the roof over their heads. But where could she go and what could she do?

She shared her troubles more and more with Tom who tried his best to reassure her that something would occur to solve her problems. Though their friendship deepened, he held back from taking the step which might release her from the trials of Hacker's Yard. He was afraid to act too soon. He did not want to alienate her feelings when Reuben was still strong in her memory by overstepping the bounds of convention.

Things went well for Gennetta at work. The rapport between her, Joey and Davey made the drudgery of sorting bearable. Most of the men in the workshop had come to accept her. There were a few who saw it as no place for a woman, still wanted it to be exclusively a man's world. Matt Harrison and his two cronies, whose eyes followed her whenever she came into the workshop, left her in no doubt as to what they would prefer.

Having left home early one morning to try to avoid the women of Hacker's Yard, she arrived at the workshop to find only Matt, Jake and Tully there.

'Ah, our little lady,' said Matt, mockery in his voice. 'And all alone.'

Gennetta's steps faltered. Her glance swept round the workshop to find it deserted except for the four of them. 'Where's John?' she asked, knowing that the foreman was the only one of the workers to have a key.

'Forgotten his grub, slipped home for it,' Matt informed her with a smile. 'Only us here, no one else.' He looked at his two companions and winked knowingly, an action he made sure Gennetta saw.

She drew herself up and started towards the sorting room. Her heart was fluttering, her stomach felt hollow, but she was determined they should see no sign of her unease.

As she neared them Matt Harrison stepped in front of her, making sure she could not pass. 'Now, the little lady wouldn't be leaving us so soon, would she?' he said smoothly. 'I'm sure we could entertain her before work starts.'

There was a chuckle from Jake and Tully. They'd play along with Matt. They always did, no matter what.

Gennetta's eyes smouldered. She met Matt's challenging gaze. 'Step aside, Matt Harrison,' she said firmly, suppressing the tremor which threatened to reveal her true fear.

136

'Oh, Mrs High and Mighty, are we?' he mocked. He paused a moment, eyes narrowing. 'Don't come that with us. Thee's down and out, no better than one of us. At least our folk don't resort to little boys. It's a man thee wants to show thee a thing or two.'

Gennetta's emotions spilled over in anger. Her hand lashed across his face with a resounding crack.

He flinched at the pain but swiftly composed himself, his eyes narrowed with the desire for a revenge which he knew would defile her the most.

'Want us to hold her, Matt?' There was glee in Tully's voice at the thought of what he might witness.

Before he could reply, the door to the workshop opened and John Young came in.

The three men turned away as if nothing had happened. It was on the tip of Gennetta's tongue to reveal the truth but she felt Matt's eyes on her and knew he would deny it, and that he would have the backing of Jake and Tully. She bade John 'Good morning' and went on to the sorting room.

As she passed Matt his low voice carried only to her. 'I'll have thee for that.' And his fingers touched his cheek.

Chapter Twelve

Two weeks passed and Harrison's threat had faded from Gennetta's mind as she found herself more and more occupied with her new life. Work took up most of the day, while evenings were spent with her children and then Joey and Davey. She was grateful to Rose for what she did in the house, always seeking a chance to improve things. Living as they were, they became close in a way that never would have happened if they had not had to move to Hacker's Yard. Gennetta was pleased that Rose was developing a relationship with Caleb and saw that it had every sign of going beyond mere friendship. He called frequently, doing odd maintenance jobs whenever he was in port, ignoring the invitations he received from some of the other occupants of Hacker's Yard.

Gennetta's visits to the children were the highlights of her evenings but she also found rewards in the progress the two boys were making with their drawing, and in her companionship with Tom.

He always expressed pleasure at her arrival. On one occasion she had stayed later than usual. She had not noticed that time had passed so quickly. The lessons had gone well, and when they had finished the two boys were so happily engrossed in Davey's model ships that it seemed a pity to disturb them. Gennetta was swept up in Tom's talk about jet and the trade which had become one of Whitby's mainstays. She found it fascinating and her desire to know more was roused.

'Let me see you home?' he offered when she and Joey prepared to leave. 'It's getting dark.'

'There's no need,' replied Gennetta, expressing her thanks. 'I'll have Joey as far as the workshop and then I'm nearly home. You see Davey to bed, he's tired. We shouldn't have stayed so long.'

'I've enjoyed it,' said Tom.

'So have I. Good night.'

The light was fading fast as she and Joey stepped out into Henrietta

Street. They were soon into Church Street where the buildings on either side seemed to close in on them as if forced by the multitude of houses behind rising precariously up the steep cliff. In the dim light it was easy to be transported into an imaginary world where the houses assumed grinning faces filled with evil. Narrow alleys, inhabited by scurrying rats, ran down to the river which assumed the darkness of the oncoming night.

Joey gave a little shiver. 'Thee all right, missus?' he asked, more as a token reassurance against the fear which assailed his own mind. Used as he was to being on his own, even when foraging at night from his shakedown in the workshop, he felt uneasy as they hurried along Church Street. Tonight the atmosphere felt strange. For once no one else was about and the raucous sounds from the inns plying their nightly trade seemed more remote, adding an eeriness to the silence which enveloped them.

The shock when they were grabbed by powerful hands and dragged into a dark alley running to the river prevented any attempt to scream, and then it was too late as their mouths were shut for them.

Gennetta twisted and struggled against two men as she was dragged deeper into the alley. Joey hit out at the man who held him but his blows brought only a deep-throated chuckle from his assailant.

'No use, boy, no use,' he muttered harshly as he switched his grip to Joey's throat.

In that brief moment of release, the boy acted. He brought his knee up sharply into the man's groin. The grip on him slackened and he twisted away from the man to burst into Church Street at full tilt. Without looking behind him he headed for Henrietta Street as fast as he could. He must not waste one moment, the missus was in danger! His feet flew across the uneven ground. He must get help and that lay in Henrietta Street.

In a matter of moments, though to him it seemed as if he would never reach the house, he was pounding on the door and yelling, 'Mr Tom! Mr Tom! Quick!'

'Joey, what's wrong?' Tom asked.

Even before he'd finished the question, Joey was urging action. 'We was attacked. Three of 'em. They've got the missus! Matt's one of them. Come on!'

Tom needed no second bidding. He could guess who the others were. 'Get Caleb!'

Joey was away to the house two doors down.

Tom turned to Davey who had followed him to the door. 'Stay here, Davey. Lock yourself in. Don't open to anyone but me.' He stepped outside.

Joey was already racing back to him with Caleb close behind.

There was no need for words. Joey knew he had to show the way.

'In here,' he called as they reached the alley.

Halfway down the narrow opening they were aware of a tangle of bodies.

Gennetta, driven by frenzy, still struggled even though Tully and Jake pressed her against the wall. Matt was in front of her, his left hand at the neck of her dress, his right gripping her chin, forcing her head back against the stone. He grinned at the fear in her eyes and revelled in the power he held over her. His lips came down hard on hers and at the same time he ripped her dress open.

The sound of pounding footsteps distracted him from his purpose.

'There they are!' Joey's voice rang down the alley.

'Thought you said the boy was out cold?' snarled Matt. Furious, he took a swipe at Tully, sending him hard against the wall. His grip on Gennetta slackened.

Tom was straight at Matt with the full weight of his body. He was thrown away from Gennetta. Off balance, he was unable to avoid Tom's fist which pounded into his mouth, splitting his lip. He spun round against the wall, stiffened his back and threw a punch which caught Tom high on the head. Determined Matt would pay dearly for his attack on Gennetta, he ignored the blow and punched hard and fast at the bully who threw up his arms to protect his face. He ducked round his assailant and ran.

Caleb hit Tully before he could recover from Matt's blow and he pitched to the ground, unconscious. Caleb did not pause but launched himself at Jake who, overcome by the swiftness of the assault, had no time to defend himself against Caleb's weight and huge fists. Two blows to his stomach had him doubling up, gasping for breath. As he staggered forward, Caleb spun him round and propelled him towards Church Street with a well-aimed kick.

Breathing hard, Tom turned to Gennetta. 'Are you all right?' he asked with deep concern. He wanted to take her in his arms and hug the confidence back into her but made his voice merely reassuring. He did not want her to think he was taking advantage of the situation.

Gennetta drew air deep into her lungs, trying hard to calm herself and master the fear in her body. She nodded. 'Yes,' she gasped, though her flesh still crawled with the touch of Matt's hands. She shuddered.

'Put these round you, ma'am.' Caleb held out her cape and shawl which had been ripped from her by her attackers.

Gratefully she reached out, then held back, embarrassed to recall her torn dress. She pulled it together quickly, covering her breasts,

140

and tucked it so that it would hold up. Caleb draped the cape around her and she took the shawl.

These actions brought some measure of calm to her and with an effort she controlled her voice.

'Thank you, all of you.' There was still a catch in her voice. 'A good job you got away, Joey.'

'I gave Tully a kick where it hurt most,' replied the boy. 'Thought it best t'get Mister Tom.'

'You did right,' Tom praised him.

There was a moan beside them as Tully regained consciousness. He tried to sit up. Tom reached down and pulled him to his feet by the neck of his shirt. The action brought realisation back to Tully. There was fear in his eyes as he looked around the little group. Tom pushed him hard against the wall.

'Scum,' he hissed. 'You'll hear more about this tomorrow. Now, on your way.' He pushed him towards Church Street. Tully staggered a few yards, looking back over his shoulder, then gathered his wits and ran. 'Come on, Gennetta, we'll see you home.'

As they started off, Tom realised he had used her Christian name for the first time. Silently he said it to himself again, savouring it. It felt right. He hoped it would be right for her too in the future.

When they reached the house in Hacker's Yard, Rose was surprised to see Gennetta's escort. Her questioning glance changed to one of concern at the sight of the dirt on her mistress's cloak and shawl, but when she saw the torn dress she became openly alarmed.

'I'm all right, Rose,' Gennetta hastened to reassure her. 'Thank goodness Tom and Caleb arrived in time, due to Joey's quick thinking.'

'Who was it?' she asked as she fussed around Gennetta. 'They want horse-whipping!'

'I'll see the authorities deal with them tomorrow,' said Tom firmly.

Gennetta saw the resolve in his eyes. 'No,' she said. 'I'll deal with them in my own way. This was an act of revenge.' She went on to tell them of the incident when she had arrived at work early. 'I think what happened tonight was partly a result of that. If we take this further, Matt will bear a further grievance which he'll want to take out on me. I'd be in fear of another attack. I cannot go on like that. Let me deal with this in my own way.'

'But ...' Tom started to protest.

Gennetta silenced him by raising her hand. 'You three punished them tonight. Let me finish it off.'

'You must be careful, ma'am,' warned Caleb, his face serious as he shot a glance at Rose, seeking her support.

141

'I will be.'

'But what can you do?' asked Tom, seeing danger if Gennetta wasn't cautious.

'You'll see tomorrow if the opportunity arises. But I must ask all of you to say nothing about what happened tonight to anyone.' She looked round them all, seeing doubt in their eyes.

'The authorities should be told,' protested Rose.

The others agreed.

'It could happen again,' Tom pointed out, not convinced that Gennetta was right.

'Not with Matt and his cronies. Please do it my way.'

They all reluctantly agreed.

'Remember, not a word ever to anyone. Promise?'

They all did so.

The following morning, when Gennetta arrived at the workshop, most of the workmen were already there and she heard them chaffing Matt, Jake and Tully about their cuts, bruises and black eyes.

She smiled to herself at their sullen excuses but cast them a withering glance of contempt as she passed them by. She saw disquiet in their eyes and knew they were wondering if she was going to inform the authorities – if she had not already done so.

As the midday break approached Gennetta took Joey to one side. 'Go to Matt and tell him quietly that I want to see him and Jake and Tully here in the sorting room, and tell Tom as well. But do it quietly so no one else hears.'

'Yes, missus.' He scurried away to the workshop and when he returned, a few moments later, gave her a nod signifying he had done as she wanted.

Tom had seen Joey speak to Matt before he came to him and, surmising he had given Matt the same message, made it his concern to have a word with Gennetta before they all arrived.

'What's going on?' he asked.

'You'll see,' was the only reply she would give him.

'Be careful,' he insisted.

'That's why I want you here, Tom, just in case they turn nasty. But I don't think they will.'

The door opened and Matt, followed by his two cronies, came in. She could see from their tentative approach that they were apprehensive.

She drew herself up, exuding an air of authority, though she knew she really had none. But she felt, as a result of their actions and the consequences of the previous night, that she had the upper hand. She watched them with a steely eye, her gaze fixed firmly on them but giving nothing away.

They stopped in front of her, Jake and Tully halting a step behind Matt. They shuffled uneasily, their eyes cast down. Matt stood firm, ready to defy her denunciation to those in authority. She met his gaze with cold contempt.

'What you did last night deserves prison and I've a good mind to see you get that punishment.' Her voice lashed them like a whip.

Jake and Tully stopped shuffling. They looked up at her with alarm on their faces. 'No, missus, no!' They shrank from the thought of prison.

'Thee wouldn't!' Matt's hiss was almost inaudible between his tight lips. His eyes flashed angrily.

Tom saw it and took one step forward to emphasise his presence.

'But I'm not,' Gennetta went on firmly. 'If I do there would be scandal for your families to face. A prison sentence for you would mean hardship for them, and you would not have a job to come out to.' She could sense the relief come over the three men. Jake and Tully looked at each other and grinned broadly. Matt, while relieved, was wary. He eyed Gennetta with suspicion. 'I'm not doing this out of pity for you, but for your families.' She left a momentary pause to let her words sink in and then put ice into her voice. 'But if ever you try anything like that again, I'll reveal what happened last night and your punishment will be doubled.'

'Thanks, ma'am, thanks.' Jack and Tully touched their foreheads and, reading dismissal in her look, scurried away.

Matt started to turn away but stopped and looked back. He smiled the smile of one who has got away with something through no effort of his own. As she met his eyes Gennetta saw open admiration. She felt uneasy as his gaze went right through her, but hid her discomfort. 'Thank you, Mrs Briggs.' He leaned forward slightly and lowered his voice. 'You're a fine woman. You can't blame me for wondering what ...' He grinned and turned for the door.

Tom tensed at the remark. He made to step after Matt but Gennetta restrained him and shook her head.

'And, Matt, you and your cronies keep your snide remarks to yourselves in future,' she called after him.

He did not stop, did not turn, but raised his arm in acknowledgement.

When the door closed behind him, Gennetta relaxed, and only then did Tom realise the strain that the confrontation had been for her. 'Well, he won't bother me again,' she said as she sat down.

Gennetta was right and life began to settle down for her. The catcalls and comments of the inhabitants of Hacker's Yard grew fewer and fewer as they realised that they were having no effect on either Gennetta or Rose. They began to offer greetings instead and Gennetta and Rose even exchanged friendly words with their neighbours.

But life for Gennetta was marred one evening on her way home from work when she met Cyrus Sleightholme in Church Street. He was immaculately dressed in grey trousers, black waist-hugging tail coat, grey waistcoat, white shirt and black cravat. He wore a black top hat and carried a black cane. Gennetta's heart raced when she saw him and she recalled the occasions when she had seen the figure in black. She remembered the disquiet she had felt and now, in broad daylight, face to face with Cyrus, wondered if she had been right in assuming that figure had been his.

'Why, if it isn't Gennetta. Good day, my dear.' He doffed his hat and bowed slightly.

She was conscious of her grubby appearance, with dirty, torn dress, smeared face and hands needing a wash. She felt his grey eyes run over her.

'Good day, Cyrus.' She tried to be pleasant. 'I trust you are well?'

'I couldn't be better, my dear. And you?'

'I am in good health.'

'I'm pleased to hear it,' he replied smoothly. 'But what of other matters?'

'I am still not over losing Reuben.'

'That is only natural,' he sympathised.

'But I'm coming to terms with my loss.'

'Good.' He pursed his lips and gave a little shrug of his shoulders. 'Life must go on.'

'True,' she agreed, 'but it's not easy.'

'I hear you are living in Hacker's Yard and sorting jet?' He pulled a face.

'It could be worse.'

He gave a little sneer and a quirk of his eyebrows. 'Not much.' He leaned forward slightly, taking his weight on his cane. 'Just think, you'd have had none of this suffering and humiliation if you'd married me. I warned you that nothing good would come of your marriage to a sailor.'

Gennetta detected gloating in his voice. 'But something did,' she replied. 'I had Reuben's love.'

'And what did that get you? Widowhood!'

'No, love didn't get me that. Those murderers did, or someone behind them.' She was watching him closely but saw no reaction to her final words, only a dismissive comment.

144

'Someone behind them? My dear, you are letting your imagination run away with you.'

'Am I?' Gennetta's mind was racing. Might she learn some unpalatable truths? The past had faded to some extent but this meeting was awakening unpleasant memories. She half expected to hear the cry of geese. 'Wouldn't you have liked to see Reuben out of the way? Aren't you pleased that he is? Now you can wait until my official period of mourning is over and then you can propose, hoping I'll accept to escape the likes of Hacker's Yard.' Gennetta was wound up. The words poured out. Her face was tight with anger. 'Didn't you appear on the quay the day that Reuben sailed on his last voyage, just as you did on other occasions, a symbol of ill omen and ...'

Cyrus broke in. 'Just a minute, Gennetta.' His words were mingled with laughter. 'You are accusing me of instigating Reuben's death just so I could marry you?' His amusement infuriated her but before she could lash out again he went on, 'No, my dear. You should know I would never stoop as low as that. On my word of honour, I had nothing to do with it. As for my appearances ...'

'So you admit you were the figure in black? I was not seeing a ghost?'

'Ghost? I'm as solid as you are.' He chuckled deep in his throat. 'And black? Well, even you should know it's what I usually wear. My dear Gennetta, you have caused yourself anguish with your over-active imagination. I'm sorry if seeing me caused you pain. That was never meant. On some occasions I felt I should be present, such as the christening. That day I thought it could have been our child, an heir to the Turner and Sleightholme jet businesses. On the quay the day Reuben sailed? Merely coincidental, my dear. I didn't even know he was sailing.'

Gennetta was confused. She knew Cyrus well enough to know he wasn't lying. She had made a fool of herself. 'I ... I ...' she spluttered, trying to find the right words.

'Don't apologise, please.' The amused twinkle in his eyes did not escape her.

'But I must. I've harboured a suspicion which had no foundation.'

'Think nothing of it, Gennetta. Banish it from your mind. Maybe I will come calling one day.' He bowed and stepped past her before she could say any more. She was left staring after him with his amused laughter ringing in her ears.

Cyrus's denial was confirmed and the truth revealed only a week later, just after she had returned from seeing the children. Rose was visiting Caleb's mother and Gennetta was bustling around gathering pencils and paper for the drawing lessons at Tom Unwin's. Answering a knock on the door, she was surprised to find Captain Barrick standing there.

'Ah, Mrs Briggs, at last I've found you,' he said briskly. 'I had no idea you were living in the notorious Hacker's Yard and eventually went to see if your brother Jack knew where you were. He told me you were here.'

She saw his puzzled expression as she invited him to step inside. 'It's a long story, Captain Barrick, from which my brother does not come out very well,' she said, indicating a chair.

'Ma'am, I don't wish to pry. But I am sorry it has come to this.' His glance encompassed the room. 'Though I am glad to see that you are making the best of it. And I have something which may help a little.' He fished in his pocket and drew out an envelope. 'Our last voyage went well and was highly profitable for the owners who gave the crew a bonus payment. They made a unanimous decision and insisted that part of it come to you as Reuben's share.' He held out the envelope.

Astonished and moved by the generous gesture, she stumbled over her thanks. 'But he didn't sail ...'

'Nevertheless the crew wanted to help. Reuben was well liked. He would have made a fine captain.'

'It's most kind of them. Please thank them all. I'll be for ever grateful to them, especially for thinking so highly of my husband.'

Captain Barrick had been watching her intently. She was young enough to be the daughter he had never had. He had taken a great interest in Reuben and had been pleased that he had married a girl as sensible and pretty as Gennetta. He realised that they could have had a golden future together which had been shattered by Reuben's murder.

'My dear, you have created an oasis in the midst of squalor.'

'It is mostly my maid Rose's doing. She insisted on coming with me,' explained Gennetta, wanting to give credit where it was due.

'A pity it doesn't rub off on some of the other folk in the yard. Is there no chance of your finding somewhere else?'

'None at the moment but one day I hope ...' She left her words hanging.

'If there's anything I can do at any time, don't be afraid to ask.'

'That's extremely kind of you, Captain Barrick. I will remember your offer. And thank you for this.' She indicated the envelope. 'I'm not destitute but my wage is meagre. This will ease things.'

'There's one other matter, Mrs Briggs. It may be some consolation to you to know that the two men who murdered Reuben have been apprehended.'

146

'What!' She was startled by the news. Strong emotions swept over her like an enormous wave. There was relief that the perpetrators of the crime had been caught, and horror as it brought back memories of that fateful day.

'I pursued the matter. After all, apart from the murder of one of my crew, I was concerned to try to recover the money. I employed some men to investigate while I was away. Suffice to say they were successful. The men are in custody and most of the money recovered.'

Gennetta heard his explanation through a haze of remembrance. She had thought that if ever the day came when the men were caught she would rejoice, but that was not her reaction now. Instead she felt just a glimmer of satisfaction that there had been an arrest but this was overlaid by the numbness of remembering her great loss that day.

'It appears,' Captain Barrick went on, 'that it was just by chance that these two spotted Reuben coming out of the bank and, recognising him as Mate of the *Diana*, reckoned he had been collecting the wages for the crew. It was a spur of the moment attack, with no intention to murder.'

She nodded, her mind grasping the fact that here was confirmation that her suspicions of Cyrus had been ill-founded. What he had told her had been the truth. And it must also be true, as he had indicated, that she had put the wrong interpretation on the figure in black. She frowned, perturbed by her own misjudgement.

'My dear, I'm sorry to have put you through this.' The captain had seen her distress but only knew the reason for part of it. 'I wouldn't have told you but I thought you ought to know. Besides, I'd rather you heard it from me than from someone else.'

Gennetta started and drew her mind sharply back to the captain and his words.

'I'm pleased that you did. You've settled something about the murder which has troubled me from time to time. Now I can cast that from my mind.'

He smiled kindly. 'Then I am satisfied I did the right thing.' He rose from his chair. 'I must not intrude on you any longer.'

She crossed the room with him. At the door he paused and turned to her. 'Don't forget, if there is anything I can do at any time, please ask.'

'Thank you. You are so kind.'

Captain Barrick took his leave. When the door closed, thoughts of Reuben overwhelmed her. She sank on to a chair and wept.

Ten minutes later, her tears dry, she hurried to Henrietta Street.

'Sorry I'm late,' she apologised to Tom when he opened the door. 'I had a visit from Captain Barrick.'

Tom sensed she had been distressed and looked concerned when he asked, 'Nothing wrong, I hope?'

'No. He came to tell me that Reuben's killers had been found.'

'That must be a relief to you?'

'I suppose so. But there's more to it than that.'

He gave her a querying look but said nothing.

'We must get on with the lesson now.' She paused then added, 'Tom, I need to talk to someone. Will you walk on the cliffs with me on Sunday, after I've been to the morning service, if the weather is fine?'

'It will give me great pleasure. And I can promise you, I am a good listener.'

After she had passed pleasantries with the vicar and other regular churchgoers, Gennetta threaded her way between moss-covered gravestones to a newer one which proclaimed Reuben's resting place.

Her eyes were swiftly damp. 'Oh, Reuben, we didn't deserve what happened. So much happiness awaited us.'

After a few seconds of silent communication she raised her eyes and glanced in the direction of the path along the edge of the cliffs. A lone figure looked out to sea. Tom.

Confusion rent her heart. She bit her lip and looked down. 'Reuben, I love you, I always will, but I'm alive, I'm me. I mean no betrayal of my love for you. Tom is so kind and gentle, yet strong in the way you were strong. I need someone ...' She swallowed hard, brushed away the dampness from her eyes and turned slowly away from the grave.

By the time she reached Tom she had taken a grip on her feelings and composed herself.

'Good morning, Tom,' she said brightly as he turned on hearing the rustle of her dress in the grass.

'Hello, Gennetta.' His eyes were soft with pleasure. 'You couldn't have picked a nicer morning.'

The warm air was troubled only by a slight breeze. A few drifting clouds marked the blue sky and the sea was calm with waves hardly able to break against the cliffs. The whole scene was so peaceful.

They turned along the path, Tom matching his stride to hers.

'Thank you for coming, Tom.'

'The pleasure is mine. You said you needed someone to talk to? I'm always here if you want me for that.' He drew back from saying more. He knew she would have visited her husband's grave after

148

coming out of church and did not want to intrude in any way on those moments.

Gennetta hesitated, wondering what would be the best approach, then said sharply as if it was something she hadn't wanted to ask yet felt she must, 'Tom, do you believe in the Gabriel Hounds?'

Surprised by the question, he glanced at her and saw that she was serious. 'Well,' he said slowly, 'I've seen the geese fly over. I've heard their cries, but to me that's all they are. I know some folk look upon them as a sign of ill omen but ...' He paused slightly. Deciding to alter tack before he passed any more opinions, he said, 'Why do you ask?'

She moistened her lips. 'Well, it's a long story.'

'I'm a willing listener, if you want to tell me?' he replied in a persuasive voice.

As they walked slowly past the gaunt stonework of the ruined abbey, mellowed by the bright sun, to the cliffs above Saltwick Bay, she told him her story from the point where she left home. She emphasised the appearances of the figure in black and of the Gabriel Hounds and told him of her fears and her suspicions after Reuben's murder. 'Then, the other day, I met Cyrus in Church Street and in the course of our conversation I challenged him about his possible involvement in Reuben's murder. He denied it and I believed him. Any suspicions I had left were finally eradicated when Captain Barrick visited me.'

'So what do you want from me?' asked Tom, who had listened intently. He was pleased to have heard what she had to say. Now he knew more about Gennetta's life and also about her thoughts and feelings. 'I've served as someone for you to talk to and I believe that has helped you, but I think you have answered your own doubts.'

'Not quite. Remember my first question?'

'The Gabriel Hounds?'

'Yes.'

He stopped and she turned to face him. She saw earnestness in his face, and concern for her, and knew she had a solid and steadfast friend. When he spoke, his voice was quiet but firm. 'I told you, to me they are just geese. I believe some folk link two events because of a belief, a supersitition, which has grown up. They see or hear the geese and something unfortunate happens so they link the two, just as you've done. They could connect an upset with anything – say, seeing a woman in a green dress – and after that they'd be expecting something to happen whenever they saw the same thing.'

She nodded thoughtfully. 'You could be right.'

He smiled. 'I know I'm right. Folk could just as easily connect the

149

geese with a happy event, a sign of good fortune. Forget them, Gennetta. The Gabriel Hounds can't affect events. They would happen whether the birds flew or not.'

She turned and walked on but after three steps stopped and faced Tom who had not moved. He was watching her closely. He saw from the look on her face that he had won. He had driven the superstition from her mind, and he was glad.

'Thank you, Tom. You have been a great help,' she said.

'I hope I can always serve you,' he said humbly, his gaze intent, holding an expression which revealed more than mere friendship.

He admired the wisps of silky fair hair which had escaped from the sides of her small bonnet and imagined them released, tumbling like a shimmering waterfall. He wanted to take away the sadness which could cloud her face and leave in its place only the joyful sparkle which he knew could light up her eyes.

Their gazes met and held. The gap between them was no longer a barrier. He stepped forward and reached out to her shoulders. The first time they had touched. He would remember this moment for the rest of his life. It sent a magic coursing through him, something he had thought he would never experience again after his wife died. But now here was someone special, whom he had grown to respect, care for, and – he could not deny it – love. He had kept his feelings to himself but now he could hold back no longer. He took heart from the fact that she had not tensed against his touch, nor drawn away, and from the look in her eyes he saw that he had released something within her.

He drew her gently to him, searching her face as he said, 'Gennetta, I love you.'

He saw wariness in her eyes, as if she was afraid of her feelings. He started to draw away. Her hands reached out to prevent him. 'Tom, please.' Her voice was hoarse, charged with emotion. 'Hold me.'

His heart sang with joy, but he moved gently when he enfolded her in his arms.

Within their embrace she felt safe and cared for. She had felt like this with Reuben. Now she knew she loved Tom but was reluctant to admit it just yet.

Reuben! She swallowed hard. Was she betraying him? Doubts began to fill her mind. She had to be rid of them. She looked up at Tom. 'Kiss me,' she whispered.

He looked longingly and lovingly into her blue eyes as his lips met hers, just brushing them gently. The feeling sent a shiver down her spine. She responded with a kiss which matched his, and when he would have pulled away, held him to her. Pleasure sparked between them.

'I think a lot about you too, Tom,' she whispered, when their lips parted.

Swept up in the joy of that revelation, he hugged her tightly. 'That makes me so happy. I believe we ...'

'Hush, Tom, say no more,' she broke in, putting a finger to his lips. 'Please leave things just as they are between us.'

Concern clouded his face. 'Oh, Gennetta, I'm sorry. I'm intruding on your love for Reuben. All I want is your happiness. Why not leave work and Hacker's Yard behind you?'

'You mean, if I married you?'

He nodded. 'There's nothing I want more in the world.'

'You would lose your job if you married me,' she warned. 'My brother wants to humiliate me by keeping me in Hacker's Yard sorting jet. If I married you he would no longer be able to do that, but would take his revenge by sacking you. And he'd see no other jet manufacturer employed you. You'd have no work. I can't let that happen. It wouldn't be fair to you or Davey.'

She saw him start to protest but stopped him. 'Please try to understand, and give me time to adjust to our newfound love.' She reached up and kissed him and Tom knew he could not deny her request. 'Please be patient. Something will turn up to solve my problem with my brother.'

She tried to sound reassuring, though how Jack's enmity could be eradicated she could not see. She was not prepared for the unexpected.

Chapter Thirteen

The drawing lessons which Gennetta conducted most evenings, leaving Saturdays and Sundays free, went well. Tom took pleasure in watching her encourage Joey and Davey and was struck by the progress she'd made in bringing out their talent. But more than that, he admired her own work when she was demonstrating.

One day she asked him to take three etching tools home with him. He did not query her request, and when she arrived at the house in Henrietta Street that evening, she found the home-made tools – nails with sharp points embedded in pieces of wood for handles – laid on the table.

She produced three pieces of jet ground ready for etching.

'How did you manage that?' asked Tom, alarm in his eyes. 'If you'd been caught ...'

Gennetta smiled impishly. 'I wasn't. And none of you will tell.' She looked at the three of them in turn.

'No, missus, we won't breathe a word,' said Joey with a serious face.

'Right,' said Gennetta, removing her cape from her shoulders and the shawl from her head. She passed them to Tom who hung them behind the door. 'We'll start with simple etchings and see how we get on.'

They sat down at the table while Tom stirred the fire beneath the kettle hanging on the reckon.

'In my bag there's some cake that Rose made,' she informed him.

While he prepared the refreshments they usually had halfway through the evening, she directed the boys in what she wanted them to do.

By the end of the evening Gennetta was pleased by what she and the boys had produced.

Over succeeding weeks she smuggled more jet out of the workshop under her dress. She made light of what she was doing, and, though Tom was alarmed for fear she'd be seen, he played his part and also passed on valuable tips picked up from the etchers in the workshop.

At the end of a month Gennetta selected several pieces and announced that tomorrow she would show them to John Young, and if the foreman had an eye for talent, they would be moving out of the sorting room.

'But that will mean admitting you took the jet,' Tom protested.

'It will,' Gennetta agreed, 'but don't you worry about that. Leave it to me.'

The next morning she sought out the foreman as soon as she arrived at work. 'Can I show you something, John?' she asked.

He gave her a friendly nod. He liked Gennetta, admired the way she had coped with work she was never made for. He wished he could make things easy for her but with his employer's weekly checks, which could come at any time, he dare not.

She fished in her bag and produced the etched jet, placing it in front of him.

His eyes widened at the unexpected sight and his face was serious when he looked hard at her. 'Where did thee get this?' he asked. 'It's not the work of any of my men,' he added, seeing styles he did not recognise.

'You're quite right.' Gennetta gave a faint smile.

'Then why bring it to me?'

'Because it's the work of some of your employees.'

Mystified, his frown demanded an explanation.

'Joey, Davey and myself,' she announced with a touch of pride.

'What? But ... ' Realisation that she must have taken the jet without permission struck him. 'Thee stole the jet from here?'

'No, John, borrowed. You'll get it back plus the talent you see there.' She indicated the jet.

He eyed her, suspicious of the excuse she was offering.

Before he could say anything she went on, 'Come on, John, you must agree there's talent there.'

'Aye,' he admitted, and bent to examine the pieces more closely. His eye travelled over the lines carefully. His years of experience showed that here were three different artists. One showed the boldness of a young hand that needed guidance and training, but in that boldness there was a gift of interpretation beyond the years of the etcher. There was a talent here which would stand still for a while without any evident progress then suddenly bloom and never go back.

In another he recognised the work of an observer who could

153

remember and translate what he had seen into delicate lines which made an instant impression on the beholder.

In the third he saw a natural flowing grace which moved him with its beauty. Here was the hand of an artist who required no more training, who could be left to develop this individual style which would soon be sought after.

He gave a little grunt in which Gennetta recognised satisfaction at what he saw. He looked up at her. 'They're good,' he admitted. 'Amazing when most men need years of practice.'

She gave a wry smile. 'Drawing skills help. They're more than good, and you know it. And they'll continue to improve.'

'Maybe,' he muttered. 'Maybe.' He pointed at the three pieces in the order in which he had looked at them. 'Davey, Joey and thissen.'

'You're a shrewd judge, John.'

He puffed out his chest at the praise.

'Well?' she queried. 'Do we move out of the sorting room into the workshop?'

He pursed his lips thoughtfully. 'I certainly could use that talent to improve our output. But Davey's a bit young.'

'I thought you'd say that and I would be inclined to agree but you can see the potential in his work. Grasp that now and it will blossom, possibly become the best of the three. Disappoint him by leaving him out and you may stifle that talent and waste the possibilities. Give him the chance along with Joey. I ask nothing for myself.'

'But thee's the best. Thy work would sell immediately. Joey's needs a bit of refining.'

'Give us the chance,' urged Gennetta enthusiastically. 'It will benefit the firm.'

John rubbed his chin as he pondered the situation. 'Mr Turner should approve but he's away for a fortnight.'

'Then we'll have more work to show him when he gets back and he'll have a better chance to assess it.'

John hesitated then said, 'All right, Joey and Davey can move into the workshop but I can't have thee in. The men wouldn't stand for it!' His expression showed regret and apology.

'All right,' she agreed. Though disappointment pricked her she would not show it. 'I'll tell the boys. And I'll do some more etching when I can in the sorting room.'

Relieved by her suggestion but wanting to be helpful, John made a concession. 'If thee want any advice or have owt to show me, come into the workshop. I'll see the men don't mind, provided the visits are short.'

* * *

The next two weeks went quickly. The boys, pleased to be out of the sorting room and free from the rough work of handling the unsorted jet, settled into their new work with zest. Davey was pleased to be working at the same bench as his father, who was not only delighted that his son's talent had been recognised by John Young but touched by the way the rest of the workers accepted one so young into their midst.

Gennetta enjoyed etching even though she was on her own and had to fit it in between sorting. She was pleased that John Young was delighted with her work.

'Young!' a voice boomed, bringing everyone's attention to the door. Jack Turner, dressed in a brown, double-breasted frock coat and matching stovepipe hat, stood there like the figure of doom. 'What the hell's she doing in here?' He swung his cane to point at Gennetta, who had just come from the sorting room with her latest etching of two swans.

Everyone held their breath. He was clearly angry at the sight of his sister consulting with his foreman. Tension sparked.

Gennetta felt the muscles in her neck stiffen and her body tense. She started to turn away but felt the restraining hand of John Young stop her.

'Mrs Briggs has shown a natural talent for etching so I allowed her to do some in the sorting room, only coming in here when she had summat t'show me.'

'And these two?' snapped Jack, pointing at Joey and Davey.

'They showed a talent which I thought need encouraging.'

'You had no right until you'd consulted me.' Annoyance flared in Jack's eyes. 'You're not here to make decisions but to see that my orders are carried out.'

John was annoyed at being ticked off in front of the men but knew better than to let it show. Instead he said, quietly but firmly, 'Sir, you were away. I thought they could do some pieces before you returned so that there would be a selection for you to see. They will add to what you have to sell, especially those done by Mrs Briggs.' He had excused himself, and touched the one spot he knew would tempt his employer, namely that there would be more money in his pocket. And by adding, 'If you think not, then they can easily go back to the sorting room,' he acknowledged that Jack's word would be final.

His boss grunted and gave a reluctant nod. 'Show me.' John produced some pieces and laid them out for his employer to see.

Jack picked up each piece in turn and examined it closely. He kept his reactions to himself but recognised that he was holding marketable jet, especially those pieces his foreman had indicated were his sister's work. The scenes she had depicted were almost alive. They would

155

certainly sell well but he was not about to let her know that.

He became aware that the room was still. He glanced up and saw all his workmen watching him. They knew Gennetta's work was good and expected him to acknowledge it. 'Well,' he snapped, 'get on with your work. Don't waste what is *my* time!'

As one everybody turned their attention back to what they had been doing when their employer had arrived. Grindstones, driven by pedals, started to turn again and tools rasped on jet.

'Yes, good,' said Jack in a flat tone so that his enthusiasm for the pieces would not be betrayed. He still said nothing directly to his sister but moved on to look at Joey's work. 'I can use some of these,' he said after a few minutes, having realised that here was someone who with more practice could become a leading etcher.

Tom Unwin held his breath when Jack leaned over Davey to finger the jet which had been marked by the young boy. The decision, which would be delivered in a matter of moments, could make or break his son's enthusiasm which had so far been encouraged, nurtured and developed by Gennetta. For what she had done he would always be grateful, and he hoped for her sake too that Mr Turner would see some merit in Davey's work.

Jack was struggling with himself. He had expected to toss this work aside for he had no idea that such striking etching could be done by one so young. He realised it was a gift which had been caught and nurtured at the right moment, and wished he had been able to do that with a son of his own. 'Davey Unwin,' he said gently, his initial anger on entering the workshop mollified by what he had seen, 'you work hard and you'll become well-known for your work.'

The boy's apprehension vanished. Pleased at the praise, he smiled up at Mr Jack and then, wondering what his father was thinking, glanced at him. A proud Tom smiled back and winked at him, and Davey's day was made. His father was pleased.

He shot a look at Gennetta. He so wanted her to be pleased too. He was delighted when she gave him her customary warm smile and inclined her head in a nod of approval.

Jack turned his attention back to Joey. 'Now ...' He hesitated, realising that he did not know his surname, and nor for that matter did anyone else. It just seemed he had always been there and had never been called anything else but Joey. 'Now, Joey, can you make me three more like that in the next two weeks?' He held up a piece of Joey's work.

'Aye, I can, sir,' he said with conviction. 'Six if thee likes?' he added enthusiastically.

Jack gave a doubting chuckle.

156

'I can, sir, easily,' returned Joey, a touch hurt that his ability should be questioned.

'All right, lad.' Jack's attention was on another piece of his work. 'Do that one as well. Three of each.'

'Yes, sir!'

Jack glanced at Gennetta. He still did not acknowledge her and his eyes were cold but he said, 'I'll take all you do in the next three weeks, plus all that you have here.'

She judged he would be selling them but he did not enlighten her as to where. She only learned that after he had selected work from other workers and had left the premises. John announced that in three weeks' time Mr Turner was going to the London Exhibition where he would be displaying their work.

Excitement ran high in Turner's workshop after Jack had collected all the pieces he wanted to take with him. If he was successful, then demand for their jet would grow.

Knowing how hard everyone had worked to fulfil Mr Turner's requirements, John closed the workshop early.

'It's a pleasant evening, would you like a walk on the cliffs?' Tom suggested to Gennetta as they left work.

'Love to,' she replied.

They talked little as they climbed the Church Stairs, the effort robbing them of breath. Reaching the edge of the cliffs, they stopped to regain their composure after the climb.

The evening was still, the sea calm. A hush seemed to have settle over the town and it accentuated the movement of the *Amelia* as it sailed down the river towards the piers.

'There goes our jet,' commented Tom.

'I wish Father could have known about it,' said Gennetta. 'He would have been excited at the jet being shown in London and the prospect of more work, though he wouldn't have shown it. His heart and soul was in his business.' Her voice hardened. 'And that's why I never had any love from him. The firm took him away from me after he blamed me for my mother's death.'

'What?' Tom looked shocked.

Her hesitation was only momentary, then she poured out her story to the time she left home. 'And,' she concluded, her eyes narrowing, 'some day the Turner business will repay me for my father's antagonism. It deadened his feelings for me. I deserve something back.'

'But how?'

Gennetta shrugged her shoulders. 'Who knows? But I'll await my opportunity.'

Tom was startled and troubled. As she'd unfolded her story he had witnessed a side of her he had never seen before. There was a ruthless belief that some day this desire could be achieved, and he saw her determination to seize every opportunity as it arose. Could her attitude threaten their relationship? Would she, like her father, come to see one goal only at the expense of all other feelings?

He frowned. He had seen what ambition could do when it had taken his father from the east side of the river to better himself on the west side. Then had come disaster, ruin, his father found floating in the river – a suicide. His mother had died of a broken heart two weeks later. At that moment Tom, aged eighteen, had determined to develop his skills as a carver and create and maintain a safe, comfortable way of life, without any of the pressures which had wrecked his family. He had married a girl of like feelings who wanted nothing more than to be a good wife and mother and was content with the security they found together in Henrietta Street.

'And your brother shares your father's attitude?' he asked.

'You've seen evidence of that.' She gave a little snort of disgust.

'He could have acknowledged your work with more enthusiasm. After all, your pieces will most likely fetch the best prices and in all probability bring more requests for your work. He's going to profit by it.'

'Yes, he will, but does it matter? I'm not worried if he doesn't acknowledge me or my work. It's all for the good of the firm, which one day will pay me back!'

They stood watching the *Amelia* meet the first caress of the sea. Her bow cleaved through the dancing waves. She moved a safe distance beyond the coast before turning to head for London.

At that moment Gennetta's eyes were drawn skywards. Birds in a V-formation flew along the coast, heading in the same direction as the ship.

A chill fastened around her heart. 'The Gabriel Hounds!' she whispered. She stared at them, transfixed by their flight.

'What?' Tom's attention was taken from the ship.

'The Gabriel Hounds,' she returned, without taking her eyes off the birds.

He followed her gaze and saw the birds flying steadily just off the coast. 'They're just geese,' he said firmly.

'No. Gabriel Hounds. Listen.' Her voice held a tremor of fright. The cry of the birds reached them.

'That's just normal,' replied Tom quickly, trying to divert her mind from what he guessed she was thinking.

She proved him right when she said, 'Ill omen.' Her thoughts racing, she looked back at the ship then turned to Tom, eyes wide with horror. 'Jack! Something terrible is going to happen to him.' There was a wildness in her voice which threatened to turn into hysterics.

Tom gripped her by the arms. 'Nonsense!' he said forcibly. 'Nothing's going to happen to Jack. I told you, they could be regarded as a good sign if you look at it like that. They could mean Jack is going to be successful at the London Exhibition.'

Gennetta stared at him, drawing reassurance from the look in his eyes. 'I hope so,' she whispered, and found comfort in his strong arms as they watched the *Amelia* sail away from them.

Jack Turner took a stroll around the deck and then leaned on the rail to watch Whitby grow smaller and smaller as the ship cut through the water.

She plied the London route from Whitby regularly with light cargoes and passengers. Her hold was full of butter, pickled fish, potted lobster, hams and flour bound for the dining tables in the capital. She also carried dressed sheepskins and linen, prized by London ladies.

Only six passengers had embarked on this voyage. Jack had passed the time of day with two of them but knew he would have to be more sociable when they dined with the captain that evening. For now he wanted to be alone with his thoughts. Whenever he sailed out of Whitby, he enjoyed these moments alone, looking back at his home town.

Those sailings had been more frequent over the past year as he first explored the possibilities of exhibiting his jet wares, and then confirmed and organized plans to do so at the Great Exhibition, to be held in the enormous glass conservatory designed by Joseph Paxton and built as the Crystal Palace. Jack had seen the possibilities of boosting British trade by the exhibition and did not share the views of critics of the Queen's Consort, Prince Albert, who accused him of meddling in national affairs. Jack believed that Royal sponsorship would give the venture the extra boost it deserved and was determined to make the most of it to enhance Turner's business.

He had kept his plans very close to himself, with only Grace knowing the reasons for his trips to London. He hoped he might be the only jet trader to be exhibiting but had recently heard rumours that the Sleightholmes were going to be there too. But that did not detract from his enthusiasm for he was sure that they would not have the quality pieces that now lay carefully packed in a large bag in his cabin. He inwardly acknowledged that these had been enhanced by the contributions of his sister and Joey, though he would not admit that aloud.

It amused him to think that she was contributing to his wealth while she received a meagre wage and, to fulfil his conditions of employment, had to live in Hacker's Yard. But it was no more than she deserved after going against their father's ambitions to unite the Turner and Sleightholme businesses.

He straightened up from the rail and breathed deep of the salt air. Life was good and an even brighter future beckoned. The business would thrive, expand on the trade from the exhibition, and Grace might still give him a son and heir.

Pleased with the prospects, he took two more turns around the deck before going to his cabin to wash and change for the evening meal. There was no one else on deck. Sailors were tending their chores at the bow and the stern and others were tending the sails to take advantage of any wind. It was these moments he had come to like the best, when he seemed isolated from the world. No one could reach him here. The swish of the sea along the side, the creak of the ropes, the slap of the sails and groan of the timbers, were not intrusions on his narrow world but a part of it, emphasising its confines.

He paused at the door which would take him below deck, breathed deeply, looked around at the gently moving sea, and with a nod of satisfaction went inside.

Jack leaned back contentedly on his chair. The meal had been most enjoyable, the conversation stimulating without being intrusive, and the captain full of good seafaring tales which held his six passengers spellbound.

The gentle motion of the ship began to increase but it had no effect on any of the people round the table. The captain had just passed the port when the *Amelia* rolled even more.

'Excuse me, gentlemen.' He stood up and left the saloon with the businesslike step of a man who liked to be in touch at all times with any changes during the voyage.

The passengers continued to enjoy a feeling of well-being, enhanced by the wine while exchanging news and comment and ignoring the rolling of the ship, coupled now with an extra shudder as its bow dug deeper into the waves.

When the captain returned ten minutes later he was heavily clad in a thick cloth overcoat for protection against the weather. 'Gentlemen, I'm sorry to have left you but regret to report that the wind has increased and a heavy sea is running. The storm is coming from the north-east which does not augur well for a comfortable voyage. I would ask you all to return to your cabins and be prepared for an unpleasant night.'

Comments were exchanged and the concern on some faces brought a hasty reassurance. 'Gentlemen, there is nothing to be alarmed about, but I thought it best to warn you that we could be in for a rough night.'

The passengers hastily drank their port or left it where it was and, bolstered by more confident words from the captain to each of them, hurried to their cabins.

Jack lay down on his bunk fully clothed and soon the sounds of the ship weathering the gathering swell, together with its predictable motion, lulled him to sleep.

He was awakened by a sudden loud knocking at his door. He swung from the bunk, steadied himself against the pitch of the ship and staggered with its roll to the door. Supporting himself with one hand against the wall, he pulled the door open to find the steward there.

'Captain begs to inform you, sir, that due to the heavy weather conditions he is making a run for Yarmouth.'

'Thanks,' returned Jack. 'Much worse, is it?' Even as he put the question he realised how ridiculous it sounded. Repeated shudders were running through the ship as her bow met the heavy seas and she rolled viciously. Only his hold on the door knob prevented him from being thrown across the cabin. When he looked back at the doorway the sailor had gone, his sealegs enabling him to withstand the roll and move on to the next cabin.

Jack closed the door, steadied himself, and as the ship lurched again worked the motion to his advantage to get to his bunk. He gave a little curse as he flopped down on it. This would mean a delay in reaching London. It irritated him that his plans would be thrown out, but it was no killing matter for he had allowed himself an extra couple of days in case there were any snags. But he had hoped to take in the latest play on the London stage and now he might have to forfeit that.

An hour passed, physically the most unpleasant of his life as the *Amelia* battled against the wind and the waves, which seemed determined to spin her to her doom. The gentle swish of water along the side of the ship had been replaced by the pounding of vicious foam-flecked waves. The gentle breeze had turned into a howling wind which shrieked through the rigging like the cry of a ghostly tormentor. Though not a religious man, Jack prayed.

'All hands on deck! Everyone on deck!' The shouts along the gangway held an urgent note. A banging on the door startled Jack with its life-or-death warning. He swung from the bunk and lost his balance as he shrugged himself quickly into his topcoat. He struggled against the heaving ship to regain his feet. He looked round desperately, panic beginning to engulf him. His precious jet! He must save

161

it. The exhibition would be a waste of time if his jet lay at the bottom of the sea. He grabbed his bag just as he was propelled across the cabin to the door. He yanked it open. Water swilled around his feet as he stepped into the gangway. A body, charged with terror, only thinking of self-preservation, pushed past him. Jack staggered, almost fell, but with an overwhelming desire not to lose his jet, kept a tight grip on his bag. He lurched along the gangway with the now unpredictable motion of the ship.

He reached the deck to be met by a scene of frightening violence. The sea ran high, huge waves chasing the ship, crashing over the stern, threatening to swamp her. Dark grey water seemed to be everywhere, merging with a dark grey sky to unite in one element bent on the destruction of the ship. The wind howled in fury, driving the sea at a ship now made even more helpless as with a loud crack the mainmast broke. Alarm filled Jack as he looked up. For one moment the timber seemed to hang in mid-air then slowly it tumbled, dragging rigging with it to crash across the deck.

Through the driving rain and spuming spray he glimpsed men trying to launch boats but it was a hopeless task in such a heavy sea. Huge white-capped towers rolled alongside, carrying the helpless *Amelia* onward at their will. The ship shuddered, her stern beaten down by a monster wave. The bow came out of the water and then, released as the wave broke, plunged into the trough with an impact which seemed to stop the vessel in her tracks. Then she was carried on by the ocean swell.

Desperate, Jack looked for escape but there was none. He was at the mercy of uncontrollable elements. The ship lurched and he was sent scudding across the deck. In the automatic, desperate desire to preserve life, he reached out and grabbed the rail. Gasping for breath as water pounded over him, he hung on grimly. He was aware of no one else. Everyone was fighting their own private battle.

The bow plunged. The ship shuddered as if it had hit a great wall. Every plank and spar protested at the sudden impact. The sea lifted her up, rolled her on and, releasing its hold, let her hit again with a juddering backbreaking smash which tore her heart out and left her stranded, at its mercy, on a treacherous sandbank.

Jack, holding on to the rail with one hand, saw a huge black wave towering above them, the wind whisking its edge into streaming white spray. The monster beat down and down with a great roar, pounding the helpless ship.

His grip was no match for the violence of the impact. His frightened cry was swept away on the wind and the sea took him, one hand still holding on to the bag of jet.

The *Wanderer* slipped quietly out of Yarmouth, her crew thankful that they had been in port when last night's violent storm struck the Norfolk coast. Bound for Whitby and ports to the north, she now carried the sad news of the loss of the Whitby ship *Amelia*.

News of the tragedy had come overland from Cromer. There, the first indication of disaster had been the sighting of flares in the direction of the dreaded Cromer Banks. The lifeboat had put out but, in spite of the bravery and determination of her crew, had been driven back by the dangerous seas around the Banks. There were no sightings of crew or passengers and with the ship breaking up rapidly it was unlikely that anyone had survived. The lifeboat crew had reluctantly turned for home having recovered a piece of flotsam which identified the stricken ship as the *Amelia* of Whitby. With the authorities knowing that the *Wanderer*, at berth in Yarmouth, was bound for Whitby, news had been rapidly relayed to her.

'Look, Davey, the *Wanderer*. Let's go and see her tie up,' called Joey, indicating the ship which was sailing up the Esk towards the bridge.

The two boys were watching the activity on the river from the fish pier, as they often did during their midday break.

'Right, race you!' Davey was off with a shout and a laugh.

They ran off the pier and through the narrow street, past the Shambles and the Market Place, weaving their way through the stream of people going about their business. They glimpsed the vessel passing through the open bridge and ran down Grape Lane, knowing they would reach the quay in time.

They had regained their breath amidst much banter as they watched the *Wanderer* tie up. They were near the gangway when it was run out and the master came ashore and immediately engaged in serious conversation with one of the harbour officials.

Joey caught their exchange as did other nearby folk who immediately sought confirmation that they had heard correctly.

'Aye,' said the captain, 'it's official. The *Amelia* went down with no survivors.'

'Hear that, Davey?' cried Joey. 'Come on!' He started to run.

Davey put an extra spurt to catch him up. 'What's wrong?' he panted.

'*Amelia*'s gone down. Heard missus say Mr Turner was on board, ganning t'London.'

They drove their feet faster. They had important news.

Their sudden eruption into the workshop startled everyone. John

Young scowled angrily but the words which sprang to his lips were stilled by Joey's outburst.

'The *Amelia*'s gone down! On Cromer Banks.'

His immediate exclamation of 'What?' was followed by a stunned silence.

Sensing their disbelief, Joey went on, between gasping for breath, 'It's true, isn't it, Davey?'

'Aye,' nodded the younger boy, his face flushed from the run.

'*Wanderer*'s just in from Yarmouth and brought the news,' Joey added. 'No survivors.'

The foreman's face was grave as he rose from his stool. Without a word, he walked quickly to the sorting room.

'What's wrong?' Gennetta asked when she saw his serious expression.

'Bad news, ma'am,' he replied. His slip into formality surprised her. Something terrible must have happened.

'The *Amelia* has gone down with all hands.'

'No!' Gennetta gasped.

''Fraid so, ma'am. Lost on Cromer Banks. *Wanderer*, just in, brought the news.'

Genetta felt numb. Her immediate emotions were in turmoil. Regret and sorrow were mixed with some measure of relief. Jack would no longer have a hold over her. She could escape the degradation of Hacker's Yard without jeopardising her job. But she had lost her own flesh and blood. Now she had no one. Then one thought shattered the rest – the Gabriel Hounds!

'John, I must go to my sister-in-law.'

He nodded. 'Come back when thee's ready.' He paused, then added as she started for the door, 'And, ma'am, if thee can find out what we should do, we'd be grateful.'

'I will, but I expect it will be to carry on as normal.'

As she entered the workshop the low murmurings between the men ceased. Silence hung over the room like a pall. No one spoke as they watched her leave.

Tom followed her and as she stepped into Church Street, detained her. 'Gennetta, I could tell what you were thinking, but the geese had nothing to do with it.'

'Believe what you will,' she replied, and hurried away.

She made a brief stop at her house in Hacker's Yard to change from her workclothes and inform Rose of what had happened. She said she was going to see Grace and Rose must expect her back when she saw her.

As she hurried through Whitby's streets she shivered at the thought

164

of the Gabriel Hounds. Tom could think what he liked but she knew the associations they had for her.

Before she reached Bagdale, she had controlled her anxiety and begun to wonder what the future held for the Turner business as Grace knew nothing of that side of Jack's life. It must not be lost. Gennetta knew that before long the Sleightholmes would be viewing it with greedy eyes. Her mind churned with possibilities. Had Jack's death come to save her? Could this be the opportunity for her to take repayment for the love her father had denied her? By the time she turned into the garden of Grace's residence she was wondering if Tom's interpretation of the Gabriel Hounds could be right. Maybe they were a sign of good omen – for her.

Chapter Fourteen

When the door was opened by a serious-faced maid whose eyes were red-rimmed, Gennetta knew that the shocking news had reached Grace.

'Mrs Briggs! Thank goodness you're here. Madam is past herself.' The maid indicated the door to the drawing room and, without waiting to be announced, Gennetta went straight in.

She found Grace's personal maid trying to console her distraught mistress who was sitting in a chair to one side of the fireplace, racked with grief. Her slender body heaved with sobs as she dabbed at the tears which flowed constantly down her cheeks.

They both looked up at Gennetta's unheralded entrance. She detected some relief in the maid who realised that here was someone to take over the role of comforter.

'Gennetta!' Grace saw her sister-in-law through a haze of tears. 'What a terrible day!'

As the maid hurried away, Gennetta crossed the room and dropped to her knees beside the chair. She took Grace into her arms and let her weep in the comfort of knowing there was a relation with her.

'Thank you for coming,' she said between sobs.

'I came as soon as I heard.' Gennetta's eyes were dry. Though she felt the loss of a brother, his treatment had hardened her. She felt sorrow but could not weep.

'I wish I had your strength,' moaned Grace.

'It's not strength,' returned Gennetta. 'Weep if that's what you need. It will be best for you. I cannot.'

Grace made no comment. She knew exactly what Gennetta meant and could not blame her.

One Grace had composed herself they had to consider what was to happen.

'It's going to seem strange without a funeral,' said Grace.

'You could have a memorial service?' suggested Gennetta.

'I suppose the vicar will expect it.'

Gennetta saw from her glum expression that she was not altogether happy with the prospect. 'There's no need if you don't want one.'

'It means everything will be dragged up again just when I should be getting used to being without Jack.' Her voice caught at the mention of his name. She tightened her lips, resolving not to burst into another flood of tears.

'Then don't have one.'

'But what will the vicar say? What will people think?' wailed Grace.

'Would you like me to speak to him?' Gennetta suggested.

'Would you?' Grace said with relief.

'You'll have to be prepared for callers,' Gennetta warned.

Grace let out a low moan of despair. 'Oh, please help me with that.' She looked pleadingly at her sister-in-law. 'Please!'

'All right,' Gennetta agreed, though she did not relish the thought of listening to all the praise and eulogies which would pour out from people who did not know the whole truth. 'Would you like me to stay the night?'

Grace brightened. 'Could you?'

'If you would like me to?'

'Oh, yes, and a few days longer until I get settled down.'

'We'll see. Now you should have something to eat.'

'I don't feel like it.'

'You need to keep your strength up. I'll see Cook and arrange something light.' She rose and left the room before Grace could protest any more.

When she returned she sat down in the chair opposite Grace's. 'Cook will have something ready shortly.'

'You'll share it?'

'I thought you wouldn't mind. Then I'll go and get some things for tonight.'

'And for a while longer,' pressed Grace.

'All right.' Gennetta smiled to herself at the relief on her sister-in-law's face. It might just ease the way for what she was about to suggest.

'Grace,' she said seriously, 'I know you won't have given it a thought yet but you must, and the sooner the better. What will you do with the business? It will be yours now.'

She looked aghast. 'It hadn't entered my mind.'

'I'm sorry to mention it, but it's something which is better faced at the outset. I feel sure that there are people in Whitby who'll be

167

wondering what you will do. It would be wisest to have something in mind.'

'I know nothing about it.' Grace threw up her arms in despair. 'Jack ran it. Told me nothing. Not that I wanted to know, it didn't interest me and Jack wouldn't have wanted it.' She shrugged her shoulders. 'I suppose the obvious thing is to sell it.'

'Oh, Grace, you can't do that,' Gennetta protested, her voice quietly persuasive. 'Jack wouldn't want you to. He'd want the business to go on under the Turner name.'

'But I can't run it. No, it will have to be sold.'

'Well, you are the sole owner so it will be up to you to decide.' Though the thought of Turner's going to someone else, most likely the Sleightholmes for she felt sure they would top anyone else's bid, riled her, Gennetta kept her voice level. She did not want to distract Grace from what she was about to say. 'But may I make a suggestion?'

'Yes, do.'

'Well, since I've been working with jet I've learned a lot about the trade. Would you consider letting me run the business as manager?' She was watching Grace closely for her reaction, hoping it would be favourable.

Grace was taken aback by this unexpected suggestion. 'You? But do you know enough? It's a man's world.'

'There's no reason why a woman shouldn't succeed. I could do it.' Gennetta pressed her case with enthusiasm. 'I know the workings of the workshop and feel sure I would have the respect and cooperation of the men after working there. What I don't know, I could soon learn from Jack's book-keeping – the way he kept his accounts, who his customers were and so on. I know he hoped that by displaying at the London Exhibition he would expand the business. That chance might be lost but I could try and salvage something from it.' She saw Grace was pondering her words carefully. 'Jack would want you to keep the business,' she urged. 'I know he would. Whether he would want me to run it is another matter but that decision is now up to you. You would be employing me as a manager and paying me the appropriate wage. I wouldn't want any of the business from you.'

'Then he could have no objection,' Grace said quietly, weighing up the situation with care. She may not have a head for business but at least she could see the pros and cons of situations. At this moment her mind was toying with something which could come out of Gennetta's suggestion, something that would be to her own advantage apart from having the business run for her.

Gennetta read the signs that she had said enough. To press too hard

168

might disrupt the thoughts which were running through Grace's mind.

'Right,' she said, her mind made up, 'I'll employ you as manager of Turner's. I'll expect you to maintain its present income and hopefully to expand.'

'I will, Grace, I will.' Excitement danced in Gennetta's eyes. 'You'll not regret the decision. I'll do all ...' She stopped in midflow as Grace raised her hand.

'There's more,' she cut in. 'My manager cannot live in a place like Hacker's Yard. I expect her to move.'

'But I have nowhere ...'

'You have here.'

Gennetta gaped at her sister-in-law. She swallowed hard. 'You mean, come and live here?'

'Yes, why not? You can bring the children. I'd love having them around. It will be like coming home for you. This house is too big for me alone. It was really too big for Jack and me, but he wanted to live in the family home. It will have a family again if you'll come. And you'll be company for me.'

Speechless, Gennetta stared at Grace. Her mind was in a turmoil at this unexpected offer.

'Well?' Grace gave her a little prompt.

Gennetta started: 'What can I say? This is so unexpected.'

'Say you'll come?' urged Grace.

Gennetta's face lit up with a broad smile. 'Of course I'll come.' She jumped from her seat and hugged her sister-in-law. 'How can I thank you enough? Your generosity means so much to me. To have my children under the same roof as me ... I've missed that so much.' She leaned back and looked hard at Grace. 'You'll never regret it.' She hugged her again before saying, 'I must pay for ...'

'Only contribute to the housekeeping, the rest is ...'

'... part of my wage,' Gennetta finished the sentence.

Grace shook her head. 'No. Over and above your wage. You must get back to your situation as it was before you lost Reuben.'

'You're too kind.' There were tears of joyful appreciation in Gennetta's eyes.

'It will be a good thing for us both,' said Grace. 'I'm sure we'll get on.'

'Just one more thing,' said Gennetta. 'May I bring Rose with me as my personal maid? She has been so good to me since I had to move to Hacker's Yard. I can't leave her there, and she is so fond of the children, she'd love to be back with them.'

'Of course,' Grace readily agreed. 'You must have someone.'

'Then it's all settled?'

169

'Yes.'

They kissed each other on the cheek and sealed their unwritten agreement.

Excited by the prospect of being united with her children again, Gennetta lost no time in making her way to Mrs Shaw's. Her arrival at this time of day surprised them, and when she told them her news they were as excited as she.

'Today, Mama?' cried Nathaniel, jumping up and down, hardly able to contain himself.

Gennetta laughed as she hugged Flora. 'Not today, love. I have things to arrange. Tomorrow.' She glanced at Mrs Shaw's damp eyes. 'Is that all right with you?'

She nodded, trying to muster a smile. 'We'll miss the bairns. We knew we would lose them one day but now it's here ...' Her voice choked.

'We'll visit you,' put in Nathaniel, and ran to her to give her a reassuring hug.

'You'll be welcome any time, love.' She ruffled his hair affectionately and kissed Flora who confirmed her brother's promise.

Gennetta gave her heartfelt thanks to Mrs Shaw and arranged a time to call for her children.

Gennetta made her way back to the east side of the river to collect some belongings, marvelling at the sudden change in her fortunes. From being tied by Jack to an alien life, amidst poverty and degradation, she was now free of it and he, in death, had freed her.

As she and Rose sorted out the belongings they wanted to take with them, a loud knocking on the door interrupted their packing. Rose hurried downstairs to see who demanded entry so insistently. She returned a few moments later to inform Gennetta that Tom Unwin was asking for her.

When she came into the room she saw Tom's eyes were bright with excitement. 'After you left, I suddenly realised what the loss of your brother meant.' His words came fast. 'You're free! He has no hold over you! You need no longer to stay here for fear of losing your job. You can marry me without risking his wrath being turned on me as well.' He grabbed her arms. 'We can get married, Gennetta!'

His enthusiasm slipped slowly into bewilderment when she did not respond as he had expected. He had assumed she would be overjoyed but instead he saw hesitation and doubt in her. 'What is it?' he asked. The puzzled expression in his eyes sought an explanation, pleading for it not to mar the elation which had gripped him.

She turned her head away as if she dare not look into his eyes. She realised how much she was going to hurt him, yet she must. His suggestion was something which, in her concern for Turner's, had never entered her head. Now she realised that naturally it had come to Tom. His reaction emphasised the depth of his love but now, because she had not reacted in the same way, she began to wonder if she could ever match it.

He placed his fingers beneath her chin and slowly turned her head. 'Tell me,' he said gently.

Her eyes were damp as she looked at him, hoping he would understand. 'Tom, I can't, not just yet.'

'What do you mean, not just yet? This is our chance. What are you putting in its way?' His voice began to have an edge on it.

'I'm not putting anything in the way. But I have to have time to see to the business.'

'The business?' He frowned, baffled by her statement.

'I can't let Turner's go! Grace can't run it. She has no knowledge of it. She would sell it and that would mean the Sleighthholmes getting it.' She looked at him desperately. 'I can't let that happen, I just can't. Both Father and Jack would turn in their graves.'

'Then let them,' snapped Tom. 'You owe them nothing.'

'Maybe not, but I can't let the Sleightholmes get it. It's a Turner business and that's what it will always be. Besides, as I told you, it owes me for the father's love I missed. This is my chance.'

'But if the business belongs to your sister-in-law, you've no say in it.'

'I've persuaded her to let me manage it for her.'

'You?' Tom's eyes widened. 'You've put the business before us! Did you never think of the chance which is now ours, no barriers to our marriage? Did our love mean nothing to you?' He half turned away in disgust.

She put out a hand. 'Tom, please try to understand,' she pleaded. 'There's more. Grace has offered a home with her for me and my children.'

'You could have had that with me and you know I'd have welcomed Nathaniel and Flora, but I see now that wouldn't have been good enough for you.' His voice was filled with sarcasm. 'I should have known all along that I wouldn't be right for someone from the other side of the river. I should have dismissed all ideas that Mr Turner's daughter could love me.' He turned for the door.

'Tom, wait!' she cried. 'I need your help.' He stopped and turned round. Hope sprang to her heart. 'You've taught me a lot about the jet business but I'll still need advice. Say you'll give it?'

171

He looked at her coldly for a moment. 'I'll give it because I want to keep my job and not give my boss the chance to sack me and get me out of the way.'

His barbed words tore at her. 'Tom!' she cried, tears springing to her eyes. 'Don't be ...' The crash of the door behind him as he left the house obliterated her words. She stared at the blank wood and let out a low moan. 'Oh, Tom, I do love you.'

Gennetta and Rose settled into their new surroundings that evening, though for Gennetta it was like stepping back in time and for a while it seemed as if she had never left home. But she was reminded of the intervening time the next morning when she brought Nathaniel and Flora to the house in Bagdale.

They were delighted to be living with Aunt Grace in a big house where they each could have a room of their own and a garden to play in. And they were more than pleased to have Rose with them again.

Once they had settled in and had cajoled Rose into taking them to the sands, Gennetta sought Grace's permission to examine the books and documents relating to the firm. The first bunch of letters she examined revealed what had been occupying her brother's time prior to his sailing. They referred to the Great Exhibition and when she studied the arrangements he had made, she realised that there was still time to take advantage of them. Excitement gripped her as a plan began to form in her mind.

It was still enthusing her when she hurried to the workshop that afternoon. She had dressed smartly, but not showily. She did not want to overdo the transition from the working clothes the men had been used to seeing her in. She wore a woollen day dress of simple cut falling from a drawn-in waist with only a slight flare. She had chosen one with a high neck around which was a piece of blue lace, the colour matching the pale blue stripes alternating with red in her dress. A red shawl draped her shoulders and was accompanied by a matching bonnet.

When she arrived at the workshop she found that work was going on as normal and expressed her gratitude to John Young when he came to her on seeing her enter the building. She added, 'I'd like to say something to everyone.'

He called the men into a group and from their exchange of expressions with one another she knew they were commenting on her appearance and wondering what had brought about this change in the woman who but yesterday was working alongside them.

'I've talked with my sister-in-law who is shattered by this terrible blow. I knew you would all be anxious to know about your jobs so

172

let me reassure you that they are safe. The workshop will continue to operate as it has always done.'

Murmurs of satisfaction ran through the men. When these subsided she continued, 'Mrs Turner knows nothing about the business and has appointed me as manager.' Low comments were exchanged and some eyebrows raised but they all realised that Gennetta, having worked among them, was not a novice, though whether she had the ability to run the business as her brother had done they did not know. 'I want you all to carry on as you have always done. Mr Young will remain as foreman and Mr Unwin as under-foreman.' She glanced at Tom as she mentioned his name but he avoided her eye. 'I want to make this the most successful firm in Whitby and I am sure you'll all help me do this. Thank you.'

The men, talking amongst themselves, went back to their work.

'John,' Gennetta turned to the foreman, 'as you know, my brother was going to display our jet at the London Exhibition. I've been through his papers and now know what his arrangements were. I see no reason why we cannot continue. We will be late taking up our stand but that can't be helped. What we need as quickly as possible are pieces suitable for display.' Her enthusiasm was catching. 'We will make a selection from what we have left and get some more ready between now and sailing. I want you to come with me.'

His eyes widened at the suggestion. 'But, ma'am, I've never been out of Whitby.'

'Nor have I.' Gennetta smiled. 'It will be a new venture for both of us.'

'Take someone younger. Tom, maybe.'

As much as she would have liked that, she deemed it prudent not to do so after their disagreement. 'You have more experience of jet and that will be invaluable in dealing with customers. I want you to come.'

John lifted his hands in surrender and raised his eyes as he said, 'What will the missus say, me ganning to London?'

'We'll take her with us, John. All expenses on the firm.'

He could not hide his surprise at this change of outlook. Jack would never have countenanced such an expense.

Gennetta guessed what he was thinking. 'A new broom, John, but it's all for the good of the firm. It's settled then?'

He nodded.

'Good. I'll have a word with Tom. He'll be in charge while we are away. Then we'll choose some pieces to take with us.'

The foreman crossed the floor to Tom who was busy carving a locket. A brief word passed between them. Tom laid down his

173

carving tool and jet and rose from the bench. He showed no emotion when he reached Gennetta. She felt chilled. He was treating her as if she was a stranger. She met his cool stare.

'Tom, I want you to take charge when John and I go to the Great Exhibition in London.'

For one brief second she saw surprise flicker in his eyes then it was gone. 'Yes, ma'am,' he replied in a voice which merely accepted her statement. He started to turn away.

'Tom,' she said quietly, detaining him.

'Yes, ma'am?' He spoke as an employee, as if there had never been anything between them. It stabbed her to the heart.

'Please, Tom, don't be like this. I need your support in what I want to do.'

'You have it, ma'am. After all, I am employed by you and as such you have my full support.' The indifference in his attitude, signifying an end to their friendship, hurt. He moved away and this time she did not stop him.

A dampness filmed her eyes but she checked her tears. She must not let her emotion show before the men. She pulled herself together and crossed the floor with a purposeful stride to engage John in choosing the best of the jet pieces. When they had done so and she was leaving the workshop, she stopped to have a word with Joey and Davey.

'That's coming along,' she commented, admiring some gulls flying low over waves which were taking shape on Joey's piece of jet. 'And yours, Davey.' She bent to take a closer look at the bold lines of the inventive pattern. 'Keep at it, I need some more to take to London.'

Joey's eyes widened. 'Thee ganning t'London, missus?'

'Yes.'

'What about our lessons?' His expression switched from one of surprise to concern, as if the whole future had taken on a sombre, uncertain quality.

'We'll see, Joey, when I get back. We may have to make other arrangements.'

'But nobody can teach us like thee,' he protested.

She smiled, appreciating his faith in her. 'Oh, I'll teach you, but the lessons may not be as frequent and you may have to come to Mrs Turner's house in Bagdale.'

'Does that mean you won't be coming to us in Henrietta Street any more?' queried Davey in a voice filled with disappointment. His father had told him last night that this might be so.

She smiled wanly. 'We shall see.' To prevent any more questions

174

she called John over. 'Let's go and see Mrs Young and persuade her to come to London with you.'

Once that was achieved by no little persuasion, for Mrs Young imagined London to be a teeming bed of iniquity, Gennetta found that she was able to book passage on the *Majestic*, sailing in three days' time.

Chapter Fifteen

The *Swan* bound for Whitby from London, was nearing its destination. She had enjoyed a voyage on calm seas, the slight swell lending a gentle motion to the ship. The weather was fine, the breeze right. Altogether there was an air of well-being about her.

On deck, enjoying the tang of the salt air, Gennetta had that same feeling. Her two weeks at the Great Exhibition had been profitable. Their jet had attracted attention, sold well, and resulted in more orders, especially from two of London's leading jewellers who expressed a desire to continue purchasing after the exhibition closed.

Though the stand obtained by her brother had been for only a fortnight, she had negotiated to display for a further four weeks, split into two separate periods, one to coincide with the closure of the exhibition.

Flamborough Head was falling away behind when she turned to see John Young and his wife come on deck.

'Soon be off Scarborough and then not long before we see home,' she informed them as they joined her.

'That'll be a right pleasure, ma'am,' said Mrs Young. She huddled deeper into her plain brown three-quarter-length coat with its wide collar.

'I hope that doesn't mean you haven't enjoyed the visit to London, Emma?' said Gennetta, showing concern. 'And that you will consider my offer to accompany us on our next two visits?'

'I wasn't too happy about coming, especially on all this water, but I enjoyed it. But it'll be nice to be home again after all that crowding and bustling in London.' Emma had taken to the voyage as if she had been born to the sea. She suffered no ill effects and had expressed sorrow when the voyage was over. Gennetta had enjoyed her company and had no qualms about suggesting that she should help them at the exhibition. Emma had worn necklaces and brooches, showing them off to their best advantage to possible customers. She seemed to derive pleasure and satisfaction from this new role and now confirmed it by saying, 'I'll be delighted to help thee again, ma'am, if that's what thee wants?'

'Good, then that's settled,' beamed Gennetta. 'Happy about it, John?' she asked, turning to her foreman.

'Aye,' he replied. 'Thee's created a demand I never expected. Folk were so enthusiastic for our jet. More than they were for Sleightholme's, from what I heard when I nosed around their stand.'

'Good. We'll consolidate our position on our next two visits now we know the type of thing the customers want. Now,' she added, dismissing all talk of business, 'let's enjoy our sail into Whitby.'

The workmen were pleased at the success of the first visit to the London Exhibition and worked with a renewed interest and vigour to have as much jet as possible for the next two visits.

Four days after her return, when Gennetta visited the workshop, she was confronted by Joey. All the men had left work. He asked, in the presence of just Tom and Davey, 'Missus, are we going to have any more lessons?'

'Yes, some time, but I'm so busy at the moment.' She saw the disappointment on his face and immediately regretted the offhand way in which she had answered him. 'All right,' she added quickly, to try to rectify the situation, 'we'll have one tomorrow evening, and then make arrangements as we go along. I can't have them every evening. And you'll have to come to Mrs Turner's in Bagdale.'

Pleased that the lessons were to resume, he was nevertheless disappointed that they were to be less frequent. 'Yes, missus.'

Gennetta glanced at Tom for confirmation that this arrangement would be all right for him.

'Sorry, Davey won't be able to come,' he said tightly.

Gennetta was taken aback by the refusal.

'Why, Pa?' his son asked plaintively.

'Because I say so. Now wait for me outside. You too, Joey.' The stern look he gave his son brooked no argument.

Davey's lips trembled. The disappointment which welled inside him was almost too much to bear, but he fought down the tears which threatened. He was now in a man's world and men don't cry. He looked at Joey who put one arm around his shoulders as they left the building.

Gennetta glared at Tom. 'Why?' she demanded. 'Look what you're doing to the boy.'

He met her gaze. 'I'm not having my son seeing the likes of life in

Bagdale. It will only give him ideas that cannot be fulfilled. He'll see things and want things that I cannot give him.'

'Rubbish! The boy's sensible. What's wrong with seeing another side of life?'

'It'll make him dissatisfied.'

'Could give him the ambition to achieve it.'

'And take him from me.'

'He'd never desert you.'

'You did.'

Gennetta tossed her head. 'So that's it, Tom Unwin, you're taking it out on the boy because you couldn't understand or accept my reasons.'

'You thought more of this business than of me. You saw it could take you back to the old life you were used to and I had no part in that.'

'That's not true!'

'How could I ever be a part of it? No, Gennetta, if you'd really loved me, you'd have accepted my way of life.'

'And what do you think would have happened to all this?' She cast her glance over the shop. 'It would have gone to the Sleightholmes and more than likely some jobs would have been lost, maybe even yours.'

'So now you're putting yourself up as a saviour?' He gave a snort. 'You did it for your own selfish reasons – a return to luxury on the other side of the river.'

The contempt in his eyes pierced her heart. She knew nothing she could say would convince him.

'Don't destroy your son,' she said quietly, hoping it might make him see reason, at least about allowing Davey to resume the lessons.

'If anyone destroys him, it will be you.' Tom's words were meant to hurt. 'He looked forward to your visits. To him you were like the mother he lost.' His voice tightened. 'If anyone is to blame it's you! But you wouldn't sacrifice your own wants. Mind they don't ruin you.' He swung on his heel and strode quickly from the building.

Shocked by the severity of his tone and the contempt in his eyes, Gennetta felt drained. She could not raise her voice to stop him, to tell him that he was wrong, that she loved Davey, that she loved him. Then the pain of his words hit home. It shot through her like a thousand arrows, numbing every other feeling. Exhaustion dragged at her and she sank on to a stool beside the bench. Thought did not exist. In its place was an empty void. It remained like that until the squeak of the door made her aware of her surroundings again.

It moved slowly and she saw Joey step inside. He closed the door

178

behind him so that it clicked quietly into place. He walked towards her as if he had no right to intrude and yet needed to.

She did not speak but watched him, a boy with nothing in life who had befriended her. He still had little but he did have a natural talent which she had been pleased to discover and nurture. At least she could go on doing that.

He stopped in front of her, his face glum.

He said quietly, 'Missus, I won't be coming for lessons if Davey isn't.'

He did not wait for her to speak but stepped past her and went to the sorting room. The enormity of what had happened pressed down on her like a huge fist. Had she sacrificed happiness for the business? But this was the Turner business. There was no other like it. She was beginning to understand why it had obsessed her father. Now it was taking hold on her, but she would make it pay for the love she had lost and it would keep her in the life she once knew, never again to suffer Hacker's Yard. She could not throw away that chance. She must go on.

Gennetta threw herself into her work with renewed vigour. She recognised that, apart from attempting to further the business, this was an attempt to purge herself of the attitude of Tom and the boys. Besides dealing with all the paperwork – letters, bills and orders – she was a frequent visitor to the workshop, selecting and planning with her foreman what to take to the London Exhibition on her next two visits. Tom and the two boys kept out of her way.

She had settled well with Grace. They were compatible and fond of each other and, though neither voiced it, both realised that their relationship had been prevented from blossoming by Jack's intransigent attitude to his sister.

It was a joy to have her children with her, to be able to show them love and guide their lives. But when Gennetta played with them, enjoyed their company and listened to their chatter, which at times seemed to be endless, she felt the loss of her former close contact with Joey and Davey.

Whenever she visited the workshop she received nothing but polite coldness from them. Still she made suggestions when examining their work, and though they only replied in dull monosyllables, appearing to ignore what she was saying she noticed that what she said was acted upon.

She realised that their attitude grew out of Tom's, for he remained distant and cold, keeping conversation purely to his work, without any hint of enthusiasm for her presence. He had become a stranger

179

and, though she knew the real Tom was still there, it pained her to feel the gap between them widening.

But the business demanded her attention and she realised that if her next two visits to London were as successful as the first then the Turner trade would flourish. Gennetta knew that Grace had liked the luxury provided by Jack and was determined to go on providing it for her and become indispensable. In that success she saw her own security and a resumption of the life she had always known on the west bank of the river.

She was elated on her return from London after the closure of the exhibition. Queen Victoria, on one of her frequent visits, had visited Turner's stand. She had showed a great interest in the jet and, surprised to find a female in charge, had questioned Gennetta about it and the jet trade before buying some pieces which Gennetta recognised as being by Tom and Joey. They would be delighted at the news.

She wanted her workers to share in the success as soon as possible and immediately on landing made her way, with John Young, to the workshop on Church Street.

She called the men around her so she could address them from the doorstep.

'We have had a very successful visit to the exhibition. We have received several good orders and numerous enquiries, but most important of all – we sold some pieces to the Queen.' An excited murmur ran through the group. 'And this, of course, has led to orders from the Queen's jewellers. When that becomes more widely known, I'm sure it will mean more work for us all. The business is thriving, thanks to you.' She gave them the rest of the day off work.

As they were leaving she asked Tom, Davey and Joey to stay behind. They waited uneasily until the last man had gone.

'I thought it wisest not to announce to everyone whose pieces the Queen bought, but I thought you would like to know that it was yours, Tom, and yours, Joey.' She saw a flicker of excitement in Tom before he masked it.

'The Queen has one of mine?' Joey gasped in wide-eyed amazement.

'Yes, she has,' smiled Gennetta.

'What about that, Davey?' Joey turned to his friend.

The youngster gave him a dig with his fist. 'Congratulations, Joey!'

'I'm sure she'll go on buying jet,' said Gennetta, 'so some day she'll be buying yours, Davey.'

'Of course she will,' cried Joey, wrestling with Davey in his

180

excitement over what had happened. Davey broke free and ran off with Joey in chase.

'And that'll be putting more money into your pocket,' commented Tom, keeping his voice low but audible enough for her to catch the words. 'Keeping you in luxury across the other side of the river.'

'Keeping money in the firm so that it thrives and keeps you in work,' she replied testily, anger at Tom's attitude rising. 'And what's wrong with wanting to live on the west bank? The town's expanding, there's more space over there. Have you no desire for a better life?'

'Henrietta Street is all right,' he retorted tightly, annoyed by what he took to be her criticism.

'Yes, it is,' she agreed, 'it's better than a lot in Whitby. But don't you have any ambition?'

'If I'm content and Davey's happy that's all that matters,' he replied.

'But you could be better placed, give him a chance to see a better life.'

'And that could ruin him,' Tom snapped, irritated by her attitude which he saw as meddling. 'Look what it did to us. You could have been content with me. We were happy until you saw a way of returning to your old life. Why you wanted to go back, I'll never know. It hadn't brought you any happiness.'

Gennetta bristled. Her eyes narrowed with fury. 'Don't you question my life with Reuben. I *was* happy with him. The other side of the river does not necessarily bring unhappiness, just as this side doesn't guarantee it.'

'You'd have been happy with us but you had big ideas.' His voice ran on, his thoughts out of control. There was a stinging hurt in his words. 'A woman's place is not running a business. That's men's work. You should be at home tending ...'

'So that's the sort of life I would have had with you, kitchen sink and bed? Well, I'm glad I escaped, Tom Unwin.' She pushed past him and was out of the building without another word.

He watched her with cold eyes but as the door slammed recognised a yearning within him which wanted their relationship to be restored. But he would not humble himself to go after her.

'We did well at the exhibition, but not well enough,' growled Robert Sleightholme, standing with his back to the fire. There was annoyance in the way he drew on his cigar. He looked at his son who was sitting in a wing-back chair to one side of the fireplace, a glass of Madeira in his hand. 'Let me tell thee, jet will be very fashionable now the Queen has bought some.'

181

'You know who she bought it from?' Cyrus asked casually.

'No?' Robert looked at his son curiously for he detected knowledge behind the question.

'Turner's.'

'What!' Robert's face went red at the news. His temper exploded like a volcano. He plucked the cigar from his mouth, swivelled round and hurled it into the fire. 'Damn!' He faced Cyrus again and poked a finger at him to emphasise his words. 'That should have been us. How the hell did they manage it?'

'Exceptional pieces, I'm told, though I did not see them. But I have no doubt Gennetta used her charms.'

'Women! Meddling in things that don't concern them.' Robert's mouth tightened with exasperation. 'If she hadn't interfered, Grace Turner would have sold the business and I'd have got it.'

'It's never too late,' replied Cyrus casually, unmoved by his father's near apoplexy.

'What's thee getting at?' Robert, knowing his son could be a schemer, eyed him closely.

Cyrus smiled slyly. 'Gennetta's only managing the firm, she has no share in it. The firm belongs solely to Grace.'

'So?'

'I could marry Grace. Her period of mourning is over.'

For a brief moment Robert examined the implications behind the statement. 'Thee conniving devil,' he chuckled finally, deep in his throat, relishing what this could mean. 'But how do thee know she'll have thee?'

'Ah.' Cyrus gave a knowing look. 'The Sleightholme charm and my persuasive powers. Don't underestimate me, Father.'

Robert stiffened. Doubt clouded his face. 'Wait a minute. I want a grandson, an heir to the business. Grace can't have children.'

'That's only your assumption. It was generally thought that was the case, but don't forget she did become pregnant, only to lose the child when she fell. Remember?'

Robert nodded and looked thoughtful. 'So thee think there's every chance she might ... again?'

Cyrus spread his hands. 'Why not?'

'Why not?' repeated Robert with a grin.

Cyrus smiled and raised his glass to his father. Robert took another cigar from his case with a satisfied air.

Cyrus laid his plans carefully, first hinting to his mother that they should have a few friends for dinner round about Christmas and use it as an occasion to bring Grace back into society after her period of mourning.

182

'We'll have to include Gennetta. After all, she is living with Grace,' his mother pointed out.

'It will do her good too after the traumatic experience of being forced to live in Hacker's Yard,' he agreed amiably.

'I'll never understand how Jack could do that,' said his mother with a shake of her head.

Cyrus made no comment but directed her thoughts back to the guest list.

Two days later the sisters-in-law opened their invitations.

'Splendid!' cried Grace with delight when she read the neatly written card. She had grown tired of leading the life of a mourning widow. Now she could resume the tea parties at which she could exchange Whitby gossip.

Gennetta, while commenting favourably so as not to upset Grace, viewed the invitation sceptically. She sensed Cyrus working behind his mother's invitation. If that was so, had he some ulterior motive for inviting her? After all, since she'd turned down his marriage proposal they had not exactly been friends, and by walking out on her father to marry Reuben she had severed the friendly relationship between the two families.

'How exciting it will be, Gen! We must get new dresses. We can enjoy shopping together. You've been working so hard, you must take a day off.'

'But ...' she started to protest.

Grace raised her hand and gave a little shake of her head. 'I won't listen to any objection. You must come with me.' She gave a slight smile accompanied by a teasing chuckle. 'And that's your employer speaking.'

'All right. I give in.' Gennetta gestured surrender. She realised that she had been working extra hard and had given no thought to her own pleasure except for the time she spent with the children. It would be nice to choose new clothes, spend time getting ready and then enjoying good food at leisure while relaxing in pleasant company, though she was still suspicious of Cyrus.

'What a beautiful evening,' commented Grace as they stepped outside for the short walk to the Sleightholmes' house.

'It really is,' agreed Gennetta. She breathed deeply, enjoying the cold feeling as she drew crisp air into her lungs. Myriads of diamonds pricked the heavens and the moon bathed Whitby roof-tops with a silvery sheen. The still night seemed to hold the world suspended in time. Gennetta loved such nights for at this time of the year they seemed to herald the peace of Christmas.

They picked their way briskly to the Sleightholmes' house and when the door was opened to their knock an atmosphere of well-being flowed out to embrace them. Stepping from the cold into the warmth, to be greeted by Robert and Maud with jovial remarks, they were promised a pleasant evening.

As the maids took her calf-length cape, bonnet and gloves, Gennetta felt sure she was going to enjoy herself. It was good to be experiencing such times again. She had done so when her father entertained and when she accompanied him to friends, and again with Reuben when he was in port. Only now did she realise how she had missed the relaxation, the chatter and social contact. She had seen her father turn them to his own advantage to further his business. Maybe she could do the same. She must be alert for such chances, for she felt sure more invitations would follow this one and that Grace would be organising similar evenings now that she was out of mourning.

'What a beautiful dress!' exclaimed Maud with raised eyebrows as she stepped back to admire Grace's dress of pink silk muslin with pink and white stripes cascading into three wide frills. The pointed waistline accentuated her slim waist and the sweeping width of the skirt. The neckline dropped slightly from the top of her shoulders and was trimmed with net and lace which merged into the short sleeves. Her hair, which she had waved slightly, was drawn back into a neat bun at the nape of her neck and decorated with a pink bow.

'Oh, Gennetta and I had such a pleasant time choosing them. Isn't Gen's simply exquisite?' replied Grace, directing attention to her.

'Simply delightful, my dear,' Maud exclaimed with marked admiration of the white silk dress with its large striking pattern of red roses. The pointed bodice came tight to the waist and left Gennetta's shoulders bare. The three-quarter sleeves were pleated to match the skirt. She had drawn her fair hair to the top of her head and banded it in such a way that it was allowed to tumble down to the back of her neck. 'And I do like your hair style, but you have such beautiful hair to manage. Don't you think so, Robert?'

Her husband, who had been standing by enjoying seeing the ladies admire each other, bowed slightly as he said, 'Delightful to have such beauty in my house. Now come along, warm punch and the other guests await you.' He ushered them into the large drawing room, amply lit by oil lamps nestling in brackets around the walls. 'I think you know everyone,' he announced, drawing attention to the new arrivals.

Cyrus detached himself from a group and came to them. 'You look exquisite,' he said as he bowed to Gennetta, his smile warm and friendly.

'Thank you.' She inclined her head in acknowledgement, thinking to herself that such words could not have been put to her on their last meeting in Church Street.

'And you, Mrs Turner.' His eyes held hers in a way they had never done before.

Grace felt a little shiver of pleasure run down her spine. 'Grace, please.'

He bowed his acknowledgement. 'Come, a glass of warming punch?' He led the way to a side table where he ladled two cups of steaming punch.

Grace and Gennetta turned to mingle with the guests. As they did so Cornelius Mitchell excused himself from the young lady to whom he was talking and came up.

'Ah, Mrs Briggs, it is good to see you again and in more propitious circumstances,' he said smoothly, his head nodding up and down as if he was agreeing with himself.

'I survived,' replied Gennetta without emotion.

'I was sorry the way things turned out, but I had to do the best for my client.' He spread his hands and hunched his shoulders in a gesture of regret.

Gennetta sensed he was just making contact without any real meaning behind his words. 'Think nothing of it, Mr Mitchell. It's over and done with, and maybe I gained something from the experience.'

'Well, you're back where you belong, this side of the river.'

She cocked an eyebrow at him. 'Do I, Mr Mitchell? Do I?'

'Of course you do.' He tried to sound emphatic and threw up his arms in mock horror that she should think otherwise. 'From what I hear you are making a success of the business. Mrs Turner is fortunate to have you. If there's anything I can do for you, let me know. Miss Briggs thought highly of my services.'

'Thank you. I will remember.' She glanced around, seeking an escape. 'Now, if you will excuse me, I must have a word with Mrs Sleightholme.'

'Of course.' He bowed and stepped to one side to let her pass.

Relieved, Gennetta eagerly fell into conversation with her hostess.

The evening passed pleasantly for her after that. She enjoyed stimulating talk and a meal the like of which she had not experienced in a long time. She savoured the soup rather than the oysters and followed it with goose served with an excellent green sauce in which green wheat, gooseberries and melted butter had been blended to perfection. She chose that in preference to the succulent sirloin of beef which stood invitingly alongside it on a long sideboard. This feast was served with a smooth tangy wine which stimulated the palate.

When the servants cleared the main course and started to load the table, which seated sixteen people comfortably, with jellies, fruit pies, cakes and sweetmeats she thought of Joey and wondered what he and Davey, and for that matter Tom, would have made of all this.

Tom ... She thought of him with regret for what had come between them. She wished that they were still friends and that he could have understood and accepted the reason for the course she had taken. Someday he might see she was right but then it could be too late to restore their happy relationship.

'Gennetta! Where were you?' Cyrus's voice made her start.

Embarrassed, she glanced along the table. 'Oh, I'm sorry, I was miles away. You were saying?'

'Share your thoughts?' someone called.

Other voices lent support to this prompting.

She laughed. 'Oh, no, I couldn't.'

'Where were you, at least tell us that much?' cried Grace, not to be denied some information.

'No further than Whitby,' she replied, then added quickly to stop any more enquiries, 'You were saying, Cyrus?' She turned to him, seeking relief.

His lips twitched with amusement at her dilemma. 'We were saying that your visit to the London Exhibition was successful. No doubt those Southerners were surprised to see a lady in such prominence on your stand.'

Gennetta rose to his observation and the topic continued throughout the rest of the meal.

'I enjoyed that,' remarked Grace after they had said goodbye to Cyrus who had insisted on escorting them home. 'It was good to be out and about again, and I mean no disrespect to Jack.'

'I'm sure you don't,' agreed Gennetta. 'Though you may not forget the dead, you cannot go on mourning forever. You have a life to lead.'

'I'm pleased to hear you say that,' said Grace giving her sister-in-law a hug. 'We must give some dinner parties ourselves.'

They made for the stairs and, after they had said good night, Gennetta slipped into the children's bedrooms and, with all the love she had for them, gave them a silent goodnight, moved by their peaceful expressions. She hoped she could keep life so for them. To this end she resolved to make sure the business prospered.

* * *

Over the succeeding months she threw herself into advancing the firm. She found new outlets for jet locally, improved the deal with the jet miners in her favour, made savings in production, and by visiting London to keep personal contact with the jewellers she had met at the exhibition, increased their orders for her products. Recognising the exceptional talent which had gone into some of the jet pieces, they insisted that those particular workers should supply more. This put more work on Gennetta herself as she was determined to keep her hand in at etching, something she enjoyed. Time became precious and though she wanted to re-establish the lessons for the two boys on a twice-weekly basis, it was only by holding them at Bagdale that she could give the time. Tom still refused his permission for this arrangement, so all she could do was to give them the occasional hint and direction when she examined their work at the workshop.

Occupied as she was, she had little time for socialising and was never part of the tea parties which brought Grace into contact with the ladies of Whitby society. But Grace insisted that Gennetta should have some relaxation so she attended the dinner parties which her sister-in-law organised and often accompanied her when invitations took them to the houses of merchants, shipowners, shipbuilders, and all those engaged in reaping the benefit of Whitby's prosperous trades.

Some time later she became aware that Cyrus was seldom missing from these events and that he was very attentive to Grace. At first Gennetta put it down to polite socialising, for he was always pleasant to her too at such times. It was only after Rose had made an innocent remark that Mr Sleightholme was becoming a frequent visitor to Grace's residence, particularly when Gennetta was out, that she began to wonder about his intentions.

She brought the matter up one evening after the children had gone to bed and she and Grace were relaxing in the drawing room.

'You seem to be seeing a lot of Cyrus these days, Grace,' she remarked casually. 'And he's always very attentive when we meet socially.'

'Yes,' Grace agreed brightly. 'I find him very pleasant to be with. And he's so considerate. You may not be aware, you're so busy, but we've been out several times together, taking meals at places outside Whitby where he is known. They have been very pleasant occasions.'

Gennetta noted the emphasis on the word 'very'. 'I'm pleased for you,' she replied, 'but can I give you a word of warning?' She fixed serious eyes on Grace. 'Be sure he has no ulterior motive. The Sleightholmes have always had their eyes on Turner's.'

Grace was taken aback by the insinuation behind these words.

187

'Nonsense,' she said indignantly. 'Cyrus never mentions the business. He's shown no interest in it even when I say how well you are doing.'

'That's when he's at his most dangerous.'

'Dangerous?' Grace gave a little laugh. 'You think I'm naive?' she said indignantly. 'He isn't concerned at all about our business.'

'You be careful, Grace. Don't let him fool you. Be on your guard.'

'I've nothing to guard against.' Her eyes flared as she added, 'It's all in your mind. Maybe you're jealous because he's paying more attention to me than you.'

'What?' Gennetta screwed up her face in disgust. 'I wouldn't want him to, not ever.'

'Then don't criticise me,' snapped Grace.

'I'm *not* criticising.'

'You are. Your so-called warning is an oblique criticism of what I'm doing.' Grace stood up and glared down at Gennetta. 'It's my life and I'll live it as I want, so don't impose your ill-found opinions on me.' She tossed her head and swept from the room.

Gennetta sighed with regret at upsetting her sister-in-law, and with it came worry, for she detected in Grace's attitude either infatuation or love and either could be dangerous. What she had thought of as stability could be precarious, based as it was on Grace's generosity.

Chapter Sixteen

Gennetta realised, with trepidation, that Grace's relationship with Cyrus was becoming serious. She felt helpless to avert what she saw as a disaster.

Each time she pointed out the danger behind his attentions, Grace would have none of it. She found Cyrus charming and attentive, as Gennetta knew he could be, and insisted that there was nothing devious about him. Gennetta saw that Grace was besotted and at times behaved like a love-sick girl.

She tried all sorts of ways to make her sister-in-law see reason. She employed subtlety and outright warnings but each time it only led to fierce arguments. Grace would not be moved. Gennetta became aware that if she continued to criticise Cyrus, she could put her own position in jeopardy. Her sister-in-law had been only too ready to point that out during their last altercation.

'Remember this, Gennetta, you are here thanks to my generosity. Don't abuse it.' Her words were cold, her attitude haughty. 'You might find yourself out of a job with nowhere to live, otherwise.'

Although taken aback by the threat, Gennetta spoke out. 'And you remember, I've worked hard for your firm. It's prospering as it has never done, and that benefits you. Don't let Cyrus take it away from you.'

'What I do with the firm and my life is my affair,' replied Grace testily.

Gennetta was stunned. The enormity of the statement almost overwhelmed her, but she summoned the strength to hit back. 'Don't you ever let the Sleightholmes get their hands on what my father, my brother – your husband, might I remind you – and I have built into the most important jet firm in Whitby. Let Cyrus run it and he'll ruin it. He has little business sense. For it to survive it would need his father behind him and that would mean they'd want full control. I'd fight before that happened.'

'You might fight in vain. What I do, I do for my own good and you can't stop me!' replied Grace, angry determination flashing in her eyes.

All Gennetta could hope for was something to trigger a change of mind. Though she did not see that materialising it still came as something of a shock when Grace, returning from an afternoon with Cyrus, was deliriously happy to announce, 'I'm to marry him next month!'

'Grace! You can't!' All Gennetta's dismay and fear were evident.

Grace looked hurt. 'Oh, Gen, please don't rake up all your old arguments. Do be happy for me.'

Gennetta was cold with anger at what she saw as a betrayal of the Turners' ambitions but could not deny the pleading tilt of Grace's head, the pouting lips and troubled expression. Remorseful that she could hurt Grace at this moment, she came to her and hugged her. 'If that's what you want then I'll say no more.' She kissed her on both cheeks. 'I hope you'll be happy.' Though her tone had a genuine ring to it, her mind held doubts.

Grace smiled. 'Thanks, Gennetta, I'd hoped you'd give me your blessing. Now as regards the business, Cyrus assures me that he has no interest in it, so you can go on running it for me in your own way.'

Though she made no comment, Gennetta regarded Cyrus's attitude with the gravest suspicion. She had no doubt that some time in the future he would be more than interested.

'Where will you live when you're married?' she asked, needing to be clear on her position.

'Here,' replied Grace.

'Then you'll want me to move?'

'Well ... I'm sorry ...' Grace looked regretful.

'That's all right. It's what I expected.' Her voice held no malice.

'Thank you for understanding. I'll help you find a pleasant residence, a gift for what you are doing for the firm.'

'That's kind of you,' replied Gennetta, genuinely touched by the offer.

Two days later, thanks to Grace's generosity, Gennetta made her way to see Cornelius Mitchell. Even though she did not particularly like the man, she thought he might be keen to help and make amends for his attitude after Reuben's murder now that money was no problem.

Recognising her, Benjamin fussed as he showed her into his employer's office.

'Ah, Mrs Briggs, it is a pleasure to see you.' Cornelius came quickly from his desk to greet her. He shook her hand with a limp grip and ushered her into an armchair at one side of his desk. He turned his own chair to face her and sat down. 'I don't expect this is a social call.' He gave a little chuckle. 'So how can I be of service to you?' He reached out and drew a notepad and pencil to him.

'I want to buy a house,' she stated.

He gave a harsh little cough as he raised his eyebrows at this unexpected announcement.

She noted his surprise and added, 'You will hear soon enough, if you have not already done so – my sister-in-law is to marry Cyrus Sleightholme, and as they will be using her house as their home, I will have to leave.'

'My dear,' he replied smoothly, 'your reasons don't concern me.'

Gennetta smiled to herself. You hypocrite, she thought, you love a bit of gossip.

'How soon will you require one?' he asked, covering his mouth as a cough racked his chest. 'Pardon me,' he apologised.

Gennetta acknowledged his concern with a slight nod. 'As soon as possible,' she replied.

'Any particular area in mind?'

'The west side of the river. Oh, nothing like New Buildings or Bagdale. Something a bit more modest than those, but it must be well-appointed, comfortable and pleasantly situated.'

Cornelius nodded thoughtfully. 'I might know of the very thing but I don't think it will be available for two weeks.' He riffled through some papers as he searched for the one he wanted. His breath came sharply and he broke into a fit of coughing, causing him to drag a large handkerchief from his pocket and hastily put it to his mouth. He gasped for breath as the coughing stopped. 'I'm so terribly sorry,' he muttered, his face showing lines of exhaustion.

'Are you all right, Mr Mitchell?' Gennetta asked with concern. 'Should I get your clerk?'

Cornelius shook his hand, dismissing her suggestion. 'No. Nincompoop wouldn't know what to do.' He swallowed hard, then having regained his breath, returned his attention to the papers. 'Ah, here we are.' He held up a sheet of paper triumphantly then laid it down in front of him and studied it for a moment. 'Probably the very thing for you.' He glanced up at Gennetta. 'A house in Well Close Square, built about seventy years ago. A fine Georgian building. Three storeys so plenty of room. Maybe too much for you?'

'Probably not. I like lots of room. Used to it in Bagdale and New Buildings and I appreciate it more after Hacker's Yard.'

'No doubt. I'm sure.' He fussed over his words, embarrassed at the mention of Hacker's Yard for it pricked at his conscience that in turning her out of New Buildings he might have been responsible for her experience. 'It has a large kitchen and a small secluded garden, ideal for the children.'

'Sounds interesting. When can I look round it?'

'Any time.'

'Now?'

'Yes. I'll take you there.' He rose from his chair and went to take his coat from the stand close to the door. As he reached up he started coughing again and had to wait for it to subside before he could shrug himself into the garment.

'I do think you should see the doctor about that cough, Mr Mitchell,' Gennetta advised.

He nodded but pulled a face. 'I suppose so but I have an aversion to them. They'll always find something wrong with you.' He opened the door and gave a slight bow as she passed him. He paused to inform Benjamin where they were going.

Within half an hour they were back. A deal had been struck for what Gennetta thought was a reasonable price, made more so by the occupiers who were eager to have everything settled before they left Whitby for York in two weeks.

There had been spasmodic coughing from Cornelius on the way to and from Well Close Square, and as she left the office Gennetta reminded him to see the doctor.

Nathaniel and Flora were excited by the prospect of moving to a place of their own and Rose was delighted to be going with them, for she would no longer feel an intruder in a house where every other servant was employed by Mrs Turner. The three of them were thrilled that they might be united with Mrs Shaw again when Gennetta indicated that she would be asking her to resume her old job.

'And I'll be asking Mr Shaw to help us again with moving furniture when the time comes.'

'I'll mention it to Caleb. I'm sure he'll help.'

'Thanks, Rose.' Gennetta gave a wry smile. 'I'm going to lose you to him one day.'

The children overheard the remark and rushed to Rose, flinging themselves against her. 'You won't leave us, Rose? You can't,' they cried.

Blushing at Gennetta's meaning, she laughed at the children's pleas and gave them a hug. 'I won't leave my bairns, even if I marry Caleb. I'll still come and work for you.' She gave Gennetta a querying look.

'Of course you can. We'll always want you.'

Rose looked down at the children. 'There you are then.' She gave a little smile. 'But he hasn't asked me yet.'

'Oh, I'm sure he will,' Gennetta commented knowingly.

The next week was hectic for Gennetta. Grace had agreed that as she would still be manager it would be more convenient for her to have all the documents and paperwork necessary for running the business in her new home. There was a lot of sorting out to do, and that, on top of arranging what furniture she would want and organising the removal, occupied most of her time. It was five days before she was able to pay a visit to the workshop.

Though she liked to call there more frequently she had no worries that all would be well for she knew she had an exceptional foreman in John Young. She arrived just before the works closed for the day and, while she was having a word with him, got the impression that Tom was hanging back, pretending to be busy. She noticed too that when he had had a word with Davey and Joey, the two boys left with the other men.

'Haven't thee had enough for the day, Tom?' John asked.

'Just want to put the finishing touches to this piece, ready for that shipment to London tomorrow.'

'Right. Thee lock up after seeing Mrs Briggs out.' John looked across at Gennetta who was examining some of the jet for the Queen's jewellers. 'Is that all right, ma'am?'

She glanced over her shoulder. 'Yes, John. Won't keep you long, Tom.'

He did not reply but when the door closed behind the foreman, he said casually, 'You have to move again?'

'Who told you?' Gennetta straightened from the jet brooch she was examining and turned towards him but he went on with his carving.

'Caleb.'

'Ah, of course. Rose was asking him to help with the move.'

He laid down his tool and swung round on his stool. His eyes were intent on her as he said, 'You aren't coming this side of the river?'

'You know I'm not,' she replied, anticipating that Caleb would have told him where she was going.

'Ever think about it?'

'That you asked me to marry you – yes. But living over here – no.'

His lips tightened. 'The two go together.'

She shook her head. 'Not necessarily.'

'You've grown too big for your own boots,' he snapped. 'All you can see is this firm and you think that means living the other side of the river.' Disgust had come into his voice.

193

'No, Tom, I don't. You know what this firm means to me. You know what I've done for it. My sister-in-law assures me that I need fear nothing from her marriage to Cyrus Sleightholme but I think otherwise. I had to move out of her house.'

'Then why didn't you come to me? I still love you. Don't destroy that by thinking too much of what the business owes you.'

'It's paying me now.' The light of triumph came to her eyes. 'Grace has bought me the house in Well Close Square.'

'What!' Tom gulped, and then eyed her seriously. 'Be careful where that attitude might take you. I've seen how ambition can destroy people.' He started telling her the story of his parents again, hoping it might make her see the value of his attitude to life.

'Tom, I'm sorry about what happened to your father and mother, but it won't happen to me. I can't just stand by and see the Sleightholmes get their hands on Turner's. As long as I am still manager I can have control and be near my sister-in-law to keep an eye on anything devious Cyrus might dream up. Please try and understand.'

'I understand it's still between us.' He bit his lip regretfully.

'Tom, now that I'm moving into my own house in Well Close Square, we could resume the drawing lessons for the boys.' She put enthusiasm into her voice as she tried to win him over with this suggestion. He hesitated. She pressed the matter. 'I've just been looking at their work. It could blossom even more if we captured their talent and developed it now.'

Tom grunted.

'You were bothered about Davey getting big ideas by seeing life in Bagdale, but he'll not see that kind of life with me,' she went on, urging him to see her point of view. 'It will be different from Henrietta Street but you know I won't spoil him. Say yes, Tom.' Her eyes searched for his reaction. 'It will mean we can see more of each other,' she added, an enticing tone in her voice.

She saw a different light come into his eyes with her last remark, but he looked thoughtful. 'Being in your own house could be different. I'll think about it.'

'Good. I hope you'll say yes for Davey's and Joey's sakes.' She was glad she knew the reasons for Tom's suspicions and could understand them. She reckoned that he had once been ambitious like his father. Maybe the desire to better himself lay dormant, and maybe, just maybe, she could make him see that life across the river held something for him too.

The succeeding days were filled to the full. Preparations to move

194

were added to Grace's excitement at her forthcoming wedding. The household was in a turmoil and Gennetta felt relieved when the occupants of the house in Well Close Square vacated the property and she was able to move in.

Seth Shaw and Caleb were ready with their carts, and their willing hands carried and placed furniture as Gennetta required. Rose kept the children busy without curbing their excitement. It was a hard exhausting day but everyone made light of it and was in a good mood when they all sat down together to a meal prepared by Mrs Shaw who had agreed to come back as cook to Gennetta on the same basis as before.

Caught up as she was in her own affairs while attending to the business, Gennetta had little time to consider her promise to be in attendance on the bride, but all went well. Robert Sleightholme was in no mood to stint things. This was his only son who was getting married and in his eyes this was no ordinary marriage. He would be a proud man the day he had a grandson who would inherit both firms and unite them under the name of Sleightholme.

He smiled to himself as he watched bride and groom walk down the aisle. Jeremiah would turn in his grave if he could see what was happening.

Cyrus sought Gennetta out at the reception at the Angel Inn and thanked her for the part she had played that day. 'And also for the way you brought Grace through her mourning period. You were a rock on which she could rely. And may I say how much I admire the way you have handled the Turner business? Your father would have been proud of you, though he would have been surprised to see a woman doing it – something he would never have condoned had he been alive. I hope while we are away, and long after, you will continue to serve us? I know Grace has great faith in your ability and wishes you to go on with the good work.'

Gennetta still harboured her suspicions. Cyrus could talk smoothly and at the same time be planning for his own ends. She noted the term 'serve'. It was as if he was reminding her that she held no more status than any other employee.

With the honeymooners away for a month Gennetta dismissed her doubts and enjoyed settling into her new home. That was easy, for the house had a friendly feeling, and the children, Rose and Mrs Shaw took to it as if they had always been there.

Once she had everything to her liking she called at the house in Henrietta Street, enjoying the walk to the river and across the bridge to Church Street.

Unpleasant memories were revived as she passed Hacker's Yard but she had put them to the back of her mind by the time she approached Tom's house and tapped on the door.

'Gennetta!' There was pleasure as well as surprise in his voice.

'Hello, Tom.'

Taken aback, he hesitated only a moment but it felt endless. Then, embarrassed at what he thought was a discourteous delay, his words came quickly. 'Come in, come in.' He moved to one side and said as she stepped past him, 'This is an unexpected pleasure.'

'Hello, Davey,' she greeted the boy who was sitting at the table across which were spread small pieces of wood and cloth of various sizes. 'Another model?'

His smile expressed his pleasure at seeing her. 'Yes, Mrs Briggs. It's going to be Captain Scoresby's whale ship, *Henrietta*.'

'Let me take your cape, and please sit down,' said Tom.

'Thanks.' Gennetta slipped the cape from her shoulders and, after adjusting the position of an armchair slightly so that she didn't have her back to Davey, sat down.

'You'll have a cup of tea?' Tom offered, and on receiving her acceptance went through to the small kitchen where he put a kettle on the fire. 'Have you got settled?' he asked on his return.

'Yes, thanks. It was a rush with the wedding and all that it entailed, but we managed.'

'Good.'

'You'll have to come and see it,' she suggested. Tom made no comment but merely nodded, so Gennetta decided to come straight to the point of her visit. 'Tom, have you thought over what I suggested about resuming the drawing lessons?' She saw Davey prick up his ears.

'I have,' he replied. 'I think it would be a good idea. I shouldn't prevent the development of the talent you see in Davey.'

Gennetta felt relief sweep over her, dismissing any doubts she had had. 'Good.' A broad smile lit up her face.

Tom's heart jolted. That smile enveloped him in its warmth and enhanced her beauty. Her joy was catching.

'You're going to start teaching us again, Mrs Briggs?' cried Davey excitedly.

'Your father has agreed.' Gennetta laughed at the boy's wide-eyed enthusiasm.

'And Joey?' he asked with an urgency which showed that he hoped his friend was included.

'Of course,' replied Gennetta.

'Can I go and tell him, Pa?' Anticipating his father's approval, he jumped from his chair.

'Off with you,' grinned Tom.

Without another word Davey shot from the house like a whirlwind.

Both Gennetta and Tom laughed at an enthusiasm which would not be denied.

Their eyes met. Laughter faded slowly leaving an unspoken admiration for each other. Tom stood up. He stepped towards her, his hands extended. Gennetta rose from her chair, her eyes never leaving his, her heart racing at the tension which sparked between them. She reached out. Their hands met and a shiver ran through her at his touch. Tom's were broad hands with long fingers that could work delicately and now were gentle in their expression of love. Their eyes never left each other.

'Mrs Briggs, I think I'm falling in love with you,' he said softly. He shook his head slowly as he added, 'No, I *am* in love with you.'

There was adoration in her eyes, and a longing she had thought never to experience again swept over her. 'And I think I have met the man I would like to spend the rest of my life with,' she said slowly, each word carefully chosen. 'I love you, Tom Unwin.'

'Gennetta,' he whispered as he drew her to him.

'Tom.'

Their lips met, gently, tenderly, and then moved in unbridled passion as his powerful arms closed round her and held her tight, as if they would never let her go.

The following evening, immediately upon leaving work, as planned by Gennetta, Tom accompanied the two boys across the bridge to the house in Well Close Square. The wind blew in from the sea, rippling the river and easing the congestion on the bridge as folk were not eager to linger. They hurried along Flowergate and into Skinner Street before turning into Well Close Square.

Tom opened the gate into a small garden and approached the door. There was nothing fancy about the frontage with its eight tall windows, each an exact replica of the others. Its three storeys gave it a narrow appearance, but no doubt the house would be snug and cosy.

So it proved. Tom stepped inside to a warm welcome from Gennetta and her two children, who were excited about meeting Davey and Joey.

'Now, before we do anything else, we are all going to enjoy a meal prepared by Mrs Shaw especially for your first visit,' Gennetta announced as she led the way into the dining room.

'Crikey, missus, thee lives *here*!' Joey gasped staring about him in wonder.

'Yes, Joey.'

'Crikey!' He was incredulous. 'And to think thee lived in Hacker's Yard!'

Gennetta laughed. 'Those days are gone.'

'I should think so, missus, seeing all this.'

As they moved through the hall and into the dining room, Tom could imagine what the rooms on the two upper storeys were like and he marvelled at the space after his own two rooms downstairs, two upstairs in Henrietta Street. Could he ever again come to terms with life on this side of the river?

He cast such thoughts aside. Let the future take care of itself. For he was prepared to enjoy this evening. After all Gennetta and Mrs Shaw had gone to a lot of trouble.

For the sake of the young ones, Mrs Shaw had kept the meal simple: soup, roast beef and Yorkshire pudding with potatoes and carrots, and bread and butter pudding or apple pie. Joey was speechless at it all but tucked in with a relish which both pleased and amused Gennetta. Davey, who sat between Nathaniel and Flora, chatted to them both and neither Gennetta nor Tom did anything to curb the noise, they were too pleased that the children had immediately taken to each other.

Tom enjoyed not having to get a meal ready for a change and savoured it with the relish of a man who liked good plain food.

'That was wonderful,' he said as he sat back after doing justice to both the apple pie and the bread and butter pudding. 'I must make a point of thanking Mrs Shaw.'

'Do that,' agreed Gennetta. 'She will be pleased.'

After Rose had taken Nathaniel and Flora to prepare for bed, Gennetta set Joey and Davey a drawing project. Once they were settled she asked Tom if he would like to see the rest of the house.

They visited the kitchen first where he was able to praise Mrs Shaw's accomplishments as a cook. Gennetta saw he was taking everything in and knew he must be comparing the size of her kitchen, with its big wooden table in the centre of the room and highly polished two-oven range, to his own where his cooking had to be done on an open fire with a small oven beside it.

As they went round the house she could see he was captivated by its spaciousness. He showed his interest by the questions he asked and the comments he made and she began to wonder if she was stirring an ambition which had lain dormant in him.

'Did you mind moving from your family home?' he asked when they sat down in the parlour.

'Not really. I'd left it once before and Grace's marriage made it necessary for me to leave again. And I knew I was going to love this house immediately I walked in. I felt at home straight away.'

'Do you think Mrs Turner's marrying Mr Sleightholme will make any difference to the business and our jobs?'

'You're wondering if Cyrus is going to have any influence?'

'He could. After all he's now Mrs Turner's husband and the Sleightholmes are in the jet trade. Who knows what might happen?'

'Grace has assured me that nothing will change. She's asked me to carry on in my present role. She is highly satisfied with what I have done.'

'So she should be,' said Tom firmly with admiration in his eyes. 'You made the firm more prosperous.'

'And I hope that will persuade Grace to keep it. But I'm always suspicious of the Sleightholmes. They'd hoped to get their hands on the firm through me.'

'You?'

'Yes. They had Cyrus marked out for me, and my father was all for the marriage because he saw it as a means of taking over Sleightholme's.'

'And you spiked them all by walking out and marrying Reuben Briggs?' Tom chuckled. 'So this may be a Sleightholme move to ...'

'It may well be, but I'll do my best to prevent it. If it happens I'll not rest until I get it back.' The determination which had come into her voice left Tom in no doubt where her priorities lay. It hurt him, but he held his peace, not wanting to spoil this first visit to Well Close Square.

'Ah, the newly weds.' Robert Sleightholme beamed his welcome as the honeymooners entered the house in Bagdale. He took his son's hand in a firm grip. 'And Grace! How splendid thee look,' he added as she hugged her mother-in-law.

Grace turned to him and he stooped to kiss her on both cheeks.

Maids fussed around taking capes, coats, bonnets and hats. The coachman brought the cases into the hall where they were whisked away upstairs.

'We didn't expect you to be here,' said Cyrus. 'We'd anticipated a quiet arrival at our house.'

'Couldn't think of it,' boomed Robert. 'I came down and made arrangements with the servants and cook to have a welcome home party. Thought thee'd like it?' He shot a glance at Grace, hoping his heartiness was not misplaced.

'A splendid idea,' agreed Cyrus enthusiastically, wanting to keep on the right side of his father.

Grace, almost overwhelmed by the reception, could do nothing but agree.

'Come along, my dear, I'm sure you could do with tidying up after your journey.' Mrs Sleightholme took Grace by the arm and started towards the stairs. Two maids followed.

When they returned they found the two men in the drawing room enjoying a glass of Madeira and a cigar. Grace gave a little frown. She had told Cyrus that, while she did not mind people smoking, she did not want it in her drawing room. He had deliberately ignored her wishes and that, coupled with the fact that Mr and Mrs Sleightholme had prepared this reception here, made it seem that they had taken over.

However, she said nothing now but would mention it to Cyrus later, for she did not want to spoil the evening. After all, she supposed Mr and Mrs Sleightholme had intended it as a kindness.

The evening passed in splendid style. Robert had spared nothing. The food was excellent and the wine flowed. He became more expansive the more wine he consumed, and by the time he was leaving was a little unsteady on his feet.

With goodnights said, Robert paused in the doorway. He looked at Grace. 'Well, my dear,' he said with a slight slur, 'when can I expect an heir to the Sleightholme and Turner businesses?'

Grace blushed as she met his knowing gaze.

'Robert!' Maud rebuked him.

'I'm only asking,' he pleaded in mock innocence. He looked back at Grace. 'The sooner the better.' He turned to Cyrus and gave him a tap on his shoulder with his bunched fist. 'Get on with it, lad, get on with it.'

Maud gave him a push to propel him outside. She turned to Grace. 'Take no notice of him,' she offered as an apology.

As she lay in bed awake, half hearing Cyrus's heavy breathing in sleep after his passion had been spent, Grace recalled Robert's parting remark to him and wondered if there was more behind it. Should she have heeded Gennetta's warning about Cyrus's deviousness?

Over the succeeding weeks nothing further occurred to raise her suspicions. Cyrus was a charming and attentive husband. She noticed he spent little time at work and appeared to rely on his father to run the business. He was politeness itself when Gennetta visited to report on the activities at Turner's.

But though he appeared to take little notice of these transactions, Gennetta had no doubt that he took everything in and felt sure it would all be reported to his father. She would have liked to exclude him from these meetings, which took place twice a week, but dare not suggest it when Grace showed no inclination to do so. She prayed

Cyrus had changed and that he would give Grace no cause for concern, for she appeared to be happy with him.

Gennetta's life settled down to a routine of work, time spent with Nathaniel and Flora, and lessons with Joey and Davey twice a week. She enjoyed teaching them and having Tom there.

She had been at Well Close Square two months when late one afternoon Rose announced that Mr Archibald Cooper would like to see her.

'Good heavens, my old drawing tutor.' Surprised by this unexpected visit, she added quickly, 'Please show him in.'

A few moments later Rose returned, announced the visitor and stood to one side as he came into the room.

'Mr Cooper! How delightful to see you. It has been so long.' Gennetta met him with outstretched arms, her eyes shining with the pleasure of seeing him again.

He had changed little, looked older perhaps, more lined. Maybe his shoulders drooped a little more than she remembered. But his eyes were the same: alert and observant. She saw they were summing her up in a sort of apprehensive way, as if embarrassed that she might be able to read his thoughts and guess the purpose of his visit.

'Mrs Briggs, it is my pleasure.' He took her hand in his and she felt the sensitivity in those long fingers she remembered so well directing a pencil to his will and turning out the most exquisite and delicate drawings. His voice too was the same: quiet, gently caressing. 'It is kind of you to see me.'

'You are an old and dear friend and I am ashamed that I have not kept in touch with you.' She was suitably contrite. 'Do sit down.' And she indicated a chair.

He gave a small shrug of his shoulders. 'That is life. We get swept up in what we are doing and time passes.'

'So true,' agreed Gennetta, 'but really it's no excuse for neglecting people, especially someone like you who taught me so much.'

'Ah, but you were a willing pupil with talent which only needed guiding and nurturing. I always looked forward to our lessons. Reuben's too. That was a terrible tragedy.'

Gennetta gave a wan smile. 'Yes, it was devastating.' She forced herself to change the subject. 'Now, are you still giving lessons? Wait, you'll take tea?'

'Well ...' Mr Cooper hesitated to say yes.

'Of course you will.' She stood up and pulled the cord beside the fireplace.

'That's very kind of you,' he replied.

201

When the maid appeared Gennetta asked for tea and a few minutes later it appeared, together with scones, jam and cake.

Mr Cooper's appreciation was obvious as he tucked in, and Gennetta was delighted that he was enjoying himself.

'You must be wondering why I have called on you?' he said finally as he wiped his sticky fingers on his napkin. 'Well, I know how well you can draw, and have seen some of the jet work you have done. I have also heard that you are taking two boys for drawing lessons.'

Gennetta tensed a little. Was he going to object, thinking that she was setting up in opposition? 'Only in connection with my work at Turner's,' she put in hastily. 'I saw talent, they couldn't afford lessons, so I said I would teach them as part of their training.'

Mr Cooper gave a wry smile. 'My dear, I'm not objecting. But I wondered if you might like to have more pupils? You see, I am thinking about retiring and concentrating on my own work.'

Gennetta, surprised at the unexpected suggestion, was at a loss for a moment or two. 'It's very kind of you to think of me and make this offer.' She paused thoughtfully. 'But I really have enough to do. I manage the firm for my sister-in-law, and that, coupled with my caring for my own children, takes up all my time. And, as I say, I'm only teaching these two boys because of their talent in working with jet – which of course is all to the good for Turner's. I'm sorry, Mr Cooper, but I really will have to say no.'

Disappointment clouded his face. 'I understand,' he said quietly. 'It was just a thought.'

'And a kind one,' she said. 'I do appreciate it, and I'm grateful for your confidence in my ability.'

'There's no doubt about that,' he assured her. 'Well, I'll carry on a little until I can find someone who has the ability I'm looking for.'

They resumed their conversation about local people and affairs until Mr Cooper left, saying how much he had enjoyed his visit.

'I'm sorry, Mrs Sleightholme, but I'm afraid that fall you had did more damage than we first thought.' Dr Witham looked gravely at Grace. 'I would say that it is very unlikely you will ever conceive.'

She stared at him disbelievingly. Her whole world seemed to be tumbling around her. She knew Cyrus had set his heart on having a son and now she must break this shattering news to him. Would he behave like Jack all over again?

'You're sure?' she asked tentatively.

'As near certain as I can be,' replied the doctor. 'You have never been straightforward in this respect, as you know. I think the fact that you did conceive with Jack was merely by remote chance. The fall which followed was disastrous.' He spread his hands in a gesture of helplessness. 'I'm sorry, Mrs Sleightholme, that I can't give you any more hope.'

Grace left the doctor's in a daze. She was not aware of anything around her as she walked home. Her mind was on Cyrus and how he would take this news. She feared to tell him. His hints about wanting a baby had become more and more marked, especially as his father had promised him not only a good slice of the Sleightholme business but also a say in the running of the firm, when he could present him with a grandson.

Grace had wondered at the wisdom of the last part of the promise for she had come to realise that Cyrus had little business acumen. She could see that when she compared his attitude to that of Gennetta. It had also come to her knowledge that her husband did not spend much time at the Sleightholme jet works. He was more likely to be found with a set of moneyed friends in the more salubrious inns around town, usually gambling at cards with them in private rooms. It disturbed her to discover this but she could not fault his attitude towards her. There were times when he was impatient to learn whether he was to be a father, though whether that was from a paternal instinct, or because of what it would bring him, she was not certain.

Now this! How could she break it to him gently? How could she placate him? What could she do?

By the time she reached home an idea had sown itself in her mind and that evening, as she waited for him to return, it had grown into a determination which would not be sidetracked.

Cyrus was later than usual and was surprised to see a light under the parlour door. On opening the door he was astonished to see Grace, sitting with her hands crossed on her lap, staring at the fireplace.

'My dear, you still up?'

She noted the slight slur in his voice and it brought back bad memories of Jack. It surely couldn't happen again. It mustn't. It wouldn't!

He leaned over her and with a leering look said, 'I thought you'd have been in bed waiting for me. After all, we do want that baby, don't we?' He straightened with a chuckle and looked down at her.

'Don't be disgusting,' she exclaimed, as if she would prefer to be away from him.

He swayed in front of her. 'I'm not. I'm merely stating a fact.'

She looked up and met his gaze squarely. She must not show weakness but face the next few moments with a fortitude that he could not break. Her eyes never left his as she came straight to the point.

'Cyrus, I saw the doctor today. I can't have children.'

The announcement was cold, stark, and for a moment made no impression on him. Then its finality hit him. He stared incredulously at her.

'What?'

'I can't have a baby.'

His eyes widened. His mind swung between rage that she had not fulfilled his expectations, anger because a fortune would slip away from the Sleightholmes, and despair that now his father's promises would mean nothing. He wanted to hit out at her, to pound it into her that what she was saying was not true, but there was no denying her air of seriousness. It told him that this was a stark fact. It had a sobering effect on him. Tension drained from him, leaving a feeling of hopelessness. Those few words had shattered his whole world. He stared at her for a moment and then sank slowly on to a chair, his expression betraying his helpless disappointment.

'What will Father say?' he muttered, half to himself. 'He'd set his heart on a boy, an heir to our jet empire. He'd promised me ...' The words stuck in his throat and he sank his head into his hands in a gesture of despair.

Grace was suddenly overwhelmed with sorrow. The reaction she had expected had not shown itself. The initial flare of anger she had seen had gone almost before it was evident. She could not help but compare his reaction with Jack's, and was thankful that violence had not been threatened again. She stood up and came to him. She sank to her knees beside him and put her arm around his shoulder.

'I'm sorry, Cyrus, so terribly sorry. I wanted a child as much as you did.' She stroked his hair gently.

He looked up. 'I'll lose such a lot. Not only money but responsibility – I saw this as a chance to prove myself.'

With this revelation of his expectations an idea came to Grace. Though for one fleeting moment Gennetta's words of warning about the Sleightholmes came to her, she dismissed them quickly. This man was her husband. He had been kind to her, said he loved her; she could find no fault with him. He had brought her happiness when she'd thought she would never find it with a man again. Gennetta was wrong.

'Cyrus, you *shall* have responsibility. I'll give you half of Turner's.'

'You mean ...?'

She smiled at his astonishment. 'Yes. You and Gennetta can run it between you!'

Chapter Seventeen

'You meant what you said last night?' Cyrus put the question to Grace shortly after they awoke the following morning.

'About the business? Yes.'

He rolled over, propping himself on his elbows to look at her. 'You're an angel.' He kissed her lightly on the lips.

'I wanted to lessen your disappointment.'

'And you have.' He kissed her again, letting his lips linger.

Her arms came up round his neck and she returned his kiss with an ardour which overwhelmed and enticed him until their passion was sated in a way that erased any sadness that their intimacy could never result in a child. They could still share and enjoy each other.

As they lay in each other's arms, Cyrus contemplated his change of fortune. One minute his world had been shattered by Grace's announcement and then in a moment a few words had turned it topsy-turvy and it had come out to his liking. A fifty percent share of the Turner business! His father would be pleased and Cyrus hoped it would ameliorate his obsessive desire for an heir through whom he had hoped for total control of Turner's jet.

An hour later Benjamin was showing Grace and Cyrus into Cornelius's office.

'Mr and Mrs Sleightholme, it is a pleasure to see you.' Cornelius rose from his chair and, leaning across the desk, shook hands with them before they sat down.

Grace almost recoiled from the bony touch of his hand. He smiled but it was only with his mouth; she saw no warmth in his eyes. Instead they had a distant look, as if he could not raise much interest in anything. His face was pale and drawn and the cough which he tried to stifle with his handkerchief seemed to pain him.

'I'm sorry about this,' he apologised. 'Now, my dear people, what can I do for you?'

'Mrs Turner wants me to have a half share of her business and we would like you to draw up the necessary documents,' Cyrus told him.

'Very well.' Cornelius gave a dry cough and glanced at Grace. 'This has your approval?'

'Yes,' she replied.

'Freely given?'

'Of course.' She sounded indignant.

Cornelius raised his hand in apology. 'I meant nothing by it, ma'am, but I must ask.' He could tell from her demeanour that this request held no sinister undertones. 'Very well, I will see to that for you.'

'Can it be done straight away?' Cyrus requested casually.

'Yes, I suppose so. It's a simple document and will only take a few minutes for Benjamin to write out.' Cyrus picked up a pen and wrote quickly, his action interrupted by further coughing. As soon as he was satisfied with what he had written, he read it out. Finally, he glanced at Grace. 'Is that satisfactory?'

'It seems perfectly clear to me,' she replied, and glanced at her husband. 'Is that right, Cyrus?'

'Perfect, my dear,' he answered, approving the simple statement that as from today half of Turner's belonged to him.

'Good.' Cornelius rose from his chair, steadied himself on the desk and crossed to the door. He went to Benjamin's office and a few moments later returned, only to have to support himself against the door as another spasm racked his body.

Grace watched him in alarm. 'Are you all right, Mr Mitchell?' she asked with concern.

He nodded as he gasped for breath.

With an awful feeling of wanting to help but knowing they couldn't, they could only watch until he was able to regain his composure and retake his seat. He was full of apologies as he sat down.

Cornelius dismissed their worry with a flick of his hand. 'Think nothing of it.'

'I think you should see a doctor,' put in Grace, a little hesitantly, for fear of offending with her suggestion.

Cornelius nodded. 'I really must.'

A few minutes later Benjamin appeared with two identical documents written in a neat copperplate hand.

'Thank you, Benjamin,' Cornelius said as he scanned the words. 'Capital, capital,' he added in approval. Benjamin started to leave. 'Wait,' called Cornelius. 'I want you here as a witness to the signatures.' He placed the two sheets in front of Grace, dipped a quill in the glass inkpot and handed it to her. 'If you will sign both papers, here and here ...' He pointed to the places where he wanted her to sign.

Cyrus watched with satisfaction and was only too ready to sign as the recipient.

The signatures were witnessed by Cornelius and Benjamin and the documents given a seal of approval.

Cornelius, who had fussed throughout the proceedings, picked up the documents, folded each in turn with precision, slipped them into two envelopes and handed one to Grace and the other to Cyrus. 'You are now equal partners,' he announced with satisfaction.

Cyrus stood up. 'Thank you, for your efficiency.' He leaned forward and offered his hand to Cornelius jovially. It felt good to possess something he'd wanted so long, something with which he could triumphantly confront his father.

Grace joined her husband in his thanks and, when Cornelius's throat rattled with another sharp spasm, reminded him to call on the doctor.

Cyrus felt as if he was walking on air as he went to see his father, after taking Grace home and drinking a glass of Madeira with her to celebrate the new partnership.

By the time he reached his father's office a few doors from Sleightholme's jet works, Cyrus was anxious to make his announcement.

His father looked up from the documents he was studying when Cyrus walked in, and frowned. 'Thee's looking glum, what's wrong?' he snapped. 'Thick head again, I expect.'

He leaned back in his chair and pointed a finger at his son. 'Pull thissen together, thee's a married man now with responsibilities. And thee'll have more when thee produce that son. That'll mean getting down to work. Thee's had an easy life long enough on my money. Thy drinking and gambling will have to stop.'

Cyrus's innocent expression irritated his father. 'I damn' well mean it. I'm tired of paying thy debts. Two more yesterday. Well, that's the last. I'll pay no more!'

'Now hold on, Father. I've something important to tell you.'

Robert's annoyance turned to suspicion. When his son mentioned important matters he was generally wanting something. 'Well?' he snapped, prompting Cyrus to explain, 'Grace saw the doctor yesterday. She can't have children.' His voice was quiet but it struck home.

'What!' The shock brought Robert springing from his chair. His face tensed as he glared at his son. The muscles knotted in his neck.

207

His face went a bright red. He thumped the desk. 'Damn! I still can't lay my hands on that firm, still can't outsmart ...' He stopped in mid-flow as Cyrus, no longer able to contain himself, burst out laughing. 'What the hell are you laughing about? It's no laughing matter.'

'Your face.' Cyrus slapped his thigh in merriment. 'Read that.' He thrust the envelope he had fished from his pocket at his father.

Mystified, Robert took it, looked askance at his son and withdrew the sheet of paper. He unfolded it and read. A hush descended on the office. Robert stared disbelievingly at the paper. He read it again and then looked up at Cyrus. 'What?'

'Exactly what it says,' replied Cyrus with a triumphant smile. 'I now own half Turner's. I played on my disappointment at not being able to have a son and Grace split the business with me – a sop to lighten my gloom.'

Robert listened intently, taken by his son's deviousness. He chuckled. 'Well done, Cyrus, well done! Jeremiah will be turning in his grave. It's a pity Grace can't conceive ...' His voice trailed away and his disappointment faded with the idea that he might yet have found a solution. 'We'll have our heir.' He gave a nod of satisfaction.

'How?'

'Thee knows our servant – Eliza?'

'Mother's personal maid?'

'Aye. She's expecting. If it's a boy, thee and Grace can take him.'

'That's all very well, but do you know the father? The brat might be coming from good-for-nothing stock.'

'Aye, I know the father.' Robert paused then added quickly, when he attracted a look of suspicion from his son, ' I got it out of the girl. I can't disclose who he is, Eliza wants no fuss and indeed is being well paid to keep quiet, but he is of very good stock. I think thee'll be proud. So there's the heir we want, and if it isn't a boy we'll try again. Persuade Grace it's a good idea, play on her motherly insincts.'

Cyrus smiled. 'Easily done.'

Throughout her meeting with Grace and Cyrus, Gennetta felt a little uneasy. There was an atmosphere of expectation, but why she could not say. Cyrus seemed to be more interested than usual in her report, though as usual he made no attempt to interfere. She detected he was more relaxed and sensed he was pleased with himself.

'So with two more enquiries from London jewellers, one of whom I regard as needing personal attention, I think it might be wise for me to pay them a visit,' concluded Gennetta.

'I can do that.' Cyrus's words came crisply as if that was all there was to it.

'You?' Her puzzled look went from him to Grace and back again.

'Yes. Now I own half of the business, I'll be taking a more active part and this will be a good start.' His words struck like a dagger. His smirk of triumph chilled her heart.

She looked at Grace. 'What have you done?' she demanded.

'It's right,' replied Grace gently, hoping her soothing tone would lessen the impact and assuage the hostility she saw mounting in her sister-in-law. She went on to explain quickly.

'I'm sorry that you cannot have a child,' Gennetta commiserated, 'but to hand over half the business ...' She raised her hands in a gesture of disgust. Her voice thinned. 'I warned you against the Sleightholmes. I told you they wanted to get their hands on Turner's and now that's just what they're getting. They've outsmarted you.'

'Now see here,' rapped Cyrus, 'I brought no pressure to bear on Grace. It was her own suggestion. Isn't that so?' He glanced at his wife.

'That's perfectly true,' she agreed. 'If I want to share the business with my husband, then that's my affair. It has nothing to do with you.'

The snub angered Gennetta. Her eyes blazed. 'I thought you and I meant more to each other than that? And look what I've done for the firm. For you. It would have floundered like a stricken ship if I hadn't come forward to run it for you. I've expanded, I've made you money, yet *this* is how you treat me.'

'Letting Cyrus have a share should make no difference to your running of the business,' retorted Grace, irritated by Gennetta's hostility.

'If you believe that, you'll believe anything,' she snapped. 'He's already taken the London visit out of my hands.'

'Only to help,' he replied. 'If I go, you'll be able to keep an eye on things here.'

Gennetta gave him a scornful look. 'Grace, please reconsider. Withdraw your offer.'

'Too late,' put in Cyrus smoothly. 'Everything was signed this morning.' His triumph was obvious and it heightened as he added, 'And you might like to know that we are arranging to adopt a child and bring him up as our own so the Sleightholme name will be perpetuated in Whitby's jet trade.'

'And Turner's disappear.' Gennetta's anger turned to fury. She rounded on Grace. 'See what you've done! He married you for only one thing – possession of Turner's, a business which was more successful than Sleightholme's. Now he's done just that, and the half share you still have is as good as his through this child. You've betrayed Jack and my father, and all that the firm meant to them.' Gennetta was trembling with rage, her eyes dark with anger. 'Well, no part of me will help you destroy it. I'm finished with you. See what he makes of the business.'

She stiffened her shoulders and, with head held high, determined not to let her defeat show, stormed from the room.

Grace, hurt by Gennetta's attack, made as if to stop her but Cyrus touched her hand. He shook his head. 'Let her go,' he whispered.

She bit her lip, quelling the tears which threatened. She hadn't wanted things to turn out like this. She hadn't wanted Gennetta's enmity. Grace couldn't see why her sister-in-law and Cyrus couldn't work well together.

Gennetta paused only to fling her coat around her shoulders and cram her bonnet on her head. She tried to calm the ferocity of her feeling of betrayal. Unconsciously she clenched her fists until the nails bit into her palms. Her flesh crawled at the thought of the firm falling into the hands of the Sleightholmes. She might never be able to win it back but somehow she would see the day come when Turner's name was one to be reckoned with in the jet trade. If only she had enough money to start a firm of her own!

Her steps were fast and determined as she strode across the bridge, and her face grim when she turned into the workshop.

She drew the foreman to one side, out of earshot of the rest of the workers. 'John, you must be the first to know: I will no longer be working for Mrs Sleightholme. Her husband will be taking over.'

From the grimace he made after the initial look of astonishment she knew he did not fancy the idea of working under Cyrus. 'I'm sorry to hear that, ma'am. It's been a pleasure working with thee.'

'Thank you,' replied Gennetta. 'And thank you for all you have done. Now, I'd like a word with Tom.'

He nodded, but before he called to Tom, said, 'May I wish thee good luck, whatever thee do?'

Gennetta smiled and waited for Tom to approach her.

'Something wrong?' he asked, eyes searching her face.

She nodded.

'Thought so from your expression when you walked in.' He looked at her anxiously.

'My sister-in-law has given her husband a half share in the business and I will not work with him. I've resigned. As of now, I'm finished with this business.'

Tom was shaken. 'But what are you going to do?' His brow was furrowed with anxiety.

'I haven't thought about that,' she replied. Her mind was gripped by the sudden realisation that she would have no income. She saw the suggestion which was springing to his lips and spoke quickly to stop him. 'No, Tom, don't say it!'

'But surely it's the answer.' He put all the urgency he could muster into his voice. 'You'd have no more worries and if we ...'

'And how long do you think you'd last in your job once Cyrus knew you and I were married?'

'He wouldn't!'

Gennetta gave a half laugh. 'Oh, wouldn't he? You don't know him. You can't afford to lose your job.'

'I'd get another one.'

'Maybe. Maybe not. I'll not let you risk it. It wouldn't be fair on Davey.'

He saw how adamant she was and thought it best not to pursue the matter further. 'All right. But I want you to promise me that if you need any help, you'll come to me?'

She nodded. 'I will, and thanks. You're a good man, Tom. I don't want to hurt you, but I'm determined that the name of Turner will one day be in the forefront of the jet trade again, hopefully in the premises my father started. So keep me informed on what happens here, and how Cyrus copes.'

As she walked home Gennetta's sense of uncertainty heightened. Should she have stayed on in her employment, and tolerated Cyrus? She reckoned he would have made life unbearable for her, and that would have been too much. He would have forced her out to make sure the firm was under his sole control. No doubt his father would be revelling in the situation and that thought made her all the more determined to hit back. Her immediate problem was what she was going to live on. The money she had put by wouldn't last forever.

That evening as she gave the boys their lesson the answer came to her: Mr Cooper's suggestion that she should take over his pupils. It would enable her to enjoy some income while she thought about the long-term outlook.

The next morning she visited him, to be received warmly and to find, much to her relief, that he was still teaching, and was just as eager to pass his pupils to her.

Her immediate problem was solved.

'Benjamin, I'm going home, I'm not feeling too well.' Cornelius's words were interrupted by coughing fits.

'A wise precaution, if I might say so,' replied the clerk. 'That cough has been troublesome for some time, and particularly bad since you saw Mr and Mrs Sleightholme three weeks ago.' He squinted at his employer, doubled up with an unusually severe seizure as he gasped for breath. His face was paler, and more drawn than usual but Benjamin decided it would only alarm Cornelius if he commented upon it.

Bringing the spasm under control, he straightened. 'I might go to my brother's for a few days. I'll be well looked after there. All important business has been taken care of here. You can deal with the usual things.'

'Of course I can, Mr Mitchell,' Benjamin replied ingratiatingly. 'You can depend on me. Don't worry about a thing. Anything important that I think needs your attention, I'll send to you. But I'll try not to worry you.'

Cornelius nodded but warned, 'Don't assume too much authority. And remember, the motto of this firm is discretion.'

'I know. You can depend on me.' Already Benjamin was looking forward to an easy time on his own.

Cornelius eyed him for a moment, wondering just how much he *could* rely on him.

That night, Cornelius's attempts to sleep were so interrupted by vicious bouts of coughing that the next morning he decided he must make the effort, as painful as it might be, to go immediately to his brother's in Scarborough. There he knew he would receive the careful nursing of his sister-in-law. He wished he hadn't to make the journey but it was what became of being a bachelor with no one to care for him through the trying days of sickness.

The coach journey was a nightmare for him. His fits of coughing were viewed suspiciously by his fellow passengers. Not one glance of sympathy was cast in his direction, which only served to heighten his embarrassment and make him huddle further into the corner seat which he had been fortunate to obtain.

Arriving in Scarborough eager to reach the comfort of his brother's house, he forced his legs on, even though every step was a painful effort. Spasms of coughing, stifled by the handkerchief pressed to his mouth, caused him to stop several times and it was with some relief that he reached the house, only to suffer a worse fit as he pulled the doorbell.

When the maid opened the door, alarm seized her at the sight of him leaning against the doorpost, racked by a vicious bout of coughing. She turned and ran.

'Mrs Mitchell! Mrs Mitchell!' Her voice resounded through the house.

She burst into the drawing room without knocking. Hannah was already on her feet, drawn by the alarm in the maid's voice.

'Mary, what is it?' she asked, concern mixed with agitation at the upheaval which had suddenly come to shatter this normally tranquil household.

'Mr Cornelius, ma'am ... '

'Cornelius?' She did not wait for an explanation. The expression on Mary's face made her realise that there was something drastically wrong. She ran into the hall and was seized with anxiety when she saw her brother-in-law in great distress. 'Cornelius, what's the matter?' The change she saw in him startled her. His face was drawn in pain, cheeks hollow, his eyes sunken and black-rimmed.

He pushed himself from the doorpost, trying to recover some of his composure, but staggered and would have fallen but for her support. As she helped him into the hall she was shocked to feel his bones through his clothes, and as he sank against her was alarmed by his lack of weight. He had never been a heavy man but his present condition horrified her. He felt so brittle.

'I just had to come,' he gasped weakly. 'I felt so ill and had no one to care for me. I knew you would, Hannah.' The words came with a tremendous effort as he forced his feet on, trying to match her steps.

'You did right,' she confirmed. 'Mary, get the doctor – quick!' The maid started towards the kitchen. 'Then go to Mr Mitchell's office and tell him to come home immediately.'

Hannah helped Cornelius up the stairs. It was a slow, painful climb and she marvelled that he had made the coach journey. It must have taken a lot out of him. She took him to the bedroom he usually occupied on his visits. There she sat him in a chair to regain some strength and await the doctor.

Worried by the news brought by Mary, and alarmed by the urgent summons, Thornton and James left the office.

When they reached the house they went straight upstairs to find Hannah waiting anxiously outside Cornelius's room.

'Thank goodness you're here.' Her expression was filled with relief now responsibility for Cornelius had been removed. 'The doctor's with him now.'

Thornton nodded and glanced at James, saying, 'Stay with your mother.' With a comforting pat on his wife's arm, he went into the bedroom.

The doctor glanced up as he leaned over the bed. 'Ah, Thornton, I'm glad you're here. I'm just about finished.

When he reached the bedside he was shocked to see his brother's condition. Cornelius looked like a bag of bones. Eyes dimmed by pain stared at him from sunken sockets.

He mustered a wan smile of recognition. 'Sorry, Thornton.' His apology for the upset he was causing rattled in his throat.

'No apology needed,' he replied with a gentle pat on his brother's emaciated shoulder. 'You should have come sooner.'

The doctor straightened and looked down at Cornelius as he pulled the bedclothes up to the patient's chin. 'Now,' he said in a commanding voice, 'you must stay in bed and try to eat something. You need nourishment.' He looked at Thornton. 'I'm sure your cook will be able to tickle his palate.' Thornton nodded. The doctor looked back at Cornelius. 'I'll leave you some laudanum. I'll tell Mrs Mitchell the dosage.'

'Thank you, Doctor,' Cornelius croaked.

'Only family visitors, for short periods.' He looked at Thornton. 'He doesn't want tiring.'

'We'll see he isn't,' said Thornton, who recognised from the doctor's inclination of the head that he wanted to see him outside.

He followed the doctor from the bedroom to encounter the anxious faces of Hannah and James.

When the doctor spoke, after he had glanced at the door to make sure it was closed, he kept his voice low. His face was grave. 'Your brother should have seen his doctor in Whitby long ago. I'm afraid his condition is serious.'

'Oh, no!' gasped Hannah.

'How serious?' asked Thornton solemnly. 'Don't keep anything from us.'

The doctor pursed his lips thoughtfully as he shot a glance at each in turn. He saw they all needed to know the truth. 'I'm afraid he won't recover.' Hannah grasped her husband's arm tightly. 'Things have gone too far for anything to be done. He has bad pains which will get worse. The laudanum will give temporary ease. He could go in two days, or it could be two weeks.'

Hannah's face blanched at the shock. She swallowed hard as tears came to her eyes. James moved closer to her and took her arm, as much for his own comfort as hers. He stared disbelievingly at the doctor. This couldn't be true – not Uncle Cornelius who loved the challenge of chess.

Thornton's face had drained of all colour. He was about to lose his only brother and already sensed the parting. 'So soon?' His voice was hoarse.

'It's only an estimate but I don't think it will be far out,' replied the doctor, wishing he could have given the family some better hope.

* * *

214

The doctor proved to be only a couple of days out. Cornelius died ten days after his arrival in Scarborough. They were days of increasing pain, though the Mitchells did what they could to make things easier for him and to take his mind off his illness.

Hannah kept him as comfortable as possible. Though he ate little, she saw that the food presented to him was tempting.

James spent time telling him about life in Scarborough, and recalled the games of chess they had enjoyed.

Thornton exchanged reminiscences of their boyhood and was reassured that the important matters in the Whitby office had been taken care of before Cornelius left.

The funeral, in a church high on the cliff in the shadow of the ruined castle, was a small affair, for Cornelius was not known in Scarborough and only a few of Thornton's friends attended out of deference to his loss. With a heavy heart James watched the coffin lowered into the ground, not far from the grave of Anne Brontë who had died in Scarborough and whose novel, *The Tenant of Wildfell Hall*, he knew his uncle had admired.

A sudden squall, driven by the bleak wind from the sea, sent the mourners scurrying to their coaches. Reaching home, Thornton, threw off his damp coat and called for hot drinks. Along with Hannah and James, he sought the warmth of the fire in the parlour.

'A sad day,' he commented, standing with his back to the fire and glancing at his wife and son who had sat down on either side of the fireplace so they could catch a glimpse of the dancing flames behind him. 'But Cornelius wouldn't want us to mourn him, rather be thankful that he is released from pain.'

He ran his tongue over his dry lips and was about to continue when a knock on the door heralded the arrival of a maid with tea and hot scones. Once she had left and Hannah had started to pour the tea, he went on,' I brought his will from the office. I have it here.' He withdrew a long envelope from his pocket and took out a sheet of paper, unfolded it and said, 'It's short and simple.' He glanced down and read, '"I, Cornelius Mitchell, being of sound mind, do hereby bequeath my worldly belongings to be divided equally between my brother, Thornton Mitchell, with thanks for being a steadfast friend, Hannah Mitchell, for being a kind and generous sister-in-law, and James Mitchell, an upstanding nephew who gave me much pleasure in watching him grow into a young man."'

A charged hush settled over the room as if everyone sensed Cornelius there, nodding his approval and verifying that he had done the right thing.

Thornton broke the silence. 'Cornelius has left everything neat and

215

tidy. He has been a thrifty man and we will benefit by some two thousand pounds each.'

Hannah gasped. 'So much?'

James's eyes widened with surprise.

Thornton smiled at their reactions. 'Indeed. In many ways Cornelius presented an unassuming exterior. In financial matters he did seek my advice but was shrewd, especially when it came to investing money. We should be thankful for his foresight.' His eyes settled on James who was taking a cup of tea from his mother. 'Add this to the money Miss Briggs left you, James, and you will be well off. Now, I have one more thing to add.' He nodded his thanks as Hannah placed a cup of tea in front of him. 'I think it's time for you to take on more responsibility within the firm. I would like you to run the Whitby office.'

James gaped at him. This was his second great surprise in the space of a few minutes. 'But I . . . ' he started, trying to take in what this meant.

Thornton laughed at his son's bewilderment. 'You're quite capable. I have every confidence in you.'

James regained his composure but his eyes betrayed the excitement which his father's announcement had brought. Independence! Here in Scarborough he had always been under his father's watchful eye. He had been happy enough and Thornton had never been overbearing, though he had a meticulous efficiency which at times could be irritating. Whitby offered James an escape. To run an office in the way he wanted, use his own ingenuity, make his own decisions and offer his own advice to those who sought it. He was determined to succeed in the role which had suddenly been thrust upon him.

'Thank you,' he replied crisply. 'I'll do my best.'

'And that will be good enough for me,' added Thornton proudly.

'I'll miss you,' put in Hannah sadly. 'Your father told me of his intention yesterday. I know you'll do well.'

'And I'll miss you,' replied James. 'But Whitby is not far away.' He looked back at his father. 'When do you want me to go?'

'As soon as possible. Benjamin is capable of seeing to the routine things but it requires you there quickly to keep the office running efficiently.'

'Then I can get ready tomorrow and leave the next day.'

'Splendid,' Thornton agreed. 'Take accommodation at the Angel, it's the centre of Whitby's social life. Stay there until you've looked around. I believe the tenancy of the house Miss Briggs left you might become available. Benjamin sent word that the tenants are thinking of leaving. You might like to make it your home. But I leave that to you.'

James was attracted by the idea but decided to reserve judgement

216

until he'd had time to settle in Whitby. Two months or so should give him the opportunity to weigh up all his options.

Two days later James alighted from the coach at the Angel amidst all the bustle which usually accompanied its arrival. Stablemen hurried to unhitch the horses and lead them away to be rubbed down and fed. Boys ran from the inn to grab the passengers' luggage as it was handed down from the coach. The coachman paid his passengers the courtesy of bidding them goodbye. Lookers-on watched with curiosity, speculating as to what had brought the new arrivals to Whitby.

James saw his bags taken by one of the boys, who looked around to see who owned them. 'Here,' he called.

'Where to, sir?' asked the round-faced boy.

'Here, the Angel,' replied James.

'Follow me, sir.' The boy set off towards the door of the inn which had been opened wide on the arrival of the coach.

James was soon settled in a comfortable room, the landlord pleased to oblige a customer who was likely to need it for a few weeks. After taking some lunch, he decided that he may as well pay the office a visit. It had been seven years since he was last in Whitby and he enjoyed the stroll, once again seeing the river slipping leisurely under the bridge to run between the piers down to the sea. Ships were tied up at the quays taking on board goods destined for the Continent, or unloading precious imports of spices, silks and tea. Other ships lay at anchor in mid-stream, awaiting their next voyage. Hammers rang out from the shipyards. People bustled about their business or idled away time in talk, all making up the cosmopolitan life of this busy Yorkshire port.

James entered the building to see the door to the room on the right, where he would have expected to find Benjamin, open and no one inside. The door on the opposite side of the corridor, which led to what had been his uncle's office, was closed. He opened it and surprised Benjamin who swung his feet from the desk and sprang from the chair.

'Ah, Benjamin, sorry to disturb your snooze,' he remarked with a hint of admonishment.

'Oh! I ... Mr James, I ... I ...'

Flattered that the clerk remembered him after seven years, James gave a little smile. He dismissed the attempted explanation with a casual gesture. 'We'll have work to do from now on, Benjamin, so I think you had better resume your own office.'

He swallowed. 'We?'

'Yes, we. My uncle died and I'm taking over.'

Benjamin's eyes widened. 'Died? Oh, I'm sorry. I didn't know.'

'How could you?' replied James as he came over to the desk.

'A tragedy,' commented Benjamin, hunching his shoulders and rubbing the palms of his hands together. 'I remarked how bad Mr Cornelius's cough was but he was reluctant to go to the doctor.'

'A pity he didn't but I doubt whether anything could have been done for him.'

Benjamin nodded. 'Your uncle and I rubbed along very well. I hope we will too?'

'No doubt we will,' replied James, fixing his eyes firmly on the clerk, 'so long as your work continues to satisfy.' He paused for a moment to let his words sink in. He noticed Benjamin tense a little and then avoid his gaze.

'Oh, it will, Mr James, it will.'

'Good. Now you can familiarise me with the work in hand and anything else of importance.'

'Very good, Mr James, very good.'

He scurried away to return a few moments later with a sheaf of documents.

Over the next three weeks James became conversant with the business his uncle had conducted in Whitby. Word soon got around that Cornelius had died and clients, while bringing their commiserations, sought reassurance that their affairs were still in capable hands.

James was reminded of his inheritance from Miss Briggs when, at the start of his fourth week in Whitby, Benjamin announced that a Mr Fairbrother wished to see him.

'Who's he?' James asked quietly.

'Mr Cornelius leased him the property in New Buildings,' replied Benjamin. 'There was some talk that they were leaving.'

James nodded as he recalled his father's words. 'Show him in.'

He judged the small man who entered his office to be in his late fifties. He was smartly dressed in light grey checked trousers with a dark grey three-quarter-length coat. A grey cravat was tied to perfection at his high shirt collar. He carried a top hat, revealing neatly trimmed dark hair, greying at the temples. His voice was gentle when he spoke.

'Mr Mitchell, I was so sorry to hear about your uncle.' He extended his hand.

James came from behind his desk. He felt the grasp of long thin fingers which he had always associated with a deft piano player and wondered if this man could draw magic from the instrument.

218

'Mr Fairbrother, it is good to meet you. I hope the relationship my uncle had with you can continue?'

Mr Fairbrother gesticulated with his hands and gave an inclination of his head, both emphasising his words. 'I regret that is not going to be possible. Alas, my wife and I are leaving Whitby in order to be nearer our daughter who lives in Boston in Lincolnshire. Earlier this year she was bereaved. She was left well off but a condition of her continuing affluence was that she should remain in her late husband's property and run his estate as he would have done. She has asked us to go and live with her.'

'Understandable, Mr Fairbrother. I hope both you and your wife will be happy there.'

'I'm sure we shall. We were always close to her, and of course we shall have the pleasure of our grandchildren.'

'So, when would you be leaving?'

'The end of next week, the rent is paid until then. I always paid your uncle two months in advance.'

'Very well, Mr Fairbrother. Do you mind if I come and look at the property? I'm staying at the Angel at the moment. I've been looking for a house so maybe this will be right for me.'

'I'm sure it will,' replied Mr Fairbrother brightly. 'Maybe a little large for one person, but who knows? That situation might alter.'

James smiled as he followed his client's lead and stood up. 'Indeed it might.' He escorted Mr Fairbrother to the door, shook hands and arranged to visit the house the next day.

When he started up the path to number seven New Buildings, James felt the house looking at him, as if trying to reach an opinion about him.

Mr Fairbrother's greeting was warm. When James stepped into the hall he sensed the house echoing that greeting. He was introduced to Mrs Fairbrother, who insisted he take some hot chocolate with them before Mr Fairbrother showed him over the house.

'It seems a friendly place,' James commented as they went up the stairs.

'Indeed it is,' agreed Mr Fairbrother. 'We have been very happy here. I'm sure you will be too if you decide to come.'

'I think I already have,' replied James.

'Splendid, my boy, splendid. I'm sure the previous owner would approve. She was a Miss Briggs. A fine lady, I believe, kept very much to herself but a staunch friend to those she encouraged. Most of the furnishings were hers. I don't know who owns it now, Mr Mitchell never said, only told us he was acting as agent.'

219

James held his counsel. He saw no reason to reveal that the house and its contents had been left to him.

As he walked through it the feeling grew stronger and stronger that he belonged here. He had a strange sensation that Miss Briggs was watching, approving, and giving her blessing to his decision. Though he had never met her, and only learned of her after she had died, he felt a special empathy with her as he moved among what had been her belongings, in a house he felt sure she had loved. And yet he had an odd notion that something was not quite right ... as if something still disturbed Miss Briggs.

That feeling remained with him when he entered his office and called for Benjamin. He was sitting at his desk, his hands clasped pensively in front of him, when the clerk came in with a questioning look.

'Benjamin,' James leaned back in his chair and fixed his gaze on his clerk, 'what was Miss Briggs like?'

The mention of her name made him screw up his face. 'Old fusspot,' he muttered.

'I take it you didn't like her?'

'Well, er, not exactly.'

James eyed him with curiosity. 'Go on,' he prompted.

The clerk wondered just what he could say. He did not want to speak ill of the dead – it could be unlucky. Nor did he wish to appear ingratiating. 'She demanded attention as soon as she walked in.'

'Don't all our clients expect that?' James raised his eyebrows.

'I suppose so,' Benjamin agreed reluctantly, as if he thought James was defending her. 'But she'd tap her walking stick impatiently if she was kept waiting even for one second.'

'Had she any family – relatives?'

'Only a nephew. Well, the son of her nephew. She took him in when his parents died. She brought him up. Tragic, his murder.'

'Murder?'

'He was Mate on the *Diana*. Was set upon after he had collected the crew's wages.'

'That would have been devastating for Miss Briggs?'

'Oh, no.' Benjamin shook his head. 'She was already dead – heart attack two years previously.'

James's mind jolted at this information. The boy she had brought up was still alive when she had died! Why hadn't she left him her money and property? Why had James, a perfect stranger, inherited? His thoughts made him only half aware of what Benjamin was saying.

'The Master of the *Diana*, Captain Barrick, was friendly with Miss Briggs. He could tell you more about her than I can.' He sought an easy way to escape from having to express what he knew would be a biased opinion.

James nodded. 'Thank you, Benjamin.' He gestured with his hand that the interview was at an end. He wanted to be left with his own thoughts.

Half an hour later he was no nearer understanding why he had been the beneficiary. Maybe he could learn something from Captain Barrick. He got the captain's address from Benjamin and, ten minutes later, was climbing the seven steps to the front door of a house in Poplar Row. Its variegated bricks stretched three storeys high.

His knock was answered by a maid neatly attired in black dress, white apron and mob-cap. Her cheery smile spoke of contentment in her situation and gave James the impression that he would be meeting a kindly man and thoughtful employer.

'Captain Barrick at home?' he asked pleasantly.

'Who shall I say is calling, sir?'

'Mr James Mitchell.'

In a few moments she was back, inviting him to step inside.

As she closed the door behind James a ruddy-faced man, well-built, his eyes bright, came from a room on the right. He held out his hand. 'Mr Mitchell, I'm pleased to meet you.' His deep voice seemed to fill the small hall.

'And I you, sir,' returned James.

'I take it you are Cornelius Mitchell's nephew, now running the business in Whitby?'

'Indeed you are right, sir.'

'Sad about your uncle, but I'm pleased to see that the firm will continue here in Whitby. Now come along in.' He led the way to the room he had just left.

James found himself in a room that had been turned into Captain Barrick's study. One wall was lined with bookshelves. A desk stood crosswise in one corner and two wing chairs were placed on either side of the fireplace. Paintings of ships hung on the walls, with one area devoted to depictions of the whaling trade. The whole room conveyed the feeling of a man contented with and steeped in a job that he loved.

'Do sit down, Mr Mitchell, and tell me what I can do for you? You are fortunate to catch me. I sail in two days' time.'

'Then I am lucky. And please, sir, I'm James Mitchell.'

Captain Barrick nodded. He was a man given to sizing people up quickly and liked what he saw. James struck him as alert; he had noted how quickly the young man had taken in his surroundings and no doubt had formed an opinion from them. He liked the open face and the crispness in his voice.

James sat down in one of the wing chairs and Captain Barrick took the other.

'Well, sir, I believe you were friendly with Miss Edith Briggs and I wondered if you could tell me something about her?' He saw the captain look questioningly at him and went on quickly, 'She was a client of my uncle's and there are one or two things I want to make sure have been cleared up, regarding the house in which she lived.'

'A fine woman. Knew her own mind. Made decisions and stuck by them. Could be a formidable person and always appeared so to strangers because they imagined she was viewing them with suspicion. She wasn't really, it was just her way of presenting herself. Behind that exterior – and she was no beauty – was a warm-hearted person.' He paused then added, 'She did not make friends easily – or rather, she did not encourage many on a close basis, but those she did were always assured of a warm welcome at her home. She loved that house, stamped her personality on it.'

James recalled the strong feeling he had experienced when he had visited it. 'She had no relatives?'

'Only Reuben, the son of her nephew. A fine young man. Had his heart set on the sea. Though Miss Briggs was not for it, she saw that he would do well in anything he really wanted to do. She came to me and I took him under my wing.' He added quickly so that there should be no misunderstanding: 'No privileges. He had to start at the bottom. But he had ability and was soon promoted. He would have gone far.' The captain shook his head sadly. 'A tragedy when he was murdered. And for what? One might say a handful of silver. Thank goodness Edith was not alive to know it.' Again he shook his head as he recalled, 'It devastated his wife.'

James looked at him sharply. 'He was married?'

'Oh, yes. To a fine lass, Gennetta Turner, daughter of Jeremiah who founded Turner's jet business. She walked out when he insisted she marry Cyrus Sleightholme, and took Reuben instead. Jeremiah cut her off. Edith gave them a home. She loved having them and doted on the two children, Nathaniel and Flora.'

Again James was puzzled. If that was the case, why hadn't she left everything to them? Seeking a clue without revealing his true interest, he asked, 'What happened when she died?'

'They stayed on in the house, but when Reuben was murdered Gennetta couldn't afford to live there.'

'It wasn't theirs?'

'No. It appears Edith left the place to someone else. I don't know who. Gennetta turned to her brother, Jack, for help but he was a hard bastard.'

James was struck by the venom which had come into the captain's voice and knew why when he heard what had happened.

'But she was strong-willed,' the captain concluded, 'survived and seized the opportunity to run the business, knowing her sister-in-law, Grace, couldn't after Jack was drowned. Then Grace ups and marries Cyrus Sleightholme, and once again Gennetta sees her position in jeopardy.'

'Why?' asked James.

'The Sleightholmes are rival jet workers. Always had an eye for the Turners' business.'

James nodded his understanding.

'Gennetta couldn't stomach the idea of their taking over Turner's,' the captain went on. 'I suppose she thought that Cyrus had married Grace for that purpose.'

'And so?'

'She left. She bought a house in Well Close Square and is managing by teaching drawing.'

'It sounds as though she deserves some luck,' commented James thoughtfully.

As he walked to his office he turned over in his mind what he had learned, but was no nearer finding the reason why he had benefited from Edith Briggs's will when it seemed that Reuben and, after him, Gennetta, should have done so.

Chapter Eighteen

The slashing rain did nothing to improve Tom's temper as he made his way to the house in Well Close Square together with Davey and Joey.

Watching them take off their wet coats in the hall, Gennetta could tell there was something wrong.

Tom greeted her politely and though he was eager to unburden his annoyance, waited until she had given the boys their initial instructions and settled them down to the task she had set them. She noticed that on a couple of occasions Joey seemed set to say something and then drew back. She wondered if it had anything to do with Tom's mood and if he had had instructions to say nothing.

Once the boys were devoting their attention to their drawing, though she had a feeling that they were not concentrating as hard as they usually did, Gennetta and Tom crossed the hall to the parlour.

'Now, Tom, what is it?' She put the question even before the door had clicked shut. 'You're in a mood, something's upset you.'

His lips were tight with annoyance as he paced the floor. His eyes darkened stormily and did not lighten with his outpouring. 'That damned Cyrus Sleightholme! He's ruining a good firm. Turner's will disappear, I can see it coming. I don't like the way his father keeps visiting the workshop, telling Cyrus what to do. The business has nothing to do with him. He's a bombastic busybody who'll ride roughshod over anyone.'

Gennetta was startled. Something really *had* upset him. But the information did not surprise her. She had expected something like this to happen when Grace had given Cyrus half the company. She had always thought he was incapable of running it and Grace certainly was not strong enough to interfere and control him. 'Tom, calm down. Come and sit down and tell me calmly what's happening.'

He flung himself into a chair opposite her. There had been a time

224

when such events would not have bothered him, but since his association with Gennetta his interest in Turner's had sharpened. Even though they had their differences of opinion, he recognised that her business acumen was for the good of the firm and was beginning to understand her reasons for not wanting it to fall into the hands of the Sleightholmes.

'In the last nine weeks, Cyrus has been to London twice and is planning to go again tomorrow. That must be costing the firm money.'

Gennetta raised her eyebrows in surprise. She had never found it necessary to go as frequently as that, but she offered no comment on his judgement. 'That's all right, if he's getting good orders.'

'He did the first time he went. In fact, more than we could deal with in the delivery time. I know for a fact that he slipped in some work from Sleightholme's workshop. Saw it myself. Inferior stuff. Not good for Turner's image.'

'What?' Gennetta sat up. 'That's the way to lose orders! What about his second trip?'

'Nothing. No orders. It was too near the first, unless he was going to attract new clients which he didn't. I'm not sure that was the purpose of his visit.'

'What are you implying?' Gennetta's brow furrowed with a puzzled frown.

'I overheard a conversation in the Black Bull. Cyrus was one of five men discussing where they were going to do their gambling that evening. He suggested that they make the stakes bigger, like those he had played for in London – they made the game more exciting apparently.'

Gennetta, understanding the insinuations he was making, stared at him. 'Going to London, paid for by the firm – and you think he could be gambling with Turner's money?'

'I've no proof of that, but it's possible. There are ways and means.'

Gennetta sighed in despair. 'And there's nothing we can do about it! Challenge him and he'd deny it. Go to Grace and she wouldn't believe us. Go to his father and, even if he did believe us, he would deny it and do nothing for he'd see it as ruining Turner's and a chance for him to buy Grace out cheaply when the business has run down. Maybe he's even conniving in what his son's doing.'

'I'm afraid there's more bad news.' Tom looked dispirited.

'What now?' she sighed.

'He's upsetting the men. Sacked a couple of them for no reason at all as far as I could find out. Undermined John's authority as foreman. Takes him all his time to curb his tongue, but John needs that job, can't afford to lose it. And today he got rid of Joey.'

'What?' Gennetta was shattered. 'I thought he was itching to tell me something. What happened?'

'Cyrus criticised what Joey was etching in a way he didn't like. Joey spoke back, sticking up for what he was doing, saying that was the way you had taught him. Cyrus told him to forget what he had been taught by you, and in doing so spoke ill of you. Joey didn't like that and told Cyrus what he thought of him, so Cyrus sacked him there and then and told him to clear his things out of the building.'

'Oh, no! Doesn't he realise he's losing one of the best assets the firm has?'

'And he lost another.'

'Who?' Gennetta's eyes widened. 'Not you?'

'No. Davey.'

'Yelled at Cyrus not to do that to his friend and promptly kicked him on the shin.' Tom gave a little chuckle, recalling the incident, and Gennetta had to smile as she pictured Cyrus hopping around on one foot, trying to soothe a shin which must have been causing him great pain.

'He didn't turn on you as Davey's father?' she asked in concern.

'No. Yelled at me to punish my brat for kicking his elders. But Davey was long gone. I was tempted to leave too, but, like John, I need that job. Besides, you need someone inside that firm to report what's going on.'

'Thanks for that, Tom. What's happening to Joey? Where's he gone?'

'His things, few as they are, are at my house. He can sleep in a chair tonight but it's no permanent solution, small as the house is.'

'He can stay here. There's a spare room at the top.'

'Are you sure you want that?' Doubt crept into Tom's voice.

'He's a good-hearted lad.' She gave a smile. 'You're thinking of his rough edges, the life he's led?'

'Well, you have Nathaniel and Flora to think of.'

Gennetta's smile broadened. 'Listen who's talking – the man who criticised me for wanting to live on this side of the river!'

'Well, I was only ...'

'Don't worry, they'll cope. And if I know Joey, he won't try to influence them. But come, we'll let him decide.' She rose from her chair and Tom followed her from the room.

A few minutes later Joey was staring wide-eyed at her suggestion. 'Me, stay here, missus?'

Gennetta smiled. 'You have nowhere else, have you?'

'No.'

'Then why not?'

'For good?'

'As long as you want. You may not like it here.'

'Like it? Who wouldn't?' He looked round him in amazement. Him, living in a house this size? He couldn't believe it.

'We'll see how you like it. I'll show you where you will sleep, but you have to remember to abide by certain rules.'

'Anything thee says, missus.'

Gennetta was at the door. Joey leaped from his chair and ran after her. 'Can Davey come?' he called.

'Of course.'

She led the way up three flights of stairs to the top floor. She opened a door into a small room which held an iron bedstead on which there was a straw-filled mattress. Blankets, neatly folded, lay on top. 'I'll tell one of the maids to bring sheets and make up the bed.'

'Sheets? Never slept in 'em before,' gasped Joey. 'And a maid to make me bed?' He couldn't believe what was happening.

His eyes ranged round the room as the others stood watching, amused by the changes of expression on his face.

A chair with a wicker seat stood beside the bed while a chest of drawers with a mirror, and a table which held a basin and ewer, were the only other items of furniture in the room. The wooden floor had rugs on either side of the bed.

Gennetta smiled when he looked into the ewer. 'Wash regularly, Joey, morning and night. Always come to a meal clean, neat and tidy. If you can do that and behave yourself, we'll get along famously.'

'Yes, missus. And thank thee.'

'All right, that's settled.'

For two days after visiting Captain Barrick, James pondered as to whether he should call on Mrs Briggs. The answer was made for him when he decided to put two drawers in his desk to better use. He had given them little attention until now as a glance had told him that they contained only notepaper.

Having dealt with the morning's mail which demanded his immediate attention, James started on the top right-hand drawer. He took out notepaper and envelopes, stacking them into neat piles on top of the desk. When he leaned down to make sure he had cleared the drawer he saw that two sheets of paper still lay there. He fished them out and as he placed them on one of the piles, became aware that there was something written on one of them. He recognised his uncle's writing in what appeared to be a scribbled note.

He read: '1 June 1848. Draw up new will for Edith Briggs – everything to Reuben. In event of his death, all for Gennetta.'

James sat staring at the words. Obviously they must have been made during a visit by Miss Briggs. She must have issued instructions for her will to be changed. His thoughts raced. If that had been done he wouldn't have inherited ... unless she had changed her mind again? He tried to recall the date of the will which had left him everything, but failed.

'Benjamin!' James's shout brought the clerk scurrying into his office.

'Sir?'

'Do we still have a file on Miss Edith Briggs?'

'Yes.'

'Bring it to me.'

A few moments later Benjamin handed James a folder. He acknowledged it and dismissed the clerk with a wave of his hand.

He flicked the folder open and searched through its contents. Documents relating to Edith's inheritance from her father, how Cornelius had invested it, and records of the growth of her assets. He stared at the next folded sheet of paper he picked up. Just what he was looking for. The neat copperplate writing announced it to be 'The Last Will and Testament of Edith Briggs'. The date leaped out at him: 1st August 1823.

He opened it and saw the words he had last read in Scarborough.

Her will had never been changed.

Why? Had his uncle forgotten his note of 1 June 1848? James's mind went back over the year his uncle had spent some time with them. When had it been? In the summer he was sure, but when exactly?

'Benjamin!' he yelled, bringing the clerk hurrying into the office.

'Benjamin, cast your mind back. The year Miss Briggs died ...'

'Yes?' He cocked his head to one side like an inquisitive sparrow.

'Did she visit my uncle prior to her death?'

'Yes.'

James eyed him sharply. 'You have no hesitation in saying that?'

'None. I remember it well because she came to the office several times after that – your uncle was with you in Scarborough – and the old battleaxe was more agitated every time she came to hear Mr Cornelius wasn't here. If I remember rightly she was expecting some sort of document from your uncle. Took it out on me when it wasn't here. Thought I wasn't passing her messages on to him. But I did.'

'Any idea what that document was?'

'No, sir.'

James looked thoughtful for a moment, then said, 'Thanks, Benjamin. That will be all.'

James sat staring at the will and the scribbled note. It seemed as though Edith Briggs had wanted to change her will but her wishes had not been carried out. Why? Even though his uncle had been in Scarborough, the necessary document could have been drawn up. Yet it hadn't been. He was puzzled because his uncle had always struck him as being efficient and it was unlike him not to carry out a client's wishes as soon as they were made. James began to feel that the inheritance from Miss Briggs shouldn't be his. It had been her wish for it to go to her only relative, distant though he was, and in the case of his death, to his wife, the Gennetta Captain Barrick had told him about. Maybe he should go and talk to her after all? He was on the point of deciding to do just that when he reckoned it would be better to make sure that Miss Briggs had really meant to alter her will. His father might be able to give him the reason why it had not been done.

There was a fine drizzle coming off the sea when James climbed into the coach for Scarborough the following morning. He made conversation with the other passengers though his mind was still troubled by the thought that he had inherited against Miss Briggs's real wishes.

The rain had ceased by the time the coach reached Scarborough, though low cloud still hung close to the Norman keep on the promontory between the two sweeping bays. The grey sea looked cold and uninviting. James turned up the collar of his coat and hurried to his father's office.

'This is a surprise, and a nice one at that,' cried Thornton, coming from behind his desk, his hand held out to shake James's fondly.

'Nice to see you too, Father,' he returned, and then shook himself out of his coat.

'Come, sit down. A glass of Madeira to warm you? It won't have been a pleasant ride on a day like this.' Thornton went to pour two glasses and as he brought them back to the desk said, 'How's life in Whitby? Settling in all right?'

James took the glass, raised it in acknowledgement and took a sip. 'Yes, everything is going well. I've moved into Miss Briggs's house.'

'Splendid.' Thornton beamed as he leaned back in his chair. 'That will be a great asset when you start to entertain. It will be good for business.'

'I don't know whether I should have it.'

There was a moment's silence. 'What do you mean?' Thornton frowned at the unexpected statement.

'I found this at the bottom of a drawer.' James passed over the scribbled note.

Thornton read it. His mind raced. What fool thing had Cornelius done? Why the devil hadn't he destroyed any note he'd made regarding Miss Briggs's wishes? He looked up, keeping his irritation under control. 'But this is only a note. It has no legal standing.'

'True. But I believe Miss Briggs wanted to alter her will in favour of her nearest relative. Why didn't Uncle Cornelius do it?'

Thornton spread his hands. 'I don't know,' he replied, then added, 'if that really was the intention. Maybe Miss Briggs had second thoughts and cancelled this?' He poked a finger at the note.

'I think not,' replied James with a sharp shake of his head. 'Benjamin remembers it as a time when Uncle was here in Scarborough. He had several visits from Miss Briggs in that time. Seems she was expecting a document from Uncle.'

'That could have been about anything.'

'I think it was a new will. And I believe that she was anxious to get it signed and sealed because she knew she was dying. She did soon after. If you remember, Uncle Cornelius returned in time for the funeral.'

'But that's only theory,' protested Thornton, trying to make light of the matter, though his mind was troubled by where James's suppositions might lead him.

'But probably near the truth. I can't understand why Uncle Cornelius didn't attend to the matter there and then. Have you any idea?'

Thornton shook his head. 'No. I admit it's unlike him but there must have been a good reason.'

'It almost seems as if he was avoiding doing it.'

'Nonsense,' Thornton rapped, rather sharply. He wanted to put an end to this conversation, but James went on.

'Well, I don't feel happy with the inheritance. After all, I was a stranger to Miss Briggs and she had a relative to whom I believe she intended to leave everything.'

'But Reuben Briggs was murdered so ...'

' ... everything should have gone to his wife.' James finished off his father's sentence in a different way from the one he'd intended.

'She's no direct relation, only by marriage,' Thornton pointed out.

'Miss Briggs must have thought highly of her to mention her in that note. I'm going to see her, she's still in Whitby.'

'What on earth for?' Thornton asked cautiously, trying to dissuade James.

'If I think she should have had my inheritance, then I'll give it to her.'

'You'll be going against Miss Briggs's wishes,' Thornton warned.

'Will I? I wonder.'

'But you'll be giving money away to a stranger!'

'I'll make my mind up after I've met Mrs Briggs.'

'Give her a hint and she'll probably play you for a fool.' Irritation at James's folly was creeping into his father's voice. 'Forget this nonsense!'

'I can't and won't until I know what Miss Briggs's real intentions were.'

'And how do you expect to find that out?'

'See what Mrs Briggs knows. Talk to Benjamin again, see if he can throw any light on that note.'

Thornton's mind was racing. Cornelius had been careless. Had he been even more careless in mentioning this to his clerk? Had Miss Briggs told her nephew and his wife what she was going to do?

'I think you are wasting your time. Miss Briggs left everything to you. She wouldn't have done that if she hadn't intended you to have it.'

'But that note seems to indicate otherwise.'

'It's only a piece of paper,' snapped Thornton. 'It means nothing.'

'Then why was it made? Uncle Cornelius wouldn't have made those notes if he hadn't been approached by Miss Briggs, and that seems to indicate it was her intention to leave her belongings to her nephew, and in the event of his death to his wife. I think I should respect the wishes of a person I never knew. What was I to her? Just someone she'd heard of through Uncle Cornelius. This Reuben and Gennetta were far more to her.'

At James's words Thornton's temper began to rise. 'They weren't,' he snapped. 'Forget it, James, forget it. Don't overturn your mother's will to satisfy a whim that's arisen through a note with no legal binding.' The disclosure was out before he realised it.

'Mother? What has this to do with her?'

'Er, nothing ... I ...' Thornton was flustered. His face was turning bright red. His normally calm exterior had disintegrated.

James was surprised by the change in his father. He had never seen him so flustered as he was now.

'There's something you know that you aren't telling me,' said James. The steel in his voice told his father that he meant to find out and would not be put off. 'It's do to with those words, "mother's will".' He repeated them half to himself, this time as if he was pondering what might lie behind them. They came to his lips once more, silently. His eyes widened. The possible solution shocked and puzzled him. Surely what he was thinking couldn't be right? But

231

Thornton had said 'your mother's will'. They had not been discussing his mother's will, they had been talking about Miss Briggs's will, and yet Thornton had used that term in relation to it. He stared at Thornton. 'Miss Briggs was my mother?' The words came out slowly, quietly, but charged with emotion, demanding an answer.

Thornton hesitated. He bit his lip, regretting his slip.

'I want to know!' There was no mistaking James's determination to have the truth.

Thornton moistened his lips with his tongue as he nodded. 'Yes, Miss Briggs was your mother.'

'But ...' James looked bewildered.

Thornton knew that there was nothing for it but to tell him the truth.

'When she was pregnant she went to your uncle for advice. She would not reveal your father's name but didn't want you to bear the stigma of being illegitimate. Knowing that Hannah and I wanted a child, Cornelius arranged for her to come to us. With doctor and nurse sworn to secrecy we took you as our own as soon as you were born.

'So there it is,' he concluded. 'I'm sorry you ever had to learn the truth and that it had to be in this way.'

James nodded slowly. His thoughts were in turmoil and now he regretted all the more that he had never met Miss Briggs – his mother. 'So that is why she made me the sole beneficiary in her will?'

'Exactly,' verified Thornton, hoping this would eliminate all thoughts of contacting Gennetta Briggs.

'Then why the note I found in the drawer, and dated so recently? And why didn't Uncle Cornelius carry out what appeared to be a change desired by Miss Briggs?'

'Because he knew you were her legitimate heir and to change the will would have meant that you would have lost everything which was rightly yours.'

'But he had no right to do that! As a solicitor he should have carried out his client's wishes.' James found his good opinion of his uncle being sorely tested. 'I shall visit Mrs Briggs as soon as I get back and tell her what I intend to do.'

'Think what you will lose if you ...' Thornton began, trying to dissuade James, but he cut him short.

'You won't talk me out of it. That note refers to my mother's wishes and I mean to see they are carried out. Besides, I don't need the money. Maybe Mrs Briggs does.'

Two days later, on a pleasant afternoon, James sought admittance to the house in Well Close Square. His request to see Mrs Briggs was granted and as he walked into the parlour he was struck by the delicate beauty of the woman he had come to see.

'Mrs Briggs, I am sorry to intrude on you like this. I would not have done so had it not been important.' His voice was apologetic.

She extended her hand. 'Mr Mitchell, I don't think we have met but you are welcome.'

It was a handsome man who stood before her. James's smile was warm and friendly and she liked his open face and soft caressing voice. His hair was so black it reminded her of the finest polished jet.

'Please, do sit down. You'll take tea?'

Not wanting to trouble her, he was on the point of refusing when he detected a genuine offer of friendship and realised he would disappoint her if he said no. 'That would be kind.'

He watched her closely as she went to the bell-pull beside the fireplace. Her silky fair hair was plaited neatly at the back of her neck and draped carefully over her right shoulder. He found himself imagining it loose and flowing down her back like some cascading stream. As she turned to take a seat on the opposite side of a low table, he was struck by the beauty of her pale blue eyes. After the enquiries he had made regarding Gennetta Turner, or Gennetta Briggs after her marriage, and the way life had treated her, he was surprised to find that she seemed so tranquil and content.

'I understand that you are continuing the practice which was run by your uncle?' she observed as she smoothed the front of her dress.

'You could put it that way,' he replied.

His answer struck her as a little odd when all she had expected was confirmation. But she made no comment. Instead she said, 'So you come in an official capacity?'

'Not exactly,' he replied, and then left her wondering while tea was brought in.

'Well?' she prompted as the door clicked shut.

'I come about the house I own – seven New Buildings.'

Gennetta paused in pouring the milk and looked at him. He was shocked to see an expression bordering on hostility had come into her face. '*You*? You are the person so mysteriously named in Miss Briggs's will?'

'You saw it?' he asked, and then waved his hand as if to dismiss the question. 'But, of course, you must have.'

'Yes. As my husband was her only relative, it was only natural that your uncle should make it known to us.'

'Quite right,' he agreed.

'So you are also the person who, by charging an exorbitant rent, made it difficult for us to stay? When Reuben was murdered it was impossible for me to meet the amount stipulated and your uncle made it clear that there were new tenants wanting to move in.' Her words poured out, laced with anger.

'But I never fixed a rent! My father said I should leave all the arrangements to Uncle Cornelius. I don't think he made an exorbitant charge.'

'Sixty pounds, not exorbitant?' Gennetta was disgusted at his opinion.

'Sixty pounds!' James gasped. 'You paid sixty pounds?' He recalled his father telling him that his uncle had negotiated a rent of twenty pounds. It did not take much imagination to see where the other two-thirds had gone – split equally between the two brothers. He felt revulsion and shock at what they had done. 'Let me assure you, Mrs Briggs, that I had no knowledge of this and am sorry for any hardship which may have resulted from it, and from the actions of my uncle following the death of your husband.'

The plea in his voice and the way his face had paled could not be denied. If ever Gennetta had seen a man who was genuinely embarrassed, he was sitting in front of her. She continued to pour his tea. James read this, along with the fact that her face had softened a little, as a sign she believed him.

She handed him a cup of tea. 'Help yourself to sugar.'

'Thank you.'

She passed him a scone and as he buttered it, he asked: 'I take it that you loved that house and were happy there with Miss Briggs?'

'Oh, yes. She was a wonderful person. So kind. She did so much for Reuben when he was orphaned. Brought him up like her own son.'

'And that's why you were surprised when she left everything to me?' He took another bite at his scone.

Gennetta nodded. 'Not that we wanted it. We didn't crave it. If that's what Aunt Edith wanted, then so be it. But I must admit it hurt a little at the time, more so for Reuben.' She gave a shrug of resignation and stirred her tea thoughtfully as she recalled that interview with Cornelius.

Pondering his next approach James watched her, imagining, from what he had heard about her, the steel behind her gentle exterior. He knew he was sitting with a woman of great determination. She was a person who would prefer him to come to the point and this was evident when she looked up and met his gaze without looking away.

'Mr Mitchell, I don't think that you came here to tell me about the house, I think more lies behind your visit.'

He smiled. 'You're right, Mrs Briggs. I merely introduced the topic of the house to assess your feelings, especially towards Miss Briggs. You have told me ...'

'So little,' Gennetta interrupted.

'Ah, more than you know. The look in your eyes when you mentioned her told me you loved her dearly.'

'So very much. And not only me but also Reuben and the children. We were all devastated when she died so suddenly.'

'You were with her?'

'Yes.'

'I'm pleased to know that she had someone with her who loved her and whom she loved. I wish I could have been there.'

Gennetta was startled by this last statement. She was curious. Where was this conversation leading? 'I never heard her speak of you.'

'I don't suppose she did. I never met her and never knew her, yet I was her son!'

The shock of this unexpected announcement robbed Gennetta of words. She stared at him disbelievingly, and yet from this person whom she judged to be utterly genuine, it must be the truth.

When she spoke her voice was quiet but perfectly under control. 'Son? Then that answers the question of the will. Reuben wasn't her nearest relative. We never knew.' She gave a slight pause then asked, 'Your father?'

'No idea. Even my adoptive father did not know. My mother kept it her secret. I did not know any of this until two days ago.' James went on to tell her his story. As he finished, he fished a piece of paper from his pocket. 'It all came out because of this, which I found at the bottom of a drawer in my uncle's desk, covered by other papers.'

She took the paper from him, looked down at it and read. She gazed at it for a few moments longer, the words burning into her mind. Then she looked up slowly to find James watching her intently.

'But this date is shortly before Aunt Edith died. I don't understand?' She looked bemused.

'It seems to me that my mother wanted to change her original will in favour of you and your husband. For some reason Uncle Cornelius never did it. I have my own ideas why, but I'll not go into those. They are irrelevant to my reason for coming to see you.'

Gennetta's mind had been racing. She could make a lot of trouble but it would not overturn the legality of the original will and would only hurt the young man sitting opposite her.

'I would like to honour my mother's wishes, and I believe those to be that your husband and, following his death, you, should inherit. So I propose that everything that came to me should be handed over to you.'

She gasped at the proposition, and stared at him. 'But I couldn't.' She shook her head.

'Why not? It's what my mother wanted.'

'Maybe, but I couldn't take it from her son.'

'I won't be badly off. There's my uncle's business, which is thriving. I think she knew this and realised that what she had would benefit you more than me. I think she loved us all.'

'I'm sure she did. But I couldn't accept this from you. I wouldn't feel comfortable with it.'

'But Gennetta ...' He pulled himself up short. Her name had come out before he realised it. He blushed. 'Oh, I ... I'm sorry.' He gathered himself. 'Please may I call you Gennetta? I feel that through my enquiries, made from the best of intentions, I have come to know you so well. And now meeting you ...'

Delighted laughter interrupted him. 'Of course you may ... Mr Mitchell,' she added with teasing formality.

He held up one hand. 'James – please.'

She acknowledged this with an inclination of her head. 'It is very kind and thoughtful of you to make this offer but I can't possibly accept.'

'But it's what Mother wanted.'

'But you were her son, you have the greater right.'

James looked thoughtful, wondering how he could persuade her.

'More tea?' she interrupted his thoughts.

'Please.' He watched her as she poured the tea. As he took it he said, 'This has come as a surprise to you, if not a shock. You know what I would like to do. Please think it over before you reach a final decision.'

She hesitated, then agreed.

As James was leaving he said with deep sincerity, 'It has been a pleasure meeting you. I hope to hear from you soon that you will accept my offer.'

Gennetta was thoughtful as she returned to the parlour. James and his proposal occupied much of her thoughts for the rest of the afternoon and interrupted her sleep that night. By morning she thought she'd found a solution, one which she hoped might result in her getting her father's business back, if she planned carefully and acted decisively.

After breakfasting with the children and Joey and leaving them in Rose's care, she made her way to James's office. It was a pleasant morning so she did not hurry but savoured the atmosphere of the busy port. It gave her the opportunity to reconsider what she had decided and by the time she had reached the building she had confirmed to herself that it was a good idea.

'I'm pleased to see you again so soon.' James greeted her with a

236

welcoming smile. He indicated a seat and as he sat down behind his desk, added, 'I take it you have come to a decision?'

'Yes.' Gennetta nodded. 'You want me to accept, and I don't want to take what I believe is rightfully yours, so I've thought of something which I hope will be acceptable to both of us.' She paused a moment, then seeing his interest was roused, went on: 'Why don't we use the money to set up a business from which we could both benefit?'

Intrigued, he asked, 'What sort?'

'I know the jet trade.'

'Set up a new firm?' James pondered. 'Is this a good time?' he asked cautiously.

'I can see boom times ahead. I have the knowledge and the connections.' Gennetta pressed her case eagerly.

'A rival to your father's old firm?'

'Yes. Why not?' Her voice hardened. 'Cyrus Sleightholme tricked my sister-in-law into letting him have half the business and now he's ruining it. I want it back and our firm could help me do that!'

James nodded. He knew her story and he sympathised with her. 'If I agree, you must do nothing illegal,' he said cautiously.

'Of course not,' said Gennetta, an edge to her voice. 'But I'd take so much business from him that it wouldn't survive.'

'And he'd sell cheaply?'

'That's what I'd expect.'

'And you, or rather we, would buy?'

'Yes.'

'But wouldn't his father bail him out or take over just to be rid of the Turner name?'

'That's a possibility but I'd deal with that somehow, depending on developments.' She warmed to her subject and pressed her case. 'This is a golden opportunity for both of us. Say yes, James. Your mother would be pleased if we did this together.'

'She would, wouldn't she?' From the descriptions he had had of her he could just imagine Edith looking down on them and nodding her approval. 'All right,' he agreed enthusiastically.

A broad smile spread across Gennetta's face. 'Good! You'll put it all on a legal footing?' she insisted.

'Of course.'

'And one more thing, and I won't take no for an answer. Seven New Buildings is not involved in this. That house is yours.'

'But it was your home. Wouldn't you like to move back there?'

'No. I'm settled and happy in Well Close Square.' She knew Tom was getting used to visiting her there on this side of the river. She had seen his confidence growing stronger and the ambition which had been drained from him in his youth returning. A chance to be part of a new jet firm might fire it even further, but to suggest moving to a bigger and finer house now might destroy what she had gained. 'The house is to be yours and that's final.'

'All right,' James agreed with a smile. 'But I know it meant a lot to you so I hope you will visit as often as you like.'

Chapter Nineteen

By the time Gennetta left the office their preliminary plans had been made. She had insisted that they should start straight away. Tomorrow they would look for suitable premises. James would see to any paperwork relating to the purchase and would set up a fund for running the business. He would also organise any alterations she wanted to the building and see to any repairs that might be required. She would see to the purchase of the equipment and recruit the necessary workers.

The prospects for this new venture, the opportunity to get back into the jet trade, preoccupied Gennetta so entirely that she could not wait to tell Tom. Her footsteps quickened as she threaded her way among the crowds crossing the bridge and then hurried along Church Street to Turner's jetworks. She hoped that Cyrus would not be there. It would be unlucky if he was, for, according to Tom, he was spending less and less time there.

She entered the workshop and sensed tension the air when the men saw her. As she paused, looking around for Tom, John Young hurried to her.

'Mrs Briggs, nice to see thee again.' There was query behind his greeting.

'John, can I talk to Tom for a few minutes?'

'Of course.' He looked round. 'Tom,' he called, just as he emerged from the sorting shed.

Surprised at seeing Gennetta, he dropped the two pieces of jet he was carrying beside one of the lathes.

'Mrs Briggs wants a word,' said John, and moved away.

'Hello, Gennetta, what ...?' Tom was mystified as to why she should be here and puzzled by the excitement he sensed emanating from her.

'Walk with me,' she said, and turned for the door.

239

'But I ...'

'John's given permission,' she reassured him

'It must be important to bring you here,' he commented when he joined her outside.

'It is.' She started in the direction of the Church Stairs.

'What is it?' he pressed.

Though she was bursting to tell him she waited until the crowds had thinned and they had started to climb the steps to the church. They were halfway up. There was no one near. She stopped and turned to him.

'Tom, we're starting our own jet firm.' She smiled broadly, enjoying the shock she had given him.

'You're what?' He was unsure if he had understood her.

'Starting a new jet firm, and I want you to be part of it.' She took his hand. 'Come on, I'll tell you all about it.' They climbed the rest of the way to the churchyard and then walked beyond, on to the path by the cliff edge. As they walked she told him the whole story, from the time she had opened the door to James yesterday until this present moment. 'It's so exciting and could be the means of getting Turner's back from the Sleightholmes. There is one thing – James doesn't want it known that he has an active interest in the firm. He pretends to be merely acting on our behalf as a solicitor.'

'Gennetta.' Tom stopped her and turned her to him. His face showed deep concern as he said, 'Be careful. It is admirable what you and Mr Mitchell want to do with Miss Briggs's money but you could lose it all.'

'Tom, don't be so pessimistic. This is the opportunity I've always wanted, and with Cyrus acting as you've reported, we could force him to the point where he would want to sell.'

'And you could lose your money. Don't forget, I've seen it happen, seen my father ruined by an investment gone wrong, seen poverty because of it. You've experienced Hacker's Yard, you don't want that again.'

'That won't happen,' she pressed. Her eyes beseeched him to see things her way. 'Neither I nor James will let it. Look, Tom, I want you with us. You've a wonderful talent. We need that. And Joey's and Davey's – their future can be assured. The shadow of poverty need never hang over any of us again. Tom, forget the past, forget what happened to your father, look to the future, look what there could be for Davey. Look what there could be for us – you and me. It is in your hands, Tom. You must decide.'

'You'd do it without me?' he asked quietly.

She nodded. 'Yes, I would. But it will be easier with you because then I would have the man I love at my side.'

'I can put nothing in but my talent.'

'That's all I need – and your love.'

A silence lengthened between them. In the depths of their eyes, fixed on each other, there was love filled with understanding.

'It is yours,' he said quietly. His hands came to her waist and he drew her to him. Their lips met, sealing the promise.

As they walked back along the cliff and down the steps to the town, Gennetta talked enthusiastically about the new venture, bolstering Tom's growing interest.

'Let me do the recruiting for you,' he said. 'I know the men who would be the greatest asset to us.'

Pleased that he had used the word 'us', she readily agreed, as she did to his suggestion that they should proposition John Young. 'I know he doesn't like working for Cyrus,' he concluded. 'I'll bring him out now,' Tom said when they reached the workshop. 'We'll see what he says.'

A few moments later he reappeared with John. Gennetta could tell from his questioning look that Tom had told him nothing, except that she wanted to see him.

'John, would you like to come and work for me?' His surprised look demanded an explanation. 'I'm starting a new jet firm. Tom has agreed to come.'

He glanced at Tom, who gave a little nod of confirmation. 'I'd like nowt better,' replied John, enthusiasm charging his voice. 'I'm fed up with interference, especially now Mr Robert Sleightholme visits us more than his son, supposedly acting for him.'

'Good,' replied Gennetta. 'We'll arrange all the details later. Tom said he will recruit the necessary workers when we get everything else set up. In the meantime, you both carry on here and say nothing to anyone.'

'Just one thing, ma'am,' said John. 'Is thee employing me as foreman?'

'Of course. Tom understands that. He will be your deputy so the working relationship is exactly the same as it is now. I want him to be able to concentrate on his carving and to recruit some others.'

'So we'll be back to the same team – with you and Joey and Davey etching?'

'Yes,' she confirmed. 'I want the London trade. And with the same people as we had here, the London jewellers will soon recognise us.'

The following morning Gennetta and James found suitable premises in Flowergate and once the purchase had been agreed James saw to the conclusion of the transaction that afternoon.

At six o'clock she eagerly awaited the arrival of Tom and the two boys. Joey and Davey, enthused by the news that they would be working again, had spent the day together and met Tom when he left work.

'Something's pleased you,' observed Tom as she rushed into the hall to greet them.

'I've had a wonderful day,' Gennetta replied. 'Tell you about it while we eat.'

'Smells good, missus,' said Joey with relish. 'What is it?'

She laughed. 'Yorkshire pudding with onion gravy, then Mrs Shaw's special potato and onion pie, and your favourite bread and butter pudding.'

'Can't wait, can we, Davey?' grinned Joey. He started towards the dining room.

'Hold on – wash first.' Gennetta's crisp tones brought them to a halt.

'Come on, lads.' Tom knew the routine when he came straight from work.

Nathaniel and Flora rushed down the stairs, shouting greetings to the two boys, and ran into the dining room.

Ten minutes later they were all starting into their Yorkshire puddings.

Tom looked across at Gennetta who seemed to glow with excitement. He could guess the news but wanted to hear it from her. She felt him looking at her and, glancing up, caught his gaze. 'Well? Don't keep us waiting any longer.'

'We've got premises in Flowergate,' she announced proudly.

'Good.' Tom's eyes brightened. 'Now we can get started. Flowergate?' An amused smile twitched his lips. 'You're determined to get me this side of the river,' he added above the shouts of Joey and Davey, who were joined by Nathaniel and Flora, eager to add to the noise.

'Of course.' She returned his smile, laughter on her lips as she looked round the excited faces. 'Quiet, quiet!' she called, bringing order to the noise. 'We'll forget drawing lessons for this evening, and after we've eaten we'll go and look at what will become our new jetworks!'

The following two weeks were filled with activity. The building needed only a little repair and no alterations. Benches were put in place, lathes and grindstones installed, tools and polishing boards bought, and men engaged.

John Young oversaw the whole operation, arranging the workshop to his own liking to give the best use of space. Tom recruited two more carvers: one whom he knew was a master at carving flowers and fruit while the other was an expert at cameos. Two engravers seized the chance to work for the new firm when they knew they would be employed by Mrs Briggs.

For the time being Gennetta had decided to purchase jet from a rough jet dealer. While it would not give her flexibility, and would be a little more expensive than buying direct from the mines, she would eliminate sorting for that would have already been done and she need only purchase the precise amount she wanted. She came to an agreement with a dealer in Baxtergate who used tenement property where each floor was allocated to a particular type of jet. She also made it known that she was willing to consider jet brought from the shore, for this already had its skin worn by the action of the sea.

Three weeks from the day of the purchase of the premises, the new firm, known as Briggs Jetworkers, produced their first piece of craftwork: a replica of the west front of Whitby Abbey.

'Cyrus what's all this I hear about Gennetta and a new business?' Grace put the question in an enquiring tone as she faced her husband across the dining table, a tureen of soup between them.

'Yes, she's started one, though where she got the money to do so I don't know. She must have a backer, but who?' He shrugged his shoulders.

'How long have you known?' she demanded testily.

'She's started today, so it will be just over a week.'

'Why didn't you tell me? Why did I have to hear of it at one of my tea parties?' There was a touch of annoyance in her voice.

'I didn't want to bother you with such trivia.'

'Trivia?' She raised her voice in horror. 'How can you take a rival firm, and one run by Gennetta, so lightly?'

'It will amount to nothing,' he said dismissively, turning his attention to his soup. He did not want to tell her that both John Young and Tom Unwin had left to go to the new firm and that he had heard from his father who did not take the matter lightly.

'Gennetta did well when she took over after Jack died,' Grace pointed out.

'She already had an established firm to build on. This is different, she is just starting,' he replied. 'And don't forget, we have the London trade.'

'Well, see that we keep it. Don't forget I own half that firm and I don't want to see my income dwindle away through your carelessness.'

'It won't, my dear. I assure you, you have nothing to fear. Now let

243

us enjoy our meal without any more talk of business.' He smiled sweetly at her, reached for his glass of wine and raised it to her.

'Off to London again, Cyrus? Really, is it necessary?' Grace was indignant. 'This is the ninth time in as many months and I don't like your being away.' She looked at him intently, trying to decipher what was behind his bland expression.

'Of course it's necessary, my dear,' he answered smoothly. He was already dressed to leave and his bag, top hat and cane awaited collection in the hall. 'It's for the good of the firm. If we can keep our London trade on a solid foundation and expand, not only will we see more profit but we'll make any rivals, including Gennetta, think twice about trying to trade there.'

'Gennetta didn't think it necessary to go so often.'

'Then she wasn't thinking of the firm. Frankly, my dear, the less we hark back to her time, the better. I'm running things now.'

'I knew more about what was happening then. We met regularly, you remember. You don't bother to tell me much now.'

'I tell you what is necessary. You know you have no head for business.'

'I agree, but I like to hear what is happening.'

'You have and you shall. But I don't want to bother you with trivial things. I'm only thinking of you, my love.'

'Then hurry back. I miss you when you aren't here.'

'And I miss you.' He bent to kiss her lightly but Grace rose from her seat to return his kiss. Her arms came round his neck and held him tight whilst her lips met his with unbridled passion.

'To tempt you back quickly,' she said seductively.

'Soon,' he promised, and slid out of her arms.

She came with him into the hall, received a kiss on the cheek, then watched him as he hurried down the path, hat set at a jaunty angle, cane in one hand, his bag in the other. He paused at the gate, looked back and raised his cane, then he was gone.

Five days later Cyrus breathed a sigh of relief as the *Speedwell* slipped its ropes and moved out into the centre of the Thames. This had been a disastrous visit to London and he would be only too pleased to get back to Whitby with miles between him and the capital. Would anyone bother to search him out so far away just to settle a gambling debt? He had promised to send the money, his word as a gentleman being accepted at the same time as he wrote the IOU for one thousand pounds. But how could he keep his word? Where could he raise that amount? Go to his father? Cyrus quaked at the thought.

Hadn't Robert laid down the law in a fierce lecture, saying he would no longer meet the gambling debts his son was incurring in Whitby? It was a good job he did not know the real reason for Cyrus's visits to London and the debt his latest visit had incurred.

Thank goodness the ship was now under sail. He could go on deck without a qualm. He knew he had been watched when he had left the gaming tables but reckoned he had given them the slip, that they would not know where he was staying or the ship on which he sailed. He had kept to his cabin until they left just to make doubly sure that no one should accidentally spot him from the quay.

He donned his coat and hat and made his way on deck. It would be good to have some fresh air.

Stepping from the companionway, he paused, breathed deeply and looked around. Several passengers stood beside the rail, watching London slide by. There were two elderly couples engrossed in the various activities on shore, and two well-dressed gentlemen, whom Cyrus did not recognise as Whitby residents, were deep in conversation.

Beyond them, half turned to face the bow, as if she was enjoying the breeze now playing with her fair hair where it peeped out at the sides of her bonnet, was a smartly dressed young woman. He decided that she had good dress sense. Her travelling coat was ankle-length and belted at her slender waist. Its collar was turned up against the wind and left the two shoulder capes showing to their best advantage. Its bold colour, a deep red, caught the eye, and a large muff of the same colour seemed to draw even further attention.

He smiled confidently to himself as he stepped in her direction. She could make a pleasant travelling companion and take his mind off the trouble he was in. That could wait, and if his London creditors did eventually find him, the matter could be circumvented then. For now, at least he had the pleasure of female company.

As he came up behind her, he said, 'Good day, ma'am, I see you are travelling alone. May I offer you my services on this voyage?' He doffed his hat and bowed as she straightened from the rail and turned around.

'Why, Cyrus, how gallant of you.'

He looked up sharply, stunned by the voice. 'Gennetta!'

Her amused chuckle revealed the delight she felt in the shock she had given him.

'I didn't know you were on board,' he spluttered.

'How could you? And you wouldn't recognise my clothes, they're new, just bought in London. Like them?' She smiled teasingly at him and turned around to show her coat, hat and muff off to advantage.

245

'Delightful,' he replied, more from obligation than with any enthusiasm for his mind was already pondering why Gennetta had been in London, though he believed he knew the answer.

'Been on business, Cyrus?' she asked coyly.

He nodded. 'Yes.'

'Successful, I hope, for Grace's sake?'

'It was,' he replied, though he wondered if she was playing with him. Could she know that he had contracted no business deals this trip? Hadn't even attempted to. He'd been here for one purpose only and had lost.

'Good, I'm pleased.' She made her pleasure seem genuine though she knew he was lying. She had visited the customers she had cultivated when she was managing Turner's, jewellers she had met through the Great Exhibition, men who could recognise genuine craftsmanship and were eager for it. They had told her that they had been disappointed in the work they had been receiving from the firm now run by Cyrus Sleightholme, which came nowhere near the standard set by her when she was in charge. When she showed them the goods she had brought to London they recognised at once that she had not only assembled the talent she had had before, but had enhanced her stock by the products of new and skilled hands. They were genuinely pleased to switch to the new firm of Briggs Jetworkers. Gennetta was in a happy frame of mind as the ship left the Thames and headed north. She was looking forward to breaking her good news to Tom and to James.

'And you, Gennetta, what brought you to London?' Cyrus probed.

She gave a little shrug of her shoulders. 'I thought it would be obvious,' she said, lifting her arms so that his attention was drawn to her clothes.

He raised an eyebrow. 'Business must be good?'

She smiled but made no comment.

'There are all manner of rumours still going around as to who financed your venture,' he commented, hoping to draw information from her so that he could judge how formidable an opponent he faced.

She laughed. 'I've heard them. None of them is true, but you'll believe what you will.'

'This may be fortuitous meeting,' he went on smoothly. 'Up to now I've not had the opportunity to come and see you, to welcome you back into the fraternity of jet manufacturers and say that I hope there is no animosity left between us. I do want our working relationship in the future to be amicable.'

She acknowledged his gesture with an inclination of her head, though she reckoned this was glib talk and that he had purposely avoided visiting her. Cyrus would never wish a rival firm, especially one run by her, good luck. 'That's nice of you, particularly when some of your men came to work for me.'

He made a gesture of dismissal with his hands. 'One of those things. I had no trouble in replacing them with men of equal calibre.'

'Good, then I needn't feel guilty.' Not that she had ever done so. She had seen the move only as a step towards regaining control of Turner's. 'Now, if you'll excuse me, I think I'll take a rest,' she added, putting an end to their conversation.

He bowed, doffed his hat and watched her walk away, wondering how much of a threat her business was to his own security.

The sea ran fair, the wind filled their sails and, with the Yorkshire coast in sight, the *Speedwell* made good progress towards Whitby. An alteration in course took the ship beyond the reach of the menacing finger of Flamborough Head, its white cliffs glistening in the morning sunshine. The captain held out beyond Filey Brigg, the Devil's Bridge, came closer to Scarborough and swung with the curve of the coast for Whitby.

'Hello, my dear. I trust you slept well?'

Gennetta half turned from the rail at the sound of a familiar voice. 'Hello, Cyrus. I did, thank you. You've slept late. A sleep like mine, I hope, without worries,' she added, and doubted the truth of his reply.

'It was.' He glanced in the direction of the abbey, high on the cliffs some distance ahead.

'We should soon be home.'

'And I will be glad. The less I need to go to London, the better I will like it.' She took a deep breath of the sharp salt air as if to emphasise her joy at being relieved from London's grimy atmosphere. 'I hear tell your visits are becoming more frequent. Getting a taste for London life?'

'Ah, little birds have been chattering?' he returned in a tone contemptuous of any rumours she might have heard. 'Business, my dear, business. You will need to visit the capital more frequently if you are to compete with my firm.'

She stiffened at the word 'my'. 'Yours?' she asked testily.

He gave a grin touched with sardonic triumph. 'Yes, mine.'

Gennetta's heart skipped a beat. Surely Grace hadn't signed everything over to him? Relief followed quickly as he went on. 'After all, I run it. Grace has no business sense, as you know. It's a pity you and I weren't partners.'

247

'Partner's? Never.' Her defiance was icy. 'You, a Sleightholme, running the firm my father created? He must be turning in his grave. But one day I'll have it back and purge it of any contamination. I tried to warn Grace what would happen if she married you but she wouldn't listen. You besotted her with your easy charm.'

She started to turn away but he grabbed her by the arm. His eyes narrowed, his piercing gaze conveying menace.

'You'll never see that day,' he hissed.

'Won't I? From what I hear, you're ruining that firm. Sell me your share now – you'll get a better price than later.'

He threw back his head in a contemptuous laugh. 'You haven't enough money to buy me out. And you shouldn't heed everything you hear. I have the love of your sister-in-law and that could easily bring me the rest of the firm.'

Anger at the thought of what might happen clouded Gennetta's face. She felt his grip on her arm slacken and wrenched herself free. But as she was about to walk away, Cyrus stopped her again.

'Listen!' His voice was low, as if even that utterance would mask what he had heard. The uncanny gleam in his eye unsettled her.

'What?' She found herself keeping her voice as low as his.

'There!' He had heard it again.

She strained to catch what he wanted her to hear. Then it was there, borne on the wind. Her whole body stiffened. He felt it do so and chuckled. It came from deep in his throat and seemed to add menace to the distant cry of the geese.

'There!' He pointed to them, flying above the cliffs, barely visible though their unmistakable haunting cries identified them.

She stared, transfixed, held by him as if he was forcing her to watch, as if he was identifying himself with the Gabriel Hounds as a sign of ill-omen.

The geese flew on, their cries becoming fainter and fainter as they hovered over Whitby and disappeared beyond the town.

'They bode no good for you, Gennetta.' There was delight in his voice.

She saw it in his eyes as well. She tore her arm free and rushed away from him, but his chuckle seemed to follow her and was even audible when she slammed her cabin door behind her. Trembling, she sank back against it. Her chest heaved from her haste to escape but there was no freeing herself from Cyrus's laugh. She shuddered and clamped her hands over her ears, trying to shut out the cry of the Gabriel Hounds which mingled with his malevolent taunts.

She became aware of warm tears flowing down her cheeks. They had a cleansing effect. Gone were the noises in her head. She let her arms fall to her side. She closed her eyes with relief and realised that the thoughts which had tormented had been replaced by memories of Tom and his comforting words that the Gabriel Hounds could equally be a sign of good luck as bad; it all depended on how a person viewed them in relation to events. Could they possibly be a good sign for her? Wasn't she returning from London with news of orders? She knew Cyrus had none, at least not from the firms she thought important. Could the Gabriel Hounds be a mark of ill-omen for him?

When she went on deck again the *Speedwell* was already running between the piers and there was something comforting in the quiet flow of the river, even though all around there was the activity of a busy port.

There was no sign of Cyrus, for which she was thankful.

As she stood by the rail watching the *Speedwell* manoeuvre next to the quayside, a sailor, designated to the task, asked if she would like her bags brought on deck. When he reappeared a few moments later, she stopped him from moving to the gangway which had been run out. She had seen Cyrus and wanted him to get ashore before her. She watched him disembark and then started across the deck followed by the sailor with her two bags. Gennetta said goodbye to the captain and nodded to the two men who raised their top hats and smiled pleasantly at her before becoming engaged in a conversation with the master.

'Carry your bags, missus?'

'Carry your bags?'

Barefooted urchins eager to earn a copper crowded round her as she stepped ashore.

Gennetta laughed at their enthusiastic jostling and looked round their eager, upturned, dirty faces. 'You, and you!' She pointed at two of them, enjoyed their cries of triumph and turned a deaf ear to the moans of disappointment from the others. The two boys took the bags from the sailor and prepared to follow Gennetta. She paused a moment and searched the crowds who flowed along the quay until she saw Cyrus and was certain that he did not intend to turn back.

If he had he would have seen the two gentlemen passengers still in conversation with the captain. He would also have noticed that their gaze was turned in his direction. If he had been able to overhear the words passing between them he would have known that the two had just come into possession of his address, and that in seeking accommodation they had been directed to the Angel Inn.

'Presents, Mummy, presents!' shouted Nathaniel and Flora as they ran across the hall to greet Gennetta. Her laughter, filled with pleasure at seeing them again, resounded round the hall as she stooped down and swept them into her arms.

'All in good time,' she said as she hugged them. 'But have you been well-behaved while I've been away?'

'Yes! Yes!'

Gennetta raised a querying look to Rose who stood close to the foot of the stairs, her face wreathed in smiles at the exuberance of the children.

'They have, ma'am. Good as gold. Just the usual mischief.'

Gennetta straightened up. 'Come, I must change.'

'I'll bring your bags, ma'am.'

'Thanks, Rose.' She started for the stairs with Flora holding her hand and Nathaniel racing ahead.

With bags unpacked and presents distributed, Gennetta changed into a workaday dress in a simple pinafore style, ankle-length, flaring only slightly from the narrow waist. She went to the kitchen and enjoyed a cup of tea with Mrs Shaw.

'I've got all our London orders back,' Gennetta informed her. 'I think that calls for a celebration.'

'Of course it does, ma'am,' agreed the cook enthusiastically, for she liked doing something special.

'Good. I'll invite Tom and Davey, of course, and Mr and Mrs Young, and Mr Mitchell.'

Eager to break her news to everyone connected with the business, Gennetta called at James's office on the way to the workshop.

Benjamin showed her straight into his room, following instructions he had been given regarding Mrs Briggs if his employer were not otherwise engaged.

'Gennetta, you're back!' cried James. He leaped to his feet and came round the desk quickly to greet her, taking her hands in his. 'You look well. The sea voyage must have done you good.' He admired the glow in her cheeks and sensed her feeling of well-being.

'I'm pleased to be home.' She smiled, aware that he still held her hands.

'And I'm glad you are. I've missed you.'

She gave a small laugh and pulled her hands from his. 'I've not been away a week.'

'I know, but I still missed you.'

She was alarmed by the sensation which his tone sent through her. They had spent a lot of time together, setting up the business. They had become close, good friends, or at least she had seen it as nothing more than that. But now the warmth of his welcome after her absence

250

made her wonder if she had deluded herself in thinking that their relationship could be nothing more than a working partnership. She didn't think she had encouraged anything but that. But a likeable, good-looking, eligible bachelor and a pretty young widow – wasn't that a recipe for more than friendship?

She veered away from the possibilities. 'James, I've good news,' she cried enthusiastically.

He started, his mind brought back to the mundane world from the fertile images of Gennetta's beauty which haunted him and made him want to take her in his arms.

'The London trip went well?'

'Better than I hoped.'

'Wonderful. Tell me all about it?' He gestured to a chair and returned to his behind the desk.

'I got back all the London customers I cultivated when I was running Turner's.'

'All of them?'

'Yes.' She laughed with the joy of it.

'Excellent.'

'They recognised the talent which was there before and wanted pieces by the same workers,' she explained.

'A blow for Turner's.'

'Yes. Cyrus was on board the *Speedwell* coming home. Don't know how long he'd been in London. He said he'd been there on business, but I know he didn't get any orders – I got them. In fact, he hadn't even visited the jewellers, hadn't done so for some time, they told me. So what he was doing in London, I don't know.'

'We'll keep our eye on developments at Turner's. When the business starts to go down, the time will be ripe to make a move for it.'

'He wonders where I got the money to start up again. He quizzed me on the ship.'

'Did you tell him?'

'No.'

'So he doesn't know I'm involved?'

'No.'

'Just as well, when I'm handling his affairs and those of the Sleightholmes.'

She jumped to her feet. 'Now I must be off and tell our workers the news.' She started for the door before he could come out from behind his desk. 'And, James,' she called over her shoulder, 'a meal at my house – half-past six?'

She was gone and the door closed before he could reach it.

The thought that he might be trying to take their relationship further than she wanted troubled Gennetta as she hurried to the work-shop in Flowergate. She could not deny that she had a liking for him. He had good looks, a charming manner and an integrity that left her in no doubt that he was a man she could trust. He was attentive and had put much enthusiasm into their venture, but more than anything, in this latest meeting, she sensed that he was investing deeper feelings than mere friendship into their association.

These thoughts were cast to the back of her mind when she entered the workshop. Everyone looked up from their work to see who had come in and an air of expectancy charged the atmosphere when they saw her. They knew she had been to London and that a great deal would rest on what she had achieved.

Tom laid down his tools and crossed the floor to meet her. His pale blue eyes glowed with the pleasure of seeing her again, and now there was a desire to share his thoughts and feelings with her. Their sadness, born in the hard events before she knew him, had been banished. 'I missed you,' he said quietly when he reached her, and then added a little louder, 'You look pleased with yourself. Good news?'

She gave him a slight nod and a look which was only for him. Aloud she called, 'Everyone, can I have your attention?' She paused a moment as the men turned to her. 'As you know, I have just got back from London. I'm pleased to tell you that I have a full order book and that the jewellers I had dealt with in the past were delighted to be dealing with us again. Our work ... your work ... is wanted.'

A buzz of excitement ran round the room. It quietened again when John Young stepped forward. 'Ma'am, this is good news. Can I, on behalf of everyone, thank thee? It can't have been easy.' He gave the smile of one who has some new knowledge and added, 'While you were away we had several enquiries which were followed by firm orders. Our reputation is spreading – York, Scarborough, and Middlesbrough.'

'Marvellous. With the London orders we'll have to employ more men.'

She saw John glance at Tom. 'Thee tell her.'

When he hesitated, her eyes darted from one to the other. 'Tell me what?' she pressed.

Tom looked a little uncomfortable. 'Well, with John's approval, I took it upon myself to find two more etchers and one carver. They start tomorrow. I hope I did right, but with orders piling up and antic-ipating your success ...'

'Splendid, Tom. You did right.' She saw his expression of relief. 'Where did you find them?'

A flicker of satisfaction crossed his face. 'Sleightholme's,' he announced triumphantly.

'What!' She felt a tingle of excitement at this news.

'I know these three. Their work is some of the best in Whitby.'

'But not quite as good as ours?' she put in.

'No, but close enough to benefit by working with us, and therefore in the near future benefit us. I also knew that some of their work was being diverted to bolster Turner's output so it will be a double blow to our rivals, my persuading them to come and work here.'

'You did well.' She was more than pleased that he had taken this extra responsibility upon himself, it showed he was throwing aside the caution that had always held him back. 'It strengthens our position and maybe brings the day nearer when I can regain my father's firm.'

And how delightful to learn that Cyrus would have more problems on his hands.

Chapter Twenty

'I'm so pleased to see you back.' Grace greeted her husband with an affectionate kiss, then, as the maid took his bags, helped him off with his coat. 'I hope you had a successful visit to London?' she asked, taking his arm and leading him to the parlour, knowing that the maid would bring his favourite hot chocolate in a few minutes. 'Come, tell me all about it.'

'Not a lot to tell, my dear.'

She noted his serious expression and thought it was put on to tease her. 'Come on, Cyrus, don't keep me in suspense,' she cajoled. 'You must have got some good orders? They were due.'

'Nothing's due, Grace,' he returned quietly.

She detected a note of regret and it tempered her exuberance though she still thought he was joking. 'What do you mean?' she asked cautiously.

'I got no orders,' he replied.

There was incredulity in her eyes as she fixed them firmly on him. 'No orders?'

He shook his head and looked away from her. 'None.'

'But why? I thought when there were none last time, you would surely get some this visit. Did they give any reason?'

'None. Just said they had sufficient for the time being.' He dare not tell her that he had never visited their customers, that he had hoped to make more money from his gambling but it had gone wrong.

Grace brightened a little. 'Then next time will be better.'

Cyrus was relieved when there was a knock on the door and the maid entered with a tray on which there were two cups of steaming hot chocolate. It brought a change in topic, though little relief to his homecoming.

'I've just had a visit from your father,' Grace informed him as she took her cup from the tray.

Cyrus raised an eyebrow. 'What did he want?'

She gave a half laugh. 'Wasn't in a good mood, I can tell you. Seems he's lost his two best men.'

'Oh?' He looked up sharply from stirring his chocolate. 'How's that?'

'Getting better pay from Gennetta's firm.'

'What? Someone approached them?'

'Tom Unwin, I believe.'

Cyrus grunted. 'Getting back at us.'

'I don't know about that,' said Grace, doubting the justice of his view. 'But I do hear tell that Gennetta's firm has a lot of work, and that's why they were looking for more workers.'

'Has Father done anything about it?'

'He didn't say but he did make a suggestion.'

Cyrus eyed her curiously as he waited for her explanation. What was his father up to now?

'He suggested that Sleightholme's and Turner's amalgamate. Said it would make us stronger, and made sense particularly as Gennetta's new firm seemed to be doing well. He thought together we could resist and outdo any inroads she is making.'

Cyrus nodded. 'I can see his point.' He looked thoughtful as if weighing up the suggestion. 'It has possibilities,' he agreed, though he was really thinking what it could mean to him. He chuckled to himself. His father was a wily bird, never one to miss an opportunity! He must have seen this as a chance to gain control of Grace's part of the company.

'There was some sense to it but I gave him a firm no.'

'You did?' Cyrus raised his eyebrows.

'Yes, I did,' went on Grace, even more emphatically. 'You've got a half share already, I don't want to lose the other half.' Robert's approach had reminded her of Gennetta's warning, and it had put her on her guard as to his ultimate intentions.

'But you wouldn't. You'd have a share in the bigger company.'

'And your father would run everything. No, Cyrus, I'm not having that. You've got to put more time and energy into the business.' She eyed him with a gravity that made him wince. 'Put more thought into it instead of your gambling and drinking. Don't look so shocked, I hear these things. You said you could run it when I gave you a half share. I think you should let me see you do so.'

He put down his cup and came to her. 'I will, my dear, I will.' He smiled in the way he knew could soften her heart and take her mind off the more mundane matters of life. 'But this is no homecoming for me. I've missed you so.' He reached for her cup and she willingly let

255

him take it. He placed it on the table and, looking directly into her eyes with an expression filled with desire, reached for her waist.

She smiled seductively at him, letting him know she could read his intentions and had no objection to them. She raised her head to meet his mouth which swept her into an ecstacy she had never known with Jack.

As they walked hand in hand up the stairs, she marvelled at the change her love for Cyrus had wrought in her. The feeling of being oppressed had gone. In its place there was an assurance that she meant something to her husband. In return she made much more of her appearance and always relished the praise Cyrus heaped upon her. Her blue eyes glowed with a new enjoyment of life and were filled with promise as they climbed the stairs.

Gennetta knew her enthusiasm and excitement over what she had achieved in London, and what it meant to the firm, had spilled over to Mrs Shaw and that the celebratory meal that evening would be something special.

While Rose prepared Nathaniel and Flora, for their mother said they too should share in the festivities, Gennetta primped herself. After failing to decide over three dresses, she finally made her choice. The deep black of her skirts, falling half-full from a tight waist, brought out the fiery aspects of the vivid scarlet jacket she wore above them. Slightly pointed at the waist, it was trimmed with black velvet. The sleeves, wide at the elbows, came tight at the wrist but allowed a glimpse of her white blouse which also peeped out around the neck. She brought her fair hair into a bunch at the top of her head and secured it with a jet band which Tom had worked in a leaf motif. The open pattern of a jet brooch was highlighted by the white silk on which it was mounted and made an eyecatching feature at her throat.

Having been warned about the special occasion, Joey had taken care to be presentable, wearing the fawn trousers, green jacket, new shoes Gennetta had bought him. He was pleased to receive her approval when they met on the stairs on their way to the hall.

His response of: 'And thee don't look so bad thissen, missus,' brought a smile of amusement to her face.

They went to the parlour to find Rose already there with Nathaniel and Flora. A fire burned brightly in the grate and Gennetta noted that the decanter of Madeira had been filled and stood on the oak sideboard with the appropriate glasses, beside a jug of home-made lemonade for the children.

Gennetta took over from Rose the game of snakes and ladders she was playing with the children, but a few minutes later she handed over to Joey when she heard the doorbell resound in the depths of the house.

'Mr Mitchell, ma'am,' the maid announced on entering the parlour.

Gennetta rose from her chair to greet him with a warm smile. 'So pleased to have you here for our celebration, James.'

'It is my pleasure.' He took her hand as he bowed. As he straightened, he cast an admiring glance towards her. 'You are looking wonderful.'

'Thank you.' She gave an inclination of her head, showing her pleasure at gaining his approval. At the same time she noticed he had taken particular care about his dress. He wore a black tail-coat of broadcloth. His white silk waistcoat was patterned in black and his trousers, of small black and white checks, were perfectly tailored. His only concession to colour was the pale blue cravat tied neatly at the throat of his white shirt. The choice of clothes set off his handsome square-cut features, and though black dominated it seemed to bring out the colour of his black hair and the depth of his dark eyes.

The children had paused in their game and he saw he was under close scrutiny.

'Children, this is Mr Mitchell.' Gennetta went on to introduce them, 'Flora and Nathaniel, and Joey who now lives with us. He'll be a noted artist and jet engraver one day.'

'Hello, all of you.' James's smile enveloped them all. He realised immediately that he must put himself on good terms with the children. 'What's this, snakes and ladders?' he said with enthusiasm. He promptly sat down beside them on the floor. 'Who's this?' He pointed at a token two squares from a snake.

'Me! Me!' shouted Flora, excited that her token had been picked out.

He looked intently at her, a teasing twinkle in his eye. 'I'll bet you shake a two and land on that snake.'

'Shan't! Shan't!' she shouted, and immediately gave the die in its container a sharp shake. She tipped it out and sent the die rolling across the board. All eyes watched it, anxious to see the result. It slowed, gave another roll, tottered and fell still.

'Three!' Flora yelled with glee, as moans of disappointment came from Nathaniel and Joey and laughter broke out from everyone.

James knew he had made three friends.

'Glass of Madeira, James?' Gennetta offered as he counted Nathaniel's throw, which brought a shout of delight from the boy but groans from Flora and Joey when James moved the token up a ladder.

'Please,' he called over his shoulder.

As she poured the drink, Gennetta felt pleased that James had

257

immediately made himself at home. She sensed that the children had taken to him. Now she wondered how he and Tom would get on.

Five minutes later, with James enjoying his drink while still participating in the game and drawing Gennetta into the excitement, the doorbell rang, to be followed by a knock on the parlour door.

'Mr Unwin and Davey, ma'am,' the maid announced.

Gennetta jumped from her seat and was halfway to the door by the time James scrambled to his feet.

'Hello, Davey,' she said as he ran into the room, to give James only a passing glance as he joined Joey, Nathaniel and Flora with the question, 'Who's winning?'

'Tom.' The pleasure in Gennetta's voice was not lost on James and he felt a pang of jealousy. 'Come and meet Mr Mitchell.'

'Mr James Mitchell, Mr Tom Unwin.' She made the introduction, smiling at each one in turn.

'Mr Mitchell.' Tom nodded affably as he held out his hand but his mind was buzzing, wondering why Gennetta had invited the solicitor.

'Mr Unwin.' James took Tom's hand in a firm grip and smiled warmly, but he wondered why this man had been invited. All he knew of Tom was that when setting up the company Gennetta had mentioned his skill as a carver, naming him as a key member of the workforce.

Tom eyed James's smart attire and felt drab beside him. His dark grey frock coat, with no waist detail, was of equal length all round and hung to the knees. He wore it open revealing a plain matching waistcoat and trousers of the same colour. The only splash of brightness was the red cravat tied around his plain white collar.

'Can I pour Tom some wine?' suggested Joey, leaping to his feet. It was something he had come to like doing. It made him feel important and he was fascinated to watch the rich liquid against the sides of the sparkling glass.

'Of course,' Gennetta approved, amused at his enthusiasm.

When Joey handed Tom his glass, he turned to James. 'Some more for you, Mr Mitchell, sir?'

'Thanks, Joey.' As he passed his glass to the boy, James added, 'I hear you are good at drawing?'

'Aye, sir, thanks to the missus.' He glanced at Gennetta.

'He has a natural talent, I've only helped him to develop it and channel it in the right direction,' she pointed out.

'I'd like to see some of your drawings,' said James.

'And Davey's,' put in Joey, not wanting his friend to be left out. 'He's good.'

'Yes, and Davey's,' agreed James, wanting to keep on the right side of those of the younger generation who were close to Gennetta. He turned to Tom. 'Your son draws too?'

'Yes. Like Joey, his talent has been brought out by Mrs Briggs and both of us will always be grateful to her for what she has done. I only wish his mother had lived long enough to see how good he is.'

'I'm sorry,' offered James politely.

Any speculation as to why Tom Unwin was here was, to James's mind, answered when the maid announced the arrival of Mr and Mrs John Young.

'So kind of thee to invite us.' They both expressed their appreciation to Gennetta.

'It's my pleasure,' she returned. 'As foreman you are an important part of the firm, John, and deserve to celebrate the success of my London visit.'

James now knew that all the people on whom the success of the firm depended were here and that Tom Unwin was part of them and probably nothing more. He smiled to himself when he recalled the jealousy he had felt when the jet carver arrived.

When everyone had charged their glasses Gennetta proposed a toast of 'Briggs Jetworkers', and then ushered everyone into the dining room.

They enjoyed a sumptuous meal which Mrs Shaw had taken delight in preparing.

Gennetta was pleased with the whole evening for everyone had mixed so well and James had taken particular interest in the children, even being cajoled by Flora into reading her a story before she went to bed. The moment Rose took Flora and Nathaniel upstairs Tom took his leave, for Davey was turning sleepy too. He was reluctant to do so as James showed no sign of leaving. He had experienced pangs of jealousy every time the solicitor was attentive to Gennetta. He recognised that James's handsome features, his poise and articulate conversation, would be attractive to the opposite sex. And now he would be alone with Gennetta. But Tom's despondency was short-lived and he felt a little touch of pleasure when the maids brought James's overcoat along with his, having assumed both were leaving. When Gennetta made no suggestion that he stay, James could do nothing but leave.

As he walked home, enjoying the sharp night air and his feeling of well-being, James's thoughts were all of her.

A week later, when Gennetta was at the workshop, a letter from London was delivered to her, having been brought by ship.

Her curiosity aroused, she slit the envelope open and extracted a

259

sheet of paper. As she unfolded it she saw that the address on the top was that of the leading jeweller's whom they supplied with jet.

She read the letter quickly and excitement gripped her. Then she read it more slowly to make sure she had understood its contents correctly. She was looking at a special order for three pieces of carved jet which were to be presented to three prominent members of a leading society. She realised that not only was the order valuable in itself but it could easily lead to similar commissions. The jewellers suggested that she visit them to discuss the order in detail, but even as she read the words again an idea was forming in her mind.

It would be better if Tom, who was the obvious choice to do this work, were able to discuss the project personally. She saw it as an opportunity to give him more responsibility, to deal directly with customers, and thereby foster an ambition which had long been stifled.

She called him to one side. 'I've just received this letter from London.' She handed it to him.

He read it, and when he looked up there was an intent expression in his eyes. 'This is splendid. When will you go?'

'I'm not going.'

'But ...' The spark of enthusiasm was replaced by a look of bewilderment.

'You are!'

'Me? But ...'

'You're all buts,' she teased, and laughed at the astonishment on his face. 'You'll be making these pieces so it's far better if you discuss them with the commissioner. You can put your own ideas forward so the customer will get a better product and be more satisfied.'

'But I've never been out of Whitby.'

'Then it's time you did.'

'But what about Davey? I can't leave him.'

'There you go again, another but. Stop trying to put obstacles in the way. Davey can come to me, you know that, and no doubt he'll enjoy being with Joey, Nathaniel and Flora.' Her lips tightened in a determined line. 'So that's settled. You can find no further excuse. You go to London.'

Tom knew that she was right. It would be far better for him to deal directly with the customer about an order such as this. 'Very well.'

Before he left work Gennetta had briefed him about where to stay, how to get to the jeweller's, and the personalities of the owners of the shop with whom he would be dealing.

The following day she saw Tom leave Whitby on his first sea voyage, having tried to reassure him that he would enjoy it.

As the ship slipped away from the quay and the gap between them widened Tom realised how much he would miss her. He saw her most days, even if some meetings were only in the course of work, but now it would be five days before he would see her again. He felt a sense of loss, a heaviness in his heart, and realised how deeply he loved her. He wanted to jump ship and sweep her into his arms, telling her over and over again how he felt and that he knew why she wanted to live on the west bank of the river. It was a place with the standing that was necessary to further the business. It had nothing to do with snobbery, as he had once thought. Because this parting had brought a deeper understanding of his love for her, he was now willing to storm the barriers to marriage she had raised through her burning desire to repossess her father's business. He would even move across the river to achieve his ambition – marriage with her – and work with her to help her attain hers.

If only he had told her all this before he had left! But it had needed this widening gap to make him see what he should have seen before. Now he would have to wait five days. And in the meantime James ... Jealousy flared at the thought of what might happen. Had Gennetta deliberately sent him to London, wanting him out of the way so she and James ... He raged at himself – what a fool for falling into the trap!

Two days later the mate of the *Speedwell* left the ship as soon as it docked mid-afternoon in Whitby. His left hand was dug deep into his pocket, holding an envelope as if to make sure there was no chance of losing it.

He ignored the activity on the quay and the people around him as he hurried to the bridge and crossed it to Baxtergate. Reaching the Angel Inn, he stepped inside to be confronted by a porter who eyed him up and down suspiciously for this was the entrance used by residents and the well-to-do, and this man looked neither but exactly what he was – a man who had just stepped off a ship.

'What does thee want?' cackled the porter, trying to straighten shoulders stooped by carrying bags and boxes over the years.

'Mr Brown and Mr Smith 'ere?' asked the sailor.

Then porter half closed his eyes and peered at the speaker, as if trying to probe the reason for his question. 'Who wants t'know?' he demanded.

'I do,' snapped the mate, irritated that he should be questioned by this old man trying to assume a bit of authority.

'They might be,' returned the porter.

The mate's lips tightened. He knew there must be no delay in delivering the letter. 'Well, are they?' His voice was tinged with anger.

'Wait 'ere, wait 'ere.' The porter turned and shuffled away in a parody of a run.

The mate waited impatiently but was relieved when a big man, smartly dressed in loud-coloured clothes, appeared. His round florid face indicated a liking for ale and good food with his bulging midriff he looked every bit the landlord of a good hostelry.

'Publican?' asked the mate.

'Aye. Charlie tells me thee wants Mr Brown or Mr Smith?'

'He tells thee right.'

'May I ask why?'

'I've a letter to deliver.'

The landlord had been eyeing the mate up and down and figured he was equally right in his judgement as the sailor had been about him. 'Just in from London?'

'Aye. Mate on the *Speedwell*.'

'Well, Mr Brown and Mr Smith will be glad to have that letter. They've been here ten days waiting on it. Got to know the times of arrivals from London and are always here at that time and for an hour afterwards. Seems now their waiting is over. I'll see they gets it immediately.' He held out his hand.

The mate did not remove his hand from his pocket. He shook his head. 'Sorry, I can't give it thee. Captain says I must hand this letter over personally to Mr Brown or Mr Smith. No one else must touch it.'

A fleeting look of annoyance crossed the landlord's face as he said, 'Don't thee trust me?'

'Aye, I trust thee, but it's my job I'm thinking about. If word got back to the captain that I'd handed this letter to thee, I'd be hauled up before him for disobedience. So, are they here?'

The landlord nodded his understanding. 'Aye. Come this way.'

The mate followed him into a room dotted with small tables, several of which were occupied by people taking an afternoon cup of tea. He led the way to a table tucked in a corner at which two men were sitting. They looked up when they realised that they were being approached. The mate caught their look of eager anticipation, as if something they had been expecting was about to happen.

'Mr Brown, Mr Smith, the mate of the *Speedwell* to see thee.'

The two men nodded, and when they immediately turned their attention to the newcomer, the landlord left.

'You have something for us?' Mr Smith asked.

'Aye,' replied the mate bluntly. He hesitated, eyeing each man in turn. They were young, mid-twenties he reckoned, well-dressed, maybe a little dandified but that did not detract from their air of self-assurance. There was friendliness about them too as if they were pleased to see him, though that might be because of what he carried. 'But how do I know thee's who thee says thee is?' he added cautiously. He saw the two men exchange quick glances.

'Now here's a right good fellow,' said Mr Smith, warmly. 'Your caution is commendable. You're right to want identification.' He fished in his waistcoat pocket and pulled out a gold hunter watch. He pressed the catch and it flicked open. He held it out towards the mate who bent forward and read:

The Honorable Joycelyn Smith
To Joss with love
Camilla

Mr Smith saw the mate's eyebrows rise in surprise. He smiled. 'Ah, my good man, you thought Mr Smith and Mr Brown weren't our real names, that we were travelling in disguise so to speak? Well, as you see, Smith is my real name and I can vouch that this is Mr Brown. Will that satisfy you?' He closed his watch and placed it carefully back in his pocket.

'Aye,' the mate grunted, then spluttered with embarrassment over his doubt. 'I'm sorry but I ... '

'Never mind, there's no harm done,' cut in Mr Brown. 'You did perfectly right. Now the letter, please.' He held out his hand.

The mate took the envelope from his pocket, passed it over and left the Angel with a quick step, eager to be back among his ships and away from these 'posh' folk.

Mr Brown slit the envelope open with a knife. He pulled a single sheet of paper from the envelope and read: *'Nothing is forthcoming. Take the necessary action.'* There was no signature. They didn't need one. They knew who it was from. They had been expecting it.

'Now?' queried Mr Brown.

'There's no time like the present,' returned Mr Smith. 'The sooner we get this over, the sooner we can get back to London.'

Mr Brown nodded his agreement. They rose from the table, picked up their top hats and walking sticks and left their tea half-finished.

Less than ten minutes later they were ringing the bell of Cyrus's residence.

Mr Smith appreciatively eyed the maid who answered the door. 'Mr Cyrus Sleightholme at home?'

263

'No, sir,' she replied, blushing under his gaze. 'And Mrs Sleightholme is entertaining.'

Mr Smith raised his hand in a gesture of understanding. 'Do not disturb the good lady. Just tell us where we might find Mr Sleightholme?'

'I expect he's at work, sir.'

'And where might that be?'

She directed them to the workshop on Church Street and they took their leave.

'Pretty little piece,' commented Mr Smith as they walked down the garden path.

'Keep your mind on what we have to do. You'll soon find plenty to amuse you in London,' replied Mr Brown.

'Gad, how I've missed them,' sighed Mr Smith. 'But I've been a good boy, no involvements here in Whitby as you warned. The fewer folk who know about us the better.'

They walked briskly to the bridge where they were irritated by the crowd impeding their progress but once in Church Street their pace quickened again. Their entrance into the workshop brought a man from one of the benches.

'Good day, sirs, what can I do for you?' He had summed them up as customers and as instructed by Mr Sleightholme showed them every attention.

'We would like to see Mr Sleightholme.'

'I'm sorry, sir, he's not here.'

Mr Brown gave a tut of annoyance. 'Do you know where we can find him?'

The man hesitated.

'Come, it is urgent and important to Mr Sleightholme. He'll be very annoyed if we don't contact him as soon as possible.'

The man, judging it might be something of importance to the business, said in hushed tones as if confiding a secret in them, 'Well, I don't exactly know but if y'want my guess, I think y'might find him in the White Horse, just along the street.'

'Good man.' Mr Brown brightened and started to turn away.

'Here, sirs, don't tell him I told you. It's more than my job's worth. Doesn't like being disturbed when he visits the White Horse.'

'He won't hear it from us,' replied Mr Smith, giving the man a reassuring pat on the shoulder.

They were soon walking into the noisy bar of the White Horse. All the tables were taken and customers lined the counter where three buxom barmaids were serving beer as fast as glasses were cleared. Mr Smith and Mr Brown searched the room from the doorway and spotted Cyrus sitting at a table with four other men. They were obviously in a buoyant mood and as Mr Smith and Mr Brown neared their table they caught a part of the conversation as one man proclaimed the venue for tonight's gambling. On hearing it Mr Brown raised an eyebrow as he glanced at his companion. When they stopped at the table the five men fell silent and looked at the newcomers questioningly.

'We are sorry to interrupt, gentlemen.' Mr Smith gave a slight bow and rested his weight on the walking stick in front of him. 'But we would like a word with you, Mr Sleightholme.' His gaze rested on Cyrus.

He looked surprised. He did not know these strangers and yet he felt there was something familiar about them. 'Me?'

'Yes,' replied Mr Smith. 'It is a matter of some importance.' He glanced round the other four men. 'If you will excuse us, gentlemen?' He was giving Cyrus no time to question him or refuse.

Cyrus rose from his chair, looking at each stranger in turn.

As they moved away from the table Mr Brown said, 'Mr Sleightholme, you obviously know this hostelry. Is there a room we could use? We know you'll want to keep this private.'

Cyrus was even more puzzled but realised the only thing to do was to play along with these men. 'Yes, follow me.' After a quick word with the landlord, Cyrus led the way upstairs to a room in which four small tables, a tray of drinks, and another table set with cards and roulette wheels showed its use as a gambling room.

'Familiar surroundings for you, Mr Sleightholme,' commented Mr Brown as he closed the door behind them.

Cyrus was startled. What did these men know about him? He made no comment but said, 'You have the advantage of me, gentlemen.'

Mr Smith gave a gesture of apology. 'Mr Brown,' he half turned to his companion, 'and I am Mr Smith.' He saw Cyrus's smile of amusement. 'Oh, I assure you, those are our real names. Show him,' he added, looking at his friend.

Mr Brown tugged a wallet from his pocket, and held it out for Cyrus to read the embossed inscription: *The Hon. Harrison Brown.*

Cyrus nodded his acceptance. 'Well, what do you want with me?'

'A little matter of a debt incurred in London,' replied Mr Smith coldly.

Cyrus's face drained of colour. His eyes widened with fright. 'Lord Sanderson!' The name was scarcely above a whisper.

'Ah, you remember that you lost a considerable amount to Lord Sandy? You said you would pay it once you returned to Whitby.'

It dawned on Cyrus where he had seen these two men before. He

265

stared from one to the other. 'You were on the *Speedwell* from London.' He remembered now that he had never been in conversation with them on that voyage, was never close to them. Now he saw why they had purposefully kept their distance: they did not want to be recognised in Whitby.

Mr Smith smiled and nodded.

'So Lord Sandy had me followed from the moment the gambling session was over?' hissed Cyrus, sinking on to one of the chairs. The realisation that he could never have escaped, even in the remoteness of Whitby, struck him like an arrow. Now he was going to have to face the consequences of his own folly.

The two men stood in front of him, seeming to tower over him, their sticks held at their sides.

'Well, what are you going to do about it?' demanded Mr Brown.

'Give me a few more days.' Cyrus glanced up at them pleadingly.

'You've had over ten days already. We've received a note from Lord Sandy telling us to take action.'

'Take action?' Cyrus looked wildly from one to the other.

'Yes. We have to have the money or ...'

'But I can't lay my hands on it just like that.'

'I don't know whether you can lay your hands on it at all,' said Mr Smith, shaking his head in doubt. 'In that case, we'll have to go to your wife.'

'No! Not that!' he cried in alarm.

'Your father, then?'

'My God, no!' He realised that in their stay in Whitby they had been checking on him so that when the time came they would know the action to take.

'Well, where can you raise the money?'

'I don't know!' yelled Cyrus.

'Well, if you can't there's only one course: we'll have to take you back to London. Accidents can happen there and no more said.' As if to emphasise his meaning, Mr Smith pulled at the handle of his walking stick and with a smooth sweep pulled a long, thin, vicious-looking blade from the stick which acted as sheath.

The implication was obvious. Cyrus shook. 'No, gentlemen, no.' His voice cracked.

'What then?' Mr Smith pointed the blade at his neck.

He flinched and swallowed hard. His mind was in a turmoil, trying to find a way out.

'Well?' Mr Brown added his threat to Mr Smith's.

'Wait, wait!' cried Cyrus. 'I'm thinking.'

'Think quick, we want action.'

266

He waved his hand as if to brush aside their impatience. In his mind he was checking through his assets but none would enable him to clear the debt. He bit his lip in exasperation. 'Can't you give me a little longer?' he pleaded.

Both men shook their heads slowly. Their eyes were cold and threatening. Mr Smith twirled his blade close to Cyrus's face, emphasising that they would stand no nonsense.

He flinched and cowered. 'Wait, let me think.'

'Don't take long about it,' snapped Mr Brown, who found his patience being tried. 'You either can or can't raise the money. And if you can't, you'll be taking another voyage to London.' There was an ominous ring to his voice.

Cyrus was left in no doubt that acting on Lord Sanderson's orders these men would be ruthless in extracting their master's revenge. He was shaking at the thought of what the result might be. Beads of sweat covered his brow in spite of the cold clutching at his heart. He wiped his hands across his face, in a gesture of desperation, as if trying to draw a solution from his mind.

He stopped, his hand across his mouth. His expression changed abruptly and he looked up at his two assailants with relief in his eyes. 'I've got an idea. I can raise the money.'

'Good. What is it?' asked Mr Smith.

'Come with me.' Cyrus's eyes darted from one to the other, seeking their agreement.

'Where to?'

'Across the river. You'll see when we get there.' He started to push himself to his feet.

'No tricks.' The warning implied dire consequences should Cyrus try to outsmart them.

He nodded, breathing deeply, trying to gain the strength to carry out the solution he had in mind.

The two men stood back, slid their blades into their sheaths and followed Cyrus as he hurried from the room.

He led the way to the west side of the river at a brisk pace. Before those two threatening blades, symbols of what his end could be, he had made a decision. The sooner it was fulfilled, the better. He wanted no time to reconsider.

He turned into the building marked 'Mitchell, Solicitor' and fairly snapped at Benjamin, 'Mr Mitchell!'

The clerk's eyes considered the three men. He knew Mr Sleightholme. The others were strangers. There was urgency in Mr Sleightholme's crisp command and he was not going to ignore it, especially as there was an air of tension about the other men. Benjamin slid off his stool and scurried past them into James's office.

'Young Mr Sleightholme wishes to see you, sir. He has two strangers with him.'

Surprise and curiosity were evident in James's face. 'Show them in.' He sat back in his chair and waited. When Benjamin opened the door to admit them, he rose to his feet. 'Gentlemen.'

'Mr Mitchell.' Cyrus bustled across the room. He paused and half turned. 'May I present Mr Smith and Mr Brown?'

James nodded to each in turn as he shook hands. 'Do please sit down.' He indicated the chairs which Benjamin was quickly arranging in front of the desk.

'Mr Mitchell,' Cyrus had caught his look of enquiry, 'you remember assigning half of my wife's business to me?'

'Yes.' James nodded, steepling his hand beneath his chin.

'Can you arrange to sell it as soon as possible?'

The query came as a thunderbolt but James held his surprise under control and said, 'Doesn't your wife want it back?'

'I want to sell it,' replied Cyrus sharply – rather too sharply for James's liking. It was as if he wanted this whole thing, which somehow must involve these two strangers, finalised and finished with quickly. 'It was signed over to me without any restrictions, wasn't it?'

'You're perfectly right,' returned James.

'Then I'm asking you to sell it. My wife must know nothing about it.' He added hastily, 'Well, not until I tell her, when I think the time is right.'

James's mind sharpened. This appeared to be a sudden decision, as if Cyrus Sleightholme hadn't thought through the possible consequences. His wife would have to know soon for the new owner would be sure to come forward and declare his interest in the business. His thoughts took a new turn. New owner? Turner shares – half the business? The possessor of those shares did not have to be a man!

'I see,' he said calmly, disguising the excitement which was coursing through him. 'Yes, I can enact a sale but it may take a day or two to find a buyer.' He knew he could do it quickly but he was not going to let Cyrus know whom he had in mind.

'It must be done quickly. It's imperative,' replied Cyrus, displaying annoyance at the fact that there might be some delay.

James threw up his hands in despair. 'I've got to find a customer, Mr Sleightholme, and then there are documents to be drawn up.'

'Tomorrow, then?'

James caught the glance he exchanged with the two men as if seeking their approval, and was in time to see their almost imperceptible nods of agreement. So they were involved. But that was no concern of his. He was only here to carry out Cyrus Sleightholme's instructions.

'All right,' he agreed. 'I'll do my best. Shall we meet again, at two o'clock tomorrow afternoon?'

'Very well,' replied Cyrus. He rose quickly as if he wanted to get away in case any awkward questions were asked. 'Good day, Mr Mitchell, and thank you.' He turned for the door. The strangers bade James 'Good day' and followed Cyrus from the office.

James sat for a while, deep in thought. This was an opportunity he was not going to miss but he wanted time to consider the course he would take.

His decision made, he called Benjamin into his office and instructed him to draw up two identical documents for signature tomorrow, and reminded him that, like all his other work in the office, this transaction must remain a secret.

'Well, Eliza, a fine, healthy son, from what I hear.' Robert Sleightholme beamed at the girl who sat primly on the opposite side of the desk in his study.

'Aye, sir,' she said, looking down at her hands.

'Then I shall pay thee the agreed sum and thee will take the child to Mr and Mrs Sleightholme.' Robert felt deep satisfaction. The longed-for heir to the Sleightholme jet business, who would also inherit Turner's, would soon be under his influence. Robert would see that he was brought up in the right way, and any disagreement from Grace would not be tolerated. 'When that is done thee will never attempt to contact the child again.' He sat back in his chair, his eyes sweeping over the girl, remembering. She was a pretty thing with an innocent look in her blue eyes. Innocent? He gave a little chuckle to himself.

She looked up and met his gaze firmly. Innocence had been replaced by ruthlessness. The change, something he had never witnessed before, chilled him. 'I'm not parting with t'boy. Thee can keep thy brass.'

He stared at her, thunderstruck. How dare she talk like this to him? His flesh crawled at her audacity and defiance – her, a mere servant. 'Thee can't! Thee agreed!' His voice was sharp, cutting through all opposition, but here it struck stone.

'I've accepted nowt.'

'Damn it all, it was all arranged.'

'Thee can't 'ave 'im. He's too nice.'

'I want him and I'll have him,' Robert blustered, his face reddening as he leaned forward, glaring angrily at her.

'Thee can't 'ave 'im and there's nowt thee can do t'get 'im.' Her tone was quietly confident. He was seeing a different Eliza. Demure? Obliging? Now she was cold, calculating, with steel in her sharp eyes.

'Thee'll be out of a job and I'll see thee never gets another in Whitby,' he stormed, the muscles tightening in his neck.

'Thee'll do no such thing, Mr Sleightholme. I could tell folk a few things.' There was the hint of a triumphant smile at the corners of her mouth.

His fury was raised to boiling point at the thought of the scandal she could cause. 'I'll give thee more money,' he offered, making every effort to keep his temper under control. Vent it and there might be even worse consequences for him.

'Threats, bribery. Neither will work,' she said firmly.

'Anything you want, anything at all, but my son must have that child.' He was beginning to plead, and with that came a sense of humiliation – he, Robert Sleightholme, begging a mere servant girl.

She smiled at the power she held and was pleased she was following her mother's instructions. 'I'm keeping 'im.'

Robert's face was taut. 'I want him.'

She shook her head slowly. Her eyes mocked him.

'Out!' he stormed. 'Not one penny unless thee hands him over.'

She did not move, keeping her eyes fixed intently on his. 'Oh, thee'll stick to our agreement. Thee'll pay me what thee said and summat each month.'

'Not unless I get the boy.'

'I told thee, I'm keeping 'im.'

'Then thee gets nothing.'

'What?' She raised her eyebrows in surprise. 'Does thee want thy wife to know who the real father is? Does thee want all Whitby to know who sired my bairn?'

Cold fingers clutched at his chest. He was cornered and there was no way out. 'You conniving little bitch,' he hissed between tight lips.

'Now, now, Mr Sleightholme, thee shouldn't be talking to one of thy staff like that,' she said quietly, taking pleasure in admonishing her employer.

'Staff? Thee's dismissed from now,' he fumed. He'd be glad to be rid of her. To see her around the house would bring too much pain at the thought of what might have been.

Eliza smiled and shook her head. 'No, no. I keep my job. Seeing me around will remind thee to pay me for t'boy. Never miss or thee'll be the talk of Whitby. And don't thee fear, my son will never be inside these walls. My ma will look after 'im.' She paused, enjoying seeing him beaten and humiliated, a just reward for what he had demanded from her whenever he had the opportunity. Then she added, 'Now, Mr Sleightholme, is that all agreed or do I ...?' She left the threat unspoken.

Robert was already nodding, a subdued and defeated man.

There was no briskness about Robert's step as he walked to his son's house where he learned that Cyrus was thought to be at the workshop and Grace had gone shopping. As he made his way to the bridge to cross to the east side of the river, he saw Cyrus parting from two strangers. Robert quickened his step and called his name.

Cyrus turned and, seeing his father, waited.

'Who's those two?' asked Robert.

'Just two men I met on the ship from London. They've been spending a few days in Whitby but are about to return.' Cyrus could tell from his father's demeanour that something was troubling him. 'What's wrong?' he asked.

Robert kept his voice low as they strolled towards the pier. 'That bitch Eliza's keeping the bairn.' His eyes were clouded with annoyance as he recalled the confrontation.

'But I thought everything was arranged?' Cyrus made a show of distress, though the prospect of a child meant nothing after his recent interview.

'She damned well changed her mind. I've tried all ways to persuade her but there's nothing I can do about it.'

Cyrus could guess the situation – his father was being blackmailed and was prepared to pay for her silence. But he made no comment.

'I'm sorry, son. Tell Grace that too. We'll have to think again about finding an heir.'

'She won't look elsewhere. She only agreed to this because you knew the father's stock.'

Robert nodded. He was silent for a moment, then straightened, drew back his shoulders and seemed to regain his confidence for having told his son. There was determination in his voice as he said: 'We'll find a way to get Turner's. After all, we're halfway there with your share.'

Cyrus made no comment.

The following day James was not surprised, after the urgency displayed yesterday, that Mr Sleightholme, accompanied by Mr Smith and Mr Brown, arrived at his office at precisely two o'clock.

'I trust you have been able to complete a sale?' asked Cyrus anxiously as he entered the office.

'Everything is arranged, Mr Sleightholme. The documents, ready for signature, are on my desk.'

'Good, good. How much were you able to get?'

'One thousand one hundred.'

A broad smile of pleasure engulfed Cyrus's face. 'Capital. Better than I expected.' With a smile of satisfaction, he glanced at the two men who had followed him into the room.

'My clerk will act as one witness,' James explained. 'And,' he looked enquiringly at the other two men, 'one of you?'

'Certainly,' Mr Smith replied, rather eagerly as he envisaged a return to the more familiar haunts of London.

'Good.' James picked up one of the sheets of paper. 'Perhaps you'll be good enough to glance through this? It details the sale of your half of the business.' He handed it to Cyrus.

'I'm sure it will be perfectly all right,' he returned, eager to get it over and done with. He started to reach for the pen lying on the inkstand.

'Wait,' James interrupted him. 'I must insist that you read it, to make sure everything is correct.'

'Very well.' Cyrus's lips tightened with irritation. He looked down at the paper. He started to read, scanning the words quickly. Then he slowed. Now each word bit into his mind, bringing with them an ominous chill. Incredulity crossed his face. He stopped reading and looked up. Anger flared in his eyes as he fixed them on James. 'Your buyer is Briggs Jetworkers?'

'Yes,' replied James politely, acting as if he wondered why Cyrus was putting such a question.

'They can't be. I can't sell to Mrs Briggs!'

'Why not?' queried James, appearing bewildered by his statement. 'You instructed me to sell. I thought her firm a likely buyer.'

'But I can't! I won't!' Alarm and panic engulfed Cyrus as he pictured himself facing the wrath of his father. With his hands on half the Turner business through his son, and with possession of the other half surely only a matter of time, Robert Sleightholme would not take lightly to what his son was doing. Cyrus's mind was a confusion of thoughts. They were brought coldly into perspective by the quiet voice at his shoulder.

'Is there some difficulty?'

Cyrus glanced at Mr Smith and saw warning in the look he received.

'Er ... no. I was taken aback. Mrs Briggs's firm is our chief rival and if I'm selling half of Turner's to her ...' He threw up his hands in despair then brought the paper back into focus. He stared at the

272

words. The name Briggs seemed to stand out more than any other, mocking him with its implication. His whole world was collapsing around him and there was nothing he could do to prevent it.

'Well, if there's no difficulty, then ...' Mr Smith pursed his lips and raised his eyebrows, making his meaning quite clear.

Cyrus turned his attention back to James. 'The pen,' he said with resignation.

James picked up the pen, dipped it in the inkwell and handed it to Cyrus. Pausing only for a moment, he signed the paper and also the copy which James placed beside him. He looked up. 'The money?'

James handed him a piece of paper. 'A draft on Messrs Simpson and Chapman for the amount agreed on.'

'Do they have a correspondent in London?' put in Mr Brown.

'Yes,' replied James. 'Messrs Barclay, Tritton, Bevan and Co.' The query had answered his curiosity. These men were from London and he guessed that Cyrus owed them money – a considerable sum if he was forced to sell his half of Turner's.

'Ideal,' returned Mr Brown. 'We'll make the arrangements.'

As he took the draft Cyrus directed his gaze at James. 'I suppose Mrs Briggs was delighted to sign this?' he commented, regret in his voice.

James did not answer but looked at the draft in Cyrus's hand.

It caused him to look at it. His eyes widened in surprise. 'But you've signed this,' he said with suspicion.

'Correct,' said James.

'But the draft is on the Briggs account.' He was puzzled.

'Right again.'

A mist was clearing from Cyrus's mind. 'I wondered where Mrs Briggs got the money from to start her firm. So *you* are her backer? The firm is really yours. *You* now own half Turner's, not Mrs Briggs.' Even in the midst of the mess he had created he found a grain of consolation in the fact that Gennetta was not getting his half share. But that hope was short-lived, defeated by James's explanation.

'No. The Briggs firm owns half of Turner's, and as Mrs Briggs and I are equal partners, she also owns part of Turner's.'

Cyrus's lips tightened. 'And that's as good as her owning half of it.' Even as he muttered them his words seemed to carry the ring of doom.

Chapter Twenty-one

James sank on to his chair with a satisfied feeling. A half smile played on his lips as he looked down at the piece of paper in front of him. The signature of Cyrus Sleightholme, scrawled across the bottom, and those of the two witnesses, signalled a triumphant conclusion to a deal he felt sure would delight Gennetta. In spending money from the Briggs account he had acted without her approval but reckoned she would not object when she saw what he had achieved.

He reached for a pen and wrote a brief note. He scanned it, signed it 'James', sealed it in an envelope which he addressed to Mrs G. Briggs and marked it in the top left-hand corner 'Personal'. He went to Benjamin's office.

'Take this note to Mrs Briggs. Deliver it to her personally. No one else. It is imperative that she gets it as soon as possible. Try the Briggs workshop first. More than likely she'll be there.'

'Yes, sir.' Benjamin got down from his stool. He took the envelope from James and his hat from a hook near the door.

'And remember, Benjamin, not a word to anyone, not even Mrs Briggs, about what you have witnessed this afternoon.'

'Yes, sir. Do I wait for an answer?'

'Yes.'

'Very good, sir.'

He left the office and soon reached the workshop in Baxtergate. He was pleased to find Mrs Briggs there for that saved him having to scour the town looking for her. Now he could take his time getting back to the office.

Gennetta was surprised to receive a note from James when, at some convenient time of day, he could easily have called on her personally.

She slit the envelope open and read:

Dear Gennetta,
Please do me the honour of dining with me this evening at 6.30. I
have some important news.

James

She read the note again quickly then looked at Benjamin who had
waited at a discreet distance. 'Please convey my regards and thanks
to Mr Mitchell and tell him the answer is yes.'

'Very well, ma'am.'

It was a pleasant evening as she climbed the hill to New Buildings.
Below her the daytime buzz of the busy port had settled to a low
murmur, marred only now and again by the raucous screech of a
disturbed seagull or an exceptionally loud command on one of the
ships preparing to sail on the evening tide. But Gennetta was only
vaguely aware of it all, preoccupied with James's news, just as she
had been from the moment she had received his invitation. She had
been unable to concentrate on anything else and at one time had
almost gone round to his office to satisfy her curiosity at once but she
knew that would not be polite. He had issued an invitation which she
had accepted and to deviate from that would have been bad-mannered.
So she must content herself with conjecture.

His news must be important if he wanted to divulge it over a meal
in the privacy of his house. Her heart gave a little flutter as she
wondered whether his news involved personal feelings? If it did,
would he have used the word 'news'? Reaching no conclusion, she
found herself assessing James as a person. He was a handsome man,
considerate, likeable and understanding, someone she was comfortable with and whose company she enjoyed.

A neatly attired maid admitted her to the house. As Gennetta
stepped inside, she felt a pang for the past and the happy times she
had spent here. The hall was just as it had been in Aunt Edith's day;
just as it was on the day she'd had to leave with her children.

James appeared from the parlour and came briskly across the hall
to greet her, smiling with pleasure.

'Gennetta, I'm so pleased you could come.' He stepped behind her
to take her cloak as she slipped it from her shoulders. He handed it
to the maid who also took her bonnet.

'I'm so sorry it was such short notice, but it all happened so
quickly,' he offered by way of apology as they went into the parlour.

'That's quite all right,' she replied, dismissing his apology. 'But, I
must say, I have been wondering all afternoon what your news could
be.'

'All in good time,' he teased, seeing how eager she was to know what had prompted his invitation.

He crossed the room to a table where a silver tray was set with a decanter and two glasses. 'Do sit down,' he called over his shoulder as he poured the wine. When he brought her a glass she sensed his excitement.

'Well, what's this important news?' she prompted.

For answer he picked up a piece of paper from the small table next to the fireplace and handed it to her with a smile of satisfaction as he said, 'A present for you.'

Mystified by this gesture, she looked down at the paper. There was a moment of silence. She turned a gaze full of disbelief on him. 'What is all this?' she asked, searching his face for answers.

'Exactly what it says,' he replied quietly, pleased by her reaction.

'But Briggs Jetworkers owning half of Turner's? I don't understand.'

He smiled and sat down in the chair opposite to her to begin his explanation.

Hardly able to believe what she was hearing, Gennetta sat silently as his story unfolded. 'So the Sleightholmes no longer have any hold over Turner's?' she mused at last when he had finished.

'Exactly,' James confirmed. 'Though the shares are in our company's name, I regard them as yours.'

'But ...'

He raised his hand. 'No buts. You manage the practical side of Briggs as I expect you will for Turner's. If I remember rightly, you said your sister-in-law has no business acumen and left the running of it to you. No doubt she will do so again.'

'I wonder what Grace will say to this when she hears about it?' She tried to picture the scene when Cyrus had to reveal what he had done.

'It would be interesting to be a spectator,' James agreed.

'You saw his reaction first-hand. I wish I could have seen his face when he realised I would be getting back a piece of the company.'

'He was so taken aback, I thought he was going to refuse the offer but the other two had certainly put the fear of God into him.'

'No doubt the settlement of a gambling debt. Thank goodness whoever he owed the money to demanded cash. Imagine if he had taken half of Turner's.' She shuddered as if it didn't bear thinking about.

'Well, he didn't, so here's to us and our success.' James raised his glass.

Gennetta raised hers and inclined her head in acknowledgement.

* * *

A leisurely meal was enjoyed in a glow of triumph. Good food and good wine utterly relaxed Gennetta. She could almost say she had achieved her ambition of running Turner's, almost made up for what it had deprived her of in her early years – the love of a father.

They had settled down over coffee in the parlour when James asked, 'Were you happy in this house, Gennetta?'

'Tremendously,' she replied. 'Aunt Edith was so kind. I wish you could have known her.'

'So do I,' he said with genuine regret.

'She was so good to me and Reuben. I don't know what I'd have done without her.'

'I sense her around me. I'm sure she has never left this house.'

'Then you have good company.'

'And you could have it too. You could be happy here again,' said James, his voice soft and caressing.

Gennetta looked at him hard. 'I'm sure I could, but surely you aren't thinking of leaving?'

'No, I'm asking you to marry me.'

She was stunned. She seemed to have passed into a world of bewilderment and uncertainty. So much was happening this evening. She gulped, 'Oh, James, I hadn't expected ...'

He put down his coffee cup and rose from his chair. He took her cup and saucer and placed them on the low table beside her. Taking her hands, he pulled her to her feet. His eyes never left hers and she felt she was being drawn into the depths of still dark pools where there would be an unknown life full of promise.

'I've loved you since the first time I saw you,' he said. 'You constantly haunt my mind. Say you'll marry me?' To add persuasion to his words he drew her close and kissed her. He gained heart from the fact that she did not pull away and let his kiss linger. He felt her lips tremble in response and sensed the passion he had always imagined would be there.

Eventually she drew herself away and buried her head against his chest as his arms enfolded her.

'My sweet, say you will?' James pressed hoarsely.

Her mind was full of confused thoughts. So far this evening she had not given Tom a thought, but now ... She had always pushed his proposals aside with the excuse that all else must wait until she had wrested Turner's from the rapacious Sleightholmes. He had seen that, and her desire to live on the west side of the river, as barriers to their love. But now she had what she wanted, they could be broken down, particularly if Tom's London trip had strengthened the ambition she had seen beginning to emerge in him. Yet here was James, a man who was as ambitious as she was, a man who had seized the opportunity to buy the shares which, unknown to him, could clear her way to a marriage with another man. In all their meetings he had been kind and considerate, and though she had dismissed the attraction he had stirred in her, telling herself that she merely found him good company, now she must admit it had been stronger than that.

'Oh, James, I don't know,' she faltered. 'This is all so sudden. I like you a lot but I don't know about ...' She let the words fade away.

He stroked her hair gently. 'Like can turn to love. I'm sure it's not far away. I'm not demanding an answer now. Take your time. Let me have hope at least.' He placed his fingers under her chin and turned her head. He saw the confusion in her pale blue eyes and was sorry that he was responsible. He kissed her again. 'I love you,' he whispered, 'and more than anything, I want you to be my wife.'

'Give me time?' she pleaded.

'All the time in the world, so long as your answer is yes,' he replied.

She kissed him gratefully.

'And, Gennetta,' he added, 'Mother would have approved.'

Sleep did not come easily to her that night. Two faces haunted her. One was clean-cut with a firm determined chin which did not detract from handsome features. She had seen the pale blue eyes sparkle with a joy for life and witnessed the final dismissal of a sadness which had long lingered there. She knew that had come about because of Tom's growing love for her, but his stubbornness held him back from finally eliminating his suspicion of life on the west side of the river, and from realising the ambitions thwarted by the tragedy of his father's death.

The other handsome face was enhanced by thick black hair and eyes which tempted with their dark mysterious depths. She had gazed into them and been lost. It was the face of someone with ambition and drive, someone who could seize a chance and make it pay, but she knew that there was no ruthlessness behind it for she had experienced only kindness, consideration and fairness from him.

It pained Gennetta to think that she might hurt either of them.

Neither face prevailed with her, each fading in and out of her fitful sleep. When the morning light woke her, nothing had come out of her dreams to guide her in her choice.

Gennetta ate her breakfast with Nathaniel and Flora, Joey and Davey having already gone to work, but left as soon as they had finished, bent on savouring her visit to Turner's.

It was a bright morning, matching her mood as she crossed the bridge and hurried along Church Street. She passed Hacker's Yard without stirring any bad memories for today was too important to be marred by those.

When she entered the familiar workshop several heads turned to see who had come in. One man stepped quickly towards her. He touched the brim of his cap. He knew who she was and was wondering what she was doing here. 'Good day, ma'am.' The intonation in his voice made it a query as well as a greeting. 'I'm Jos Parker, foreman, can I help thee?'

The man was pleasant enough, open-faced but with nothing particularly striking about him. She felt that there was no air of authority, not in the way that there was about John Young. But maybe that could be brought out once he knew where he stood with the new owner.

'Good day to you, Jos,' she returned pleasantly. 'You probably know who I am.'

'Aye, ma'am.'

'And probably are wondering what I am doing here?'

He gave a little chuckle as he confirmed, 'Aye, ma'am.'

This brief exchange of words had carried across the room and all the workmen had ceased what they were doing and were intent on hearing Gennetta's explanation.

'Well, as I now own Mr Cyrus Sleightholme's half of the company, I will be seeing to things here.'

The announcement brought murmurs of surprise from the workers.

'I don't think I'm hard to get on with, but I do expect my workers to be loyal, to do their best and try to improve their work. I do not intend to run Briggs's and Turner's as rivals but as two firms willing to exchange ideas and work together. I have full order books at Briggs's and it can be the same here but the standard of work, from what I have seen on the open market, will have to improve. That can come about if you all put your minds to it, and there will be rewards for additional effort.' She paused and then added, 'That is all I have to say at the moment.'

The men resumed their tasks, commenting on Gennetta's words to each other in low voices.

She turned to Jos. 'Are you a carver or an etcher?'

'Etcher, ma'am.'

'Let me see some of your work.'

He led her to his place at the bench on the right-hand side of the room and positioned three pieces of jet for better display. Gennetta examined them carefully and then turned to him. 'These are very good, Joss. You have a talent which wants but a little encouragement to improve even further. I suspect it has been at this stage for a long time.'

Her comment caught him unawares but it made him realise that she was exactly right. He remembered turning out pieces like this at twenty; now, at thirty, he was still doing the same. He had never received any prompting to improve. Who knew what might happen now? He had heard of Mrs Briggs's ability. 'Yes, ma'am.'

'You'll remain foreman, use that authority to the advantage of the company. See that the work is satisfactory and that everyone does his fair share.'

'I will, ma'am,' he replied, thankful that he still held his position.

'Good. Now let us take a look at some of the other work.'

She had been moving among the workers examining their pieces for about ten minutes when the door opened and Robert Sleightholme walked in.

'Parker!' he boomed.

Jos was about to scurry to him when Gennetta restrained him with a touch on his arm. He glanced at her, confused as to what he should do for he had long been used to Robert Sleightholme making this sort of imperious entrance.

Gennetta stepped away from the bench at which she had been inspecting a carved brooch. It was only then that Robert saw her.

Everyone had stopped work, alerted by the tension which had swept over the room.

Robert stared in amazement at Gennetta. 'What the hell is thee doing here?' he blustered loudly. His heavy jowls quivered with annoyance. 'Thee has no right coming here stealing our ideas. Parker, thee's fired for letting her in. Now, Mrs Briggs, get out and stay out.'

Gennetta let him finish his tirade. She knew everyone was waiting for her reaction. 'Mr Sleightholme,' she said quietly but with an icy firmness, 'it is you who have no right here. It is you who must leave.'

Robert's lips tightened, his eyes narrowed. 'I'll have none of thy impertinence. Get out!'

'No!' Gennetta adopted a defiant stance. 'I have every right here. More right than you.'

'Ridiculous!' snapped Robert. 'I come here in an advisory capacity to my son who, as thee well knows, owns half this firm.'

'And that is where you are wrong, Mr Sleightholme, he does not.'

Robert gave a mocking laugh. 'I don't know where you get such a foolish idea.' He glared at Jos. 'Parker, get her out of here and thee with her.'

Perplexed, the foreman looked from one to the other.

'Stay where you are,' ordered Gennetta. With her eyes fixed unyieldingly on Robert, she walked towards him, holding out the document which bore his son's signature. Anticipating such a confrontation, in fact hoping it would occur, she had brought it with her. 'This will show you why I have every right to be here and you don't.'

Robert snatched it from her, his eyes widening in disbelief. He blew out his cheeks in exasperation and his face went red with rising temper. But the words were there, in black and white. 'What's the stupid fool done now!' he snarled and flung the paper down on the nearest bench. He gave Gennetta one last furious look and stormed out of the building.

With every step he took through Whitby's streets, Robert Sleightholme's fury mounted. His son had thrown away the golden opportunity he had sought for years. How? Why? Even as these questions churned in his mind, he felt certain he knew the answer.

His furious ringing of the doorbell brought a maid scurrying across the hall to tug the door open in alarm. Robert stormed past her, almost knocking her over, and found himself coming face to face with Grace and Cyrus who had rushed into the hall on hearing the commotion.

'In here,' he snapped, and strode into the parlour, dropping his top hat and stick on a chair without stopping.

Grace and Cyrus shot querying glances at each other and each shrugged their shoulders, signifying bewilderment as to what had caused such a rage in him.

As Cyrus pushed the door shut, his father swung round to face them. Anger flared in his eyes; the muscles in his neck tightened. 'What the hell have thee been up to?' He glowered at his son. 'And don't try to play the innocent, I know thee's sold thy half of Grace's business!'

She gasped. This was unbelievable. Her gift to Cyrus, sold, gone? 'Is this true?' Her voice was scarcely above whisper but her words rang with accusation though her eyes implored his denial.

Cyrus had known his action would be discovered but had not expected it this soon. He had hoped for time to make some plans, find some excuses for what he had done.

He nodded. 'I had to,' he said.

'Had to! Had to?' Robert stormed, pre-empting any further query from Grace. 'Gambling, I suppose. My God, I've warned thee time and time again. I've bailed thee out. I thought when thee got an interest in Grace's business thee'd knuckle down, but it seems I was

281

wrong. I warned thee I would not meet thy debts in future. I thought that would stop thee gambling. Seems thee took no notice.' He turned away in disgust.

Bewildered by these revelations, Grace looked from one to the other. 'Is this true, Cyrus?' she demanded.

'Yes,' he replied reluctantly. 'I had to do something. You've heard Father wouldn't meet any more debts, I wouldn't come begging to you. My life was threatened, so I took the only way out.'

'Threatened?' Grace was horrified. 'By whom? Who in Whitby would do that?'

'No one. They were from London.'

'London?' She was mystified for a moment, then realisation of what had been going on dawned on her. 'Then those frequent visits to London weren't for any purpose of furthering our business but to satisfy your craving for gambling?' Contempt filled her voice.

'I did do business, you know I brought some orders back.'

'But not what we expected and sometimes none at all.'

'You can blame that on Gennetta,' he cried, trying to vindicate himself. 'She stole our best workers and recaptured the London trade with them. We'd lost it all. I tried to bring money back into the business and ...'

'What, through gambling?' Robert exploded. 'How stupid can thee get? Didn't thee learn thy lesson in Whitby before getting tied up with those sharks in London? The two I saw, I suppose?' His eyes filled with loathing. 'Thee could have beaten Gennetta by improving the business but thee hadn't the gumption to do that. Instead thee's ruined everything, destroyed my dream of possessing the firm Jeremiah built up – and it was so near.'

The fury burning inside him prevented him from choosing his words more carefully. They poured out. 'Thee'd been smart in prising half the business from Grace; the other half would have come before long. The Turner name would have been destroyed and Sleightholme's would have dominated the jet industry. Now all that's gone and the Turner name will live on now Gennetta's got your share.'

'Gennetta?' Grace gasped at this revelation.

'Aye, Gennetta,' snapped Robert.

The name hung in Grace's mind, bringing back memories of Gennetta's warnings about the Sleightholmes' ambitions. She had been right but Grace had chosen not to believe her.

Robert started for the door. 'See what thee can make of thy worthless husband,' he flung at her. He stopped and glared at Cyrus. 'If I had another son, I'd abandon thee here and now. As it is thee's the only one for the Sleightholme business, but to get it thee'll have to prove thissen and learn how to run it with me. And, my God, I'll be a hard taskmaster. Report tomorrow morning with the rest of my workers and be prepared to start on the menial jobs. If thee don't, then thee'll get nothing, for I doubt if Grace will ever trust thee again.' He flung the door open and stormed out.

Grace watched her husband cross the room and close the parlour door. When he turned round she said, 'Now, Cyrus, explain how Gennetta comes to have the half of the business I gave to you?' Her face was stern, demanding the truth with no attempt to evade it. She watched him closely as he unburdened his soul with repentance in every word.

'Tell me, was our marriage nothing more than part of a scheme to get my business?' she asked when he had concluded his explanation.

He hesitated but only momentarily when he saw her expression. He nodded. 'Yes.' There was the deepest regret in his admission. 'But,' he went on, 'I came to love you truly, you must have seen that, and I still do. I'll always regret what I have done to you. Now if you want me to leave, I will.'

Grace did not speak for a few moments but held him in her gaze. She was confused. By right she should hate this man, but she didn't. She had seen his love for her grow; he had been kind and considerate and always attentive. She had been happy with him and knew she could be in the future. She felt pity that he had succumbed to such weakness. Maybe from that a stronger person would emerge.

'I don't want you to leave. You are my husband and in spite of what you have admitted, for some strange reason I find I still love you just as much as ever.'

Cyrus closed his eyes and swayed with relief. He passed his hand over his face and there was thanks in his gaze as he looked at his wife with admiration and love. He held out his arms. She came to them and he held her tight.

'Just one thing more,' said Grace. 'I am going to make sure my firm remains Turner's. There will never be any chance of your father realising his ambition. My part of the firm will never become yours. You have the chance of taking Sleightholme's over from your father. See that you make the most of it.'

'I will.' From his tone she recognised Cyrus would endure any trial his father might impose.

Ten minutes later Grace was aware of a freshening breeze which made people hurry across the bridge to escape its bite as it blew in from the sea. She threaded her way among the crowds about their daily business in Church Street, oblivious to the sounds around her as she concentrated on what she was about to do. By the time she reached the workshop she had convinced herself that it was the only safe course to take and that it would give her great satisfaction.

Gennetta smiled to herself when she saw Grace enter the workshop. It was what she had anticipated and she was prepared for the visit, though she had no idea what course it would take.

'Gennetta, Cyrus and I have just had a visit from his father,' Grace told her after they had exchanged pleasantries.

'I thought you might, after what he learned here.'

'I'd like to go somewhere and talk.'

'Very well. Come home with me, have some hot chocolate.'

'Thank you.'

They left the workshop and in the course of their walk to Well Close Square merely passed the time of day with each other and did not broach the subject which was uppermost on their minds. That was not raised until they were settled in the drawing room and the children, excited at seeing their aunt, had been taken under Rose's care.

'Now, Gennetta,' said Grace after her first sip of chocolate, 'I believe we are partners again.'

'Yes,' she replied. 'I hope you are happy about it? I am sorry if the purchase was made due to Cyrus's misfortune.'

'You know about that?' Grace was concerned that all appeared to be known to Gennetta.

'All I know is what Mr Mitchell told me, that Cyrus wanted a quick sale and it seemed to concern two strangers who were with him. I believe they were from London.'

Grace hesitated a moment, wondering if she should leave it at that, but then decided to confide in her sister-in-law. 'Gambling, I'm afraid,' she confessed. 'Cyrus's life was threatened. He was desperate, couldn't go to his father as Robert had already told him he would settle no more debts.'

'I'm sorry,' Gennetta commiserated.

'I regret what has happened but I'm pleased his share didn't go to a stranger. You and I can take up where we left off when I was foolish enough to make Cyrus a present. You were right. I should have heeded your warning about the Sleightholmes wanting to get hold of your father's business. It all came out in Mr Sleightholme's ravings this morning. Cyrus admitted that was why he married me, but he assures me he did come to love me for myself. I loved him then and still do, in spite of his failings. I'll not cast him aside. I believe he has learned his lesson and his father's ultimatum could be the making of him.'

'I hope you're right, for your sake,' said Gennetta, but she felt a flutter of alarm in her heart and knew it had been reflected in her eyes when Grace went on quickly, in a voice full of reassurance, 'You are wondering about the half of the business I still hold. I've thought about that, so let me set your mind at rest. A Sleightholme will never get my share of the business, not even my husband. It would have been different had we been able to take that child. He would have been treated as our own, but the mother wanted to keep him.'

She put a brisker tone into her voice. 'Now, you and I are going to see Mr Mitchell and I am going to draw up a new will. I am going to leave my half of the business to Nathaniel and Flora – they are more Turner than anybody – and with your half secure it will never be anything other than the business your father and Jack wanted.'

Gennetta was overwhelmed by this magnanimity. She had what she had always wanted and there was no way a Sleightholme could get hold of it. 'Grace, what can I say? This is so generous.' She gave a troubled frown. 'But you might still find someone willing to part with a child.'

'No, not now. If we did, he would be a Sleightholme anyway. Besides I enjoyed having Nathaniel and Flora near me when you all stayed in the house. We became very attached to each other – you saw their reception of me now. They came to mean a lot to me. All I ask is that you allow me to share them with you, in the role of doting aunt.'

Gennetta smiled warmly. 'I wouldn't have it any other way. They'll love to see more of you.'

'Good,' Grace said with satisfaction. 'Now that's settled, let's go and see Mr Mitchell.'

'Good day, Gennetta.' Cyrus stepped in front of her and raised his hat with a polite gesture.

Startled by the sudden confrontation as she made her way to await the arrival of the *Speedwell* from London, she realised he must have been waiting for her. 'Spying on me? You knew I'd be coming this way?' she asked suspiciously, annoyance creeping into her voice.

'I thought you'd be going to meet your chief carver, Tom Unwin, who's returning from London.' He smiled sardonically. 'I have means of knowing.'

The pleasure in his arrogance ruffled her. 'So what do you want? she demanded.

His smile vanished. His expression changed abruptly. His hard eyes held loathing. 'I'll not forget the underhand way you got half Turner's back, and now with those two brats of yours inheriting ...'

285

His lips tightened. 'You and James Mitchell will pay one day. I'll see the Sleightholme business ...'

'Cyrus,' she cut in sharply, her eyes holding his gaze without flinching, 'you don't frighten me any more. Take my advice and be content to run Sleightholme's efficiently. With Turner's and Briggs's businesses united you'll never be able to compete otherwise.' She stepped past him and hurried towards the quay, leaving him to ponder her words.

Tom, on the deck of the *Speedwell*, enjoying the sight of Whitby drawing nearer and nearer, was anxious as to what his homecoming might reveal. The thought of Gennetta and James together had haunted him while he had been away until, without his realising it, the situation had grown out of all proportion in his mind. He began to visualise how much more James had to offer her until he was certain in his mind that he would have captured her heart.

As the *Speedwell* approached the quay, people were waving and calling as they spotted friends or relations. Their exuberance cast a shadow over him. There would be no one to meet him. He started to turn away from the rail, then stopped. Was he mistaken? Had he caught a glimpse of Gennetta? Was she there? His eyes swept the crowd on the quay. She was! He shouted and waved. He saw her searching for a face among the folk on board. Then she waved back. She had seen him. His heart raced. She was alone.

Tom was impatient as he watched the ropes thrown out, grabbed by men on the quayside and tied to the appropriate capstan. Slowly the *Speedwell* was drawn to its berth. The gangway was run out and passengers, eager to be ashore, swarmed from the ship.

'Gennetta, I'm so pleased to see you, thanks for coming.' Pleasure and admiration shone in his eyes.

'I couldn't wait to hear how you got on in London,' she replied brightly.

'Is that the only reason you're here?' A touch of disappointment tinged his words and it deepened when she avoided his question.

It had raised thoughts of James and a wish that she did not have to make a choice. 'So much has happened here, so much I must tell you, and I want to hear how you fared in London.'

He thrust disappointment aside. Maybe her change of subject had not been intentional. He looked round. 'Here, boy.' A barefooted youngster, catching the call and seeing his chance to earn a coin, ran to him. 'Take this bag to number four Henrietta Street and stay with it till I come.'

'Aye, aye, sir,' he said briskly, imitating the sailors he had heard around the harbour. He picked up the bag and was off.

'Walk on the cliff, Gen? We've so much to talk about.'

'Had a good voyage?' she asked as they started away from the quay.

'Yes.'

'Enjoy it?'

'Yes. Soon got my sea-legs and then found it invigorating and relaxing.'

'I'm pleased. It will have done you good. And London?'

'Too big, too smoky, too many folk. I'm glad to be back. But I'll have to go again, maybe a few times if you are agreeable?'

'Of course,' she approved readily, pleased by the enthusiasm in his voice. Had this visit stirred his ambition as she had hoped? She was eager to hear more but did not push him.

Tom offered no further explanation for, as they walked along Church Street, he was keen to know about his son. 'How's Davey?'

'Well. Enjoyed himself. I'm sure he liked ...'

'... the other side of the river,' Tom finished for her. 'You'll have spoilt him.'

'No more than my own or Joey,' she protested.

'I wonder how he'll like coming back to Henrietta Street?'

'He'll like it wherever you are. We talked about you every day, wondering what you were doing.'

'Now, for your news. You've something on your mind,' prompted Tom.

'Your news is more important,' she countered.

Though to him this was not so, he held his counsel and realised that the quickest way for him to find out what she had to tell him was to impart his information first.

'Well, we had a long discussion about the cameo orders. I think I impressed them with my ideas because eventually they agreed to leave the final ornamentation and layout to me, provided the basic design had a rose as the prominent feature.'

'You got on well?'

'Oh, yes. The client invited me to dine with him. A magnificent meal it was. Useful too. His wife dined with us and that enabled me to find out what London ladies prefer in their jewellery. She became so interested in my ideas that she invited me to talk to some of her friends about jet. There were twelve of them and I got orders from every one.'

They started to climb the Church Stairs.

'Tom, that's marvellous,' Gennetta praised him. Had her ploy in sending him to London worked? Her question was answered as he went on.

'Who'd have thought that I would ever go to London and do what I did, moving in London society?' He laughed as he recalled the isolation he had built up around himself and Davey until the barriers had started to crumble through meeting Gennetta Briggs.

'You know, you were right, Gennetta, there are advantages to be had on the other side of the river. It is up to us to make use of them to the best of our ability. I can see I was wrong to want to protect Davey from what I thought might be misguided ideas; wanting to suppress dreams which I thought he could never achieve. What I should do is be there to guide him and see that any ambition is channelled the right way, not doused. My judgement was fogged by what happened to my father. I became too cautious, too protective. Jet can take him into a whole new and exciting world, if he can grab the opportunities.'

Gennetta's heart was racing. It was a joy to hear Tom talking like this. Everything might just fall into place.

'Listen to me going on.' He grinned. He had never talked so much before. 'I'm sorry, I should be listening to your news.'

She smiled. 'Well, you are looking at someone who now owns half of Turner's.'

For a moment the announcement did not register, then Tom's eyes widened in disbelief. 'What?'

'It's true.' She laughed at his expression. 'And as Grace still has the other half, it means I will be running the business again.'

'But how did you get her husband's half?' Tom was bewildered.

He listened intently as she told him what had happened while he was away.

'And Grace has made sure that her half will never fall into Sleightholme hands. She has made Nathaniel and Flora heirs to her half so it means the business will always be Turner's, at least for my lifetime.'

'So you have achieved what you wanted – control of the firm?' he said thoughtfully.

She nodded. 'And there's another thing.' The sudden seriousness in her voice startled him. He looked anxiously at her. 'I've had a proposal of marriage.'

'What!' He turned away, desperation on his face. He swung back, his eyes clouded. 'James, I expect?' She nodded. 'I should never have gone to London! Why did you send me?' he cried.

'And if you hadn't gone, if you had never stepped outside of Whitby, would you ever have changed your mind about the west side of the river?'

'Would it have mattered?' He shrugged his shoulders, feeling despondency weigh heavily on him.

'Of course it would,' she cried. 'You deserve ...' Her words were cut off as her steps were halted by the sight of James standing beside Edith's grave.

Tom followed her gaze across the churchyard. 'It's him!' His low whisper was filled with regret and animosity.

'I must speak to him.' Gennetta, her heart racing, started forward.

'Aye, gan to him! He's your sort. From your side of the river. You want nowt to do with the likes of me.' Tom spat out his words venomously.

She spun round, her eyes blazing. 'And haven't you just said that you too can live on the other side of the river?'

'Seems I was wrong.'

'You weren't wrong and you know it. You wait here.' Her tone brooked no nonsense. 'Leave and I'll never speak to you again.' She swung away from him and started across the churchyard.

Tom stared after her, astonished at the cutting tone of her voice.

The rustle of her dress drew James's attention. He turned to see who approached him. 'Gennetta.' He obviously hoped he would receive the answer he wanted from her. Then, beyond her, across the churchyard, he saw Tom. James's heart skipped a beat. He had watched from the cliffs as the *Speedwell* had sailed into Whitby. Gennetta must have been on the quay when she tied up.

'James.'

He smiled, but any joy in his expression was tinged with sadness. 'I think I know what you are going to tell me. You don't meet Tom Unwin and then immediately walk on the cliffs with him unless you think a lot of him.'

'I'm sorry, James. You are a very special friend to me, but I don't love you.' How she hated doing this to him! She would have soothed the sorrow from his eyes if she could. 'Oh, please understand. Don't let it destroy our friendship, nor our partnership. They are both very precious to me, and your mother wouldn't want either of them destroyed.' She glanced at the headstone.

He followed her gaze. 'No, she wouldn't,' he said quietly. He placed his hands on her shoulders and turned her to face him. He looked into her eyes with sincere respect for her. 'Nothing will spoil what there is between us.'

'You'll find someone else,' she tried to comfort him.

'Maybe, but there'll always be a place in my heart for you. I'll be near if ever you need me.' He leaned forward and kissed her on the cheek.

He started to turn away but she detained him with a touch on his arm. She raised herself on her toes and returned his kiss. 'Thank you,' she whispered. Her eyes were damp as she watched him walk away.

Then she turned and walked back to Tom. Before she reached him she saw his face creased in a dark scowl. 'So that's it.' His voice was glum but anger was not far away. 'You've made your choice, those kisses said it all.'

'Were they the kisses of lovers?' she asked quietly, her eyes warning him not to let his temper erupt. He floundered, trying to answer honestly. 'No, they weren't,' she went on. 'And remember this, Tom Unwin, James is a partner so we'll see a lot of him and I don't want a jealous husband.'

Realisation dawned. 'It's me?' Joy lit up his face. He grabbed her by the waist, laughing with relief. He pulled her to him and looked at her with a love which needed no words as he said, 'You'll marry me?'

The cry of geese reached them on the wind. An icy chill threatened to engulf Gennetta. Were the geese warning her she had chosen wrongly? Doubt creased her face. When she glanced at Tom she knew he had noticed, for in his eyes was concern mixed with the fear that he had lost, even now, and that his brilliant future had been whisked from him by this warning of ill-omen.

'Tom,' she whispered, 'you once told me that the geese did not affect our lives, that we make our own destinies, and put our own interpretation on the Gabriel Hounds.' As she spoke, he saw the fear leave her for good. 'I believe they are a sign that my future will be safe with the man I have chosen. I love you too much to lose you now.'